RESC[...]

"You're a hero always in [...] to be rescued," she said.

There was a startled silence, then without warning, he tilted back his head to laugh with rich enjoyment. "Oh Annie, my desire for you has nothing to do with causes," he husked, his eyes blazing with a hunger that made her body clench with need. "And everything to do with a man so fascinated with a woman he can barely think straight."

"We should—" She lost the ability to speak as he captured her lips in a kiss that threatened to steal her sanity.

This was no tentative, teasing kiss.

This was a blatant, sensual demand for surrender.

His lips were hard, his tongue easing into her mouth as his arms wrapped around her and pressed her tight against his chest.

Annie gasped, stunned by the shocking pleasure as her fingers tangled in his hair. He tasted of tea and passionate male.

Hot, decadent temptation.

She felt as if she were melting beneath the forceful demand of his touch . . .

Books by Alexandra Ivy

Published by Kensington Publishing Corporation

KILL
WITHOUT
MERCY

ALEXANDRA IVY

ZEBRA BOOKS
KENSINGTON PUBLISHING CORP.
http://www.kensingtonbooks.com

ZEBRA BOOKS are published by

Kensington Publishing Corp.
119 West 40th Street
New York, NY 10018

All Kensington titles, imprints and distributed lines are available at special quantity discounts for bulk purchases for sales promotion, premiums, fund-raising, educational or institutional use.

Special book excerpts or customized printings can also be created to fit specific needs. For details, write or phone the office of the Kensington Sales Manager. Attn.: Sales Department. Kensington Publishing Corp., 119 West 40th Street, New York, NY 10018. Phone: 1-800-221-2647.

Zebra and the Z logo Reg. U.S. Pat. & TM Off.

First Printing: January 2016
ISBN-13: 978-1-4201-3755-2
ISBN-10: 1-4201-3755-7

eISBN-13: 978-1-4201-3756-9
eISBN-10: 1-4201-3756-5

10 9 8 7 6 5 4 3 2 1

Printed in the United States of America

Prologue

Few people truly understood the meaning of "hell on earth."

The five soldiers who had been held in the Taliban prison in southern Afghanistan, however, possessed an agonizingly intimate knowledge of the phrase.

There was nothing like five weeks of brutal torture to teach a man that there are worse things than death.

It should have broken them. Even the most hardened soldiers could shatter beneath the acute psychological and physical punishment. Instead, the torment only honed their ruthless determination to escape their captors.

In the dark nights they pooled their individual resources.

Rafe Vargas, a covert ops specialist. Max Grayson, trained in forensics. Hauk Laurensen, a sniper who was an expert with weapons. Teagan Moore, a computer wizard. And Lucas St. Clair, the smooth-talking hostage negotiator.

Together they forged a bond that went beyond friendship. They were a family bound by the grim determination to survive.

Chapter One

Friday nights in Houston meant crowded bars, loud music, and ice-cold beer. It was a tradition that Rafe and his friends had quickly adapted to suit their own tastes when they moved to Texas five months ago.

After all, none of them were into the dance scene. They were too old for half-naked coeds and casual hookups. And none of them wanted to have to scream over pounding music to have a decent conversation.

Instead, they'd found The Saloon, a small, cozy bar with lots of polished wood, a jazz band that played softly in the background, and a handful of locals who knew better than to bother the other customers. Oh, and the finest tequila in the city.

They even had their own table that was reserved for them every Friday night.

Tucked in a back corner, it was shrouded in shadows and well away from the long bar that ran the length of one wall. A perfect spot to observe without being observed.

And best of all, situated so no one could sneak up from behind.

It might have been almost two years since they'd returned from the war, but none of them had forgotten. Lowering your guard, even for a second, could mean death.

Lesson. Fucking. Learned.

Tonight, however, it was only Rafe and Hauk at the table, both of them sipping tequila and eating peanuts from a small bucket.

Lucas was still in Washington, D.C., working his contacts to help drum up business for their new security business, ARES. Max had remained at their new offices, putting the final touches on his precious forensics lab, and Teagan was on his way to the bar after installing a computer system that would give Homeland Security a hemorrhage if they knew what he was doing.

Leaning back in his chair, Rafe intended to spend the night relaxing after a long week of hassling with the red tape and bullshit regulations that went into opening a new business, when he made the mistake of checking his messages.

"Shit."

He tossed his cell phone on the polished surface of the wooden table, a tangled ball of emotions lodged in the pit of his stomach.

Across the table Hauk sipped his tequila and studied Rafe with a lift of his brows.

At a glance, the two men couldn't be more different.

Rafe had dark hair that had grown long enough to touch the collar of his white button-down shirt along with dark eyes that were lushly framed by long, black lashes. His skin remained tanned dark bronze despite the fact it was late September, and his body was honed with muscles that came from working on the small ranch he'd just purchased, not the gym.

Hauk, on the other hand, had inherited his Scandinavian father's pale blond hair that he kept cut short, and brilliant blue eyes that held a cunning intelligence. He had a narrow face with sculpted features that were usually set in a stern expression.

And it wasn't just their outward appearance that made them so different.

Rafe was hot-tempered, passionate, and willing to trust his gut instincts.

Hauk was aloof, calculating, and mind-numbingly anal. Not that Hauk would admit he was OCD. He preferred to call himself detail-oriented.

Which was exactly why he was a successful sniper. Rafe, on the other hand, had been trained in combat rescue. He was capable of making quick decisions, and ready to change strategies on the fly.

"Trouble?" Hauk demanded.

Rafe grimaced. "The real estate agent left a message saying she has a buyer for my grandfather's house."

Hauk looked predictably confused. Rafe had been bitching about the need to get rid of his grandfather's house since the old man's death a year ago.

"Shouldn't that be good news?"

"It would be if I didn't have to travel to Newton to clean it out," Rafe said.

"Aren't there people you can hire to pack up the shit and send it to you?"

"Not in the middle of fucking nowhere."

Hauk's lips twisted into a humorless smile. "I've been in the middle of fucking nowhere, amigo, and it ain't Kansas," he said, the shadows from the past darkening his eyes.

"Newton's in Iowa, but I get your point," Rafe conceded. He did his best to keep the memories in the past where they belonged. Most of the time he was successful. Other times the demons refused to be leashed. "Okay, it's not the hellhole we crawled out of, but the town might as well be living in another century. I'll have to go deal with my grandfather's belongings myself."

Hauk reached to pour himself another shot of tequila from the bottle that had been waiting for them in the center of the table.

Like Rafe, he was dressed in an Oxford shirt, although his was blue instead of white, and he was wearing black dress pants instead of jeans.

"I know you think it's a pain, but it's probably for the best."

Rafe glared at his friend. The last thing he wanted was to drive a thousand miles to pack up the belongings of a cantankerous old man who'd never forgiven Rafe's father for walking away from Iowa. "Already trying to get rid of me?"

"Hell no. Of the five of us, you're the . . ."

"I'm afraid to ask," Rafe muttered as Hauk hesitated.

"The glue," he at last said.

Rafe gave a bark of laughter. He'd been called a lot of things over the years. Most of them unrepeatable. But glue was a new one. "What the hell does that mean?"

Hauk settled back in his seat. "Lucas is the smooth talker, Max is the heart, Teagan is the brains, and I'm the organizer." The older man shrugged. "You're the one who holds us all together. ARES would never have happened without you."

Rafe couldn't argue. After returning to the States, the five of them had been transferred to separate hospitals to treat their numerous injuries. It would have been easy to drift apart. The natural instinct was to avoid anything that could remind them of the horror they'd endured.

But Rafe had quickly discovered that returning to civilian life wasn't a simple matter of buying a home and getting a nine-to-five job.

He couldn't bear the thought of being trapped in a small cubicle eight hours a day, or returning to an empty condo that would never be a home.

It felt way too much like the prison he'd barely escaped.

Besides, he found himself actually missing the bastards.

Who else could understand his frustrations? His inability to relate to the tedious, everyday problems of civilians? His lingering nightmares?

So giving into his impulse, he'd phoned Lucas, knowing he'd need the man's deep pockets to finance his crazy scheme. Astonishingly, Lucas hadn't even hesitated before saying yes. It'd been the same for Hauk and Max and Teagan.

All of them had been searching for something that would not only use their considerable skills, but would make them feel as if they hadn't been put out to pasture like bulls that were past their prime.

And that was how ARES had been born.

Now he frowned at the mere idea of abandoning his friends when they were on the cusp of realizing their dream.

"Then why are you encouraging me to leave town when we're just getting ready to open for business?"

"Because he was your family."

"Bull. Shit." Rafe growled. "The jackass turned his back on my father when he joined the army. He never did a damned thing for us."

"And that's why you need to go," Hauk insisted. "You need—"

"You say the word 'closure' and I'll put my fist down your throat," Rafe interrupted, grabbing his glass and tossing back the shot of tequila.

Hauk ignored the threat with his usual arrogance. "Call it what you want, but until you forgive the old man for hurting your father it's going to stay a burr in your ass."

Rafe shrugged. "It matches my other burrs."

Without warning, Hauk leaned forward, his expression somber. "Rafe, it's going to take a couple of weeks before we're up and running. Finish your business and come back when you're ready."

Rafe narrowed his gaze. There was no surprise that Hauk was pressing him to deal with his past. Deep in his heart, Rafe knew his friend was right.

But he could hear the edge in Hauk's voice that made him suspect this was more than just a desire to see Rafe dealing with his resentment toward his grandfather. "There's something you're not telling me."

"Hell, I have a thousand things I don't tell you," Hauk mocked, lifting his glass with a wry smile. "I am a vast, boundless reservoir of knowledge."

A classic deflection. Rafe laid his palms on the table, leaning forward. "You're also full of shit." His voice was hard with warning. "Now spill."

"Pushy bastard." Hauk's smile disappeared. "Fine. There was another note left on my desk."

Rafe hissed in frustration.

The first note had appeared just days after they'd first arrived in Houston.

It'd been left in Hauk's car with a vague warning that he was being watched.

They'd dismissed it as a prank. Then a month later a second note had been taped to the front door of the office building they'd just rented.

This one had said the clock was ticking.

Once again Hauk had tried to pretend it was nothing, but Teagan had instantly installed a state-of-the-art alarm system, while Lucas had used his charm to make personal friends among the local authorities and encouraged them to keep a close eye on the building.

"What the fuck?" Rafe clenched his teeth as a chill inched down his spine. He had a really, really bad feeling about the notes. "Did you check the security footage?"

"Well gosh darn," Hauk drawled. "Why didn't I think of that?"

"No need to be a smart-ass."

Hauk drained his glass of tequila. "But I'm so good at it."

"No shit."

Hauk pushed aside his empty glass and met Rafe's worried gaze.

"Look, everything that can be done is being done. Teagan has tapped into the traffic cameras. Unless our visitor is a ghost he'll eventually be spotted arriving or leaving. Max is working his forensic magic on the note, and Lucas has asked the local cops to contact the neighboring businesses to see if they've noticed anything unusual."

"I don't like this, Hauk."

"It's probably some whackadoodle I've pissed off," the older man assured him. "Not everyone finds me as charming as you do."

Rafe gave a short, humorless laugh. Hauk was intelligent,

fiercely loyal, and a natural leader. He could also be cold, arrogant, and inclined to assume he was always right. "Hard to believe."

"I know, right?" Hauk batted his lashes. "I'm a doll."

"You're a pain in the ass, but no one gets to threaten you but me," Rafe said. "These notes feel . . . off."

Hauk reached to pour himself another shot, his features hardening into an expression that warned he was done with the discussion.

"We've got it covered, Rafe. Go to Kansas."

"Iowa."

"Wherever." Hauk grabbed the cell phone on the table and pressed it into Rafe's hand. "Take care of the house."

Rafe reluctantly rose to his feet. He could argue until he was blue in the face, but Hauk would deal with the threat in his own way.

"Call if you need me."

"Yes, Mother."

With a roll of his eyes, Rafe made his way through the crowd that filled the bar, ignoring the inviting glances from the women who deliberately stepped into his path.

He was man enough to fully appreciate what was on offer. But since his return stateside he'd discovered the promise of a fleeting hookup left him cold.

He didn't know what he wanted, but he hadn't found it yet.

He'd just reached the door when he met Teagan entering the bar.

The large, heavily muscled man with dark caramel skin, golden eyes, and his hair shaved close to his skull didn't look like a computer wizard. Hell, he looked like he should be riding with the local motorcycle gang. And it wasn't just that his arms were covered with tattoos or that he was wearing fatigues and leather shitkickers.

It was in the air of violence that surrounded him and his don't-screw-with-me expression.

Of course, he'd been thrown in jail at the age of thirteen for hacking into a bank to make his mother's car loan disappear. So he'd never been the traditional nerd.

"I'm headed out."

"So early?" Teagan glanced toward the crowd that was growing progressively louder. "The party's just getting started."

"I'll take a rain check," Rafe said. "I'm leaving town for a few days."

"Business?"

"Family."

"Fuck," Teagan muttered.

The man rarely discussed his past, but he'd never made a secret of the fact he deeply resented the father who'd beaten his mother nearly to death before abandoning both of them.

"Exactly," Rafe agreed, leaning forward to keep anyone from overhearing his words. "Keep an eye on Hauk. I don't think he's taking the threats seriously enough."

"Got a hunch?" Teagan demanded.

Rafe nodded, as always surprised at how easily his friends accepted his gut instincts. "If someone wanted to hurt him, they wouldn't send a warning," he pointed out. "Especially not when he's surrounded by friends who are experts in tracking down and destroying enemies."

Teagan nodded. "True."

"So either the bastard has a death wish or he's playing a game of cat and mouse."

"What would be the point?"

Rafe didn't have a clue. But people didn't taunt a man as dangerous as Hauk unless they were prepared for the inevitable conclusion.

One of them would die.

Rafe gave a sharp shake of his head. "Let's hope we have a culprit in custody when we find out. Otherwise . . ."

"Nothing's going to happen to him, my man." Teagan grabbed Rafe's shoulder. "Not on my watch."

* * *

The small but stylish condo on the edge of Denver offered a quiet neighborhood, a fantastic view of the mountains, and a parking garage that was worth its weight in gold during the long, snow-filled winters.

With a muted blue and silver decor, the condo was precisely the sort of place expected of an upwardly mobile young professional.

Not that Annie White was upwardly mobile.

Not after walking away from her position at Anderson's Accounting just six months after being hired.

At the moment, however, she didn't really give a crap about her future in the business world. Instead she was trying to concentrate on her packing. A task that would have been easier if her foster mother hadn't been following behind her, wringing her hands and predicting inevitable doom.

"I wish you hadn't traveled all this way, Katherine," Annie said to her foster mother, moving from the bedroom to the living room to place a stack of clean underwear in her open suitcase.

The older woman was hot on her heels. Still attractive at the age of fifty-five, Katherine Lowe had faded red hair that was pulled into a tight bun at the back of her head, and clear green eyes that could hold kindness or make a child cringe with guilt.

Dressed in a jade sweater and dress slacks, her narrow face was currently tight with concern. "What did you expect me to do when you called to say you were traveling back to that horrible place?" Katherine demanded.

Annie swallowed a sigh. Unlike her foster mother, her honey-brown hair tumbled untidily around her shoulders, the golden highlights shimmering in the September sunlight that streamed through the skylight. Her pale features were scrubbed clean instead of discreetly coated with makeup. And her slender body was casually covered by a pair of faded jeans and gray sweatshirt.

With her wide, hazel eyes she barely looked old enough to be out of high school, let alone a trained CPA.

"I shouldn't have called," she muttered.

She loved her foster parents. She truly did. There weren't many people who would take in the ten-year-old daughter of a serial killer. Especially after she'd spent several months in a mental institution.

They'd not only provided a stable home for her on their ranch in Wyoming, but they'd offered her protection from a world that was insatiably curious about the only survivor of the Newton Slayer.

Now, however, she wished her foster mother would dial back on the fussing.

"You think I wouldn't have found out?" Katherine demanded.

Annie grimaced. She tried to ignore the fact that while she'd moved away from the ranch, her parents continued to monitor her on a daily basis.

Not only by their nightly calls, but by speaking with her boss, Mr. Anderson, who happened to be a personal friend of her foster father.

They only wanted to make sure she was safe.

"I don't want you to worry," Annie said.

Katherine waved a hand toward her open suitcase. "Then reconsider this rash trip."

Annie moved into the bathroom, collecting her toiletries as she struggled to smooth her features into an unreadable mask.

Overall, her foster parents had been supportive. They'd urged her to discuss her past with them as well as a trained therapist. They'd even allowed her to keep a picture of her father beside her bed, despite the devastation he'd caused. But the one thing they refused to accept was her claim that she'd seen visions of the murders as they'd happened.

And they weren't alone.

No one believed the strange images that had plagued

her were anything more than a figment of her overactive imagination.

Over the years, Annie had tried to convince herself they were right. It was insane to think they'd been psychically connected to her father while he was committing the murders.

Right?

Then two nights ago the visions returned.

The images had been fragmented. A woman screaming. A dark, cramped space. The shimmer of a knife blade in the moonlight. Newton's town square.

Annie didn't even try to deny the visions.

Either she was losing her mind—or they were real.

The only way to know was to return to the town and confront her nightmares.

"It isn't rash," she said as she returned to the living room. "I've given it a great deal of thought."

Katherine made a sound of impatience. "But what about your position at Anderson's?"

"It's possible they'll hold my job for me," Annie said, mentally crossing her fingers.

It wasn't a total lie.

Her supervisor had said they *might* reconsider rehiring her when she returned.

"Do you realize how many strings Douglas had to pull to get you a place at such a prestigious firm?" Katherine demanded, clearly not appeased. "In this economy it's almost impossible to find anything that isn't entry level."

Annie turned to take her foster mother's hands. She knew she should feel bad about leaving her position. It was what she'd trained to do, wasn't it?

"And I appreciate everything he's done for me," she assured the older woman. "That you've both done for me."

Katherine clicked her tongue. "If that was true you wouldn't be tossing it all away on this harebrained scheme."

"I get that you don't understand, but it's something I have to do."

Katherine pulled her hands free, clearly frustrated by

Annie's rare refusal to concede to her stronger will. "Nothing can change the past," she snapped.

Annie turned, unnecessarily smoothing the jeans she'd placed in the suitcase.

This wasn't about the past. The visions weren't memories. They were glimpses of the present.

"I know that," she murmured.

"Do you?" Katherine pressed.

"Of course."

There was a long silence, as if the older woman was considering the best means of attack.

Katherine Lowe was a wonderful woman, but she was a master of manipulation.

"Is this because it's the anniversary of the deaths?" she at last demanded.

The thought had crossed Annie's mind. Within a few days it would be exactly fifteen years since the killings started.

Who could blame her for being plagued with hallucinations?

But her heart told her it was more than that.

"I don't think so," she hedged.

Katherine pressed her hands together, a certain sign she was trying to maintain her temper. "Maybe you should talk with your therapist."

"No."

"But—"

"I don't need a therapist," Annie said, her voice uncharacteristically hard.

What was going on in her head couldn't be cured by sitting in a room and talking.

She had to go see for herself.

Seeming to realize she couldn't badger Annie into giving up her plans, Katherine glared at her with an annoyance that didn't entirely disguise her concern. "What do you hope to find?"

Annie flinched.

It was a question she didn't want to consider.

Not when the answer meant she was out of her mind. Or worse, that there was a killer on the loose.

"I just need to know that . . ." Her words trailed away.

"What?"

"That it's over," she breathed. "Really and truly over."

A shocked expression widened Katherine's eyes. "What are you talking about? Of course it's over. Your father . . ." The older woman hastily crossed herself, as if warding off an evil spirit. "God forgive him, is dead. What more proof do you need?"

Annie shook her head. "I can't explain."

Reaching out, Katherine placed her hand on Annie's arm, her expression anxious. "Do you know how many nights I woke to hear you screaming?"

Annie bit her lower lip. No one could have been more patient over the years as Annie had struggled to heal from the trauma she'd endured.

The last thing she wanted was to cause Katherine or Douglas even more concern.

"I'm sorry."

"Oh, Annie." Katherine pulled her into her arms, wrapping her in the familiar scent of Chanel No. 5. "I'm not trying to make you feel bad. I just don't want the nightmares to come back."

"They already have," Annie whispered, laying her head on her foster mother's shoulder. "That's why I have to go."

Chapter Two

The small café on the north side of the town square had a large front window painted with the name "Granny's Home Cooking."

Rafe didn't know if there was an actual granny doing the cooking, but the place looked like it'd been around long enough for the original granny to be long gone.

There was a chipped linoleum floor straight out of the fifties, along with aluminum tables with Formica tops. Overhead, the drop ceiling was faded a weird shade of yellow, while fluorescent bulbs flickered with a crazy light that threatened to cause a seizure.

But despite the lack of elegance or any adherence to basic health regulations, the food was actually edible and the coffee was hot and black, just as he liked it.

A good thing, since his hope of finishing the packing of his grandfather's belongings in a day or even two had been demolished the second he'd entered the small house. Hell, he'd barely managed to shove open the front door without toppling over the boxes that were stacked from floor to ceiling.

Worse, there was a garage and two outbuildings that were equally stuffed.

His first instinct was to toss the entire mess in the Dumpsters he'd had delivered the day he'd arrived. It wasn't as if the old man had anything of value.

Most of the shit looked like it'd been bought at the local flea market.

It was only the knowledge that his father would have wanted him to keep any family pictures or heirlooms that'd forced him to face the daunting task of actually going through each box.

Which meant he was stuck in Newton for at least a week, if not two.

Finishing his French toast, Rafe was waiting for a refill on his coffee when he realized the middle-aged waitress was busy with a young woman who'd entered and taken the table next to the wall while he was busy checking through the messages on his phone.

Well . . . hello. How'd he missed a beauty like that sitting a few feet away?

He wasn't a horny eighteen-year-old anymore, but damn, he wasn't dead.

Leaning on his elbows, he openly studied the pale, perfect face that was framed by a curtain of windblown brown hair. No, wait. Not brown. It was a glorious multitude of colors. Honey and gold and sunlight.

Her eyes were wide and thickly lashed, although he couldn't determine their exact color, and her lips were a lush curve that made a man think about the pleasure of having them exploring various parts of his body.

She wasn't a flashy beauty, but she had a wholesome prettiness that drew him with a fierce urgency he hadn't felt in far too long.

Ignoring the voice in the back of his head that warned he didn't have time for distractions, no matter how delectable, Rafe turned in his seat, watching as the waitress with the name tag that revealed she was Frances laid a laminated menu in front of the woman.

"You in town for long?" the plump waitress with short salt-and-pepper hair demanded.

Rafe lifted his brows.

So the beauty wasn't a local.

"I'm not really sure." The woman grabbed the menu, studying it with an unnecessary concentration, as if hoping the nosy waitress would take the hint and move away.

Rafe could have warned her that she was wasting her time.

Frances was a nice enough lady, but she wasn't shy about prying into her customers' private business.

"Visiting family?" the older woman pressed.

"Something like that."

"Well, of course you would be. Not much else in this place to bring visitors."

The stranger kept her head down. "True."

Impervious to the lack of enthusiasm, Frances bent down to get a better look at her customer's face. "You look familiar," she said. "Do I know you?"

The woman tucked her hair behind her ear in a gesture that seemed oddly nervous. "I doubt it," she muttered.

"Are you on TV?"

"No."

"Were you in the papers?"

"I—" The woman seemed to shrink into her seat, as if wishing the floor would open up and swallow her.

Before he even realized he was moving, Rafe was out of his seat and crossing to slide into a chair opposite the poor badgered stranger.

"Hey, Frances, can I get another cup of coffee and some of your world-famous French toast for my friend?" he said as both women glanced at him in surprise.

"Friend?" Frances lifted her brows in disbelief.

He flashed a killer smile. "Absolutely." He tugged the menu from the younger woman's unresisting fingers and handed it to the waitress. "And we're in something of a hurry, so if you don't mind."

The older woman studied him with a narrowed gaze. Then seeming to decide he didn't intend any harm to her pretty young customer, she turned away with a smile. "Charming rascal."

Waiting until the waitress was out of earshot, the woman leaned across the table to glare at him.

"What are you doing?" she demanded.

Rafe sprawled back in his seat, admiring the wide hazel eyes flecked with gold.

Exquisite.

Or they would be if they weren't shadowed with a hidden fear, and the skin below them wasn't bruised with weariness.

His spidey sense was on instant alert.

This wasn't a woman here to enjoy a family reunion.

She was on the run from something. Or someone.

The realization should have put an end to his fascination. After all, the last thing he needed was to get involved in some stranger's trauma. Even if his every instinct urged him to wrap her in his arms and carry her away from this place.

But Rafe had a full-blown case of savior complex.

And even recognizing the symptoms, there was no way in hell he was going to be able to walk away. Instead, he held the female's gaze and kept his voice deliberately light.

"Having endured Frances's special brand of interrogation, I thought you could use some backup," he teased. "I swear the woman should have been alive during the Spanish Inquisition."

"So you're just a Good Samaritan?" Her voice was soft. Deliciously feminine.

"We're both strangers in town," he pointed out. "It seemed like you could use a helping hand. End of story."

There was a subtle shift in her expression.

Wariness.

Suspicion.

"You don't live here?"

"Rafe Vargas. Born and raised in San Antonio, Texas, although I've recently relocated to Houston." He reached out his hand, not surprised when she refused to shake it. She was so tense she looked like she might shatter into a thousand pieces. Besides, she was clutching a newspaper as if it was a lifeline. "And you are?"

She hesitated before grudgingly offering her name. "Annie."

"Just Annie?"

"Yes."

"A woman of few words." His smile widened. "I like it."

She sucked in a deep breath, annoyance replacing the unease in her eyes.

Which suited Rafe just fine. She clearly needed a distraction from her problems.

"I don't mean to be rude, but I'm not in the mood for company," she informed him.

He ignored her warning, reaching across the table to tug the paper from her white-knuckled grip. "Is this today's?"

"That's mine," she snapped as he unfolded the front page to reveal the enormous headline:

FIFTEENTH ANNIVERSARY OF THE NEWTON SLAYER

Below it were two grainy pictures. One was an image of seven bodies in a morgue, covered by sheets, and next to it was a middle-aged man with brown eyes and a kind smile.

"Gruesome," he muttered.

"Ah." Frances reappeared at the table, refilling Rafe's coffee mug at the same time she tapped a finger to the picture of the man. "That's our local celebrity."

Rafe frowned. "Celebrity?"

"Yep. Don White murdered seven women before he was caught." Frances gave a dramatic shudder. "A terrible thing."

"Yes, murder usually is," Rafe said, covertly glancing at the woman across the table.

Her face was white, her hands clenched together.

What the hell?

Was she related to one of the victims?

"I'd forgotten it was the anniversary," the waitress continued, leaning her hip against the table. "Not to brag, but I knew him."

Rafe was barely listening, his gaze locked on Annie. "Really?"

"Oh yes. Came in for breakfast before Sunday school regular as clockwork. Brought his sweet daughter—" Frances's babbling words came to a sudden halt as she snapped her fingers and pointed toward a startled Annie. "That's it. That's why I thought you looked familiar. I never forget a face even if it has changed over the years," she said. "Little Annie White."

Panic flared through the hazel eyes before Annie was on her feet and headed toward the door.

Rafe half rose to his feet before forcing himself to resume his seat.

The woman was bolting because she didn't want to be bothered by strangers. He wasn't going to inflict his company on her.

He, better than most, understood there were times when you wanted to be left the hell alone.

"Well, well. As I live and breathe," Frances murmured. "I never thought to see her here again."

Rafe frowned. "Why not?"

"She's Annie White. The daughter of the Newton Slayer." Frances pointed toward the bottom of the newspaper that had another picture of Don White. In this one, he was standing outside a school, his arm protectively around a small girl with her hair in pigtails. "That's her with her father."

Rafe hated gossip. It was one of the reasons his father had left this town. But his unexplainable need to know more about Annie White overrode his usual aversion. "What happened?"

"A horrible story," Frances said, unable to hide her relish in regaling him with the grisly tale. No doubt she'd told it a hundred times over the years. "Of course it didn't start out that way. When Don White bought the Johnson farm, we never suspected there was anything wrong with him. It was just him and his five-year-old daughter, so we all did our best to make them feel welcome."

"There was nothing strange about him?"

"Nope." Frances paused, her brow wrinkling as if trying to recall the events of fifteen years ago. "Well, he didn't like to talk about his past, but who could blame him?"

"Why not?"

"His wife and son died in a terrible car accident."

Rafe grimaced. Jesus. Annie was just a baby when her mother and brother had been taken from her. Having lost his mother when he was just eight, he understood how painful it must have been for her. "Tragic."

"Of course, we didn't like to pry."

Rafe hid his wry smile. "Of course."

"They lived here for almost five years and he seemed completely normal," Frances continued. "And that little Annie was as cute as a button."

"Yeah, she still is," he murmured beneath his breath.

Frances clicked her tongue, trying to pretend sympathy when she was obviously relishing the knowledge she'd had the scoop of the decade dropped in her lap. Over the next few days the entire town was going to be flocking to the restaurant to hear her account of Annie White's mysterious arrival.

She was going to be a star.

"Poor thing," the waitress cooed. "I can't imagine what a burden it must be to know your father was a cold-blooded butcher."

Rafe couldn't imagine, either.

But it couldn't be good.

He glanced down at the picture of the smiling man. It seemed impossible to believe he could be a serial killer. He looked so . . . ordinary.

"They were certain he was guilty?" he demanded.

"Oh yes." Frances gave a vigorous nod of her head. "Caught him red-handed with the seven dead women in his old bomb shelter. Even had his own daughter down there. Tied up and blindfolded while he was taking a nap."

"Jesus." Rafe clenched his hand as fury burst through him. "Was he executed?"

"You could say that. He had his throat slit in his cell just hours after he was arrested."

"Another prisoner?" he asked. Not that he cared.

The bastard deserved to be chained to a wall and tortured for the next fifty years, but he couldn't be sorry that Annie hadn't had to endure the trauma of a long, drawn-out trial.

"Who can say?" A secretive smile touched Frances's lips. "God works in mysterious ways."

"He does indeed." Rafe lost interest in the dead serial killer. "What happened to Annie?"

Frances gave a shrug. "I heard she went to the loony bin for a while."

Rafe muttered a curse, his expression hardening. "Hardly surprising," he said coldly. "Most of us would need therapy after being terrorized by their father."

Frances's cheeks reddened, not missing the edge of reprimand in Rafe's voice. "Oh, it wasn't that. Or at least not entirely," she hastily said. "I heard she kept telling the cops that she could see the murders."

"Shit. He made her watch?"

"No. She said she'd seen the murders in her dreams." Frances gave a dramatic pause. "As they were happening."

Rafe blinked. Well, that wasn't what he'd been expecting.

Of course, after what she'd endured at the hands of her father, she was fortunate if all she suffered was a few nightmares.

"She hasn't been back to Newton since the murders?"

"Not that I heard of." Frances gave a sudden frown. "It's odd her turning up now."

"Because of the anniversary?"

"No, because Jenny went missing last week."

The words twisted Rafe's gut with a premonition of dread. He wasn't sure why.

Women went missing. For all kinds of reasons. It certainly

didn't mean it had anything to do with the anniversary of a serial killer.

But he'd learned a long time ago never to dismiss one of his intuitions.

There was a sudden ding of a bell from the kitchen. "Order up," a male voice called out.

Frances sent him a wink. "No rest for the wicked, eh?"

Shoving himself to his feet, Rafe threw enough money on the table to cover his bill plus a generous tip before heading out the door.

Once on the quiet street, he pulled his phone from his pocket and called the ARES office. "Teagan," he said as his friend answered. "I need your help. Send me all the info you have on a serial killer named Don White. They called him the Newton Slayer. Thanks, amigo."

He hung up before the techno-wizard could ask him whether or not he'd lost his mind. The second question was going to be why the hell he gave a damn about some long-dead killer.

The truth was, all he had was a vague fear that evil had returned to Newton.

And that Annie White was in danger.

Annie stopped at the gas station at the edge of town, filling up her tank before she headed back to Denver.

God, she was an idiot.

She'd prepared herself to discover that there was another murderer sneaking around town. Or even that her visions were a symptom of her growing mental instability.

But it'd never occurred to her that she might actually be recognized.

Now she felt raw. Exposed. And vulnerable in a way she hadn't felt for years.

God forgive her. She didn't want to be a coward, but she couldn't bear to endure another round of the lingering stares and finger pointing. Or even the sickening pity that had nearly drowned her after she'd been found in the bomb shelter with her father and the bodies.

For no reason at all, the image of a lean, fiercely beautiful male face rose to her mind.

Rafe Vargas.

He'd been gorgeous. And charming. And sexy enough to make her body tingle with appreciation, even when she'd been trying to make him go away.

The sort of male who could have any woman he wanted.

And now he knew she was . . . broken.

It made her feel ridiculously ashamed.

She shivered as the early morning air cut through her sweatshirt, and replaced the gas nozzle as she headed into the nearby building. The best thing was to return to Denver and hope she could get her job back.

Yes. She would pretend she'd never even traveled to Newton. And the visions . . . well, if she ignored them long enough they would eventually go away. Wouldn't they?

But first she had to have a cup of coffee.

The bell tinkled as she pulled open the door and entered the warmth of the convenience store that had three small tables at the back where a group of elderly men were gathered to drink their coffee and discuss the weather.

She deliberately avoided their curious gazes as she headed to the side of the store to fill a Styrofoam cup with coffee. Popping a lid on top, she moved to the front counter where a middle-aged man was filling a glass container with freshly baked pastries.

On cue, her stomach growled, her mouth watering at the sight of the doughnuts and fritters and muffins.

Yum.

Deep-fried sugar and grease.

It was exactly the sort of temptation she usually tried to avoid. But today she allowed her gaze to linger. She'd skipped dinner, and breakfast had been shot to hell.

Why not indulge?

Some days low-fat yogurt just wasn't going to cut it.

"Morning," the man boomed, ridiculously happy considering it was barely seven.

"Good morning."

"Nip in the air," he unnecessarily pointed out. "Snow can't be far off."

She kept her head bent, her gaze focused on the glass case. "Yes."

Accepting that Annie wasn't in the mood for chitchat, he got straight to business. "Can I get you something?"

She pointed to her pastry of choice. "A blueberry muffin."

"You got it."

She stepped to the end of the counter as he efficiently wrapped the muffin and dropped it into a bag. Setting down the coffee, she pulled out her debit card, her gaze captured by the poster plastered to the back of the cash register.

MISSING.
HAVE YOU SEEN THIS WOMAN?
A REWARD FOR ANY INFORMATION.
PLEASE CONTACT THE NEWTON POLICE DEPARTMENT.

Annie hissed, feeling as if she'd taken a punch to the gut. "Shit," she muttered.

Deep inside, it was exactly what she'd been expecting, and yet it still came as a mind-numbing shock.

The man placed the bag next to her coffee, studying her with open curiosity. "Something wrong?"

She nodded her head toward the poster. "Is the woman still missing?"

"Yep." He folded his arms over his barrel chest, his expression one of genuine concern. "Jenny Brown. A local gal."

"When did it happen?"

"Eight days ago." He grimaced. "She went to Des Moines and never came home. Most believe she took off with some man she met on the Internet."

She studied his broad face. Clearly he didn't buy the story. If he did he wouldn't have up a missing poster, would he?

"But not you?" she prompted.

"It's possible, I suppose. It wouldn't be the first time Jenny ran around on her husband," he reluctantly admitted. "But it's not like her to leave her kid behind."

Annie gripped the edge of the counter, her knees feeling oddly weak. "She has children?"

He nodded. "A little boy."

They always had children. Except for her.

She studied the picture in the middle of the poster, her stomach churning with fear. "She looks so young," she breathed, taking in the rounded face and big brown eyes.

"Jenny had a rough start to life," the man said, his tone defensive. Did he think Annie was judging the poor woman? She hoped not. She hated people who judged the victim, as if being hurt was somehow their own fault. "She was only fifteen when she had her son, but she's always tried to be a good mom." He abruptly halted, his blue eyes narrowing with suspicion. "Wait. You're not a reporter, are you?"

"Good Lord, no," Annie denied in fervent tones.

The press had hounded her until she'd at last arrived at her foster parents' ranch. Thankfully, Douglas had threatened to shoot them the first time he caught them on his property.

They'd eventually disappeared.

"We had one bastard down here just yesterday trying to tie Jenny's disappearance to the Newton Slayer," the man said, shaking his head in disgust.

"How could that be possible?" she asked, her voice hoarse. "The Slayer's dead, isn't he?"

The man scowled. "Of course he is. Had his throat slit in his jail cell. The sheriff claims he has a part of his ashes in that trophy he keeps on his desk."

Her fingers tightened on the counter until her knuckles turned white.

Oh God, oh God, oh God.

She couldn't think about her father now.

Even after all these years, it still hurt too much.

"Then why would the reporter suspect the missing girl is the work of the Slayer?"

"Just looking to sell his story," the man said. "Tried to imply we arrested the wrong man and the Slayer is still out there." He gave a short, humorless laugh. "We shut that down right quick and in a hurry. Then he said it must be a copycat, but if that were true another girl would already be missing. Everyone knows the killer took women every two days. Regular as clockwork. Well, except for the sheriff's wife, who was taken just the day after Kathy Benson." He blinked as Annie made a small sound of distress, and belatedly punched in the cost of the coffee and the muffin into the cash register. "I assume the reporter's next guess would have been that the Slayer's ghost was taking women, if we hadn't run him out of town," he muttered, clearly trying to lighten the atmosphere.

Annie swiped her debit card, anxious to be away from the man's distracting chatter. "Probably."

"So, are you just passing through?" the man demanded as he handed her the receipt.

Annie wanted to say yes. She'd already made the decision to leave.

Hadn't she?

Jenny, after all, was probably off playing house with some other man.

Or in Vegas with a friend.

There was no reason at all to connect her disappearance to the previous murders.

But even as her lips parted, she knew she couldn't just drive away.

"No," she muttered, turning to head toward the door. "It looks like I'll be staying."

* * *

He was standing in the upstairs of the abandoned house when he caught sight of the slender figure posed at the edge of the woods.

At last.

His heart fluttered with excitement.

It'd been so hard to wait. So terribly hard.

But he couldn't play without Annabelle.

"So you've come as I prayed you would," he whispered, his hand touching the dusty pane of glass. "Such a good girl. I've missed you, sweet Annabelle. Now we can continue our game. And this time, my love, we finish it. Together . . ."

Chapter Three

The Newton Motel was intended for convenience, not comfort.

The L-shaped building was constructed in the 1940s, with rooms that were barely large enough to fit a double bed and dresser, with an equally cramped bathroom attached.

The customers were deer hunters, road construction workers, and those people forced to attend a wedding or funeral with no desire to stay with their local family.

They'd never been intended for a visitor who was going to spend long hours trapped in the room.

After thirty-six hours of pacing the floor and waiting for news about the missing victim, or even a damned vision, Annie had to get out.

Climbing into the bright yellow Jeep that her foster father had given her the day she'd passed her final test to qualify as a CPA, she headed out of Newton to LaClede, just twenty miles to the south.

It wasn't a large town by any stretch of the imagination, but it did have a few chain restaurants along the highway where it wasn't unusual for strangers to eat. She might be claustrophobic, but she wasn't ready to face Frances and her rabid curiosity.

Taking a seat in one of the booths, she ordered a burger

and fries, keeping her gaze on the large window that offered a view of the brightly lit parking lot. She didn't actually think she would be recognized, but a young woman alone always attracted interest.

She'd demolished most of the burger and half the fries when a shadow fell across the faux wood table and a familiar male voice overrode the elevator music playing in the background.

"Now, this is a nice surprise." With an arrogance she assumed was written into his DNA, Rafe Vargas slid into the high-backed seat across from her. He flashed a smile that displayed his perfect white teeth, the warm scent of male cologne teasing at her senses. "Hello, Annie."

She frowned even as her stomach fluttered with excitement. Dammit.

He was just so freaking gorgeous. It didn't matter that his dark hair was ruffled from the brisk autumn breeze. Or that a five o'clock shadow darkened the jaw of his perfectly chiseled features. Or that he was casually dressed in a gray hoodie and black jeans.

His dark male beauty and raw charisma attracted every female in the crowded dining room like bees to honey.

"Mr. Vargas." She frowned as he made himself comfortable, his feet nudging hers beneath the table. "What are you doing here?"

"I had a meeting with my real estate agent to sign some papers." He nodded his head toward a middle-aged woman who was pulling on a trench coat as she headed out the door. "She promised this place had fantastic pies. Clearly she's never eaten my famous deep-dish apple crumb, or she would know what a good pie is supposed to taste like."

She ignored his attempt to charm her. "You're buying a house?"

"Selling one."

"Selling?" She was instantly suspicious. "I thought you said you weren't from here."

He shrugged. "It belonged to my grandfather, Manuel Vargas."

"Oh." Annie had a vague recollection of a thin, dark-haired man who drove a battered pickup. "I recognize the name. I'm pretty sure he helped my father during harvest season." She wrinkled her nose at the memory of the man's scowl whenever she tried to show him the new doll she'd just gotten for her birthday. "He used to park at the barn and walk to the field. I think he was trying to avoid me."

"Yeah. That would be him. He never was fond of kids," Rafe muttered, glancing toward the waitress who'd appeared next to the table. "I'll have a glass of whatever you have on draft."

The young woman with long, dark hair and a plump face smiled with open invitation. "You got it," she breathed, leaning down so she could display her considerable cleavage. "And anything else you might want."

There was an awkward silence as the waitress waited for the predictable reaction from Rafe. When his attention remained laser-focused on Annie, she grudgingly turned to sashay away.

Annie's heart missed a beat as she met the dark gaze that held blatant male interest.

He was good. Dangerously good.

"I don't remember inviting you to join me," she said.

"That's okay." He reached across the table to snag a french fry from her plate. "I forgive your lack of manners."

"Lucky me."

"I'd say we're both in luck."

For a scalding second she allowed herself to become lost in the dark, inviting gaze. A part of her desperately wanted to indulge in a lighthearted flirtation with this drop-dead, sexy hunk.

When was the last time a handsome man tried to seduce her?

Yeah, that would be never.

But she'd be worse than a fool to let down her guard.

She absently wiped a bead of condensation from her glass of diet soda. "Won't your grandfather be expecting you?"

"I doubt it. He died last year."

She grimaced. "Sorry."

"Don't be. I barely knew him." His tone hardened. "He wasn't pleased when my father left Newton to join the army."

"Why not?" The words were out before she could halt them. Dammit. She didn't want to know any more about Rafe Vargas. Not when she sensed he was already going to feature prominently in her fantasies tonight. "Forget that. It's none of my business."

Rafe plucked another french fry from her plate, naturally ignoring her request. "My grandfather believed my father should stay and contribute to the household income, but my father didn't want to be a farmhand for the rest of his life. The day he walked out the door my grandfather said he would never forgive him." He ate the fry in two bites. "He didn't."

Annie glanced toward the crowded dining room and then the door.

She should leave.

Not just because this man was too charming for his own good, but because she couldn't afford to be distracted. Dammit. She wasn't here for her own pleasure.

But she couldn't make herself move.

She didn't want to go back to the cramped motel room and pace the floors. Not yet.

Instead she took a sip of her soda and studied his lean face.

"You never met him?" she abruptly asked.

"Twice. At my grandmother's funeral. And then six years ago when my father was diagnosed with cancer." She didn't miss the edge of bitterness in his voice. "I had some idiotic thought that I could convince the stubborn old jackass to bury the hatchet."

She asked the obvious question. "You couldn't?"

His lips twisted. "He wouldn't even let me through the door."

"What about your father?"

"He died a year later."

Annie sensed that Rafe's sheer lack of emotion was an indication of how deeply he still mourned his father's loss. And how angry he remained toward the grandfather who cared more about his pride than his own son.

"Families are . . ." Her lips twisted as she searched for a suitable word. "Difficult."

He snorted at her eventual choice. "Some are a complete pain in the ass."

She nodded, waiting for the waitress to set down Rafe's beer. The simple task seemed to require an enormous amount of effort as the woman fussed over the napkin she placed beneath the frosty glass and brushed her hip against Rafe's shoulder.

Once again Rafe's gaze never wavered from Annie's face, the intensity of his single-minded focus sending the waitress away with a loud huff and making Annie shift uneasily against the plastic-covered seat.

What the hell did he want from her?

"I won't talk about it, if that's what you're hoping."

He arched a brow, as if genuinely puzzled by her abrupt words. "About what?"

"The Newton Slayer."

"Good," he said, reaching for his beer to take a deep drink. "I've been drowning in the past all day. Tell me what you do."

She narrowed her gaze. "What I do?"

"For a living."

"Oh." She gave a lift of her shoulder. "I'm a CPA."

"A CPA. That's . . ."

"Boring," she said with a wry smile.

"Highly respectable," he corrected. "Do you like it?"

Annie lowered her gaze. She suspected Rafe's dark eyes could see far too much.

She wasn't ready to confront her sense of dissatisfaction with her career. Not with herself. Not with her foster parents. And certainly not with a stranger. "It's a stable career with growth potential." She mouthed the words she'd heard since she was ten years old.

"Did that come on the brochure?" he teased, holding out a hand as she jerked her head up to send him a warning glare. "Okay, okay. I didn't mean to offend you. I'm just guessing that it's more functional than the job of your deepest fantasy."

She continued to glare, her hand clenching in her lap as her heart gave a renegade leap.

At the moment, her deepest fantasy included this man, a sturdy bed, and a hot fudge sundae.

A wicked desire she had no intention of confessing.

"What do you do?" she instead demanded.

"I've recently left the military," he said, something that reminded her of the dark, howling emptiness deep in her heart flaring through his eyes. Then he forced a smile to his lips. "Now that I'm back in the States, I've started a security firm with a few of my friends."

"You're a rent-a-cop?"

He gave a sudden laugh. "We're a little more specialized than that."

The underlying edge in his voice made her stiffen in warning. She studied the starkly beautiful face, allowing herself to accept what her unconscious mind had known all along.

Beneath the casual charm was a man who could kill without mercy.

She licked her suddenly dry lips. "How long have you been in town?"

He stilled, seeming to catch her sudden tension. "Four days." Slowly he lowered his hand to reach into his back pocket. "And if you're curious, I had to make a quick trip to Paris to help an old friend."

With a casual gesture he tossed a passport on the table, his dark gaze monitoring the blush that stained her cheeks.

Busted.

She cleared the lump from her throat. "Why would I be curious?"

He reached to flick open the passport, revealing the date and official stamp of his return to the country.

"Because you're an intelligent woman and you have to wonder if I had anything to do with Jenny Brown's disappearance."

She hid a wry smile. The dates certainly proved he had been out of the country, but the truth was that didn't ease her wariness.

Okay, she didn't believe this man was a crazed serial killer. Especially now he'd offered her proof he'd been in France.

But that didn't make him any less dangerous.

Like clockwork, the hovering waitress swooped forward, placing another beer in front of Rafe despite the fact he hadn't ordered it.

She also managed to drop a folded piece of paper in his lap.

No doubt it was her name and number.

Annie shook her head. Smooth. Real smooth.

"Just call if you need anything," the woman cooed. "Anything."

A portion of Annie's tension eased at Rafe's resigned expression as he swept the note off his lap and onto the floor.

Clearly the waitress wasn't the first woman to pester him when he was trying to have a private conversation.

"Maybe you should show her your passport," Annie murmured.

He reached to grab the passport and pushed it back into

his pocket. "I don't spread it around," he assured her. "Strictly one woman at a time."

"Hmm."

He pushed aside the beer and leaned his arms on the table. "Can I ask what you're doing here?"

She instinctively pressed back against the rigid cushion, afraid of getting sucked into the raw male vortex that swirled around him. "In this restaurant?"

"In Newton."

"No."

His lips twitched at her blunt refusal. "Fair enough. Then tell me what you like to do when you're not crunching numbers."

He was tenacious. She'd give him that.

"I read. Jog. Kickbox."

A genuine surprise rippled over his face. "Amazing."

She frowned. Was he mocking her? "What's amazing?"

"I jog every morning at five a.m. on the dot. A routine that started when my father began hauling my ass out of bed when I was ten years old," he said. "On the weekends I kickbox with my friends, and I have several old fractured bones and a few scars to prove they're all better than me. And when I have a quiet evening, there's nothing I like more than a bottle of wine and a good book."

Her eyes narrowed. "No doubt you also have a devoted wife and children tucked away."

"No wife. No children." He smiled, as if he knew she'd been fishing for info without coming out and asking. "I do, however, have two golden Labs who live with me at my ranch, and they're extremely jealous. But I promise I won't tell if you won't."

"You have a ranch?" Her breath caught, a pang of longing tugging at her heart.

She acutely missed her foster parents' home. Her animals. The wide-open spaces. The silence.

Katherine had pushed her to move to Denver out of the belief that Annie was becoming too isolated. She assumed it was fear that kept Annie from leaving the nest and spreading her wings.

And that could be a part of it.

Her past would never truly leave her in peace.

But most of her desire to remain had quite simply been because she loved the ranch.

"Right now it's just empty land with a house I've refurbished, a stable, and some run-down buildings." His expression revealed how much the property meant to him. "Someday—"

His words were interrupted as the waitress made yet another attempt to gain his attention. "Can I get you anything else?" she asked, the perfume she'd recently doused on herself making Annie's nose wrinkle in disgust. "Dessert? Another beer?"

Annie loudly cleared her throat.

She couldn't play this game with Rafe.

Not only was it dangerous to let herself be distracted, but she didn't do relationships.

"I'll take my bill, thanks," she told the waitress.

Rafe at last gave the woman the thrill she'd been seeking when he tilted back his head to smile. "Put it on mine," he commanded.

The woman heaved a sigh and Annie slid out of the booth.

She didn't want to be there when the waitress stripped off her uniform and crawled in Rafe's lap.

"Knock yourself out," she muttered, heading toward the door.

Sensing that Rafe was watching from the window, Annie crossed the parking lot to her Jeep. Then, climbing in, she started the engine and headed toward the highway without looking back.

It took several miles for her tension to ease and her sense of humor to return. Relaxing in her seat, she allowed her lips to twitch at the thought of Rafe trying to wrestle his way past the waitress to get to the door.

Rafe was a trained soldier, but the waitress had persistence on her side.

Then her amusement faded at the realization that now she was gone, he might have decided to accept the woman's blatant invitations.

Not that it was any of her business, she grimly reminded herself.

Hopefully by tomorrow Jenny would return home, and she could be on her way back to Denver, where Rafe Vargas would become nothing more than a pleasant memory.

In less than a quarter of an hour, Annie pulled to a halt in front of her motel room.

Crawling out of the Jeep, she locked it and headed toward the door, only to come to a wary halt.

Someone was watching her.

It wasn't the same as when she sensed Rafe's lingering gaze.

That'd felt . . . exciting.

This made her skin crawl.

"Hello?" She slid her hand into her purse, wrapping her fingers around the pepper spray she always carried. "Is there anyone there?" She cautiously backed toward her motel door. "Look, I know you're out there," she called out.

Her gaze scanned the gravel lot shrouded in shadows.

On the corner was a small coffee shop that was closed for the night, and across the road was an empty gas station that looked on the point of collapse.

The only light came from the windows of a nearby home that doubled as the motel office.

"I'm not going crazy," she breathed, her back pressed against the door.

She couldn't see the watcher, but he was out there. Stalking. Waiting. Savoring.

Her throat closed shut, but even as she was frantically digging in her purse for the key, a back porch light flicked on and the owner stepped out of his house.

"Is there anything wrong, Ms. White?" he called out.

Locating the key, she pulled it out of her bag and shoved it into the doorknob.

"No. Thank you." The lock clicked and she paused long enough to give a small wave before darting into the room and slamming the door behind her.

Oh . . . God.

She pressed a hand to her thundering heart.

It was happening again.

Hidden in the shadows of the alley, he clenched his hands and watched the woman enter the motel room.

He could hear the sound of her ragged breathing and sense the way her body trembled as she'd slammed the door behind her.

God forgive him. He hadn't meant to scare her. That was the last thing he would ever want.

His sweet Annabelle was special. So kind and gentle. Like an angel.

She was meant to be treasured. Protected.

Last time he'd failed in his duty. But now he had a second chance. He wasn't going to blow it.

But first he had work to do.

The bad woman had to be punished.

Only then would Annabelle be safe . . .

Chapter Four

Rafe forced himself to wait ten minutes before he left the restaurant and returned to Newton so he could drive by the motel and make sure the yellow Jeep was safely parked in the gravel lot.

The last thing he wanted was for Annie to think he was some psycho stalker, but he had to make sure she'd made it back to her room safely.

He told himself it was his natural protective instincts. Any man would be worried about a young female out at night when there was a potential killer on the loose.

Especially if the killer was connected to her father.

But in his gut he knew that his driving compulsion was something more.

He just didn't know what that *more* was.

Refusing to give in to the impulse to park across the street and keep an eye on her like some creeper, he turned the truck around and headed back to LaClede to pick up a few groceries. It was a chore that could easily have waited until the next day, but he wasn't anxious to return to his grandfather's house.

He'd managed to clear the boxes out of the living room, bathroom, and one bedroom, but it still felt cramped. Claustrophobic. As if his grandfather's ghost was standing at his shoulder, urging him to leave.

The bastard.

At last he returned to Newton, pulling to a halt in front of the small house built on the very edge of town.

He grimaced at the sagging roof and the wraparound porch that listed to the side. The white paint had peeled away and the hedges grown to overtake the small front yard. Long ago his grandfather had kept the property in pristine condition, but it'd been years since his health had been good enough to do the work, and he'd been too damned proud to ask for help.

Behind the house the yard stretched to the edge of an empty field, with two large sheds overfilled with boxes. So far he hadn't done more than glance inside and slam the doors shut.

The mere thought of having to dig through all the crap was enough to make Rafe wish he could toss a match and be done with the problem.

Easy peasy.

Stepping on the porch, he froze as he heard the creak of a floorboard.

Shit. Someone was inside.

Cautiously, Rafe set the bag of groceries on the porch swing and pulled out the gun holstered beneath his sweatshirt. Then, with the silence that came from years of rigid training, he was moving to press himself flat against the front door he hadn't bothered to lock. Why would he? Not only was the small town the sort of place you left your door open, but he'd be happy as hell if someone wanted to come in and haul off the shit inside.

Now he cursed his lax security.

The last thing he wanted was to have to shoot some yokel who decided to snoop around.

Easing the door open, he had the gun pointed toward the

center of the room when a familiar male voice echoed through the darkness.

"You shoot me and I'm going to be pissed," Teagan drawled. "And my mother will kick your ass."

"What the hell?"

Shoving the gun back in its holster, Rafe closed the door and flipped the switch on the wall. Instantly the room was filled with a dull yellow glow from the overhead light, revealing the large man dressed in camo pants and a black T-shirt that was stretched across the impressive width of his chest.

Rafe frowned. The last person he expected to be leaning against the crumbling fireplace was Teagan.

"How did you get here?" he demanded.

The computer genius shrugged. "Hauk flew me to Des Moines and I rented a car."

Rafe glanced out the nearby window. He'd been distracted when he'd pulled up to the house, but there was no way he'd missed a car. "Where is it?"

"I parked at the gas station on the corner." Teagan gave a dramatic shudder. The man was a freak when it came to cars, devoting his spare time to refurbishing old automobiles and selling them at an enormous profit. "I didn't want anyone to see me driving the POS."

Rafe arched a brow. "And you just decided to break into my house?"

"I didn't want to wander around town terrifying the natives."

Rafe gave a short laugh at the thought of the large male with his buzz cut and tattoos strolling down the streets of Newton.

He definitely would have caused a panic.

"Good choice," he said dryly, planting his fists on his hips. "But you wouldn't have to worry about the natives if you'd stayed in Houston."

"You asked me to get you info, didn't you?"

The faux reasonable tone did nothing to ease the spike in Rafe's temper.

He loved his partners like brothers. He truly did. But sometimes they could be worse than mother hens.

"I didn't say you had to personally deliver it," he pointed out. "This might be the boonies, but I do have Internet access."

The golden eyes narrowed. "You know I always go above and beyond the call of duty."

"Yeah, and you're as nosy as an old woman."

Teagan smiled, smart enough not to try and deny his reason for traveling to Newton. "You can't blame me for being curious why you're suddenly interested in a serial killer."

True. If the positions were reversed, he wouldn't be able to stay away. Not until he was certain his friend hadn't lost his mind.

"Where are the files?" he asked.

Teagan nodded toward the low, arched doorway across the room. "In the kitchen. Along with a few bottles from your favorite microbrewery."

"Damn." The mention of the beer had Rafe instantly on the move. He'd been enduring cheap on-tap beer for the past week. "If you weren't so ugly I'd kiss you," he said.

Teagan strolled behind him. "You're so not my type."

"Thank God." Rafe opened the fridge to pull out two beers, using the edge of the counter to pop off the caps. "I've seen your type," he told his friend, handing him one of the bottles.

"Harsh," Teagan muttered with a smile. They both knew he always chose drop-dead gorgeous females. Then, moving to the center of the cramped room, he tapped the files stacked on the dining table. "Here's the info on Don White."

Rafe pulled out a seat, flipping open the top folder and spreading the contents across the table.

"It's kind of sketchy," he muttered.

There was a black-and-white mug shot, a dozen news-paper clippings that screamed the headline NEWTON SLAYER, a copy of White's driver's license, the mortgage on his farm, and the insurance policy on a silver Taurus.

"Sketchy is the right word," Teagan growled, gingerly taking a seat across the table.

There was a creak of protest as his weight threatened to turn the hand-carved piece of furniture into firewood. They both sucked in a breath, waiting to make sure his ass wasn't going to hit the linoleum floor, before Teagan leaned forward to plant his elbows on the table.

"What do you mean?" Rafe asked.

"I can't find any info on him before he moved to Newton."

"That's weird." Rafe pointed toward the top newspaper clipping. "It says here that he was born in Fairbanks and moved to Bahrain with his family. After his wife and son died in a car accident, he moved with his daughter to Newton."

"Bogus."

"You're sure?"

"Dude. It's me."

Rafe grimaced. If Teagan said it was bogus, it was bogus. End of story.

"That's crazy," he muttered. "Granted, the police in this town are closer to Barney Fife than Sherlock Holmes, but the federal authorities had to have been involved once they realized they had a serial killer on the loose."

"The I.D. was good enough to pass most background checks," Teagan said. "Especially since they were no doubt in a hurry to close the book on the man. Once he was dead there was no reason to look any closer. Most of the evidence was boxed up and stored in the local courthouse, which burned to the ground just a few days later."

Rafe tapped his finger on the mug shot. Why would Don White have an alias?

The obvious reason was that he was on the run.

But from what?

The cops? A previous victim who could I.D. him?

At this point it was impossible to say.

He lifted his head to meet Teagan's steady gaze. "You're still digging?"

"Yep, but it'll take a few days."

Rafe pointed to the rest of the files. "What are those?"

"The victims." Teagan grabbed a folder and handed it to Rafe. "Number one. Connie Matthews." He waited for Rafe to pull out a picture of the woman with short, brown hair and a narrow, weary face that looked like it had forgotten how to smile. "Twenty-seven years old," Teagan continued. "She had one son in sixth grade. She went to the local convenience store one night for cigarettes and never came home. She was married to an alcoholic prick who regularly sent her to the hospital, so people assumed he'd finally killed her and dumped her in a ditch."

Rafe swallowed a sigh, not surprised that his companion's face looked like it'd been carved from granite.

Teagan's father had nearly beaten his mother to death before Teagan got big and mean enough to run the bastard off.

Rafe motioned with his hand. "Number two?"

Teagan handed him the second file. "Vicky Price. Taken two days later. A high school dropout and single mom."

Rafe flinched as he opened the folder to see a picture of a blond-haired girl who looked like she should be cheering for the local football team.

"She was only seventeen?" he rasped.

"Yeah. She'd just completed her GED and was about to start work at a local grocery store." Teagan grabbed the next file. "Number three was Teresa Hunt."

Rafe frowned as he pulled out the picture of an overweight, middle-aged woman with gray hair and a round face. "Forty-seven," he read from the bio that Teagan had pulled together. "Married for twenty-five years with six kids, most of them grown."

"Number four is Joyce Remington." Teagan added the

next file to his growing pile. "A thirty-year-old divorced mother of three boys. She worked as a janitor at the local school."

Rafe barely had time to glance at the grainy picture of an anemic-looking woman with faded red hair and pale skin before there was another file in front of him. "Lori Menard," he read the name on the tab.

"The trophy wife of the local banker," Teagan said as Rafe flipped the folder open to study the professional headshot of a bottle blonde with wide blue eyes and Cupid lips. A traditional Midwest beauty queen. "It was his third marriage. She'd just had their first baby when she was taken." The sixth folder was shoved in front of Rafe. "Kathy Benson. The church organist and grandmother." File seven landed on top. "And last, but not least, Sharon Brock, the wife of the current sheriff." Teagan pulled out the photo of a young woman with dark blond hair carefully styled to look windblown and a pretty, petulant face. "She was pregnant when she disappeared."

"Holy shit." Rafe spread out the pictures, pushing aside his horror at the knowledge each of the women had been gruesomely murdered. He wasn't a trained professional, but it seemed weird he couldn't make a connection between them. "I thought serial killers had a pattern."

"So did I." Teagan tapped an impatient finger on the table. "I ran a dozen different algorithms, and all I could come up with was the fact they were all women, they were all from Newton, and they all had children, except for the last, and she was pregnant."

"It's thin."

Teagan reached to gather up the files, putting them back in a pile before he placed his hands flat on the table. "Now." He had on his *don't screw with me* expression. "Tell me what the hell is going on."

Knowing the stubborn bastard wasn't going to leave until

Rafe had shared at least a part of his interest in a long-dead serial killer, Rafe drained his beer and rose to his feet.

"Come with me."

Leaving the kitchen, Rafe led his friend across the living room and out the front door. Then, reaching into the bag he'd left on the porch swing, he pulled out the poster he'd taken off the window of the grocery store.

"Here."

Teagan tilted the paper to catch the light spilling through the open door. "Shit," he growled as he read the information about the missing Jenny. "Did someone hire you to find her?"

"No." Rafe hesitated. He didn't want to share his unexpected fascination with Annie White. Not because he worried about Teagan busting his balls—that was a given—but he didn't want his friends questioning his sanity. "Let's just say I've taken a personal interest in the case."

Teagan tossed the poster back in his bag. "Do you suspect this missing girl has something to do with the dead serial killer?"

"I'm not sure."

"Does it have anything to do with your grandfather?"

"Not a damned thing."

Teagan folded his arms over his chest, his muscles bulging. "I'm going to figure it out."

"There's nothing to figure out." Rafe pointedly glanced at his watch. It was just after eleven. "Don't you have someplace else to be?"

"Not really. Hauk isn't coming to pick me up until I give him a call." Teagan flashed a smile. "We can have a slumber party and braid each other's hair."

Rafe rolled his eyes. "Even if you had hair, I . . ."

He forgot what he was saying as headlights flashed over the porch and he instinctively moved to disappear into the shadows. Since the house was the last on the block it was rare to have any traffic, and never at this time of night.

Watching the car pass, his vague curiosity sharpened to disbelief as he recognized the yellow Jeep pass by.

He muttered a curse, digging in his pocket for the keys to his truck.

"Rafe?" Teagan grabbed his shoulder, turning him to meet his puzzled gaze. "What's going on?"

"Come on." Jerking free of his friend's grasp, Rafe vaulted over the low banister that framed the porch and jogged across the yard to jump into his truck.

Five seconds later he'd fired up the engine and shoved the truck into gear. With a muttered curse, Teagan jumped into the seat beside him, barely managing to slam his door shut before they were jolting down the graveled road at a speed that threatened to snap his spine.

"Slow down, dude," Teagan growled. "Where are we going?"

Rafe kept his gaze locked on the vehicle ahead of him, keeping his lights off as they traveled past empty fields and clusters of trees. "I don't know."

"Fan-fucking-tastic." Teagan leaned down to pull a handgun from the holster he kept hidden at his ankle.

They traveled in silence, Rafe slowing the truck to keep space between himself and the vehicle ahead. Then, as the Jeep turned onto a narrow drive and halted in front of an abandoned house, he pulled to a stop at the side of the road.

"What the hell?" He watched as a shadowy figure climbed out of the Jeep and headed around the edge of the two-story farmhouse.

"Wait," Teagan muttered, pulling out his phone and tapping on the screen. "I recognize this place." He turned the phone so Rafe could see the black-and-white image of a house with a large headline above it. "Here."

"Home of the Newton Slayer," Rafe read out loud.

It took a mere glance to recognize the picture was of the same house that stood just ahead of them.

Granted, the roof was now sagging and half the covered

porch had fallen in, but the stained-glass dormer window and distinctive weathervane shaped like an owl were unmistakable.

Which helped to explain the late-night visit.

"So who are we following?" Teagan demanded, slipping his phone back into his pocket.

Rafe scanned the overgrown fields that surrounded the house, searching for any sign of movement.

"Annie White," he admitted, accepting that Teagan deserved the truth if he was going to be put in danger.

"White?" Teagan made a sound of shock. "The daughter of the serial killer?"

"Yes."

"Damn, Rafe," his companion breathed.

Rafe shoved his door open as he watched Annie return from the side of the yard, climbing onto the porch and entering the house. "Look, we can discuss this later. I'm going after her." He pulled out his gun, glancing toward his friend as the large man climbed out of the truck. "I need you to do a sweep of the area to make sure we're alone."

Teagan scowled, blatantly unimpressed with Rafe's choice of midnight activities. But with a short nod, he jogged down the road, clearly intent on starting his search at the edge of the distant field.

Rafe chose the more direct route.

Crossing the yard that had been overtaken by weeds, he cautiously stepped onto the porch that had become a minefield for the unwary—missing boards, rusty tools, and an angry opossum that hissed at him as he passed.

Not that inside was any better.

Stepping into a front room filled with furniture covered with dust and spiderwebs, he shuddered. The walls were decorated with garish graffiti that proclaimed the Newton Slayer a "Devil" and wished for him to rot in hell. And someone had dressed up a mannequin in women's clothing and smeared it with red paint, leaving it in the center of the threadbare carpet.

Christ.

The entire place would be greatly improved with a lit match and a splash of gasoline.

Moving to grab the mannequin and toss it in a distant corner, Rafe was prepared for the sound of Annie's frightened voice coming from deeper in the house.

"Who's there?"

"Rafe," he immediately called out. "Rafe Vargas."

There was a short pause, as if the woman was considering the possibility of slipping out the back door. Then, smart enough to know he would track her down, she slowly returned to the front room.

Rafe's gut twisted at the sight of her small body covered in a pair of flannel shorts and a tiny top with spaghetti straps. Her hair was tangled as if she'd just crawled out of bed, and her face was pale in the moonlight that poured through the busted windows.

She looked young and fragile and utterly lost.

Still, she didn't cower.

Oh no. Not Annie White.

Instead she tilted her chin and glared at him like a kitten preparing to hiss at a cat twice her size. "What are you doing here?" she demanded.

"I saw your Jeep drive past my grandfather's house and I followed you."

She frowned. "Why?"

"Because I was worried." He moved forward. God, he wanted to wrap her in his arms and carry her away from the evil in this place. "It's late for you to be out alone."

Her eyes widened as she abruptly pressed herself against the far wall. "No," she rasped, her gaze locked on the gun in his hand. "Stay back."

Damn. He'd forgotten he was holding the weapon. Now

he turned the weapon in his hand, angling the handle of the pistol toward her as he continued forward. "Easy."

"Please . . ." A frantic pulse beat at the base of her throat. "No."

Rafe grimaced. He could feel the force of her panic as he carefully placed the gun in her hand and wrapped her fingers around the grip.

Goddamn her psycho father.

He'd terrorized this poor woman until it was a wonder she was capable of functioning.

Of course, he wryly acknowledged, any woman would be spooked to be alone in this house with a virtual stranger.

"The safety is on, but it's loaded, so try not to shoot me unless it's absolutely necessary," he warned her, slowly releasing her hand and backing away. "Okay?"

She stared at the gun for a long second before lifting her hand and pointing the weapon at his heart with a surprisingly fluid motion.

"I went hunting with my foster father, so I know how to shoot," she warned.

He cocked a brow, his lips twitched.

Her father had tried to destroy her, but she still had plenty of spirit.

Thank God.

"Good." He met her challenging gaze with a nod of approval. "Now tell me what you're doing here dressed in your . . ." His brain searched for the words women used for the strange things they slept in. "Jammies."

She glanced around the shadowed room. "I used to live here."

"It's kind of late for a homecoming, isn't it?"

"I—"

Her words broke off with a violent shiver, and jerking down the zipper of his hoodie, Rafe pulled it off and moved to wrap it around the half-dressed woman. "Dammit, you're freezing," he growled, briefly taking the weapon so he could tuck her arms into the sleeves of the jacket. Once it was zipped, he returned the weapon to her trembling hand. "You shouldn't be here."

She glanced up, her eyes dark pools of misery. "I had to come," she whispered.

"Why?"

"I was worried."

He studied her with growing concern. There was some dark, haunting emotion that threatened to consume her.

More than just fear.

He gently grasped her shoulders. "Annie?" he prompted in soft tones.

She licked her lips, but she made no effort to pull from his touch. "I saw a woman being taken," she at last said, her voice harsh. "I was afraid she was here."

His brows snapped together, his hand automatically reaching for his phone. "You witnessed a woman being kidnapped?"

"No. I mean it was . . ." She hesitated, then with an obvious effort forced the words past her stiff lips. "It was a dream."

Rafe abruptly recalled the waitress's revelation that Annie had been institutionalized for claiming to have witnessed the murders. "A dream or a vision?"

She ducked her head as if preparing for his ridicule. "I'm not crazy."

"Annie, look at me." He hooked a finger beneath her chin, gently urging her to meet his gaze. "My mother came from a long line of psychics," he said, hoping his sincerity was unmistakable. He'd taken a lot of shit over the years for his beliefs, but he never apologized. He knew the truth. "She died when I was too young to truly understand what that meant, but I know that I've inherited some of her gift."

She searched his face, no doubt looking for any hint of mockery.

When she found none, she released a shaky breath. "You're psychic?" she asked.

He shook his head. "Not exactly, but I've learned to follow my intuition."

"Intuition?" A portion of her terror eased as her lips gave a small twitch. "I thought that was a female thing."

"I'm serious." He tapped the end of her nose, feeling ridiculously proud that he'd managed to distract her, if only for a few seconds. "Even my commanding officer listened to my hunches. Hell, he risked lives on it. So if you tell me you have visions, I believe you."

Chapter Five

Annie swallowed the lump in her throat, feeling mesmerized by Rafe's dark, compelling gaze.

In the back of her mind a tiny voice was whispering she should run.

She was standing in her father's abandoned house in the middle of the night with a man who might very well be a serial killer.

What did it matter if she had a gun? She didn't know for sure that it was loaded. And even if it was, he was close enough to snatch it from her hand.

But she made no effort to move.

She didn't know why, but when Rafe Vargas was near she felt safe.

And crazy or not, she needed to share her fears with someone.

"I don't know what's real," she whispered, afraid if she said the words too loud it might bring her nightmare to life.

His fingers tucked a stray curl behind her ear, his touch featherlight.

"Will you tell me what you saw?"

"A woman . . . but only a shadowed outline."

"Did you recognize her?" he asked.

She shook her head. "I could tell that she had long hair, but it was too dark to see her features."

His fingers traced the line of her jaw. "Anything else?"

She trembled, the images from her dream flashing through her brain. "She was running through an empty field."

"Was someone chasing her?"

"Yes." She was absolutely certain.

He nodded without hesitation and Annie had to blink back silly tears.

God. She was so used to people pooh-poohing her wild claims, trying to convince her that it was all just a dream. Or worse, looking at her as if she were out of her mind.

It felt extraordinary to have someone who simply listened.

"Were there any details that could help locate the field?" he pressed.

"I think there was a barn. Or maybe it was an old house." She grimaced. It would be dangerously easy for her mind to add in details she hadn't seen. "I don't know." She blew out a frustrated sigh. "All I remember is watching her run across the field and feeling . . ."

Her words trailed off with a small sound of distress.

His hand cupped her chin as he tilted back her head to study her horrified expression. "Annie?"

Her blood ran cold as she suddenly remembered the feel of the crisp night breeze ruffling her hair and the scent of a wood fire from a nearby chimney.

It'd felt so real.

As if she had been standing at the side of the road, watching the woman flee in terror.

"Happy," she abruptly burst out. "I felt happy that she was running so I could catch her."

"Shh. It's okay," he murmured, carefully pulling her into his arms. "Why did you come here?"

Annie leaned against his bare chest. The warmth of his body helped to ease the tiny tremors that raced through her, and the tangy scent of his male cologne . . .

She abruptly sucked in a sharp breath, realizing the sudden tingles racing through her were pure feminine arousal.

Good Lord. What was it about Rafe Vargas?

She'd never in her life been so potently aware of a man.

With a grim effort she forced herself to ignore the desire to discover what it would feel like to run her hands over the chiseled muscles of his chest. Or to tug his head down and kiss him senseless.

"The last time, my father put the women in a shelter beneath the garage," she muttered.

His hand ran a soothing path up and down the curve of her back. "Do you want me to go look?"

She shook her head. The moment she'd reached the top of the drive she'd realized that her hasty midnight trip had been a waste of time. "There's no need," she said. "It's gone. Someone bulldozed it and filled the shelter beneath it with dirt."

She felt something brush the top of her head.

A kiss?

"It's not the only building that could use a good bulldozing," he murmured wryly.

"True," she had to agree, her gaze moving toward the room that had once been filled with sunshine and happiness and childhood dreams. Now there was nothing left but . . .

"Shit." With a jerk, Annie pulled away from Rafe, instinctively aiming the gun toward the nearest window. The shadow she'd seen hadn't been a figment of her imagination. "There's someone outside."

"Whoa." Rafe reached to press her hand down, although he didn't try to take the gun. "It's a friend of mine. He's a pain in the ass but I'd prefer if you didn't shoot him."

She scowled as she watched the shadowed form move toward the dilapidated chicken coop.

"What's he doing?"

"Making sure there aren't any other midnight visitors," Rafe said, something in his voice suggesting that he was accustomed to searching for unwanted intruders.

"Oh." Without warning, Annie swayed as a tidal wave of weariness crashed over her. When was the last night she'd actually slept more than a few hours? She couldn't even remember. "I should get back to the motel," she muttered.

Perhaps sensing she was on the edge of collapse, Rafe carefully pried the gun from her hands and tucked it in the waistband of his jeans.

"Do you have anyone I can call to stay with you?"

She gave a sharp shake of her head, her teeth beginning to chatter. As much as she dreaded being alone, she wasn't going to call her foster parents.

They would do everything in their power to try and force her back to Denver.

"I'll be fine."

"You can barely stand," he growled, his expression tight with a strange frustration. As if it bothered him that she insisted on being alone. "At least let me drive you back."

"My car—"

"Teagan can drive your Jeep back to the motel." He overrode her protest, his voice warning his decision wasn't up for discussion.

If she hadn't been so damned weary, Annie would have informed him that she didn't take orders from overly arrogant men.

No matter how gorgeous they might be.

But unfortunately, he was right.

She really wasn't in any condition to be driving.

Besides, if she was being perfectly honest, she would admit that she wasn't overly eager to retrace her path through the dark country lane.

She'd been in a mindless panic when she'd left the motel. Now, however, her skin crawled at the thought of the unseen eyes that had been watching her earlier.

Without a word, she stepped around his larger form and headed for the door.

After a good night's sleep she would feel . . .

Her thought was interrupted as she kicked a small object that had been left in the middle of the floor.

Automatically glancing down she came to a sharp halt, her breath locked in her chest as she leaned over to pick up the small doll with the mass of tangled blond hair.

Britney Spears.

It was covered in dust, and the clothes were rumpled, but Annie had a vivid memory of dancing through the house with the doll clutched in her hand.

The sun had been shining and her father was laughing as he watched her silly antics.

"Annie?"

The sound of Rafe's deep voice broke her out of the past, although the precious feelings of childish joy refused to be completely dismissed.

"This house should be a place of horror, but I had such good memories," she muttered, her attention locked on the doll that looked as lost and broken as she felt since returning to Newton.

He moved to stand next to her, his hands clenching as if he was battling the urge to reach out and touch her. "You loved your father?"

"Very much," she admitted without hesitation, lifting her head to meet his searching gaze. "I know you must think it's twisted, but he was always kind and patient and funny when we were together."

"I don't think it's twisted at all," he protested. "Tell me about him." He held up a hand when she frowned. "I mean, tell me about him as your father."

Expecting the usual condemnation, Annie was caught off guard by his gentle question.

No one had ever asked her about Don White as something other than the psycho serial killer.

Tentatively she allowed herself to return to the past, the doll unconsciously pressed to her chest. "He always had two Oreo cookies and a glass of milk waiting for me on that table when I came home from school." She nodded toward the shrouded piece of furniture situated near the door. She hadn't eaten an Oreo cookie since she'd left Newton. "And he went with me to the movies on Saturday afternoon just because I said I wanted to be an actress when I grew up. And every Sunday morning he took me to the restaurant for pancakes." Bittersweet pain sliced through her heart. "I don't understand how the same man could be so evil."

"He was sick, Annie, not evil," Rafe murmured.

She hunched a shoulder. "Is there a difference?"

"Yes. I've seen men in battle," he said, a hard edge in his voice hinting at memories that were as dark and painful as her own. "Some are just naturally cruel. They enjoy causing pain because it's a basic part of their nature." His jaw clenched. "And there are others who've been ruined. By life. By war. By . . . fate. They do what they do because they can't help themselves."

Annie studied the lean, fiercely handsome face. How did he do it? How did he always know exactly what to say?

It was freaky.

"Thank you," she breathed.

He cocked a brow. "For what?"

"Most people don't want to think the Newton Slayer could have any redeeming qualities," she said, having learned from the second she'd been rescued that her father was public enemy number one. "I usually feel guilty for not hating him. He destroyed so many lives."

He brushed a hand over her tangled curls, careful to keep his touch light. "He was your father."

"Yes." He'd been more than that. He'd been her entire family. She gave another shiver. "We should go."

He dropped his hand and nodded, keeping a small distance between them as she headed out the door and across the rickety porch.

"My truck is at the end of the drive," he murmured as they reached the overgrown yard. "I'll tell Teagan to join us at the motel."

She had a vague impression of a large man who appeared

from the shadows to speak with Rafe before he was jogging toward her Jeep, but her concentration centered on keeping her feet moving forward.

Christ, she was tired.

Rafe was back at her side by the time she reached the edge of the road, opening the door to his truck and helping her to climb into the seat before he was rounding the hood and taking his place behind the steering wheel.

In silence he started the engine, flipping the heater on high before performing a U-turn. There was a brief stop as he waited for his friend to approach the truck holding her purse that he'd obviously retrieved from her Jeep. Then, placing the bag in her lap, he shoved the truck in gear and headed back to town at a pace far slower than the one she'd used to get to the house.

Annie clutched her purse, only vaguely aware of her surroundings. She had the impression of genuine leather and a dashboard that had all the bells and whistles. The sort of truck that would be functional for work around a ranch but no doubt cost more than she made in a year. But her gaze remained glued to the dark, chiseled profile of her companion.

Safely tucked in his car with the warm air beginning to ease her shivers, there was nothing to distract her from Rafe's sheer male beauty.

It was . . . nice.

Almost as if she was a normal girl being driven home by a man who she found intensely attractive.

A damned shame her brief daydream didn't last for long.

All too soon they were back in town and he was turning into the drive of the motel. Rafe pulled to a halt in the center of the parking lot and glanced in her direction.

"Do you remember where you lived before coming to Newton?"

She froze at the abrupt question, too startled to tell him it was none of his damned business.

"Most of my memories from my early childhood are

fuzzy. I think my dad said that we lived overseas, but it's really just a blur," she admitted.

It was weird. She had such a clear recollection of her time in Newton. Time with her father. Her friends at the school she'd attended. Climbing on top of the house so she could see her father in the distant fields.

But she never could capture any memories of her days before coming to Newton or the days after she'd been found tied and blindfolded in the bomb shelter.

"Why do you ask?"

"I thought you might have some family who could come to give you support," he smoothly explained.

Her gaze narrowed. She sensed there was more to his question than he was admitting, but she was too tired to try and search for any hidden meanings.

"There are just my foster parents, and I don't want to worry them," she said.

He reached into his rear pocket, pulling out his wallet.

"Then I want your promise you'll call me if you need anything," he commanded, handing her a small business card.

She took the card with a frown, asking the question that had been bothering her from the moment their paths had crossed.

"Why?"

"Why what?"

"Why are you so determined to help me?" she demanded. "I'm a stranger."

He held her wary gaze. "It's what I do."

"A hero?"

"Something like that." He pointed toward the business card. "My private cell number is printed on the back. Call me . . . any time, for any reason."

Tucking the card in her purse, she crawled out of the truck and hurried to her motel room.

Behind her there was a flash of headlights as Rafe's friend pulled into the lot in her Jeep, but she didn't hesitate as she let herself into her room.

She was too exhausted to care that he would be forced to leave the keys in the Jeep. If someone wanted to steal it, then fine. Right now she was far more concerned with crawling into the small bed and pulling the covers over her head.

For the first time since coming to Newton her thoughts weren't on the monster who might or might not be stalking the streets, but on a gorgeous, aggravating male who promised to banish her nightmares for at least a few hours.

Rafe white-knuckled the steering wheel as Teagan climbed into the truck and slammed the door.

God. Damn.

He was nearly vibrating with the need to charge through that motel room and pull Annie into his arms.

Not for sex.

Well . . . he wouldn't say no. He'd spent an embarrassing amount of time fantasizing about getting Annie White naked since he'd first caught sight of her.

But his primary interest was making absolutely certain she was safe.

It was insane.

She was a stranger, but he knew beyond a shadow of a doubt that he would do whatever was necessary to protect her.

Period. End of story.

Turning so his massive shoulders blocked out the street-light from the door window, Teagan cleared his throat.

"Now I get your sudden interest in Don White."

Rafe gave a short, humorless laugh. "I'm glad one of us does."

"She's a beauty." Teagan hesitated, clearly something on his mind. "But she's clearly in a fragile state of mind."

Rafe jerked his head to glare toward his friend. "You think I intend to take advantage of her?"

Teagan shrugged. "I'm just saying she seems vulnerable."

Vulnerable. Fragile.

And potentially in danger.

"Which is why she needs a friend," he muttered.

"Just a friend?"

Teagan's face was lost in shadows, but Rafe didn't need to see his expression to get the full effect of his skepticism.

Rafe muttered a curse as he shoved the truck in gear and headed out of the parking lot. "Stop poking your nose where it doesn't belong," he snapped.

Teagan heaved a resigned sigh as Rafe drove through the empty streets. "A young, beautiful woman in danger. A handsome ex-soldier who has a savior complex?" He shook his head. "Yeah, that doesn't have disaster written all over it."

Rafe didn't have a brilliant comeback.

Hell, it did have all the makings of an epic disaster.

But there wasn't a damned thing he could do to change it.

Pulling to a halt in front of his grandfather's house, he shut off the engine and climbed out of the truck. Then, heading straight for the door, he pulled it open and waited for his friend to join him. "Do you intend to spend the night or what?" he demanded, not bothering with the whole Miss Manners thing.

It was not only unnecessary between the five friends, but unwelcome.

Teagan clapped him on the back. "First I intend to get drunk."

Rafe entered the cramped house. "Finally, something we can agree on."

The sun was pouring through the window when Rafe managed to wrench open his eyes and roll out of bed.

His head pounded, and a glance at his watch revealed it was well past eight.

Shit.

He'd not only missed his five o'clock jog, but he'd polished off the entire stash of microbrews that Teagan had brought with him. Which meant he was once again stuck with the nasty beer on tap the locals served.

Hopping into the shower, he pulled on clean jeans and a Houston Texans sweatshirt before heading into the living room.

Expecting Teagan to be passed out on the sofa after downing an impressive amount of tequila, he was pleasantly surprised to discover his friend walking through the door with two Styrofoam cups and a white pastry bag.

"Damn, is that coffee?" he demanded.

Dressed in his usual uniform of camo pants, T-shirt, and shitkickers, Teagan headed straight for the kitchen. "Coffee, doughnuts, and the latest gossip," he muttered.

Rafe's gut cramped with fear as he followed in Teagan's footsteps, watching as his friend fired up the computer that Rafe had left on the table. "Annie?" he rasped.

"Not her," Teagan reassured him, his expression grim even as Rafe breathed a sigh of relief. "But another woman went missing last night."

Oh . . . shit.

"From Newton?"

"Yep." Teagan began to tap on the keyboard. "A Brandi Phillips. Her husband went to the cops this morning saying that she didn't come home from her shift at the hospital in LaClede."

Rafe planted his hands on the table and watched his companion work his magic. In a matter of minutes the photo of a pretty dark-haired woman appeared.

"What else do you have on her?" he asked.

Teagan brought up a screen that looked like an employment file. "Twenty-seven years old," Teagan read out loud. "Graduated from Newton High School, then went to a community college to get her LPN license."

"Children?" he demanded.

A few more clicks and Teagan had her medical records pulled up. "Two sons," he said. "Seven and five."

"Damn." Rafe straightened. She matched the sketchy profile of the typical victim chosen by the Newton Slayer. So what did that mean? "It has to be a copycat," he muttered, even as he grimaced. He didn't like the feeling he was floundering in the dark. Even a man who depended on gut instinct understood the importance of hard facts. "I need a favor."

"Name it."

"There's a small table next to the front door of Annie's childhood home."

"What about it?"

"I want you to take it to Houston and have Max pull off the fingerprints."

Teagan frowned in confusion. "A hunch?"

"Not this time," Rafe denied. "That's the one thing I'm certain Don White touched."

"Yeah, along with a hundred other people," his friend muttered.

Rafe couldn't argue. But a long shot was better than no shot.

Right?

"We might get lucky and discover the true identity of Don White," he said.

"If he has a criminal record he'll be in AFIS," Teagan agreed. "But I still don't know what it matters now."

"Neither do I," Rafe admitted, ramming a hand through his damp hair. "But it's possible something in his past might help us. If nothing else, Annie deserves to learn the truth of her past."

Teagan gave a grudging nod. "Fine, but I don't like leaving you here alone."

"Go," Rafe insisted, his mind already centered on how quickly he could get to the local motel. He didn't want Annie to be alone when she discovered there was another missing woman.

He was stepping toward the doorway when Teagan placed a restraining hand on his shoulder.

"Just as a heads-up, I put cameras in this room and the living room, so you might want to keep your hairy ass covered when you're roaming around the house," he warned, pointing toward the small device that was tucked on top of the cabinets. "And if you intend to have company over, you need to keep your activities confined to the bedroom. I don't mind watching, but only if I'm going to be invited to join the fun."

Rafe regarded his friend in genuine surprise. "You put me under surveillance?"

"Yep," he admitted without apology. "And you try to disable them and I'm going to come back and set up house with you," he warned. "Your choice."

Rafe shook his head. "Interfering bastard."

Chapter Six

He washed the blood from his hands, his body still tingling with the cathartic bliss that came after a kill.

How had he forgotten how sweet it was?

Watching the life fade from the bitches' eyes.

Catching the soft gasp of their last breath.

To know he'd rid the world of her evil.

He had to make it safe.

For Annabelle . . .

Always for sweet Annabelle.

Annie woke with a sudden start, blinking in confusion.

How long had she been sleeping?

Reaching for the cell phone she'd left on the narrow table beside the headboard, she was startled to discover it was after eight.

Amazing.

Seven straight hours of uninterrupted rest.

It was like a miracle after nearly a week of waking every fifteen minutes.

Climbing out of bed, she took a quick shower and wrapped herself in a robe as she left the bathroom. Then, crossing her fingers the ancient coffee machine would heat the water to a temperature above lukewarm, she moved to the dresser that also doubled as a TV stand, a desk, and kitchenette.

It was there she at last noticed the small envelope that'd been shoved beneath her door.

She froze, dread twisting her stomach.

She wanted to believe it was a flyer from a local restaurant, or even a copy of her bill from the motel office.

Or maybe it was simply a mistaken identity, she acknowledged, catching sight of the name that had been written in careful block letters.

ANNABELLE

She was officially Annie.

It wasn't a nickname for Anne. Or Angelina.

And certainly not Annabelle.

That didn't, however, keep her hands from shaking as she snatched the envelope off the nasty green carpet and tore it open.

Her dread only increased as she pulled out the folded paper and read the short note:

> *One for sorrow,*
> *Two for luck . . .*

What the hell?

Feeling as if she'd been contaminated, she threw the envelope and paper on the shabby chair beside the door and rushed back to the bathroom to hop back in the shower, scrubbing herself red before drying off and pulling her hair into a braid.

Then, forcing herself to return to the main room, she dressed in a pair of jeans and a lightweight sweater, her heart lodging in her throat as there was a sharp knock on her door.

Christ, now what?

She hesitated, desperately hoping whoever was out there would assume she was gone and simply walk away.

Of course, with her current streak of shitty luck there was barely a pause before there was another knock, this one louder than the first.

"I know you're in there," a male voice called out. "Open the door."

Licking her dry lips, she forced her feet forward. A serial killer didn't knock on a motel room door in the middle of the morning, did he?

Leaving the chain attached as she cracked open the door, she allowed her gaze to slide over the short, stocky man with a large head shaped like a block and thinning brown hair and brown eyes.

He looked like one of those men who drove a Ford pickup and mowed their grass every Saturday morning.

Solid. Dependable. Boring.

"Yes?"

"Well, well." He planted his hands on his hips, emphasizing the belt strapped around his pudgy waist that held the leather holster. Her heart stuttered with fear at the sight of the handgun only inches from his fingers until her brain managed to register the brown khaki uniform. Clearly he was some sort of official. "What do you know," he continued with a pronounced Midwestern twang. "The rumors are true. Little Annie White."

She frowned. Was there something familiar about the man? "Have we met?"

"I'm Sheriff Brock."

"Oh." Suddenly she had a memory of that square face appearing directly in front of her as a blindfold was removed from her eyes. "You found me in the bomb shelter."

He gave a nod. "I did."

She cleared her throat. "Is there something you wanted?"

"We need to speak."

Damn. Annie grudgingly reached to slide the chain off its track so she could pull open the door and step onto the narrow sidewalk.

The morning had barely gotten started and already it promised to be a crappy day.

"About what?" she demanded.

He glanced over her shoulder. Was he trying to see if she was sharing the room with someone?

Creep.

"Can we go inside?" he asked.

"Actually I'd rather not." She reached to pull the door shut. She didn't like the feeling he was here to snoop into her business. "Such a small space makes me claustrophobic."

It wasn't a lie.

She didn't like to be in enclosed places with other people.

Which made her cubicle at the accounting firm a place of near torture.

"We could go for a coffee—"

"If you don't mind, I'd rather you just tell me what you have to say." She interrupted the man's smooth invitation, indifferent to the hardening of his expression.

She wasn't in the mood to worry about proper manners.

"Did you hear the latest news?" he abruptly asked.

She stiffened. Was this a trick question?

"Did they find Jenny?" she asked.

"No." His jaw clenched. "Another woman is missing."

Annie wasn't even aware she was moving until her back hit the closed door. "Oh my God," she breathed, her stomach heaving with a wave of nausea. "When?"

Despite her horrifying vision last night the news still came as a violent shock, her knees threatening to give way as she met the sheriff's hard glare.

"Last night. She left the hospital in LaClede after her shift as a nurse and never arrived home," he was saying. "Her name is Brandi Phillips. Do you know her?"

She blinked in confusion. "How would I know her?"

"She was a few years older than you, but you would have gone to Newton Elementary School together."

The shock began to recede enough for Annie to realize that this man wasn't here to catch up on old times.

Did he suspect that she had some information about the missing women?

"I didn't keep in contact with anyone from Newton after I left," she snapped.

"Then why are you back?" he pressed.

She squared her shoulders, not about to reveal she'd seen both women in her visions.

It was bad enough she'd shared her secret with Rafe Vargas.

"It's personal."

The brown eyes narrowed. "Did you remember something about the previous murders?"

She abruptly grimaced. The details of the day she'd been found in the bomb shelter were sketchy, but she'd read the reports.

Not only had her father been asleep on the cot, but there had been seven mutilated female bodies stacked in the back of the bomb shelter.

One of them had been Sharon Brock.

"I don't remember anything about your wife, if that's what you're asking," she muttered.

He grimaced. "I was too late for her."

"I'm sorry."

"It's the past." The light brown eyes hardened with a combination of frustration and . . . was that anger? "Or at least I thought it was. Now I'm not so sure."

"I don't know what this has to do with me."

"Did your father have a partner?"

She blinked at the abrupt question. "A partner?"

His jaw clenched. "Was there a relative or friend that he used to spend time with? Someone he might have encouraged to follow in his footsteps?"

Annie's breath tangled in her throat at the implication that her father had groomed an acquaintance to become a killer.

"No." She shuddered. There were a lot of things in her past that were fuzzy, but not this. "If my father wasn't working on the farm, he was spending time with me or one of our neighbors. There was no one else."

The sheriff appeared unconvinced by her insistence. "And you're here alone?"

"I told you I was."

"Did you make plans to meet someone here?"

Annie was distantly aware of the sun shining in a clear blue sky, the crisp breeze tugging at her damp braid, and the sound of tires crunching on gravel, but her attention remained glued to the man who was eyeing her with open suspicion.

"Why are you asking me these questions?"

He gave a lift of one shoulder. "People are starting to talk."

She couldn't halt her small flinch as he struck at her most vulnerable nerve.

Dammit. The mere thought of being the focus of attention was enough to make her break out in hives. "About me?"

"You know how small towns thrive on gossip."

Her heart clenched with a bittersweet urge to be back at her foster parents' isolated ranch.

Maybe if she'd just stayed there she wouldn't have started having the visions and she wouldn't have come to Newton and she wouldn't have to endure . . .

No. With a stern effort she shut down the cowardly train of thought.

She couldn't hide from the world forever.

"What are they saying?" she forced herself to ask.

"They're wondering if it's more than a coincidence that you show up after fifteen years and women start disappearing again."

The fact that it was exactly what she was expecting didn't make it any easier to hear.

Being a victim of her father hadn't ever halted people from wondering if she was somehow involved in the crimes.

"You can't imagine I have anything to do with it?" she rasped.

"I'm a cop. Everyone is a suspect until I rule them out."

She wrapped arms around her waist. "Not me. I wasn't even here when Jenny went missing."

His expression remained hard with suspicion. "Where were you?"

"In Denver."

"Can anyone confirm that?"

"Several hundred colleagues," she informed him in cold tones.

He studied her for a long, unnerving minute. Was he disappointed he couldn't pin the disappearances on her?

"You still haven't explained why you're here," he growled.

"Because she doesn't have to tell you anything," a male voice drawled as a shadow fell over them. "Not unless you intend to arrest her?"

Sheriff Brock stilled, like an animal who'd sensed a predator in his territory. "And you are?" he barked, puffing out his chest as if trying to make himself more impressive.

A wasted effort.

Even dressed in casual jeans and a sweatshirt, Rafe managed to exude the sort of male dominance that made everyone around him seem . . . less.

"Rafe Vargas."

The older man frowned. "Any relation to old man Vargas?"

"Grandson."

"I heard you were in town cleaning out the house."

"I am."

The sheriff watched as Rafe moved to her side, standing close enough to hint that they were more than casual acquaintances.

"You two know each other?" he asked, his voice accusing.

Rafe placed an arm around her shoulder. "Yes."

There was a tense silence before the lawman was once again concentrating on Annie. "You said you weren't meeting anyone."

"A happy accident," Rafe assured him in mocking tones.

The sheriff gave a grunt of annoyance, his gaze never wavering from Annie. "How long are you planning on staying in town?"

She shivered, barely resisting the urge to paste herself against the man standing at her side. "I'm not sure."

"You intend to remain at the motel?"

She shrugged. "For now."

The sheriff's fingers twitched as if longing to give her a good shaking. "You might give some thought to returning to Denver."

Her chin tilted. Yeah. So easy to be brave when Rafe was her backup.

"Are you suggesting that I leave town?"

"We can't be certain it's safe for a young woman to be on her own."

Rafe pulled her closer, the heat of his body helping to ease her shivers. "She isn't on her own," he said, the hint of warning unmistakable.

"I'm speaking with Ms. White," the older man growled, sparing Rafe an annoyed glare before returning his attention to Annie. "Let me be honest. There are some in town who consider your return a bad omen."

In one part of Rafe's mind he knew he was overreacting.

Okay, the sheriff struck him as a petty tyrant who liked to use his position to intimidate others. And he was clearly being a prick to Annie. But it wasn't completely unreasonable that he would be suspicious of her return just when females started going missing. Or that he would be happier to have her out of town until they caught whoever was responsible.

But Rafe didn't give a shit about any pressure the sheriff might be under. Or his excuse for being at the motel.

All he was interested in was getting rid of the bastard before he upset Annie even more.

"I think you've said enough," he said, his voice a low command.

A flush touched the older man's cheeks, but he stubbornly refused to back down. "Look, I'm just trying to save Ms.

White from the hassle of dealing with locals who are looking for someone to blame."

"Really?" Rafe flicked his gaze toward the small knot of gawkers who'd already gathered on the corner. "Maybe you should concentrate on finding the missing women."

There was a low hiss as the sheriff grabbed the grip of his gun, no doubt imagining the pleasure of lodging a bullet in Rafe.

"Not a bad idea, asshole," the older man snarled, leaning forward to poke a stubby finger into the center of Rafe's chest. "A smart cop would start with the stranger who just arrived in town. Why don't we head to my office for a chat?"

Rafe could have snapped the finger in half. Instead he calmly reached to pull out his wallet, extracting one of Lucas's fancy-schmancy business cards with the gold edging. "You want to talk to me, you can arrange a meeting with my partner. He'll contact my lawyer."

The sheriff snatched the card to read the bold lettering, his face paling at the name.

Even small-town cops were familiar with the powerful St. Clair family.

Grudgingly backing away, the older man hitched up his pants and sent them a last glare. "I have my eye on you," he warned. *Both* of you."

The man stomped across the parking lot to climb into his patrol car and take off with enough force to send a spray of gravel in the air.

Rafe resisted the urge to flip off the blowhard, instead concentrating on the woman who was trembling from head to toe.

"God," she breathed, clearly distressed by the sheriff's confrontation.

Reaching around her, Rafe shoved open the door directly behind her and urged her into the room. "Get your things," he said in a tone that defied argument.

With a frown she turned to watch him close the door, hiding them from any prying eyes. "Why?"

"You can't stay here," he said, grimacing as he glanced around the cramped room that looked as if it hadn't been updated since the Beatles era.

Warped paneling, shag carpeting, and an orange floral bedspread.

Groovy.

Annie glared at him, but she couldn't disguise her lingering unease. "I can stay wherever I want."

Rafe forced himself to take a deep, steadying breath. As much as he wanted to toss her over his shoulder and carry her to his cave like a proper Neanderthal, he knew Annie would only take off the second his back was turned.

He needed to convince her that she would be safer with him than in this damned motel room.

"There's some madman out there kidnapping women," he pointed out in what he hoped was a reasonable tone.

"Exactly." She folded her arms over her chest, her expression set in stubborn lines. "Which is why I would be an idiot to take off with a man I met two days ago."

He held her wary gaze. "It might only be a couple of days, but you already trust me."

She hunched her shoulders. "I trusted my father."

Rafe swallowed a curse.

How did he argue with that?

He'd first feared she been traumatized by her father. But she'd revealed last night that for all his faults, Don White had been devoted to his daughter.

Still, Annie had been taught as a vulnerable child that she couldn't depend on her natural instincts.

"Wait," he muttered, pulling out his phone and hitting the speed dial. Seconds later, a familiar voice was on the line. "Hey, Max."

"What's up, my man?"

He kept his gaze locked on Annie's pale face as he spoke to his friend. "Does Teagan have the feed from my house set up yet?"

"Give me a sec." The man's lack of surprise at the question assured Rafe that Teagan had already given a full report to the others. There was the sound of Max typing on the keyboard, then a low grunt. "Yep. I got a full view of your grandfather's house. Not much to see. Damn, my man, that kitchen is filled with junk food," he muttered. "You need to cut back. That shit will kill you."

Rafe gave a short laugh. He loved the forensics expert, but the man had a serious inability to let loose and enjoy life.

Even his diet was rigidly regulated to give maximum nutrition with zero pleasure.

"Not all of us can survive on grass and protein drinks," he said dryly.

"Food is fuel." Max spouted his well-rehearsed line before returning to the reason for Rafe's call. "Looks like the cameras are working. What am I looking for?"

Rafe lowered the phone and put it on speaker. He wanted Annie to hear what Max had to say.

"I want to assure my friend that if she comes to stay with me she'll be constantly monitored," he said.

There was a confused pause. "Why would she need to be monitored?"

"To be sure I'm not a crazed psychopath."

"Ah." Max gave a low chuckle. "Your potential roommate must be the lovely Annie White."

Annie made a sound of surprise even as Rafe rolled his eyes.

"Teagan has a big mouth."

"He's worried."

"Yeah, yeah." Rafe shook his head in resignation. "Put your phone on video."

"You got it." It took a few seconds before Rafe's screen flickered and the sleek, modern furniture that Max preferred for his office came into focus.

"Show the camera feeds," Rafe ordered.

The video blurred as Max turned the phone toward the computer monitor on his desk.

"There." Rafe moved to stand beside Annie, pointing at the screen as it focused in on the monitor. "That's the kitchen and living room of my grandfather's house."

She studied the phone with a small frown. "Why do you have cameras running?"

"Because I have four friends who are overprotective pains in the ass who decided I need their protection."

The phone turned to reveal a man with short, dark blond hair, a bluntly chiseled face, and shrewd gray eyes. "You know you love us," he teased.

Rafe's lips twitched. He did love them. They were the brothers he'd always wanted.

For now, however, his only interest was easing Annie's very reasonable fears. "Once you're in my house, all you have to do is scream and one or all of my partners will hunt me down and shoot me," he told her.

Max nodded. "That's a promise, ma'am."

"See?" he murmured, lifting his hand to gently tug the end of her braid. "You'll be perfectly safe with me."

She sent him a wry glance. "So I'm supposed to feel better because I'm being watched by five strange men instead of just one?"

"She does have a point, Rafe," Max said.

"You're not helping," he informed his friend.

Max chuckled before his expression was suddenly somber. "You want me to tell her that you saved my life more than once?" he asked, his voice laced with an unmistakable sincerity. "And that you're one of the few truly good guys I've ever met?"

"Now you're just embarrassing me," he muttered. "Later." He disconnected the phone, feeling a ridiculous blush stain his cheeks. The five of them might be a tight-knit group, but none of them were comfortable with the mushy stuff.

Shoving the phone in his pocket, he placed his hands on Annie's shoulders and gazed down at her. "Come with me."

She bit her lip. "There's no reason for me to leave the motel."

He leaned down until they were nose to nose. "Either you come with me, or I get a room next door."

She made a small sound of exasperation. "Why are you being so stubborn about this?"

Rafe knew there were a thousand excuses he could use, but he didn't even consider lying.

She had to know that he would tell her the truth, even when it wasn't convenient.

"Because the thought you might be in danger makes me a little nuts," he said.

"A little?"

"Maybe a lot."

Her expression briefly softened, as if his admission touched something deep inside her. Then, as if recognizing she'd revealed more than she'd intended, her chin jutted to a defensive angle.

"I'm not helpless."

"Neither am I, but I have cameras in my home and four interfering busybodies threatening to set up camp in my backyard," he reminded her, his thumbs brushing the curve of her throat. "It's what friends do."

Her gaze lowered to his lips. "You want to be my friend?"

He gave a short laugh, his cock instantly hardening as his brain fired up all sorts of images of what he wanted from this woman.

None of them included a platonic association.

Still, his need to protect currently trumped his sexual needs.

Eventually he'd have her in his bed. He refused to consider any other possibility.

"I'm not going to insult your intelligence and pretend I'm

not attracted to you, but this is about keeping you safe," he admitted, his voice rough with the desire he couldn't disguise. "I'll sleep on the couch."

She wavered, her gaze briefly darting toward the door. He turned his head to see what had captured her attention.

No, wait, she wasn't looking at the door.

The chair?

The window?

"This is crazy," she abruptly muttered.

He turned back to study her pale face. "I have a trump card," he murmured.

The hazel eyes narrowed. "What's that?"

"I intend to find out who took those women."

Her breath caught, her body stiffening beneath his hands. "How?"

"Come with me and I'll tell you," he promised softly, knowing he'd won the battle when she heaved a deep sigh of resignation.

"Christ, I must be out of my mind."

Chapter Seven

Annie knew it was a risk to stay with Rafe.

Not because she feared he would hurt her.

At least not physically.

A man intent on harming a woman didn't announce to the local sheriff, as well as his friends, that he intended to take her to his house.

But he threatened her in a way she barely understood.

Slowly she pulled away from Rafe's light touch, acutely aware of the heat of his body that seemed to wrap around her.

What was it about this man?

Granted, he was gorgeous.

The sort of gorgeous that made her heart forget how to beat when he was next to her.

And sexy. Sexy enough that his mere touch was making her tingle in all the right places.

And he smelled divine.

A warm, spicy scent of cologne mixed with pure male skin that was intoxicating.

The fact that she wanted to tumble him back on the bed and rip off his clothes was no big shocker. There wasn't a woman alive who wouldn't be ready, willing, and eager to get Rafe Vargas naked.

But this was more.

This was a deeper, more intimate awareness that threatened her on an emotional level.

Still, she couldn't ignore the fact that she was dangerously vulnerable in this motel room.

Not only from the sheriff, and any local citizens who might decide to run her out of town, but from the weirdo who'd stuck the note under her door.

If nothing else, staying with Rafe Vargas would keep away most of the loonies.

Or at least a girl could hope.

Grabbing her suitcase, she tossed in her clothes. She needed to find a Laundromat, sooner rather than later, she acknowledged with a grimace, heading into the bathroom to gather her toiletries.

It took less than ten minutes to finish her packing, then zipping the suitcase shut, she glanced up to discover Rafe standing by the door, his expression grim.

"What's wrong?"

He pointed toward the chair where the strange note was lying in plain sight.

Dammit. Why hadn't she thrown the stupid thing in the trash?

"Do you want to explain that?" he growled.

She shrugged. "There's nothing to explain."

His jaw tightened, as if he was battling some fierce emotion. "When did you get it?"

"I'm not sure." With effort she kept the fear out of her voice. She didn't want anyone to know that she was allowing some pathetic loser to terrorize her. "I found it shoved under my door when I woke up this morning."

"Shit." He glared down at the paper, but he didn't try to touch it. "Did you tell the sheriff?"

"Why would I?" she asked in genuine confusion. "It's just some idiotic note from a crackpot."

"What makes you so certain?"

"My name isn't Annabelle."

He sent her a glance of disbelief. "That's it?"

Okay, maybe she was grasping at straws, but the thought that some crazed killer had been outside her door . . .

She gave a sharp shake of her head. No. The mere thought would ensure she would never sleep again.

"If it was the killer he would have tried to grab me, not written a creepy letter," she muttered.

Shoving aside the hideous orange and green curtain, Rafe angled his head as he glanced out the window, checking the drooping edge of the roof before shifting his attention toward the office across the parking lot.

"I don't suppose this place has any cameras?"

Annie rolled her eyes. "It doesn't even have Wi-Fi."

"Damn." Turning back toward the room, Rafe scanned the cramped space. Then with two long strides he was at the dresser and yanking the unused liner from the ice bucket. "Max will kill me for using plastic, but this will have to do."

Annie frowned as she watched him scoop the note and envelope off the chair and drop it into the bag, careful to touch only the edge.

"What are you doing?"

He folded the bag to seal in the note. "I'm going to send it to our office in Houston," he said. "If there's any clue to who shoved it under your door, Max will find it."

Annie chewed her bottom lip, torn between the urge to dismiss the note as nothing more than the work of a whacko, and relief that Rafe might be able to come up with an actual name.

"Why aren't you taking it to the sheriff?" she demanded.

His lean face tightened. "I don't trust him."

"Why not?"

He shrugged. "Your father was killed in his jail cell before he could speak with a lawyer, and the case files were burned only days later. If nothing else he's clearly incompetent," he said in flat tones. "Max, on the other hand, is a genius."

She grimaced, grabbing her bag. "I'm ready."

"Wait." Rafe moved to turn on the TV and switched on a bedside light.

"What are you doing?"

"If we leave your Jeep in the lot, people will assume you'll be back," he murmured.

"What does it matter?"

He grabbed her bag and moved to pull open the door. "I'm going to set up a motion detector camera. We might get lucky and catch the bastard who left the note."

"Oh." She allowed him to lead her to the truck parked near the edge of the lot. Rafe clearly was a man who didn't like to get blocked in. Or maybe it was about feeling trapped. Something to remember. "That's—"

He placed her suitcase in the bed of his truck and opened her door as he studied her with a curious expression. "What?"

"Unexpectedly clever," she muttered, grabbing the overhead handle to hoist herself up and into the seat.

"I have my moments," he assured her, his lips twitching as he closed the door and returned to the back of his vehicle.

She twisted around to watch as he dug through the long, silver toolbox attached to the truck bed. At last locating what he was searching for, Rafe headed back to her motel room and disappeared inside.

A part of her mind was occupied with the sight of how very fine Rafe Vargas looked in his faded jeans and sweatshirt.

The wind had ruffled the dark, glossy strands of his hair and his jaw was already shadowed with whiskers, giving him an air of untamed danger.

Something that should have terrified her, not sent tingles of excitement through her.

The other part of her mind was wondering what sort of man carried spy cameras in his toolbox.

Within minutes he was back at the truck and taking his place behind the steering wheel.

"See, I told you I had my moments," he teased.

Annie pressed her hands together, trying her best not to

consider exactly what his best moments might entail. A task that would be considerably easier if she didn't have a hot flash each time they turned a corner and she found her shoulder brushing against his hard, chiseled body.

Good Lord, get a grip, she sternly chastised herself, remaining silent as Rafe stopped by the local florist store that also doubled as a barbershop and FedEx office.

It took him only a few minutes to overnight the note to his friend, and then they were driving the short distance to his grandfather's house.

She climbed out of the truck, waiting for Rafe to grab her suitcase and lead her up the broken sidewalk. Hey, she could carry her own bag. But there were some battles that weren't worth fighting.

Glancing around the overgrown yard and hedges that needed a good trimming, Annie stepped onto the slanted porch and followed Rafe into the house.

"Sorry, the place isn't exactly the Ritz. My grandfather was eccentric, to say the least," he said as they entered a small living room. The furniture was shabby and the wooden floors worn, but the room had been ruthlessly cleaned and precisely arranged. Clearly Rafe's touch. "Bring your stuff in here." He crossed the floor to enter the bedroom that was just large enough to fit a narrow bed and walnut armoire. "I'll wash the sheets and make the bed after breakfast," he promised, placing her suitcase beneath the window. "But first . . . doughnuts."

A small smile curved her lips as they traced their way through the living room and into the kitchen at the back of the house.

Like the rest of the house, it was shabby and obviously in need of updates, but it was clean and there were boxes neatly stacked against the wall and a few next to the door.

And in the middle of the room was a Formica table where a sack of doughnuts and a computer were waiting for them.

"You do laundry?" she teased as she took a seat and watched Rafe move toward the counter to pour two mugs of coffee.

"The military teaches you to be self-sufficient," he assured her. "Cream or sugar?"

"Black." She waited until he placed the mug of coffee in front of her and took a seat across the table before asking the obvious question. "Why did you leave?"

The ebony eyes darkened with a wound that hadn't fully healed. "Long story."

She sipped the hot coffee, studying his finely sculpted features over the rim of her mug. "Were you injured?"

"Yeah."

Short. Concise.

Clearly unwilling to discuss his past.

Annie got that. There was nothing worse than rehashing old trauma.

"I'm sorry," she murmured softly.

"Shit happens." He reached to open the bag, pulling out the pastries that teased her senses with a warm, tantalizing aroma. "Apple fritters, sprinkles, or blueberry muffin?"

"Blueberry muffin."

Her mouth watered as he placed a muffin on a napkin and slid it in front of her. Rafe chose the apple fritter, and a pleasant silence filled the kitchen as they demolished their breakfast.

Odd. She hadn't even realized how hungry she was until she was licking the last crumbs.

Of course, her appetite had been as elusive as sleep over the past week.

"How do you intend to track down the kidnapper?" she abruptly demanded, not particularly wanting to analyze why her hunger had returned.

Not when she was fairly certain the reason was sitting across the table.

"If there's some lunatic snatching women, the question is how he managed to get his hands on them." Rafe reached for the computer, pulling up a local map.

She easily followed his train of thought. "They were both driving back to Newton when they disappeared," she said.

"Exactly." He nodded, pointing at the computer screen. "According to the police report, Jenny Brown left her aunt's house and was last seen at a gas station a block from the on-ramp to Highway 35."

She sent him a startled frown. "How did you get a police report?"

He shot a quick glance at the tiny red light in the corner of the ceiling. "It's better not to ask."

"Hmm," she murmured, wondering just what sort of services Rafe and his friends offered at their security firm.

Corporate takeovers?

Invasions of small countries?

He returned his attention to the map on the computer screen, using a finger to trace a path from Des Moines to Newton.

"Assuming she took the highway, this is the shortest route to Newton."

Annie placed her elbows on the table and leaned forward. "Yes."

"Brandi was driving from LaClede," he continued.

"That's the opposite direction."

"True." His finger moved to the bottom of the screen to follow the pale blue line that indicated a county road. "But she lives north of town. Their paths would have crossed here."

Annie wrinkled her nose. She'd only been back in Newton a couple of days, but it was enough to know that there were few things except cornfields beyond the city limits.

"There's nothing there," she said.

"I think we should have a look."

Her lips parted to ask if he intended to simply drive around in the hopes of stumbling across the poor women, then Rafe turned to study her with a speculative gaze.

"Oh," she breathed. "You hope I'll recognize something from my vision."

"I know it's a long shot, but . . ." His words trailed away as she blinked back the tears that threatened to blind her.

"Annie." He reached across the table to grasp her hand. "Are you okay?"

She was forced to swallow the lump in her throat, not sure she could properly explain how it felt to have someone accept her visions after a lifetime of being told she was crazy.

"You're the first one," she at last rasped.

He frowned. "The first one?"

"To believe me."

Rafe had intended to spend the day allowing Annie to settle into his grandfather's house.

It was bad enough that she'd been forced to deal with the jackass of a sheriff, but the creepy note had obviously disturbed her more than she was willing to admit.

She deserved a few hours to relax in a place where she could feel safe.

But from the second she realized he intended to discover if her visions could lead them to some clue about the missing women, she'd been fiercely eager to begin the search.

And he . . . hell, he'd been enchanted by the sight of her seated at his kitchen table, licking the crumbs of blueberry muffin from her fingers.

It was more than the usual fantasy of getting a beautiful female naked. Or the pleasure of seducing her into his grandfather's antique bed.

It was the primitive male urge to make sure she was well fed and comfortable in a place he was providing for her. And that nothing and no one could get past his defenses to harm her.

Dangerous, dangerous thoughts.

Suddenly a distraction seemed like a very good idea.

And if they managed to find something that could lead them to the missing women . . . so much the better.

Now he slowed the truck as he veered off the main road

and into the parking lot of the chain convenience store that doubled as a gas station.

"Here," he said, pulling to a halt at the edge of the brick store.

Rolling down his window, he stuck his head out and scanned the area with the eyes of a potential kidnapper.

There were a few downsides.

The front of the store had large front windows that allowed the employee inside to keep an eye on the two gas pumps, and the lot was surrounded with tall floodlights that would make the customers visible at night.

But a closer glance revealed there were no other businesses or houses within miles. And more importantly, all you had to do was step to the side of the building to be completely out of sight.

If a woman was to pull into the lot and park, it would take only seconds for someone to leap from the shadows and be in her car.

It wasn't like anyone locked their doors.

Not in Newton.

"A convenience store?" Annie muttered in confusion.

"It's probably the only place open all night in this town," he said, grabbing his phone to type in a short text.

Annie leaned across the seat, the scent of her shampoo teasing at his nose.

"What are you doing?"

"I want Teagan to check and see if Brandi and Jenny were smokers."

Rafe had never been addicted to cigarettes, but he had friends who would walk through a fucking minefield if they needed a pack. It was the one sure reason for a young woman to stop at the store. No matter how late it might be.

"You think the stalker has been taking women from here?" Annie demanded.

"It's where I would choose," he said, shoving the phone back in his pocket as he put the truck into gear.

Annie made a sound of surprise. "Aren't we going to see if anyone saw them the night they went missing?"

He shook his head. "If either of the women had made it inside, the employee would have told someone," he pointed out. "It's not often you get to be the last person to see a potential murder victim."

Annie grimaced. Was she recalling all the whackos who'd no doubt been anxious to talk about their connection to the Newton Slayer?

"That makes sense," she conceded, her brow furrowed. "But if they were taken from the parking lot, what happened to their cars?"

Rafe drove past the wide, empty space that surrounded the sides and back of the store. "If the killer was waiting at the edge of the building, he could easily get into a car and force the driver to go wherever he wanted."

She gave a slow nod, her expression distracted as he pulled out of the lot. "He would have to be staying close enough to walk here," she abruptly said.

Avoiding the highway, Rafe turned onto the county road. "Assuming the kidnapper is a reasonably healthy male in his prime, I'd say within a five- or ten-mile radius."

"That's still a lot of territory to search."

It was.

Unfortunately he didn't have any bright ideas how to narrow it down.

Not yet.

"We'll start with this side of the road."

He took a right at the first gravel road, driving for a mile before taking another right. He would expand his search outward after he made sure there were no abandoned homes or barns that offered a view of the convenience store.

Coming to a crossroads, he stomped on the brakes as Annie grabbed his arm.

"Wait," she rasped. "Turn left."

He obeyed without question. "Do you recognize something?"

She leaned forward, her hands resting on the dashboard as she studied the recently harvested fields and rolling pastures filled with cattle grazing on bales of hay.

"Not from the visions, but this place is familiar," she said, her expression distracted.

Ten minutes later she pointed toward a narrow path that was lined with trees. "That way."

He sent her a teasing smile as they bounced over the deep ruts. "Why, Ms. White, are you trying to lure me into some isolated spot so you can have your wicked way with me?"

She rolled her eyes. "I'm pretty sure I could have my wicked way with you in the middle of a shopping mall."

Rafe gave a short burst of laughter, instinctively reaching out to give her braid a light tug. "I like you, Annie White."

"You sound surprised."

Did he? He turned his head long enough to catch sight of her delicate profile and the stray curl that brushed her smooth ivory cheek. "I'll admit you're the last thing I expected when I traveled to Newton," he confessed.

"What did you expect?"

"Annoyance. Frustration." He grimaced, recalling his reaction to the message from his Realtor. "Regret."

"And instead you're chasing a potential serial killer."

His fingers trailed down the slender length of her throat, his gaze deliberately lowering to the full curve of her lips.

"That's not all I'm doing," he said, his voice husky.

She sucked in a sharp breath, her cheeks heating with a flustered awareness.

"Have you considered the fact that your interest in my

problems is a perfect way to deflect from dealing with the loss of your grandfather?" she demanded.

He turned his attention back to the narrow road. "You sound more like a psychologist than an accountant."

"Considering the hours I spent in therapy, I could probably qualify as a shrink," she said dryly.

"There's nothing to deflect," he said, his voice firm. She wasn't saying anything that he was certain his friends weren't thinking, but they were all wrong. When he wanted to take his mind off his troubles he got shit-faced drunk and sang karaoke in a country bar. This was . . . okay, he didn't know what it was, but it had nothing to do with his lack of a relationship with Manuel Vargas. "My grandfather was a stranger to me." He gave a lift of one shoulder. "I'll admit it pisses me off that he was such a cantankerous old shit and that he turned his back on my father, but in the end he only hurt himself."

"You're still—"

"My interest in you has nothing to do with my grandfather," he interrupted.

There was no way in hell he was going to let her try and diminish what was happening between them.

He rounded a curve in the road, tensing as he caught sight of a red pickup blocking their way.

"Rafe," Annie breathed.

"I see him."

"Oh my God."

Coming to a halt, Rafe covertly reached beneath his seat, pulling out the handgun he'd placed there before heading out.

"Here." He pressed it into Annie's fingers, his gaze locked on the middle-aged man who was walking directly toward them, a shotgun in one hand. "Don't be afraid to use it if necessary."

Chapter Eight

Hitting the automatic locks, Rafe waited until the man was standing next to his door before rolling down the window a few inches.

The stranger was dressed in a flannel shirt with jeans and heavy work boots. His hair was hidden beneath a well-worn seed cap and his round face was deeply tanned and chapped from the hours he spent in the sun.

He looked like a typical farmer, but Rafe wasn't in the mood to take any chances.

Not when the stranger was carrying the shotgun like he was willing to use it.

"Is there a problem?" Rafe asked, keeping his tone polite.

The man eyed Rafe with open suspicion. "You folks lost?"

"Just out for a drive."

Lifting the gun, he used it to point down the road. "This here's private property."

"We didn't mean to trespass." Rafe had his fingers curled around the handle of his door. The farmer was standing close enough that Rafe could easily shove it open and knock the weapon out of his hand. "Like I said, we're just out enjoying the day."

Seemingly unimpressed with Rafe's explanation, the man leaned to the side to glance at Annie.

"We don't get many strangers here."

"I'm Rafe Vargas. My grandfather was Manuel Vargas." Rafe turned in his seat, doing his best to block the man's view of Annie. "And you are?"

"Mitch Roberts."

Intent on the stranger, Rafe was too late to prevent Annie from leaning around his shoulder to stare at the man with a searching gaze.

"You knew my father," she said abruptly.

The man frowned. "Who . . ." He narrowed his dark eyes, his blunt features softening with genuine pleasure. "Annie? Annie White?"

A tentative smile touched her lips. "Yes."

"Well, I'll be damned. It's been—what—ten years?"

"Fifteen."

"Fifteen?" Mitch took off his cap to scratch his thinning gray hair before replacing it. "Huh. Doesn't seem like that long. What are you doing back in Newton?"

Rafe tensed, but Annie wasn't a fool. She knew the danger of revealing they were out searching for the missing women.

Not only from the stalker, but from the local law.

Sheriff Brock was clearly looking for someone to hold responsible for the kidnappings. And Rafe doubted he truly cared who he managed to pin the blame on.

"I'm not really sure," Annie hedged. "I hoped I could have . . . closure."

Mitch gave a slow nod, the expression on his ruddy face difficult to read. "My house is just down the drive." His gaze remained on Annie. "Why don't you join me for a lemonade?"

"I'd like that," Annie instantly agreed.

"Good." With a tiny nod toward Rafe, the man turned to make his way back to his vehicle.

"You don't mind, do you?" Annie asked as Rafe put the pickup in gear and followed Mitch down the road.

"Not at all."

Driving at a snail's pace, he kept his eyes peeled for any hint of danger.

A part of him remained anxious to continue the search for the missing women, but he understood this was important to Annie.

It was far too easy to believe that Newton was filled with jackasses like the sheriff who were eager to make her feel responsible for her father's sins. She needed to know there were others who could see her as the little girl who'd been an innocent victim.

Eventually they reached a white, two-story farmhouse with a screened-in porch and black shutters. The roof was steeply slanted, with a dormer window that overlooked the front yard and a red brick chimney sticking out the top.

In the distance he could see several outbuildings and grain bins, but Rafe would guess the nearest neighbor was several miles away.

Rafe did a U-turn at the end of the drive so he was parked in the direction that would take them out of the isolated property. He always liked to be prepared for a quick getaway. Then, reaching over, he took the gun from Annie's hand. "I think he has something he wants to say to you."

"Yeah, me too," she muttered, climbing out of the vehicle before Rafe could get around to help her.

He did, however, manage to reach her as she was moving up the flagstone walkway. Wrapping an arm around her shoulders, he held the handgun in his right hand.

Mitch was waiting for them at the door to the screened-in porch, his gaze lowering to the weapon.

"No need for the gun."

Rafe shrugged. "Annie isn't going anywhere unless I'm armed."

The older man grimaced. "Fair enough. Can't be too careful these days," he muttered, clearly aware of the missing women. Crossing the narrow porch, he led them into the kitchen that had the original cabinets that looked like they'd been recently slapped with a white layer of paint, and a long, deep sink that was now the fashion.

It smelled of fresh-baked bread and spearmint gum.

Mitch pointed toward the wooden table in the center of the floor.

"Have a seat," he said, moving to the white fridge that chugged like a two-cylinder engine and removing a pitcher of lemonade.

Then, gathering the glasses, he moved to join them at the table.

"Thank you," Annie murmured as she slid into one of the chairs and took a sip of her drink. "It's delicious."

Rafe took a seat next to the wall, not touching the offered beverage although he was polite enough to keep the gun under the table instead of pointed directly at the man's head.

See? Who said he didn't have manners?

"Is there anyone else here?" he asked, glancing toward the attached dining room that was piled with boxes and old magazines. It looked as if it hadn't been used in years.

"Nope." Mitch heaved a sigh. "My wife died years ago and we never did have any kids." Pulling out a handkerchief, he wiped his face before taking his own seat and focusing his attention on Annie. "How have you been?"

Annie forced a strained smile to her lips. "Surviving."

"I tried to find you after . . . after your father died, but no one could tell me where they took you."

"My therapist thought a clean break from my past would be for the best."

Mitch muttered a curse beneath his breath. "I don't have much use for therapists."

Rafe leaned forward. "Why did you want to see her?"

Turning his head, Mitch studied him with a considering gaze. "She your gal?"

"Yep, she's my gal," Rafe said without hesitation.

It was true.

He didn't know exactly what it actually meant. Or where it might lead him.

But Annie White was his gal.

Mitch drained his glass of lemonade in one long swallow.

"None of it set right with me," he finally said.

"What do you mean?" Rafe demanded.

Placing his glass on the table, Mitch leaned back in his chair. "I spent a lot of time with Don White."

"I remember." Annie glanced toward the window over the sink. "We used to come here and I would play out back."

"Yep. You always had a dozen dolls with you and you'd have a tea party beneath the apple tree while your father helped me learn how to use that damned computer." He waved a hand toward the computer that was placed on the dining room table. "Organized my accounts for me."

A fond expression softened the older man's face, and Rafe had to hide a smile.

He didn't doubt for a second that Annie had been utterly charming as a kid. Big hazel eyes. Freckles on her nose. Her hair pulled into pigtails.

And then her childhood had been ripped away.

Rafe would be damned if she would have to suffer any other loss.

"And you never thought there was anything suspicious about him?" he asked the older man.

"Why would I?" Mitch muttered, his tone defensive. "He was a decent, churchgoing man who devoted himself to his daughter and building a new life in Newton." There was a pause as the man glared down at the table, one beefy hand shoving aside his glass. "Never did make any sense to me. Hell, it still doesn't."

Rafe froze, realizing this man didn't believe his friend was responsible for the killings.

But why?

Was he just a man who didn't want to think he could be so mistaken in his friend?

Or was it something more?

Rafe abruptly realized he needed to know.

Not just for Annie's sake, but for the two women who were missing.

Taking a long moment, Rafe silently considered how he

could convince the man to express his reasons for believing his friend could be innocent despite all the evidence.

Mitch Roberts had a shrewd, taciturn nature that made it difficult to urge him to reveal more than he wanted.

"Did anyone here know Don White before he moved to this area?"

Mitch took a long minute before he answered. "I don't think so."

"Strange he would choose to move to a place without any friends or family in the neighborhood."

"Don didn't like to talk about the past," the older man said slowly, as if considering each word.

"You didn't think that was odd?"

"Not really. He was still grieving for his dead wife and son. I didn't want to pry."

It would have been a natural reaction.

Most people didn't like to poke at old wounds.

Which is why someone who didn't want awkward questions about his past might invent such a tragedy . . .

"Were you surprised when he built a bomb shelter beneath his garage?" It was a question that had been nagging at him.

How many people had an airtight hidden room built beneath the ground that was a perfect place to stash dead bodies?

"He didn't build it, the previous owner, Sam Johnson, did," Mitch growled, his brows pulling into a deep frown. "Along with a dozen other farmers during the Cold War scare. I was the one who suggested to Don that he keep it stocked with supplies in case of a tornado."

Ah. Rafe was forced to reevaluate his original assumptions as he received the unexpected information.

A specialty for him. And why he'd been so effective in the field.

Few people could think on their feet as quickly as Rafe.

"So any local would know it was down there?"

"You wouldn't have to be a local," Mitch corrected, his dark gaze assuring Rafe he knew exactly what he was trying to do. "All you had to do was walk into the garage and there was a door leading down to the shelter."

"Could it be locked?"

"Yeah." Mitch nodded his head toward Annie. "But Don kept the key in it to make sure the little one didn't accidentally get stuck down there."

That made sense. "Would he have noticed if the key was missing?"

Mitch shrugged. "Not until he had some reason to go down there. Could be weeks or even months before he realized it was gone."

Rafe ignored Annie's scowl as he considered the evidence against her father.

It wasn't just the fact that the dead bodies had been found in his bomb shelter.

He'd been down there with them.

"Did White have any enemies?"

Mitch gave a shake of his head. "Not that I know of."

Rafe glanced toward Annie. "Did you ever see him having trouble with anyone?"

"I don't think so . . . Wait. There was one day at the restaurant. A man came to our table and started shouting that Dad stole his land," Annie admitted, her body rigid as they discussed the father she'd loved even when others condemned him as a monster. "I think he must have been drunk."

Mitch seemed momentarily confused, then he gave a low grunt. "That was probably the Johnson boy."

Rafe instantly recognized the name. "Is he related to the people who sold Don White the farm?"

"Yep." The man curled his lip in disgust. "They only had the one boy and spoiled him rotten. Brody always assumed he'd inherit the land, but when it became obvious he was destined to become the town drunk, they packed up and headed to Florida."

"Brody blamed my father?" Annie shuddered, clearly disturbed by the memory of the ugly confrontation.

Mitch shrugged. "He blamed everyone but himself."

Rafe knew the type.

Unfortunately.

He pulled out his phone and sent Teagan a quick text.

"Could he be violent?" he asked the older man.

"There were rumors he beat his girlfriend."

"Where is he now?"

"Don't know." Mitch's interest in Brody was clearly non-existent. "He disappeared a few weeks after the murders."

Rafe blinked in surprise. "Disappeared?"

Mitch shrugged. "Just packed up and left town."

"And no one thought that was odd?"

"Brody was a born troublemaker." Mitch grimaced. "Most people were happy to see the back of him."

Rafe was on instant alert. "Was he ever a suspect in the disappearance of the women?"

"Lots of people blamed him at first, but before he could get lynched he ran his car into the side of the VFW building in LaClede. He was locked up when two of the women went missing," Mitch said, squashing in the bud any hope that Brody could be responsible.

Adding the info to the text, Rafe shoved the phone back into his pocket. Brody might have an alibi, but the fact that he'd seemingly disappeared just after the murders was suspicious.

If nothing else, he might have noticed something. Drunks tended to wander the streets late at night, long after the upright citizens of Newton had crawled into bed.

"Anyone else who might have a grudge against Don White?" he asked.

"Hard to say," Mitch admitted. "There's always folks hoping to cause trouble, but Don usually kept to himself. He said that all he needed was to know Annie was safe and happy."

Annie made a sound of distress, her hazel eyes darkening with pain. "My father was a quiet, gentle man," she said in soft tones.

"He was," Mitch instantly agreed, his voice daring Rafe to disagree. "Not the sort to do what they said."

Okay.

Time to put their cards on the table.

Rafe leaned forward, holding the older man's gaze.

"You don't believe he's responsible for the killings?" he bluntly demanded.

Mitch didn't flinch.

In fact, he looked pleased that someone had finally asked him the question point-blank.

"Let me put it this way. When I was told Don White had murdered seven women and stashed their bodies in his bomb shelter, I found it hard to believe," he growled, his gaze shifting to Annie. "But when they told me that he had his daughter down there bound and blindfolded . . ." He shook his head, his expression tight with a long-suppressed anger. "Well, nothing will ever convince me he would do anything to hurt his Annie." Reaching across the table, he placed his hand on Annie's tightly clenched fist. "Don would have given his life to protect you."

He was hidden behind a stack of hay bales as the truck drove past him.

Sweet Annabelle.

She'd been so close he could see the honey highlights in her hair and the flush on her cheeks from the chill in the air. A pity about her hazel eyes. Those she'd inherited from her bitch of a mother. Of course, Annabelle's held an innocence that the years hadn't managed to steal, he was swift to reassure himself.

Then he frowned, his hands clenching.

Rafe Vargas was an unexpected complication.

His first thought had been to eliminate the interloper. The last time, their game had been interrupted. He wouldn't tolerate another man ruining his reunion and taking away his beloved.

But Vargas appeared to be intent on protecting Annabelle.

For now it was perhaps best to leave her in his capable hands.

Soon, however, she would be back where she belonged. With him . . .

Annie barely noticed Rafe urging her out of the homey farmhouse or into his truck. It wasn't until an odd shiver inched down her spine that she came out of her fog enough to realize they were retracing their path back to Newton.

"Aren't we going to continue our search for those missing women?" she asked in surprise.

"We'll return later."

"But—" Her words tangled in her throat as he reached out to grasp her hand.

It was no doubt intended as a friendly gesture, but the feel of his slender fingers wrapped around hers sent a warm flood of pleasure through her body.

Her heart skipped a beat, her stomach clenching with excitement.

"I sent a text to Teagan," Rafe was saying, his thumb absently stroking the tender skin of her inner wrist. "He's going to track down an address for Brody Johnson."

"Then where are we headed?"

"We'll have lunch in LaClede while Teagan works his magic." He gave her hand a squeeze. "Okay?"

"Okay," she muttered, suspecting she would agree to just about anything when he was touching her.

He turned his head, his eyes darkening as if he could sense her ready response. She snatched her hand away, clearing her throat.

It wasn't that she was morally opposed to sleeping with the gorgeous Rafe Vargas.

Hell, if she was a normal woman she would tell him to park the truck so she could get him naked ASAP.

But she'd discovered over the years that she wasn't a

normal woman. She was the daughter of the Newton Slayer. Which meant two kinds of men were attracted to her.

Those who were fascinated by the macabre.

And those who saw her as a perpetual victim in need of saving.

Until she was certain he could see her as Annie White, she wasn't getting any man naked. Or until temptation overcame her righteous self-denial, she wryly conceded.

"Why were you asking if someone had a grudge against my father?" she asked, forcing her attention back to the encounter with Mitch Roberts.

It'd been wrenchingly painful to sit next to the older man and recall the days when she'd been a happy child, drinking lemonade and playing with her dolls.

Now she could at least breathe when she mentioned her father.

Returning his hand to the steering wheel, he turned onto the county road and headed south. "Nothing more than a hunch."

She watched the passing fields, torn between her instinctive desire to keep the past in the past and a dangerous hope that it'd all been some horrible mistake.

"You don't think he killed those women?"

He took a long time to at last answer.

"I agree with Mitch Roberts. From all I've heard, your father seemed devoted to you. Even if he'd been . . ." He struggled for the right word. "Sick, it seems impossible to believe he would hurt you."

"He wouldn't," she said with absolute conviction.

"Still, the facts point to him being guilty," he grimly reminded her.

"I know." She heaved a deep sigh. Over the years she'd occasionally gone over the evidence, only to come to the same conclusion. "God, I wish I could remember."

Rafe kept his focus on the road, but Annie didn't miss the way his fingers tightened on the steering wheel. "Do you have any memories of the day you were found?"

She grimaced. Most of it was nothing more than a blur.

As if her mind was deliberately trying to protect her from the pain.

But being back in Newton had already brought memories that'd been long suppressed. Maybe she could strip away a few more layers to expose the truth.

"It was like today. A clear blue sky. A crisp breeze," she said, a shudder racing through her. "Perfect."

Somehow the fact it'd been so beautiful only made the horror of the day seem so much worse.

Rafe veered onto the highway, which was nearly empty of traffic. "Did you go to school?"

"Yes."

"How did you get home?"

"I rode the bus." She had a vivid image of jumping off the bus and racing across the yard. "I remember running into the house. I was excited because I got a hundred on my spelling test."

Rafe nodded. "Was your father there?"

She shook her head. She'd called and called for him. "No, and I was worried."

"Why were you worried?"

Annie bit her bottom lip. This was where the memories always started to become fuzzy.

She recalled walking into the living room and dropping her backpack on the floor, then she'd . . . what?

Her brow furrowed as she tried to visualize what'd happened next.

"I . . ." Her breath caught as she had a distinct impression of turning toward the small table next to the door. "The cookies."

Rafe shot her a puzzled glance. "What?"

She shifted in her seat so she could keep her gaze locked on Rafe's bronzed face.

Somehow the sight of him eased the panic that was beginning to bubble in the pit of her stomach.

"Even if my father was in the fields or out feeding the

cattle, he always made certain that my cookies and milk were waiting for me."

He slowed the truck, his expression tightening with concern. "What did you do?"

Annie's heart thundered in her chest, a pain shooting through her head as she forced herself to return to that day.

"I went looking for him," she said, able to see herself walking through the house before she headed outside.

"Did you go into the garage?"

Did she?

She remembered walking down the back steps and then . . .

She gasped as a sudden pain shot through her head, the fog returning with a vengeance. "Shit. I don't remember," she rasped, frustration blasting through her.

Abruptly coming to a halt on the shoulder, Rafe reached to undo her seat belt and pulled her shaking body into his arms.

"Hey, don't worry, sweetheart," he soothed, his lips brushing the top of her head. "We're going to get this figured out."

Chapter Nine

The office building was newly constructed in an upscale neighborhood of Houston, but the faded red brick and large windows with ornamental molding were designed to give the impression of solid age and respectability.

Exactly the atmosphere Lucas St. Clair had declared ARES needed in order to attract the appropriate client. Which meant a place where rich fucks and politicians with sensitive needs would feel comfortable visiting.

But while Lucas had been allowed the task of finding the right neighborhood, it'd been Max Grayson who'd had the final approval on the exact location.

With a budget that would make most government agencies salivate, he had very specific demands for his lab.

Now Teagan entered the long, brightly lit room that looked as if it should be in a sci-fi movie.

The floors were pure white ceramic tiles and the walls were framed with stainless steel freezers, floor-to-ceiling storage cabinets, and a waist-high counter that held a row of strange equipment. The far side of the room was reserved for Max's massive desk, which held his computer and several flat-screen monitors.

At his entrance, Max looked up from a microscope he'd been peering into and slowly rose to his feet.

The forensic specialist was a large man, over six feet, with bulging muscles despite the hours he spent in his lab.

Like Teagan, Max came from a dysfunctional home. Of course, Teagan's father had been a drunken, abusive bastard who'd nearly beaten his mother to death, while Max's parents were financial wizards who'd made millions on a Ponzi scheme before being locked up by the feds.

Still, they'd both grown up with parents serving time.

One of those weird-ass coincidences that had drawn them together.

And the reason Teagan understood Max.

Both struggled to be the complete opposite of their parents.

For Teagan, it meant keeping people at a distance. He might take lovers, or hang with his cousins at his custom-built garage, working on his cars. But he never allowed himself to become close enough to hurt or be hurt.

With the exception of his four friends.

Max on the other hand was painfully honest, loyal beyond measure, and without the charming artifice of his parents.

You always knew exactly where you stood with Max.

"What have you got for me?" Max demanded, his gray eyes narrowed as he studied Teagan's grim expression.

"This." Teagan held up the table he'd collected before leaving Newton and meeting Hauk in Des Moines. Thankfully there hadn't been any delay in leaving, and within a few hours he was back home. Not that he intended to stay long. "And a bad feeling."

Max pointed toward a rolling cart shoved in a corner. "Put it over there and tell me about the bad feeling."

Teagan moved forward and put down the table that was still covered by a dusty canvas. Then, turning back to Max, he gave vent to his smoldering frustrations. "I think Rafe has lost his goddamn mind."

Max gave a slow nod. He did most things slow. Methodical.

And he never, ever made mistakes.

"Yeah, I had the same fear when he called me to convince the daughter of a serial killer that she would be safe in his home."

Teagan's brows snapped together. He'd known Rafe was worried about Annie White, but he hadn't expected him to actually move her into his grandfather's house. "Damn," he muttered.

"Do you think she might be dangerous?"

"I don't know, and that's the point," Teagan admitted. His intuition told him that she was exactly what she seemed. A traumatized victim who was being pulled back into a shitty situation. But he wasn't worried about her being a psycho killer. It was the fact that she was obviously a magnet for trouble that worried him. She was going to get his friend pulled into her hot mess. "Rafe has always had a compulsive need to rush to the rescue, but he usually thinks with his head, not with his cock."

"True." Max sent his friend a rare smile. "He leaves that charming habit to others."

Teagan flipped his companion off with practiced ease, ignoring the reference to his wide and varied enjoyment of the female sex. "Now he meets this Annie White and he's neck deep in serial killers and missing women."

Max's smile disappeared. "Do you think there's a connection between the most recent disappearances and the Newton Slayer?"

Teagan nodded. He didn't have Rafe's flashes of premonition, but he'd grown up with an explosive father who regularly decided Teagan needed to be knocked around. Not to mention his years roaming streets that had been filled with gangbangers, drugs, and prostitutes.

He could smell danger.

"I don't have any proof, but yeah, I think there's a connection," he said.

Max folded his arms over his massive chest. The logical scientist preferred cold, hard facts to vague instincts and street smarts.

"So what do we know?"

"Not much," Teagan admitted, scrubbing his hand over his face. He needed a shower and some food, but he had an afternoon of work to finish before either was happening. "I suspect that Don White was living under an assumed name. Once we discover his identity it might give us some answers."

"I'll pull the prints today," Max promised, glancing toward the table Teagan had brought from Newton. "What else?"

Teagan shrugged. "The sick bastard had his throat slit only hours after being locked up."

"Was there an investigation?"

"Minimal. My guess is that no one wanted to look too closely."

Max arched a brow. "Because he was a serial killer?"

"Because the sheriff's pregnant wife was one of the victims."

"Awkward."

"That's one way of putting it," Teagan muttered. There wasn't a man who wouldn't snap when confronted with the SOB who'd murdered his wife and unborn child. It'd been inevitable that something bad was going to happen.

Max leaned against his desk. "The murders stopped after White's death?"

"They did in Newton." Teagan shrugged. "I ran a check to see if there were any similar killings in other parts of the country."

"Anything?"

"Not that I could find, but I'm no expert," Teagan admitted. He had the skill and equipment necessary to find any information he wanted, but it took a specialized training to pick out the patterns of a serial killer.

"And now, after fifteen years, there are two new women missing." Max scowled. "A copycat?"

"It's impossible to know without bodies," Teagan said with a blunt honesty that made both of them grimace.

"Christ." Max sucked in a deep breath. "How does Annie White tie into all this?"

"I intend to find out," Teagan assured him. Even after years in the military and being held as a POW, it was difficult to accept the horror humans could inflict on one another.

"You're returning to Newton?"

"Hell yeah, I'm returning. You think I'm allowing my friend to search for a serial killer on his own?" It'd never occurred to him that he wouldn't go back as soon as he dealt with a few loose ends. "I have some computer searches Rafe asked me to run, then I'm going to pack a few clothes and drive to Newton tonight."

"It'll be faster to fly," a deep voice said from the doorway. "We'll meet at the airport at ten."

Teagan turned to discover Hauk leaning against the doorjamb.

"There's no need for you—"

"Not up for debate," Hauk interrupted, his voice hard with warning. "Lucas is finishing up his work in DC and will meet us there."

Teagan studied his friend's lean face. "Why?"

"This is what we do." Hauk straightened, shoving his hands into the front pockets of his pale gray pants. "It'll be a good test run for the business."

A reasonable excuse, but Teagan knew there was more. "And?"

"And Rafe is my brother," Hauk said, his jaw tightening with emotion. "Nothing's going to happen to him on my watch."

That weird, still-unfamiliar warmth spread through Teagan. Until that hellhole in Afghanistan he'd had one person in his life.

His mother.

There'd been cousins who'd never escaped the streets and rotated in and out of prison, lovers who did their own sort of rotating, and partners in crime. But no one who meant jack shit to him.

Now . . .

Now he understood what it meant to have a family.

"Good enough," he said. "I'll finish up here, then go home to pack." He focused his attention on Max as Hauk turned to disappear into his own office across the hall. "What about you?"

"I'm going to hang here and do my thing." Max nodded toward the table. "First the fingerprints and then the note Rafe's overnighting to me."

"Note?" Teagan frowned in confusion. "What kind of note?"

Max shrugged. "All I know is that it was shoved beneath Annie's motel door this morning. Rafe hopes I can get an I.D. off it."

Teagan muttered a low curse. If the note had been from the killer, that would explain why Rafe had moved the woman into his house.

Dammit, he needed to get back to Newton. ASAP.

But first, he had another matter to settle.

He hadn't missed Max's covert movement to block his computer when Hauk had been in the doorway.

"Is that all?" he demanded.

Max knew exactly what Teagan was asking.

"Nope. I'm still trying to track down the bastard who's playing with Hauk," he said.

Teagan's jaw tightened.

His friend might pretend it was nothing, but they all knew that a stalker *always* had an agenda. And that the shit was going to escalate if they didn't find out who it was. "Anything new?"

"It could be nothing," Max said, always cautious.

"Tell me."

"I traced the paper the notes were written on to a manufacturer in Turkey."

Teagan hissed, his gut twisting with an icy dread. "Is it sold in America?" he demanded.

"In a few specialty shops."

"Any in Texas?"

"Nope."

The two men locked gazes, both catapulted back to the war and the enemies they'd each made.

Could one of them have followed Hauk to Houston?

"Shit," he muttered.

Max slowly nodded. "That about sums it up."

Annie polished off the last of her iced tea as Rafe glanced down at the phone he'd left lying on the table.

After leaving Newton, he'd driven them to LaClede. But with one glance at her still-pale face, he'd zoomed past the restaurants that lined Main Street and instead pulled into the local supermarket. With a promise he wouldn't be long he'd disappeared inside the store, returning twenty minutes later with two large paper bags.

Dumping them in the back of the truck, he crawled behind the wheel and drove them out of town, not halting until they were in an isolated section of a state park.

Seated on a bluff that overlooked a large, sparkling lake, Annie was leaning back on her elbows, her legs stretched across the thin blanket that Rafe had bought at the store, along with fried chicken, potato salad, coleslaw, and tea.

She didn't know how much time had passed, and at that moment she didn't care.

It was the perfect spot for a picnic. The autumn sun was warm on her face. The tall trees blocked the chilled breeze. The view was breathtaking. And it didn't hurt that she was sharing the blanket with a dark, intensely sexy man who was seated close to her side, his fingers absently toying with the end of her braid.

The world seemed very far away. Why not allow the afternoon to drift past?

Watching a crimson leaf drift from the nearby tree to land at the edge of the blanket, Annie's sense of peace was abruptly shattered as she heard an unmistakable beep.

Rafe cursed, as if he wasn't any happier than she was at the interruption.

"It's a message from Teagan," he muttered as he pulled out his phone and glanced at his screen.

She tensed, her sense of peace slowly eking away. "Did he get an address?"

Rafe nodded, the sunlight beginning to dip behind the trees to leave his bronzed face in shadows.

"Brody's living in a town in northern Missouri," he said. "It's about two hours south of here."

"So close?" she demanded in confusion. That didn't sound like a man who was trying to disappear.

Not in this small community.

"Yep. But he's living under an assumed name . . . Richard Davis."

"Good," she forced herself to say. "We should go."

As much as she wanted to stay and pretend they were just two people enjoying an intimate picnic, she knew they couldn't hide away forever.

Not when there were women missing.

Brody Johnson might be another dead end, but they wouldn't know until they talked to him.

Before she could move, Rafe lightly brushed her cheek. "Are you sure you're up for this?" he asked. "You look pale."

"We need to find answers," she reminded him. "The sooner, the better."

"Or we could shut off my phone and find a far more pleasant way to spend the evening." He leaned forward, his lips skimming her brow, then down the length of her nose. "I have several alternatives."

Her breath caught at the sizzling pleasure that raced through her.

His lips were warm, the brush of his breath even warmer.

"I suppose your alternatives include a bed?"

"Not necessarily." He nuzzled the corner of her mouth, causing her stomach to clench with anticipation. "I've been tormented by visions of seeing you spread naked across the kitchen table since breakfast."

The vivid image of being stretched over the wooden surface with Rafe between her legs seared through her brain with a shocking ease.

As if it'd been lurking there, just waiting for the opportunity to escape.

Her heart missed a strategic beat. "It's not a very big table," she muttered.

Yeah, it was ridiculous. But she wasn't exactly thinking clearly.

He chuckled, his fingers drifting down the side of her neck.

"I can be creative."

Sharp-edged desires combined with a familiar need to pull away from such raw intimacy.

"I'm sure you're creative a lot," she muttered.

Lifting his head, Rafe studied her with a faint frown. "Why are you so determined to convince yourself that I'm some sort of player?"

She trembled, but made no effort to pull away from the warm fingers that traced the neckline of her sweater.

It felt too damned good, even if it was causing tiny flutters of panic.

"You're gorgeous, sexy, intelligent, and nearly housebroken. I can't imagine women aren't constantly throwing themselves at you."

His lips twitched. "Gorgeous and sexy?"

She rolled her eyes. Like he didn't know he was irresistible. "You notice I didn't say anything about humble."

His gaze lowered to where her pulse thundered at the base of her throat.

"I had a very rigid upbringing, and even though my mother died when I was young, my father taught me that there were rules for treating women right," he assured her, his fingers dipping beneath her sweater to explore the upper curve of her breasts.

"Oh Lord," she gasped as her nipples tightened with pleasure.

His head once again lowered, his lips returning to the corner of her mouth.

An almost-kiss that was insanely erotic.

"And like I told you, since I've been home I haven't had the time to pursue a relationship." He nipped her bottom lip, his fingers tracing the line of her bra. "No, that's not true. I didn't have the interest. Until now."

Annie sucked in a deep breath. God almighty. She felt like she was drowning in sensations.

The crisp, clean scent of his skin. The searing heat of his fingers. The tantalizing promise of his lips.

Her hands lifted to press against his chest. "Rafe—"

"What about you?" He interrupted her protest, his lips moving to find a tender spot beneath her ear.

She gripped his shirt, her back arching as excitement curled in the pit of her stomach.

His touch was magic.

"Me?" she rasped, struggling to follow the conversation.

"Do you have . . ." He used his tongue to outline the shell of her ear. She shuddered with pleasure. A slow, perfect seduction of her senses. "What's the politically correct term? A significant other in your life?"

"No."

"Why not?"

It was a question she'd heard a thousand times from her foster parents.

"My therapists would say that I have trust issues," she managed to share, her voice husky with desire.

"And what do you think?"

"That I have trust issues," she wryly admitted.

He skimmed his lips down the length of her nose. "I swear

I won't hurt you, Annie," he murmured. "That's the last thing I would ever do."

She believed him.

Rafe wasn't the sort of man who would deliberately toy with a woman's emotions.

But that didn't make him any less dangerous.

"Not intentionally," she said.

He grazed a light, sinfully sweet kiss over her lips before lifting his head to study her with a brooding gaze. "What are you afraid of?"

A stray beam of sunlight peeked through the trees, blazing across his bronzed face and threading through the glossy strands of his dark hair.

Her heart twisted. Good God.

He was so beautiful.

Not pretty. Not handsome. Or sophisticated.

But raw, sculpted male perfection.

The sort that dazzled a poor female into making decisions she would later regret.

"Being a cause," she abruptly confessed.

He scowled. "What?"

"You're a hero always in search of someone who needs to be rescued."

There was a startled silence, then without warning, he tilted back his head to laugh with rich enjoyment. "Oh Annie, my desire for you has nothing to do with causes," he husked, his eyes blazing with a hunger that made her body clench with need. "And everything to do with a man so fascinated with a woman he can barely think straight."

"We should—" She lost the ability to speak as he captured her lips in a kiss that threatened to steal her sanity.

This was no tentative, teasing kiss.

This was a blatant, sensual demand for surrender.

His lips were hard, his tongue easing into her mouth as his arms wrapped around her and pressed her tight against his chest.

Annie gasped, stunned by the shocking pleasure as her fingers tangled in his hair. He tasted of tea and passionate male.

Hot, decadent temptation.

She felt as if she were melting beneath the forceful demand of his touch before he eased the pressure enough to speak against her lips.

"You were saying?" he prompted.

She blinked. Saying? Was she saying something?

Oh yeah.

"We should go," she forced herself to mutter.

He gave a low, wicked chuckle. "I couldn't agree more. As much as I enjoy the great outdoors, there are some things that demand privacy."

For a crazed second, Annie wavered.

She wanted to give in to his seduction.

Not only because her body was aching to be consumed by the desire he'd stirred to life, but because the promise of a few hours of drowning out reality with the pleasure this man could offer was nearly irresistible.

Then the habits of a lifetime returned and she was pressing her hands against his chest. "I mean we should see if we can find Brody Johnson," she said.

He kissed a path down the length of her neck before searching out that tender spot just beneath her ear.

"Brody will be there tomorrow," he assured her. "And the next day."

She swallowed a moan, giving him another push. "Rafe."

"Okay." He immediately lifted his head, a rueful smile on his lips as he gave her braid a teasing tug. "But you're going to pay for making me wait."

A strange relief poured through her. Not at his easy acceptance of her withdrawal. Rafe was clearly a man who didn't have to coerce or badger a woman into having sex with him.

They both knew he could drive to the nearest town and have a dozen women ready and willing to please him.

No, it was the insinuation that her continued hesitation hadn't destroyed his desire for her.

She managed to send him what she hoped was a playful glance. "Is that a threat?"

"A promise." With fluid ease he was upright, reaching out to pull her to her feet. Then, before she could guess his intention, he had leaned down to steal a brief, toe-curling kiss. "I intend to make you scream my name before I'm done."

Lost in the dark heat of his eyes, Annie didn't doubt him for a minute.

Chapter Ten

Annie expected the two-hour drive to be awkward.

She wasn't familiar with unfulfilled sexual tension, but she assumed it would make her time with Rafe uncomfortable.

Instead, Rafe had kept her entertained with stories of his ranch and his numerous renovation mishaps, deliberately putting her at ease.

The knowledge stole another little piece of her heart and, even more dangerous, it threatened to fracture the wall of protection she had built around herself.

His charming distraction worked until they at last pulled into the narrow parking lot on the edge of town.

Annie leaned forward, peering through the gathering gloom to study the line of brick buildings that consumed the entire block.

She grimaced. The apartments looked like rows of squat, gray blocks shoved together with miniscule balconies and a view of a nearby trailer park.

"They all look the same," she muttered, discovering a newfound appreciation for her condo in Denver.

Rafe nodded. "A perfect place to blend in."

True. The apartments looked like a million others spread around the country.

Cheap. Impersonal. Unremarkable.

The sort of place for people who'd hit hard times. Or were running from something.

"Do you think he's hiding?"

Rafe shrugged. "I think it's suspicious he disappeared just after the crimes were committed," he said.

She bit her bottom lip. Her memory of Brody Johnson was fuzzy, but she recalled a red-faced, infuriated man who'd screamed in a drunken rage before he'd taken a swing at her father. "So do I."

He unlocked his seat belt and reached beneath the seat to grab his handgun, making sure it was loaded and the safety on before he shoved it in the waistband of his jeans. "You could wait here—"

"No."

His jaw tightened at her abrupt interruption, but he reached to open the glove compartment and pulled out a stun gun.

"I thought you were going to say that," he muttered, pressing the small black object into her hand. "Here."

She sent him a startled frown. "I don't need this, I have pepper spray."

"Keep it."

"You carry a handgun under your seat, surveillance equipment in your toolbox, and a stun gun in your glove compartment," she muttered. "What kind of security do you do?"

He flashed a quick smile. "The fun kind."

She wrinkled her nose. "I'm not sure our ideas of fun are the same."

His expression softened, his dark eyes lowering to her lips. "They could be."

Oh Lord.

"Focus," she warned, not sure if she was speaking to Rafe or herself.

He grabbed her braid, tugging her forward to press a fleeting kiss to her lips before he was shoving open his door and stepping out of the truck.

Annie swiftly joined him as he crossed the shadowed lot,

his gaze in constant movement as he searched for hidden enemies.

They used the side stairs to climb to the third floor and pulled open a glass door that wasn't locked. The town was larger than Newton, but the need for security was a low priority. Then they walked down the narrow hall, which smelled like stale cigarettes and musty carpet.

Halting in front of the door marked 3F, Rafe sent her a warning glance. "Stay behind me."

Annie rolled her eyes as she gave a shake of her head. Rafe Vargas might be insanely sexy, but he was also bossy as hell.

Heaving a resigned sigh, Rafe lifted his hand to rap his knuckles on the door. There was a short pause before the man pulled it open without bothering to put the security chain in place.

He was as tall and thin as Annie remembered, but the years hadn't been kind to Brody Johnson.

His face looked gaunt, with deep lines fanning out from the pale blue eyes. His brown hair that had once been a shaggy mane had thinned to mere wisps, and his shoulders were stooped.

He might be in his midthirties, but he looked at least ten years older.

"Yeah?" he groused, clearly hoping they were the pizza deliveryman.

"Brody Johnson?" Rafe asked.

It took a beat before the man realized his cover was blown.

"Shit." He took an instinctive step backward. "Who are you?"

Quick to take advantage of the man's shock, Rafe grabbed her arm and stepped into the apartment, closing the door behind Annie.

"I just have a few questions," he said, his voice and manner filled with the sort of authority that easily convinced the nervous Brody they were there on official business.

The man held up his hands, his expression wary. "Look, I don't want any trouble."

"No trouble." Rafe folded his arms over his chest, while Annie glanced around the apartment. There wasn't much to see. A cramped living room with secondhand furniture, connected to a narrow kitchen. Through an open doorway she could see the bedroom and a bathroom that clearly needed a good cleaning. "Answer my questions and we'll be on our way."

"Fuck." Brody shoved unsteady fingers through what was left of his hair. "If this has something to do with the women who're missing in Newton, I don't know nothing about them."

Rafe narrowed his eyes. "You heard about that?"

Brody pointed toward the newspaper that had been tossed on the moss-green carpet. "Who hasn't?"

Rafe looked unimpressed. "When was the last time you were in Newton?"

"I left fifteen years ago and never looked back."

"People said you disappeared in the middle of the night."

Brody hunched his stooped shoulders. "Wasn't anything there for me."

"And that's all there was to your abrupt departure?" Rafe pressed, not bothering to disguise his disbelief.

"People move all the time."

"Yeah, but they don't change their names."

Annie remained silent during the tense exchange, watching the emotions flit over Brody's pale face.

Annoyance. Caution. And an unmistakable fear.

The questions were bringing up more than bad memories.

They were spooking him.

But why?

"I'd finally gotten sober." He tried to bluster. "I wanted a fresh start."

Rafe gave an incredulous snort. "And a fresh start included going underground and using a false identity?"

Brody parted his lips only to abruptly stiffen as he took a

closer survey of their casual clothing and Annie's obvious unease. "You aren't cops," he snapped.

Rafe moved forward, his aggression prickling in the air.

"Answer the questions."

Brody seemed to shrink beneath the force of Rafe's more dominant personality, but there was a petulant twist to his lips.

Brody was weak, but he didn't respond well to the threat of being bullied.

"Rafe," she murmured, touching his arm as she moved to stand between the two men. She patiently waited until Brody gave her his full attention. "You probably don't remember me, I'm Annie White."

"Annie who?" He frowned before his eyes abruptly widened. "Oh hell. You're the daughter."

She swallowed a humorless burst of laughter.

Once she'd been Annie White. The sweet, always-with-her-head-in-the-clouds girl with the pigtails.

Now she was "the daughter." The spawn of the Newton Slayer.

"Yes," she said.

Oddly, the fear only deepened in the blue eyes.

"Who sent you?" Brody rasped.

She raised her brows in confusion. "No one. I swear."

He sent a nervous glance toward the yellowed blinds that covered the window. "Then what do you want from me?"

She kept her tone soothing. The man was skittish about something. "I'm worried."

"About what?"

She didn't have to fake her expression of regret. Dragging up the past was clearly as sucky for Brody Johnson as it was for her. "As much as we might both wish to put Newton behind us, we can't. Not when women have started going missing again," she said with a stark simplicity. "It's up to us to try and stop it."

He shook his head, his face paling to a sickly shade of ash. "It can't be. The Newton Slayer is dead."

Annie shrugged. None of them could afford to have their heads stuck in the sand. "Then we have a new Slayer."

"You're sure?" he muttered.

"No one can be sure. Not yet," she admitted, holding his gaze as she took a step forward. Or at least she tried to take a step forward. She was brought to a sharp halt as Rafe grabbed the waistband of her jeans and tugged her back. Swallowing a sigh, she ignored the possessive hand that remained on her lower back. "But we can't wait."

Brody shifted nervously, clearly wishing he'd never opened his door. "What do you want from me?"

"I'm hoping that the past can help us find them before it's too late."

He was shaking his head before she finished speaking. "I told you. I don't know anything about it."

Without warning, Rafe was gently grabbing her upper arms and tugging her aside.

He was clearly done playing.

"Why did you leave Newton?" he demanded, pointing a finger in Brody's face as the man's lips parted. "Lie to me and I'm not going to be happy."

There was a brief hesitation before Brody gave an explosive sigh, his hand scrubbing over his face in a gesture of bone-deep weariness. "Shit. I knew this would eventually come back and bite me."

Rafe studied him with a steady gaze. "What would bite you?"

"Stay here."

With jerky motions, Brody turned to head into his bedroom. At the same time, Rafe quickly jogged the short distance to the window, pulling back the blinds so he could peer outside.

"What are you doing?" Annie hissed.

"Making sure the bastard isn't crawling out his bedroom window."

"We're three stories up."

He sent her a dark, somber, too-knowing gaze. "Men will risk anything when they feel cornered."

A tiny shiver inched down her spine.

She sensed he was intimately familiar with desperate men and the lengths they'd go to.

"I don't think he's going to run," she said.

"Why not?"

"It's not easy to live with a secret."

Rafe winced at the soft words.

He understood exactly what she meant.

The visions.

They'd not only tormented her on a personal level, but they'd become a shame she couldn't share. Not unless she wanted people to think she was crazy.

With an effort, Rafe resisted the urge to walk across the room and wrap Annie in his arms. Instead he pulled his firearm as Brody wandered back into the room, his hand digging into a small canvas bag. "Careful," he growled in low tones.

Brody jerked his head up, his gaze latching onto the gun. "I don't have any weapons," he stuttered. "Not since I blasted off my little toe when I was sixteen."

Rafe's hand never wavered. "Then what's in the bag?"

"It was supposed to be my retirement fund," Brody said in disgust, tossing the bag onto the coffee table in the center of the room. "Instead it nearly got me dead."

Rafe inched forward, keeping his gaze latched on Brody.

Of course, Annie was there before him, the stun gun he'd given her already consigned to her purse. He cursed as she reached into the bag to pull out a stack of 8x10 black-and-white photos, blatantly ignoring his glare of frustration.

Christ, once they were alone they were going to have a long talk about her lack of caution.

"Oh my God," she breathed.

Peering over her shoulder, he was immediately distracted.

The sight of dead bodies tended to do that.

"What the hell?" Plucking the photos from Annie's unresisting fingers, he swiftly glanced through them. There were seven graphic pictures of individual women stretched on a cement floor with their throats slit and their eyes staring sightlessly at the camera. And others of the bodies piled in the corner of what Rafe suspected was Don White's bomb shelter. No doubt that was how the murdered women were first discovered. His stomach clenched with horror even as he lifted his head to glare at the silent Brody. "Start at the beginning."

Brody grimaced, wiping his hands on his jeans as if he felt contaminated by simply touching the canvas bag.

Rafe knew the feeling.

"If you've been to Newton you know I wasn't exactly a choirboy," the man muttered. "I drank too much, smoked weed, hung out with the wrong crowd."

Rafe held up the photos. "Did your bad habits include any crimes?"

"None that included death or mutilation," Brody said, a visible shudder racing through his too-thin body. Rafe suspected it was real. The man wasn't that good an actor. "Mainly I was a petty thief," Brody admitted. "And occasionally I . . . sold information."

"You were a snitch?" Rafe demanded, surprised the cops would use intel given to them by a habitual drunk.

Brody shrugged. "I gave up the names of a few local dealers for the reward money."

"That must have made you unpopular in a town as small as Newton," Rafe drawled.

"I did a lot of things that made me unpopular." Brody abruptly glanced toward Annie. "I'm sorry."

She blinked, giving a shake of her head as if she was still lost in shock from the disturbing pictures. "For what?"

"For making a scene at the diner." Brody grimaced. "I was angry at my parents for selling the farm and I took it out on your father."

"It's the past," Annie said, too kindhearted to point out that he'd done more than yell at the man who bought his farm. He'd terrified a young girl.

"Yeah."

Rafe bent to tuck the pictures back into the bag before moving closer to Annie.

She'd lived through the nightmare of being in that bomb shelter. She didn't need photographic reminders.

"You were going to tell us how you got the pictures," he prompted Brody.

"My point was that people around Newton knew I'd do anything for a few bucks or a six-pack," he said.

Rafe studied the man's bleak expression. "Anything?"

"Unfortunately." Brody shoved his hands in his front pockets, his voice filled with self-loathing. "God, I was such a fuckup."

On the point of agreeing, Rafe was halted when Annie gave his arm a warning squeeze.

"We all make mistakes," she assured the older man. "Can you tell us what happened?"

Brody took a long minute before he gave a jerky nod of his head, blatantly swayed by Annie's sweet charm.

Who wasn't?

"I was living in a shitty trailer on the edge of town," he grudgingly shared, his voice hoarse. "One night I came home—drunk as usual—and someone shoved a bag over my head and pinned me against the side of my truck."

"Since I doubt it was a robbery, I assume they wanted something from you?" Rafe asked in dry tones.

"They gave me an option." His short burst of laughter was filled with more pain than humor. "I could earn three hundred dollars for burning down the old courthouse or I could have a bullet put through my brains."

"What was in the courthouse?" Annie asked the question that was on Rafe's lips.

"Nothing as far as I knew," Brody said, a strange edge in his voice. "It'd been abandoned for years."

Rafe cocked a brow. "You agreed to burn it?"

"Hell yeah." Brody looked at Rafe as if he'd lost his mind. "I had the barrel of a gun shoved under my chin. I would have agreed to set fire to the entire town." He gave a lift of his shoulder. "Besides, three hundred dollars would keep me in booze and weed for weeks."

"Nice." Rafe curled his lips. He tried to have empathy for others. No one was perfect. But this man . . .

Christ.

Brody flushed. "It's the truth."

Annie gave his arm another squeeze, her gaze remaining on Brody. "So what happened?"

The man dropped his gaze to the tips of his worn boots. "I slept off my hangover, and the next night I broke into the courthouse with a can of gasoline and a lighter."

"Was anyone else there?" Rafe asked.

"No, it was empty. Or at least I didn't see anyone when I headed to the basement," he amended. "What I did see was a shitload of boxes stacked to the ceiling."

Annie frowned in confusion. "Boxes?"

Rafe stiffened, instantly making the connection between an old government building and a timely fire that occurred only days after the Newton Slayer was killed in jail.

"Evidence," he said, slowly lowering the gun, although he kept it in his hand.

Annie gave a shake of her head. "I don't understand."

"Teagan said the evidence gathered after the murders was destroyed in a fire."

Annie sucked in a shocked breath, turning her gaze back to Brody. "You burned the evidence?"

"I didn't know what it was at first," he protested, no doubt accustomed to trying to minimize his stupid decisions. "I opened a few boxes and it looked like a bunch of worthless paper. My first thought was that it was the perfect tinder to get the fire really going." His gaze flicked toward the bag in the middle of the floor. "Then I caught sight of a box that was marked 'Newton Slayer.'"

"That's where you found the photos?" Rafe demanded.

"Yeah. They were on top of a bunch of plastic bags filled with bloody clothes and other crap from the crime scene."

"Why would you take them?" Annie asked, astonishingly innocent despite the trauma of her past.

Brody sent her a baffled frown. "I was going to sell them on eBay, of course."

Chapter Eleven

Annie knew that she'd been overly protected after leaving Newton.

Her foster parents had done everything in their power to shield her from the nastier aspects of the world. Not just because she'd been nearly catatonic when they'd first gotten her to the ranch, but because that was the type of people they were.

They protected. They shielded. And they loved.

Now she found herself floundering to comprehend a man who would agree to arson, steal police evidence, and plan to sell pictures of murdered women on eBay.

"Are you serious?" she breathed.

He hunched a shoulder, his face flushed. "It seemed like a good idea at the time."

Rafe skimmed his fingers down her back. A light caress that helped to ease the disgust twisting her stomach into knots.

"Why didn't you?" Rafe prodded.

Brody shifted uneasily, his gaze darting toward the window, then the door.

Did he expect someone to be lurking outside the apartment?

"After I grabbed the pictures I torched the place and

headed back to my trailer," he said. "I was hoping the mystery man would be waiting for me. I'd done what he asked and I wanted to get paid."

"Was he there?" Rafe asked.

"Yeah, but it wasn't to pay me." Brody's thin face tightened with anger, his hand lifting to touch his earlobe. "The bastard took a shot at me the second I stepped out of my truck. It was only because I'd already downed a six-pack on the drive home and stumbled as I was getting outta my truck that the bullet grazed my ear and didn't drill me between the eyes."

Annie made a soft sound of disbelief. Was there something in the water at Newton that caused such violence? "What did you do?"

"The only thing I could do," Brody groused. "I jumped back in the truck and drove like a bat out of hell to the bus station in LaClede. I bought a ticket to Chicago and didn't look back."

Annie glanced around the cramped apartment. She'd done her best to put the past out of her mind, but she hadn't literally tried to hide from it. "You've been on the run for fifteen years?"

"Not entirely," Brody denied. "For the first year I kept on the move, but eventually I settled here. My cousin runs a meat locker just outside of town and he pays me off the books."

Annie wondered if he'd ever considered the fact that he was living close enough to Newton to be recognized.

Probably not. Brody Johnson was a weak, cowardly man who'd survived by taking advantage of others. And sheer luck.

She gave a sad shake of her head. "Why didn't you sell the pictures?"

"After I left Newton I got sober and started thinking clearly," he said, his voice defensive. "I don't do shit like that anymore."

Rafe gave a sharp laugh. "Because you don't want a target on your back."

Brody shrugged. "That too."

Rafe didn't bother to hide his disdain. "Did you recognize the person who hired you?"

"Didn't you hear me?" Brody snapped, clearly annoyed by Rafe's reaction. "I had a bag over my head."

"Which means you knew your employer."

Brody blinked in confusion. "Why do you say that?"

"Only someone afraid you could recognize him and share the info before you completed the job would feel the need to put a bag over your head," Rafe pointed out.

"Oh." Brody shuddered, his expression suddenly guarded. "I never thought of that."

Rafe narrowed his gaze. "Was the voice familiar?"

"I don't know."

"Think. This is important," Rafe pressed. "There had to be something—"

"I was drunk. And I had a fucking gun pressed beneath my chin," Brody abruptly burst out, stalking toward the door and jerking it open. "I don't know who it was, got it?"

Rafe scowled, but obviously sensing that Brody had reached his limit, he leaned down to grab the canvas bag off the floor.

"I need these pictures."

"Knock yourself out," Brody muttered. "I just want to forget about that night."

Rafe used his shoulder to steer Annie toward the open door, keeping the gun in one hand while he clutched the bag with the other. "Let's go."

They'd stepped into the hallway when Brody broke the uncomfortable silence.

"Annie."

She turned to meet his pale gaze. "What?"

"You were right to leave Newton," he said, his tone harsh. "That place is poison."

Her lips parted, but before she could speak Rafe was urging her down the hallway. "Come on."

Annie readily gave in to the press of his shoulder, moving quickly toward the exit and down the stairs.

Every part of Brody's life, from the shabby apartment to his gaunt, pinched expression, was . . . sad.

Defeated.

She was anxious to put it behind her.

Still, they'd come there for a reason.

Answers.

Remaining silent until they were in the truck and heading out of the parking lot, she asked the question that was bothering her. "Do you think he was hired to burn down the courthouse because of the evidence boxes?"

"There's a few other possibilities," Rafe murmured, his profile tight, as if he was disturbed by his inner thoughts. "It could be a simple case of insurance fraud. Old buildings mysteriously burn down all the time."

"But?" she prompted. Neither of them believed it was insurance fraud.

"But it seems more likely that someone was trying to destroy the files in the basement," he said, turning onto the wide street that cut through the center of town. "If I'd been charged with a crime, I would do my best to get rid of the evidence against me."

"So you think it had nothing to do with the Newton Slayer?" she asked. It made sense, but it didn't feel right.

He gave a sharp shake of his head. "No, I think it has something to do with the Newton Slayer. Either the actual case files of the murders or the death of your father."

A familiar pain twisted her heart.

Few people ever mentioned Don White in her presence, and certainly none ever discussed his sudden death.

"My father?" she whispered.

He sent her a sympathetic glance. "As far as I can tell, no one bothered to investigate how he was killed."

"No." She'd made a few discreet inquiries a couple of years before with no results. The only thing she knew was that her father had been arrested, and less than eight hours later he was found dead in his cell with his throat cut. The official cause of death had conveniently been labeled a "suicide" by the local coroner. "No one cared."

He slowed, his gaze scanning the tidy rows of businesses brightly lit by street lamps.

Was he looking for something?

Annie hoped it was a bar.

She was in serious need of a drink.

Maybe more than one.

"Perhaps not in the legal system, but there were reporters and real-crime writers poking around," he said. "If there was something suspicious in his death, then it would be better to have the evidence destroyed."

"The sheriff," she breathed.

He abruptly turned his head to meet her gaze, both of them thinking the same thing.

The sheriff's pregnant wife was among the women found dead in the bomb shelter . . .

She shivered. "God."

Slowing his truck, Rafe pulled into a parking lot. "This should do," he murmured.

Wrenching her thoughts out of the dark abyss of her father's horrifying death, Annie glanced toward the three-storied beige brick hotel with large windows and a front veranda that looked like it had been built in the 1800s. There was a small, attached restaurant to one side that was surrounded by a tidy garden.

"Why are we here?" she demanded as he parked near the exit of the lot, angled to ensure he wouldn't be blocked in.

Typical Rafe.

Switching off the engine, he turned to study her with a somber expression. "I think we've had enough of Newton and Slayers for one day," he murmured, his hand lifting to stroke his fingers down the length of her jaw. "Tonight we're having a good meal, a bottle of wine, and a night without worry. Okay?"

If Annie had given herself a second to consider the invitation, and what it implied, she might have insisted on leaving.

But she didn't.

Instead, she squashed her instinctive panic and gave a slow nod of her head.

"Yes."

Rafe didn't know which of them was more shocked when Annie agreed to a night away from Newton.

He did know that he was the first to recover. And being a relatively smart guy, he was swift to take advantage of her momentary vulnerability.

Maybe not the behavior of a true gentleman, but screw that.

Only hours ago he'd held her in his arms, his body so tight with need he felt as if he was about to explode. He couldn't wait any longer to have her beneath him, his cock buried deep inside her.

First, of course, he'd indulged her with a long, surprisingly delicious dinner and a bottle of the local wine that they shared in a private table at the back of the restaurant.

They'd talked about movies and favorite songs, and argued politics. Everything and anything that didn't touch on the past or the future.

Tonight was about the now.

At last judging the time was right, Rafe had taken Annie's hand and led her up the stairs to the third floor. Then, using the old-fashioned key, Rafe pushed open the door and steered Annie into the room.

Flicking on the light, he was relieved to discover that it was not only clean but it had high ceilings and a view of the garden that gave it an open, airy atmosphere.

Not that he gave a shit about anything other than the bed that consumed a large amount of the floor, but he didn't want Annie to feel crowded.

Not yet.

Eventually he intended to push into her space, but first things first.

Closing the door, he tucked the key in his front pocket and watched as Annie took in her surroundings.

"One room?" she demanded with a lift of her brows.

"It's a suite," he assured her, moving to push open the door that opened to a small room with a single bed shoved against one wall. He grimaced. "Or at least what passes as a suite in this town," he amended.

She tossed her purse on a nearby chair, licking her lips.

"I don't have my nightgown," she muttered.

Rafe hid his smile. Annie White was nervous.

The knowledge was somehow as erotic as hell.

Stepping forward, he unzipped his sweatshirt and tossed it aside, then pulled his T-shirt over his head and held it out.

"You can sleep in this," he offered, taking another step closer. "Unless . . ."

Her gaze lowered to his bare chest, her cheeks flushed. "Unless what?"

He tossed the T-shirt on the bed, slowly reaching to wrap his fingers around her upper arms.

"Unless I can convince you to join me in my bed." He tugged her toward him, groaning at the feel of her slender curves settling perfectly against his already-hard body. "In that case, nightgowns are not only optional, but unnecessary."

Her hands tentatively lifted to grasp his shoulders, her tension easing and her eyes darkening with arousal.

"Why am I not surprised?" she teased.

Fierce pleasure raced through him. She hadn't pushed him away.

He reached to grasp her braid, yanking off the scrunchie so he could comb his fingers through the silken tresses.

"You have beautiful hair," he murmured, tilting his hips to press his erection against her lower stomach.

She trembled, her lips parted in an unconscious invitation. "It's mousy brown."

"It's honey melting in sunshine," he argued, fisting his hand in the loose strands. Giving a tug, he tilted back her head so he could bend forward and press his lips to her exposed throat. "I want to feel every satin inch sliding over my body as we make love."

"Oh."

He chuckled as she instinctively arched against him, her nails biting into his shoulders. "Do you like that?"

She didn't try to play games. "Yes."

"Me too."

He nuzzled down to the pulse that beat at the base of her throat, savoring the sweet smell of cherry blossoms that clung to her skin.

Her soap?

Lotion?

Whatever it was, it had just become his favorite scent.

Desire blasted through him.

They were alone in the hotel room, surrounded by a hushed silence, and best of all, no chance of being interrupted.

He was done waiting.

Releasing her hair, he turned his head so he could crush her lips in a kiss that demanded complete surrender.

Annie tensed, as if caught off guard. Then she released his name as a husky sigh. The sound made his erection twitch with anticipation. He'd promised that she was going to scream his name in pleasure, but that breathy exhale had been just as satisfying.

Not that he didn't intend to make her scream.

Over and over.

He reached to slide his hands beneath her sweater. She trembled even as he found her lips again.

Slow down, he warned himself.

He could sense her passion, but her nerves had been

scraped raw over the past few days. She was too fragile for him to leap on her like an animal. That would come later. After she'd accepted that she was going to be in his arms, and his bed, for a very long time.

Easing his kiss, he pulled back until their lips were just touching, waiting for her to lift her lashes. Then, carefully monitoring her reaction, he scooped her into his arms and carried her toward the nearby bed.

Her hazel eyes darkened, but not with fear.

Lowering her onto the mattress, he planted one knee on the edge of the bed, hovering over her. "Touch me," he commanded in a husky voice.

She bit her lower lip, a hint of her earlier unease returning. "I'm not . . ."

"Annie," he prompted softly. "What's wrong?"

"I don't have a lot of experience," she admitted in low tones. "I don't want to disappoint you."

Rafe released the breath he didn't even realize he'd been holding, offering her a wicked smile. "Sweetheart, I feel like I've waited for you for an eternity," he assured her. "There's nothing in this world you could do to disappoint me."

Leashing his hungry urgency, he skimmed her sweater up and over her head, baring her to his hungry gaze.

And then he . . . froze.

No other word for it.

Holy shit.

A choked sound lodged in his throat as he caught sight of the black lace bra with a tiny red bow in the center.

"Shit, Annie," he breathed.

She frowned in confusion. "What?"

"You need to warn a man," he chastised, his gaze locked on the delicate bit of black lace that was specifically created to make a male go crazy. "Do your panties match?"

A slow, astonishingly seductive smile curved her lips. "I wouldn't want to ruin the surprise."

With a low moan, he lowered his head to lick a slow path from her navel to the tiny red bow between her breasts.

"You, Annie White, are a dangerous, dangerous woman," he growled.

Annie hissed out a startled breath, her cheeks flushed. Rafe gave a low chuckle, lifting his head.

Jesus, she was beautiful.

Goose bumps raced over his skin as she arched her back in silent invitation. In wonder, he savored her honey hair that was threaded with gold as it spilled over the old-fashioned quilt. Her eyes that were for once free of the shadows from her past. Her creamy ivory skin . . .

Planting a hand on either side of her shoulders, he was careful not to make her feel trapped as he studied the rounded swell of her breasts that were barely hidden by her lacy bra. He smiled as her nipples instantly puckered beneath his scrutiny, as if begging for his touch.

Not that there was any begging required, he acknowledged. Hell, he was ready, willing, and able to touch this woman whenever she was near.

Refusing to make her wait, he teased the tight nubs that peeked through the lace with the tip of his tongue. She jerked, a groan of pleasure wrenched from her lips. Rafe grasped her hips, holding her still as he used his teeth to tug at the bow holding the bra together.

"Beautiful," he breathed as her breasts spilled free.

She lifted her hand, sliding it over his bare chest. Rafe clenched his teeth, his entire body shuddering with pleasure.

In desperation he grabbed her wrists to raise her arms over her head. Then he firmly wrapped her fingers around the slats of the headboard.

"Don't let go."

Her breathing hitched, her eyes dilating with unmistakable excitement. She licked her lips, watching him as he tugged the button of her jeans. Shit. He forced himself to slowly peel them down her slender legs, ignoring the urge to yank them off. It wouldn't take much to spook her out of her current daze of need. Besides, there was something un-expectedly erotic about revealing her body, inch by silky inch.

With one last pull he had them off, and tossing them aside, he reached to run his hands the length of her legs, mes-merized by the tiny black thong complete with a red bow.

Who the hell would have expected the shy, skittish Annie White would prefer sexy lingerie?

Mesmerized by the visible proof of her sensual nature, Rafe leaned down to trail his tongue along the edge of her panties. She made a choked sound, her hips instinctively lift-ing off the mattress as he allowed his finger to slip beneath the thin material to discover the slick heat. Oh, yeah. Rafe felt a fierce stab of satisfaction. She wanted him.

Taking his sweet time, he continued to stroke his finger between her damp folds, lightly teasing her tender nub.

"Rafe," she pleaded softly.

"What do you need?"

"More."

He chuckled. "Patience."

"I've—"

Her words were forgotten as his next stroke found the entrance to her body and slid deep inside.

Annie gasped while Rafe swallowed a groan. She was tight. So tight. She would grip his cock like a glove.

A hot . . . fitted . . . satin glove.

Oh, hell. He wanted to make this last all night, but already he was about to explode.

Shoving himself upright, he paused to pull out his wallet and extract the condoms he thankfully kept stashed in case of an emergency. Then with blatant impatience, he kicked off his shoes and wrestled off his jeans along with his boxers. Both went sailing across the room.

Glancing up, he caught Annie staring at his straining

erection from beneath half-closed lids, her bottom lip caught between her teeth.

He could almost feel her gaze as she studied him with heated anticipation.

His cock twitched, and with hands that weren't entirely steady he ripped open the condom and rolled it down his swollen shaft. He was desperate to be inside her, but there was no way he was going to miss the opportunity to taste her.

Lowering himself to his knees, he grabbed her legs and tugged them wider. She briefly stiffened, as if suddenly aware of how vulnerable she was to him.

Rafe smoothed his fingers up and down her calves, keeping his touch light until Annie at last relaxed. Only when he was certain she was once again lost in her desire did he bend his head to lightly brush his lips along the sensitive skin of her inner thigh.

She made a choked sound, her heels digging into the mattress as he nuzzled higher and higher. He took his time before he at last reached her sweet spot, smiling as he heard the headboard creak beneath the force of her grip. Thank God the furniture was original to the hotel and not the newly fabricated crap. The bed was built to be sturdy as well as functional. Grasping her hips, he held her in place as he used his tongue to stroke through the heated honey that was waiting for him.

They groaned in unison as he found her clit with the tip of his tongue and teased her with ruthless determination. Annie arched her back, her muscles clenching as he urged her toward her climax.

"Not alone," she rasped. "Please, Rafe."

He got it.

Rising to his feet, he carefully covered her body and settled between her legs. Then, grasping his cock, he pressed it against her entrance. Annie instinctively wrapped her legs around his hips, giving him all the encouragement he needed.

With one powerful surge he slid into the welcoming softness of her body.

Rafe cursed. She felt so damned good.

Tight. Hot. Sweetly inviting.

He held completely still. He wanted to savor the sensations that jolted through his body. But when Annie moved with a restless impatience beneath him, he was lost.

Slowly withdrawing until only his tip remained inside her, he claimed her lips in a demanding kiss before he thrust back forward with enough force to make the bed shake.

"Rafe," she cried out, her nails scoring his back.

White-hot pleasure seared through him, making his muscles tense as he pistoned in and out, growing lost in the sensual pleasure clouding his mind.

Somewhere in the darkness was a madman who'd already taken two women and who was tormenting Annie with hideous visions. Not to mention an unseen enemy that continued to stalk Hauk. But in this bed nothing mattered but the fierce passion that seared between them.

Locking their gazes, he picked up the tempo, sinking into her, over and over, until he felt her tense beneath him. Her fingers clutched the headboard, her eyes squeezing shut before her cry of bliss split the air. Rafe hissed as she tightened around him, the sensation tipping him over the edge. He gave one last thrust, burying himself as deep as he could go.

Then the world fell away as his orgasm exploded through him with shattering force.

Chapter Twelve

Annie released a shaky sigh as Rafe rolled to the side and gathered her in his arms.

Wow.

That had been . . .

Wow.

Even with her limited experience, she knew the pleasure that had exploded between them was rare.

And wonderful.

Insanely, unbelievably wonderful.

As if sensing her stunned amazement, Rafe pressed his lips to her temple with a soft chuckle. "I told you I'd make you scream my name."

She smacked his hard chest. "It's not nice to be so smug," she muttered, still faintly embarrassed by the knowledge she'd been so lost in sensations that she'd forgotten they were in a hotel where anyone could hear them.

Pushing onto his elbow, he gazed down at her, his dark eyes filled with an emotion that sent shivers through her body.

"I want to see you in my bed," he growled in a low, husky voice.

She blinked in confusion. "I'm already here."

"I mean my bed at my ranch." His fingers stroked through

her hair. "My father carved the headboard for my mother when she told him she was pregnant."

"I'm . . ." Her heart forgot to beat. "I'm not sure I'll ever be in Houston."

"You'll be in Houston." He leaned down, capturing her lips in a kiss of sheer possession before lifting his head to regard her with a brooding gaze. "At my ranch. And in my bed."

"You sound so certain," she breathed.

"Sweetheart, I've never been more certain of anything in my life."

Annie shivered. Not from fear. Or at least, not fear of Rafe. She'd trust this man with her life. But at the ease with which she could see herself sharing a bed with Rafe at his ranch.

She'd be a fool to start weaving fantasies around a man who she barely knew.

Especially when he was caught in the thrill of playing hero.

Her hand lifted to smooth over his chest, enjoying the sensation of rough hair beneath her palm. Rafe Vargas wasn't the sort of man who waxed. He was hard and raw and rough-edged.

"Rafe."

Ignoring the hint of warning in her voice, his hands glided down her back, cupping her butt to press her against his thickening arousal. "Hmmm?"

"This is a night of madness," she told him.

"The first of many."

She shook her head. "That's impossible."

His eyes flashed with a sensual amusement. "Never challenge a soldier, sweetheart."

Her fingers skimmed toward his ribs, halting as they hit a thick scar hidden beneath the hair. Annie stilled. During the throes of their passion she'd tried to ignore the numerous bumps and welts she'd felt on his back and across the flat plane of his stomach.

Now, however, she couldn't halt the fierce surge of fury at the thought of the injuries that would have caused the scars.

"Was it your time as a soldier when you got this?" she asked softly.

His smile remained, but she didn't miss the hardening of his jaw or the sudden wariness in his dark eyes. "I know, it's not very pretty," he said.

She held his gaze, gently stroking her fingers over the scar, a silent assurance that the sight of the imperfection didn't bother her. It was only the knowledge of how badly he'd been injured that made her sick to her stomach.

"Will you tell me?"

He hesitated, the tension in his body making Annie fear he would refuse to answer. Then, with a resigned sigh, he met her searching gaze.

"You know I was in the military." He waited until she gave a small nod. "My unit specialized in extracting and retrieving."

She arched her brows. "Extracting and retrieving what?"

"Anything." His expression was impossible to read. "Enemy leaders that our government wanted to question. Sensitive intel. Sometimes we rescued Americans who'd been taken hostage." His voice thickened, as if the memories were still fresh. "My last mission went to hell when our helicopter was shot down and I was taken captive."

She leaned forward, pressing her lips to the circular wound just above his heart. A gunshot. "Your captors did this to you?"

His hand lifted to tangle in her hair, his head lowering to brush his lips over her forehead. "Don't ask for details, sweetheart," he pleaded.

She brushed another kiss over a long scar on his shoulder. She wasn't about to press for specifics of his torture. "How did you escape?" she instead demanded.

"I shared a prison with Teagan, Hauk, Max, and Lucas."

She tilted back her head, not surprised to see his tight expression soften at the mention of his friends. "Your partners in your security business," she murmured.

"Yeah." He absently combed his fingers through her hair, almost as if he drew comfort from the feel of the thick strands sliding over his skin. "We plotted our escape for weeks and managed to elude our guards so we could disappear into the northern mountains. Two weeks later we finally reached a village with a transmitter so we could contact our base."

Annie suddenly understood why Teagan had installed cameras in Rafe's kitchen, and why Max was willing to seemingly drop everything to assist his friend.

They'd forged the sort of bond that could only come out of the horror of war.

And if she was honest, it had to be a part of why she and Rafe connected with such ease.

They both had suffered through trauma that few other people would ever comprehend.

She reached up to stroke her fingers down the line of his jaw, his whiskers prickling against her fingertips. "Do you still have nightmares?"

"Sometimes," he admitted without hesitation.

"What do you do?"

"Accept I can't change the past. I can only concentrate on the now and hope for the future."

She blinked at his soft words. "Very enlightened."

He turned his head to press his lips to the center of her palm.

"Not always," he denied in wry tones. "There are some nights I call Teagan so we can meet at the gym and beat the shit out of each other." He gave a light tug on her hair. "What about you?"

"I try to keep myself occupied," she said. "School, helping my foster father around his ranch, work."

"Did it help?"

"Most of the time. At least until . . ." Her words trailed away as a sharp shiver raced through her body.

"Annie?"

"Until the visions returned."

With a muttered curse, Rafe rolled her onto her back, covering her with the hard length of his body. "You're safe in my arms, Annie," he said, the words sounding like a solemn pledge.

Abruptly realizing that time was swiftly passing, Annie wrapped her arms around his neck.

They could discuss their screwed-up pasts later.

Tonight might never happen again.

"I'm not so sure about that," she teased. "You're lethal to poor females."

Taking her cue, he gave a low chuckle and lowered his head to skim his lips over her brow and down the length of her nose.

"Okay, you might not be safe, but I can guarantee you there won't be any nightmares." He nuzzled the corner of her mouth, reaching for a new condom and swiftly slipping it on. "For either of us."

Her blood heated as he settled more firmly between her parted legs, the blunt tip of his cock pressing against the entrance of her body. "You guarantee?" she murmured.

He kissed his way down her jaw, and then the curve of her neck. "Do you doubt me?"

"No." Annie's brain threatened to shut down as pleasure ricocheted through her, making her toes curl in anticipation.

With a measured thrust, he pressed his erection deep inside her. "You don't sound entirely certain."

Her nails dug into his nape, her hips lifting at the delicious friction.

"Rafe."

His kissed her. "Clearly I wasn't as convincing as I should have been the first time," he murmured, his lips tracing the curve of her throat as he slowly rocked in and out of her.

Excitement blazed through her as he nibbled ever lower.

"You were very thorough," she choked out.

"Hmm." His hands gripped her hips, his tongue tormenting the aching tips of her breasts. "It's possible I missed a spot. Maybe I should do a double check."

Her eyes slid shut in utter bliss.

"Or a triple check," she suggested with a soft moan.

Rafe lingered as long as possible the next morning, making love to Annie until the maid pounded on the door for the fifth time.

Even then, it was only the fierce promise to himself that he would soon have Annie moved into his ranch where he could devote hours and hours and hours to satisfying her and easing his desire for her that allowed him to escort her out of the hotel and to his truck, which he'd left parked next to the exit.

Hitting the unlock button, he helped her climb into her seat before crawling behind the steering wheel and starting the engine.

On the point of putting the truck in gear, Rafe grimaced as he caught sight of the bag that he'd left on the floorboard. Leaning down, he tucked it beneath his seat, but not before Annie was forced to recall the unsettling encounter with Brody Johnson. "What are you going to do with the pictures?" she demanded.

He met her troubled gaze. "I'll send them to Max."

"Shouldn't they go to the cops?"

Rafe shrugged. He wasn't about to allow the pictures to be handed over to the authorities until Max had first looked at them.

He wasn't a crazed conspiracy theorist, but it was human nature for cops to try and protect each other. It'd been the same when he'd been in the service.

If the sheriff had wanted the evidence to disappear, then he wasn't going to be pleased to know he hadn't fully succeeded.

Even if they didn't reveal anything about the untimely death of Don White in his jail cell.

"He'll forward them to the FBI once he has them copied," he said.

She bit her bottom lip, looking insanely young with her drowsy eyes and hair that was once again braided.

She'd tried to weave the wet strands after they'd shared an early morning shower only to have him release them the second he'd hauled her back to bed.

He liked to run his fingers through the silken strands.

Now, however, he realized he preferred the braid when they were in public.

It meant that he was the only one who knew how beautiful the honey strands were as they spread across a pillow.

Just as he was the only one to know that beneath the jeans and casual sweater were lacy undies that made a man pant with need.

"Will Brody be in trouble?" she demanded.

"I'll have Max send them anonymously."

"Good." She wrinkled her nose. "He's pathetic, but I wouldn't want to be responsible for getting him killed."

Rafe gave a slow shake of his head. After all Annie White had endured, how did she continue to have such a kind heart?

Amazing.

And dangerous.

He reached to cup her chin in his palm. "Annie."

"What?"

"Nothing about this is your responsibility," he said, his thumb brushing her bottom lip. "Not when you were a child and certainly not now."

She frowned. "I know."

"Hmm." He studied her pale face. "I'm not so sure . . . damn."

"What's wrong?"

He dropped his hand to reach into his pocket and pull out his phone that was vibrating.

He'd muted it when they'd entered the hotel last night. There was no way in hell he was going to allow their evening to be interrupted.

Now he glanced at the screen to realize he'd missed a dozen texts and an equal number of calls.

Scrolling through the messages, he muttered a low curse. He respected and truly liked his partners, but there were times when they could rub his nerves raw.

"I should have known they wouldn't be satisfied with cameras."

"Your friends?" Annie asked.

"They're in Newton." He tossed his phone on the dash. "And they're not happy I'm not home."

"Did they discover something?"

"Nothing more than how to be a pain in my ass."

She reached to lightly touch his arm. He was swiftly discovering that it was her way of offering him comfort.

And oddly, it worked.

"They're worried about you."

"Yeah."

"You're lucky to have them," she said.

"I know, but—" He cut off his words. He didn't want to terrify her by confessing his friends were going to either put her through the third degree or treat her as if she needed to be wrapped in cotton wool. "Sometimes it can be smothering," he at last said.

Beside him, Annie grimaced. "Yeah," she muttered. "I get that. My foster parents can be the same way."

He glanced out the windshield, absently noticing the sun was shining brightly and the nearby businesses were bustling with activity.

Just a normal day.

It was easy to forget that there was a potential serial killer out there who was kidnapping women.

One who might very well be obsessed with the woman at his side.

Yeah, his friends were going to be interfering jerks who poked their noses where they didn't belong, but there was no one he'd rather have at his back.

Or who he'd rather have protecting Annie.

Shoving the car in gear, Rafe pulled out of the parking lot and headed for the highway.

"Let's go face the firing squad."

Chapter Thirteen

He watched the truck pull in front of the house with a frown. He hadn't been happy that Annabelle had been gone the entire night. How could he protect her if he didn't know where she was?

With an effort he swallowed his anger.

Soon enough his work would be done and he would be able to take her someplace they could both be safe.

For now, all that mattered was that she was back in Newton, and it was time for him to return to his hunt.

Be patient, sweet Annabelle, he whispered, stepping deeper into the hedges as she hopped out of the truck and headed toward the house.

He wished he could stay and see her excitement when she found the gift he'd left for her, but he wasn't a fool. Not only was Rafe Vargas on constant guard, but there were new players who had recently arrived in town.

He couldn't afford to take any unnecessary risks.

With a last, loving glance at the honey-haired woman, he turned to vanish among the shadows.

* * *

Annie bit her bottom lip as they pulled in front of the small house, catching sight of the sleek red Jag parked at the edge of the street, along with a white SUV.

Rafe had said his friends were flying in, so she assumed they'd rented the vehicles.

Her stomach tied in knots at the visible evidence that they were inside, waiting. Last night she'd warned Rafe that their time together was limited.

Not because she was afraid he would get ideas about "happily ever after," but because she was afraid she would.

Rafe Vargas was a custom-made heartbreaker.

Handsome, sexy, fiercely protective, with just a hint of untamed danger.

Her life was complicated enough without adding in a dose of unrequited love.

Unfortunately, her little lecture didn't halt the pang of regret at the sight of the flashy automobiles.

Rafe's friends were waiting inside. And if they were as good friends as she suspected, then they were going to do everything in their power to convince Rafe to walk away.

She was trouble.

It sounded ridiculous, but it was true.

And not just because a psycho killer was quite likely hunting her.

What did she know about relationships?

She was the daughter of a serial killer. She'd barely dated. She had trust issues. She was in a job she was growing convinced she was going to hate. And while her foster parents had always loved her, she had no idea what it meant to be in a healthy family.

See, trouble . . . with a capital *T*.

Rafe's friends would be fools not to do whatever was necessary to get her out of his life.

"Maybe I should return to the motel," she muttered, slowly climbing out of the truck.

With a fluid speed Rafe was at her side, his fingers curling around her upper arm as he steered her up the crumbling sidewalk. "No way in hell."

"But if you have company—"

"They aren't staying here." He overrode her protest, his eyes narrowing as the door was shoved open and two men stepped onto the porch.

Instantly the air was saturated with testosterone.

Her attention briefly lingered on the nearest male, with the skull-shaved head and rich honey skin. Teagan. The companion who'd been with Rafe when he'd found her roaming through her old house. She'd only seen him in the dark, but he was easy to recognize.

This morning he was dressed in a long-sleeved spandex shirt that clung to every bulging muscle, and camo pants. A tiny shiver inched down her spine as she came into contact with the predatory golden gaze. Teagan might be some sort of security expert, but he looked like he invaded Third World countries on a regular basis.

She turned her head to study the man standing at his side, her brows lifting in surprise.

Unlike Rafe and Teagan, this male was dressed in sharply pressed black slacks and a white collared shirt with the sleeves rolled to his elbows. He was also blond, with a finely sculpted face that was a breath away from beautiful.

Of course, he was as muscular as the other two men, although built along slender lines like Rafe. And equally scary, with his piercing blue eyes that watched her with a disturbing intensity.

As if he could see into her very soul.

Teagan flashed a mocking smile. "Is that any way to greet your besties?"

"Annie, this is Teagan." Rafe made the formal introduction. "And Hauk."

Hauk stepped forward, his blue gaze skimming down her body before returning to linger on her mouth.

Annie would bet good money that the slow survey made most women weak in the knees.

Hell, it would have made her weak if she hadn't already met Rafe.

Now . . .

Only one man could make her melt.

"Teagan didn't lie," he said in low, smooth tones. "You are beautiful enough to make a man lose all sense."

Rafe's arm wrapped around her shoulder as he tugged her close to his side. "Back off," he growled.

Annie stiffened at the subtle insult, but she refused to rise to the bait.

Instead, she offered a polite smile that included both men. "It's very nice to meet you."

"At least one of us has manners," Rafe muttered.

The blond shrugged. "I just said she's beautiful. It's no wonder you're not thinking clearly."

"Hauk—"

"Rafe, they're worried about you." Annie hastily interrupted the brewing fight. "That's what friends do." Pulling away from his tight grip, she headed up the stairs. "I'll go inside so you can talk."

"I won't be long," Rafe promised, his voice tight.

"Take your time," she muttered.

Ignoring the lingering glances from the two visitors, Annie took a wide path around their solid bodies to head for the door. It wasn't that she was afraid they would hurt her. It was just a natural reaction to the sheer male power that sizzled around them.

Intent on her escape, Annie nearly missed the scruffy book that had been left on the porch swing.

Coming to a sharp halt, she felt an unexplainable fear blast through her.

"Oh, shit," she breathed, her gaze locked on the cover of the book.

There was an etching of a stuffed bunny along with a faded title: *The Velveteen Rabbit*.

It could have been left there by anyone. It might even be a book that one of the men had found among the stacks of boxes she'd glimpsed on the porch and in the sheds in the backyard.

But it wasn't.

She knew that with absolute certainty.

A warm arm wrapped around her waist, tugging her against a hard male body. "Annie, what's wrong?" Rafe asked in concerned tones.

She pointed at the porch swing. "That."

Rafe muttered a curse, reaching toward the book.

"No. Don't touch it," Hauk abruptly commanded, moving to stand next to the swing. "Teagan, go inside and get a large manila envelope."

Tension coiled through the air as Teagan disappeared and Hauk reached into his pocket to pull out a silver switchblade. Pressing a hidden trigger, a three-inch blade slid silently from the handle.

Then, with a slow caution, he slid the tip of the blade beneath the cover of the book and pulled it open to reveal the words that had been scrawled in black marker across the top of the page.

Three for a wedding . . .

Annie's stomach churned as Rafe slowly turned her to meet his carefully guarded gaze.

"Does it mean anything to you?" he demanded.

She bit her bottom lip, not fooled by his seeming lack of emotion. Beneath his brittle composure he was a volcano ready to explode.

"I have a vague memory of someone reading me the book when I was a child," she admitted, that irrational fear still crawling through her. "Along with a million other kids."

"What about the quote?" he pressed.

She swallowed the lump in her throat. She struggled to call up some memory, no matter how intangible. The effort scraped against her nerves until she wanted to scream, but she couldn't come up with anything.

She shook her head in frustration. "I'm sorry . . . I don't remember ever hearing it."

Rafe turned toward the silent Hauk. "Was this here when you arrived?"

The blond-haired man gave a decisive shake of his head. "Nope."

Teagan stepped out of the house carrying a large brown envelope and wearing gloves.

"You didn't notice anyone hanging around?" Rafe asked the man as he gingerly grabbed the edge of the book and slid it into the envelope.

"We were in the kitchen," Teagan muttered.

Hauk glanced toward the street, then the high hedges that framed the yard. "The house is too isolated for the neighbors to have seen anything." He pointed out the obvious.

Pressing the flap closed, Teagan straightened with a low curse. "It's also too isolated for traffic." His golden gaze measured the distance between the narrow road and the house. "I don't remember hearing any cars go past. Do you, Hauk?"

"Nope."

They all grimaced, realizing the intruder had to have walked to the house to deliver his gift, perhaps even lingering in the hedges while they'd been completely oblivious to his presence.

"It makes sense he would have come on foot," Teagan said, returning the book to the porch swing.

Annie shivered, burrowing closer to the solid protection of Rafe's body.

Hardly the behavior of Wonder Woman, but right now she just wanted to feel safe.

"How did he know I was here?" she rasped.

Hauk cocked a brow, as if her question had caught him off guard. He glanced toward Rafe. "Have you swept your truck for tracking devices?"

"No, but this is a small town," Rafe said, his voice as tightly controlled as his expression even as his eyes smoldered with a violent fury. "It's hard to keep secrets."

"I'm going to have a look around," Teagan announced, clearly feeling the need to do something.

A man of action even if he was some sort of computer geek.

And Rafe, being Rafe, instantly went into protective mode.

"Why don't you go inside?"

His words were more a command than a suggestion, but Annie refused to budge.

"This concerns me," she reminded him. She was happy to have his support, and to follow his lead when he was obviously an expert in security, but she wasn't going to have vital information kept from her. "I think I should be a part of the conversation, don't you?"

Hauk cleared his throat, his lips twitching. "I'd be careful, amigo."

"Thanks," Rafe muttered. "I don't like the thought of that bastard watching you react to his twisted gift."

She froze, her skin prickling with sheer horror. "You think he's watching?"

Rafe's eyes smoldered. "Yeah, I think he gets off on seeing you scared."

"God." The word was wrenched from deep inside. From that place she'd locked away when she was just a child and woke up in a bomb shelter with a pile of dead bodies.

Rafe leaned down and pressed his lips to her forehead. "Go inside, sweetheart."

Her heart thundered in her chest, but she fiercely refused to give in to the panic. Instead she forced herself to consider the gift from the stalker's viewpoint.

It was easy enough to imagine him taking delight in creeping around the house unnoticed. Especially if he knew that Hauk and Teagan were inside. He would feel . . . smug, superior. She could also visualize him placing the book on the porch swing and gleefully hiding somewhere to watch her discover it.

But what was he expecting when she found his book?

Terror?

Outrage?

Horror?

"It doesn't feel twisted," she at last muttered.

Rafe frowned down at her. "What?"

She struggled to put her vague confusion into words. "If he wanted to frighten me, then why didn't he send pictures of the other women he's kidnapped? Or even a threatening note?" she asked. "*The Velveteen Rabbit* is something you use to entertain a child. It doesn't make sense."

Hauk closed his knife and slid it back into his pocket. "She has a point."

Rafe gave a slow nod. "Do you recognize the quote?" he asked his friend.

Hauk pulled out his phone and swiftly typed in the words that had been printed in the book. "It's a little vague."

"Wait." Rafe was abruptly struck by a sudden thought. "Add in 'one for sorrow and two for luck.'"

Hauk sent him a curious glance. "Do you recognize it?"

"No." His voice was hard. "But it was written on the note that was shoved under Annie's motel door."

Hauk grimaced, returning his attention to his phone as he searched for the meaning. "Got it," he at last said. "'One for sorrow.' It's an old English nursery rhyme."

Rafe scowled. "Does it have any meaning?"

"Magpies. Bad luck." Hauk grimaced before he quoted the entire rhyme. "One for sorrow, two for luck, three for a wedding, four for death, five for silver, six for gold, seven for a secret, not to be told, eight for heaven, nine for hell, and ten for the devil's own sell."

Rafe shook his head. "I've never heard it before."

Hauk glanced toward Annie. "Could it be someone from your past? Someone who knew you as a child?"

She hunched her shoulders. Once again she felt the vague

sense of familiarity. As if there was a memory that danced just out of reach.

Unfortunately there was no way to know if it was genuine or a product of her fear.

"I truly don't know."

Rafe stroked the back of his fingers down her cheek, his gentle touch helping to ease the quivers that raced through her body. "Annie, was it your father who read you the book?"

She paused, gathering her courage before she forced herself to dredge up the images she'd kept buried for years.

She had spotty memories of her father sitting on the edge of her bed, sometimes reading from a book and sometimes telling her stories he made up off the top of his head. Her favorite had always been the one about a princess who slayed the dragon and saved the prince from the dungeons.

"No." She gave a slow shake of her head. "No, I don't think so."

"Your mother?" he asked.

She lifted a hand to her throat as a strange, choking darkness suddenly surrounded her. It felt as if . . .

As if she was being smothered.

Sucking in a deep breath, she forced away the frightening sensation.

"I can't remember," she said in husky tones. "I'm sorry."

Wrapping her in his arms, Rafe cupped the back of her head and pressed her face against his chest. "It's okay, sweetheart," he murmured.

Annie leaned against him, silently wondering if it would ever be okay again.

Rafe kept Annie locked tight in his arms as he struggled to contain the fury that boiled through him.

He had to give it to the sick, psychotic bastard.

He had balls.

He'd not only dared to come to this house, but he'd

strolled up to the porch like he was a Sunday visitor leaving a fucking casserole on the porch.

And now Annie would never feel safe here.

God. Dammit.

As if sensing he was on the verge of a complete melt-down, Hauk moved to provide a necessary distraction. Leaning forward, he snatched the book off the swing.

"We need to get this to Max," the older man said. "He might be able to pull some prints."

Rafe closed his eyes and counted to ten. Then counted to ten in Spanish, French, and Farsi.

Once he was certain he'd contained his violent urge to punch something, he cleared his throat and met his friend's worried gaze. "Yeah, I have some photos to send as well."

"Photos?"

"I'll explain tonight over a beer," Rafe assured his companion, his thoughts centered on Annie. Right now all he wanted was to take her inside and make her his famous scrambled eggs with chorizo and red chili sauce. It was guaranteed to cure any ill. "Where are you staying?"

"I assumed you would offer me your bed," Hauk murmured, his gaze sliding to the woman who was nestled against him. "I don't mind sharing."

Another distraction.

Or at least it'd better be.

Rafe narrowed his gaze. "You keep looking at her like that and I'll run your ass out of town."

Hauk gave a short laugh. "Teagan and I have rooms at the motel," he said. "Lucas preferred to stay in LaClede since he was convinced Newton didn't have . . ." Hauk rolled his eyes. "Appropriate accommodations. I swear to God, those were his words."

Rafe widened his eyes. He hadn't been expecting that.

"Lucas is here?"

"Arrived just an hour ago."

"Why the hell did he come?"

Hauk held his gaze. "You know why."

Yeah, he did.

It was the same reason he'd asked them to build a business together. And why Max was in Houston, tracking down Turkish paper at the same time he was trying to help Rafe protect a woman he'd never even met.

They were more than friends.

They were brothers.

There was the sound of footsteps before Teagan vaulted over the low railing that framed the porch.

"Looks like someone came through the hedge," he said, nodding toward a narrow opening that'd been carved into the overgrown bushes.

Annie tensed, and Rafe tightened his arms, not yet ready to let her go. "Any indication of a vehicle?" he asked.

Teagan shrugged. "Impossible to say."

"Damn," he muttered.

"I'll put a couple of cameras on the outside of the house," Teagan promised.

"And one of us will always have an eye on the place," Hauk added, his tone warning the subject wasn't up for debate.

Not that Rafe intended to argue.

The more protection Annie had, the better.

Of course, it couldn't be that simple. Pressing her hands to his chest, Annie stepped away from him to glance toward Hauk.

"Maybe it would be better if you didn't," she said.

It was Teagan who responded. "Why?"

"If the person leaving the notes realizes you're watching the house, it might scare him away."

"That's the point," Rafe growled, tugging her into his arms.

Stubborn woman.

She tilted back her head, a scowl on her pretty face. "Wouldn't it be better if we could use his interest in me to catch him?" she demanded. "Or even follow him to find the women he took?"

"Rafe—" Teagan began, only to snap his lips shut when Rafe pointed a finger in his direction.

"No."

Hauk ignored the warning. "Think, Rafe. It might be our only chance to stop him."

He glared at his supposed friend. "Screw that. I'm not using Annie as bait."

Annie made a sound of frustration. "Shouldn't it be my choice?"

"No." He didn't bother to glance at her, instead keeping his finger pointed at Teagan. "I left a camera in Annie's motel room . . . get it."

"Oh, wait." Annie tried to pull away. "I have the key."

"Not necessary," Teagan assured her.

"You." Rafe pointed toward the frowning Hauk. "Send the book and pictures I left in the glove compartment of my truck to Max ASAP."

Hauk folded his arms over his chest. "Rafe—"

"Got it." Teagan grabbed Hauk's arm and tugged him toward the stairs that led off the porch. "Let's go before you get your face rearranged."

"Fine." Hauk sent Rafe a threatening glance. "I'll be back."

Waiting until the two had collected the pictures and driven away, Teagan in the Jag and Hauk in the SUV, Rafe heaved a sigh and buried his face in the curve of Annie's neck, breathing deep of her sweet scent.

"I warned you," he groused. "Pains in the ass."

Chapter Fourteen

It was nearly two a.m. when Rafe quietly let himself out the back door, carrying a six-pack that had been cooling in his fridge.

"Beer?" he asked, his voice low as he watched the shadow detach from the side of the shed and stroll toward him.

Leaning against the side of the house, Hauk reached for his beer. "I thought you would be enjoying a night with your lovely roommate."

"She's exhausted," Rafe muttered, grimacing at the understatement.

The past few days she'd endured one shock after another, not to mention barely getting any sleep the night before.

It was a wonder she hadn't collapsed during dinner.

"You're worried about her?" Hauk demanded.

Rafe didn't hesitate. "Yeah, I'm worried."

Hauk tilted his head, the light from the kitchen spilling over his pale hair and emphasizing his hard expression. "And that's all?"

"You know it's not."

"I know you want to bang her."

Rafe clenched his hand. He might love Hauk like a brother,

but that didn't mean he wouldn't kick his ass. "Watch it, amigo."

Hauk took a deep drink before once again scraping against Rafe's last nerve. "And you have a compulsive need to protect the weak and the helpless."

Rafe leaned forward, his body tense with leashed aggression. "Is this going somewhere?"

Hauk took another drink. "I saw how she looked at you."

"How was that?"

"Like you're Superman."

Rafe abruptly forgot his annoyance, a heady rush of pleasure racing through him.

Annie looked at me like I'm Superman?

The mere thought sent a treacherous warmth through his chest.

"I do have several heroic qualities," he murmured.

Hauk narrowed his eyes. "I'm serious, Rafe."

Rafe heaved a resigned sigh. Okay. He got the fact that his friends were concerned, but their suspicion of Annie was going to get old quick.

"I know you're worried she's involved with the killer, but you're wrong."

"I don't think she's involved." Hauk held up a hand as Rafe scowled in disbelief. "Not after meeting her. You can't fake that kind of innocence." The older man shrugged. "I do worry she's putting you in danger, but you're a big boy. You can decide to walk away if you want."

Rafe knew that wasn't the end.

Hauk had an expression that meant he was preparing to offer advice he didn't ask for and probably didn't want.

"Then what's on your mind?" Rafe demanded. Hauk wasn't going to let it go until he'd had his say.

"What happens when the adventure is over and you return to Houston?" his friend abruptly asked.

It wasn't the question Rafe had been expecting, but it was easy to answer. "I'm bringing Annie with me."

Hauk held his gaze. "You're sure?"

"Damn straight." Rafe shrugged. "She might be kicking and screaming, but I'm sure."

"You'd better be, amigo."

Rafe studied his companion. He was obviously trying to make a point. But it was too late and Rafe was too exhausted to figure it out. "Just say what's on your mind, Hauk."

"There are women who know the score. They understand that most relationships, no matter how good, have an expira-tion date. Sometimes a night, sometimes a few months," Hauk said with the confidence of a man who devoted a great deal of time and energy to seducing the opposite sex. "But Annie White isn't one of those women. You move her into your ranch and she's going to expect to stay."

Rafe smiled with anticipation. "That's what I'm count-ing on."

"I hope so," Hauk surprised him by saying. "She seems like a nice woman and she's been through hell. It would be a shitty deal for you to break her heart."

Well, well. It seemed he wasn't the only one vulnerable to Annie's sweet charm.

Rafe abruptly stiffened, his hand reaching for the gun holstered at his lower back as a shadow appeared at the side of the house.

"There's a party and no one invited me?" Teagan demanded, stepping into the small pool of light.

"There's a beer on the step," Rafe said, nodding toward the back porch as he released his grip on the gun. Then, barely waiting for Teagan to twist off the top and down half the beer in one long swallow, he asked the question that'd been on his mind since Teagan had returned to the motel. "Anything on the camera?"

His friend grimaced. "One or two gawkers strolled by to try and take a peek in the window."

"You're sure they're just gawkers?" Rafe demanded.

Teagan gave a lift of his shoulder. "Two women who had to be seventy if they were a day, and a couple pimple-faced boys trying to act brave."

"Jesus," Hauk breathed. "Small towns give me the creeps."

Teagan gave a short laugh. "I drove up just as the boys were trying to get a better look and they about pissed their pants when I told them what would happen if I saw them near the motel again."

Rafe's gut twisted with frustration. He'd hoped they'd catch a break with the camera.

If not the actual stalker, then at least his car pulling into the parking lot.

"Damn," he muttered.

"The bastard's smart," Teagan said, leaning against the rusted railing that threatened to snap beneath the strain of holding up the big man. "Too smart to get caught by a hidden camera."

"What about the sheriff?" Rafe demanded. "Have you seen him hanging around?"

Teagan cocked a brow. "Not that I noticed."

Hauk was the first to ask the obvious question. "You think the sheriff's involved?"

Rafe did a quick recap of their encounter with Brody Johnson and the arson of the courthouse. He included his belief that someone was anxious to get rid of evidence and that the most obvious suspect would be the sheriff.

"Even if he doesn't have anything to do with Don White's death, he's eager to run Annie out of town," he said in conclusion. "I won't have him trying to intimidate her."

Teagan's face was grim by the time Rafe was done speaking. After a childhood of watching the local police ignore his father's brutality, he wasn't a huge fan of cops.

"I'll have Lucas do some discreet inquiries among his contacts in law enforcement," he said. "If there was a cover-up, then there would have been some chatter, even if no one wanted to make an official complaint."

Rafe nodded. "Good idea."

"I have my moments," Teagan drawled, his brows pulling together. "Wait." He reached into his pocket to pull out his phone. "It's Max."

"What's up?" Rafe demanded.

"He needs me to work my magic," Teagan muttered, scrolling through the text message.

Hauk moved to stand beside Teagan. "On what?"

Teagan slid the phone back in his pocket and polished off his beer before he answered. "He has a hit on Don White's prints, but he's being blocked from getting an I.D."

"Blocked by who?" Hauk asked.

"Government."

Rafe blinked. Lucas didn't have Teagan's computer skills, but he was no amateur. Plus he had a level of clearance that could get him past almost any agency firewall. "Our government?"

"Yep." Setting the empty bottle on the back step, Teagan glanced toward Hauk. "I'm going to head to LaClede and stay with Lucas. I have shit Internet coverage here."

Hauk nodded as Rafe moved to place a hand on Teagan's shoulder. "Let me know as soon as you find something."

"Will do." The golden eyes narrowed. "Be careful, Rafe. Whoever left that book is jonesing for your girl. He won't care who he has to hurt to get her."

His words of warning delivered, Teagan headed toward the edge of the house, swiftly disappearing among the shadows.

There was a long beat of silence before Hauk asked the question racing through Rafe's brain. "What the hell could the government have to do with Don White?"

Rafe's lips parted, but before he could confess that he didn't have a damn clue, a shrill scream pierced the air.

Rafe leaped up the steps and pulled open the screen door with enough force to yank it off its rusty hinges.

"Annie!"

"Sweetheart, wake up."

Annie instinctively buried against the warm body that was pressed against her, desperate to wrench herself out of the nightmarish vision.

It'd started like all the others.

The sickening sense of anticipation. The sight of the pretty young woman racing across a field, her blond hair shimmering in the moonlight. The comforting weight of the knife in her hand.

She'd desperately tried to maintain contact with the vision, to capture some sense of where she was or even locate a landmark that could pinpoint an exact location.

But even as she realized there was something familiar about the house in the background, she felt herself running forward, a burst of electric pleasure racing through her as she lifted her hand and slashed the large dagger through the air.

That was when the scream had been ripped from her throat as she struggled to pull out of the dream.

God almighty.

She couldn't bear to witness killing the woman.

She shuddered as strong arms wrapped around her. "Rafe?" she rasped.

"I've got you. Shh," he murmured, his lips brushing her cheeks, which were damp with tears. "It was just a nightmare."

"No." She forced open her eyes, blinking against the overhead light that'd been switched on. "It wasn't a nightmare. It was a vision."

His arms tightened around her. "Annie—"

"I know what I saw," she stubbornly interrupted.

"I believe you, sweetheart," he instantly soothed, moving back to study her pale face. "Tell me."

She blinked. She was so accustomed to people assuming she was crazy she'd forgotten Rafe was different.

A dangerous warmth flowed through her, helping to ease the icy fear lodged in the pit of her stomach. Tilting back her head she met Rafe's steady gaze. "An empty field."

"Was it dark?"

"Yes, but the moon was shining."

"Anything else?"

"I thought . . ." She hesitated, forcing herself to recall the images that had seared through her mind. "It looked like Mitch Roberts's house."

Rafe stiffened in shock. "You were inside it?"

"No." She shook her head, sucking in a deep breath. The clean scent of male skin and soap filled her senses, grounding her in the here and now. She was in bed with Rafe's arms around her. Not in some remote field with a knife in her hand. "It was at a distance."

"How could you know that it was the Roberts place?" he asked, his tone curious instead of accusing. "All those old farmhouses look the same."

She grimaced. "It was a feeling. I knew that I'd been there. Recently."

His fingers absently pushed her curls from her face, his brow furrowed. "Do you want to drive out there?"

She stared at him in amazement. It was one thing for him to believe her vision. It was another for him to ignore his instinctive urge to keep her protected.

She understood exactly what it was costing him to make the offer.

Her heart melted just a little more.

Dammit.

"Can we?" she asked softly.

"If it will ease your mind."

"Yes," she breathed in relief. She wasn't any more eager

than Rafe to charge through the dark in search of some psycho who was potentially murdering helpless women, but she would never be able to live with herself if she ignored her vision. What if she had the opportunity to stop the mystery stalker before he could grab another woman? "I need to know."

Tangling his fingers in her hair, Rafe tugged her head back, scorching her lips with a kiss she felt to her toes. Then, with obvious reluctance, he released his hold on her and climbed out of the bed. "Get dressed," he murmured, his gaze resting on her lips. "I'll wait for you in the living room."

Waiting for the door to close, Annie scrambled off the mattress and quickly pulled on a pair of jeans and a heavy sweatshirt.

She would have sworn that nothing could ease the horror of feeling like she was in the body of a killer, stalking a terrified woman, but she couldn't deny that the tiny shivers racing through her body had more to do with his kiss than the vision.

Nothing short of a miracle.

Opening the door, Annie stepped into the living room, coming to an abrupt halt as she caught sight of Rafe and the golden-haired Hauk standing in the middle of the floor.

There was no need to be a mind reader to sense she'd interrupted an argument.

The very air sizzled.

Feeling weirdly self-conscious as the two men turned to lock their gazes on her, Annie cleared her throat. "Is there a problem?"

Rafe deliberately ignored the man nearly vibrating with annoyance at his side. "No problem," he assured her.

A scowl twisted Hauk's starkly beautiful features. "Rafe—"

"Stay here and keep an eye on the house." Rafe overrode his friend, the tone warning that the discussion was over. "I want to know if that bastard comes anywhere near."

"Shit." Hauk folded his arms over his chest, a muscle

twitching in his jaw. This was a man who was clearly used to giving orders, not taking them. "Do anything stupid and I'll kick your ass."

Rafe moved to hold open the door, his gaze never leaving her face. "Ready?"

She scurried forward, avoiding Hauk's glare as she stepped through the doorway.

"He's not very happy with you," she muttered once they were in the truck and pulling away from the small house.

Rafe shrugged. "He'll get over it."

Annie didn't doubt that.

Watching the men interact, it was obvious they'd formed something very close to a family.

They might squabble and maybe even throw a few punches, but when push came to shove they would always have each other's backs.

Settling in the leather seat, Annie turned her head to stare out the side window.

It was late and the streets of Newton were dark. Barren. The people in this area were farmers and factory workers and teachers.

They were up at the crack of dawn and put in long days. They didn't have the energy or interest in nightclubs or trendy cafés that served tiny coffees. By ten o'clock the locals were tucked in their beds to watch the local news.

Within minutes they'd left the outskirts of town and were headed toward the highway.

"Are you okay?" Rafe demanded.

She wrinkled her nose. "Not really."

He instantly slowed the truck. "We can go back to the house."

"No." She wrapped her arms around herself, still hearing the screams of the blond-haired woman ringing in her ears. "We need to find him before . . ."

Her words trailed away as they turned a corner and caught sight of the barriers that blocked the road to the highway.

Ahead of them was a group of cars and trucks that were pulled near the gas station-slash-quickie mart where they'd stopped . . . was it yesterday? The day before?

It was difficult to remember as she studied the various police cars that were parked next to the small brick building, their lights flashing.

"Hold on," Rafe muttered, angling the truck to a halt next to the barrier where a middle-aged man with a John Deere cap was standing guard duty. With a push of a button he had his side window rolled down. "What's happening?" he asked.

The stranger moved forward, clearly enjoying his temporary position of authority. "Another woman missing," he said, turning his head to spit out a stream of tobacco.

"Damn, that's a shame." Rafe easily slid into a good-old-boy guise, slouching in his seat as his gaze moved toward the crowd of people milling across the closed road. "Who is it?"

"Cindy Franklin. She was supposed to come in to work at the gas station at midnight." Another spit of tobacco. "She's never a minute late, so when she didn't show they called her husband. He said she'd left home at eleven forty-five as always."

Rafe nodded as Annie's stomach cramped with pain.

Even knowing that the visions were genuine didn't ease the regret when they were confirmed.

As if sensing her pain, Rafe discreetly reached to grasp her hand.

"Did they find her?" he asked the man who was now leaning against the side of the truck.

"Nope, but her car was just behind the station." The man pointed toward the empty field. "The cops are looking at it now."

"A bad deal," Rafe murmured, giving Annie's fingers a squeeze as she was tormented by the memory of a young woman with blond hair running through the darkness.

"We're waiting to see if they want to do a search," the man

said, leaning forward to peer into the shadows of the truck. "You're Vargas's grandson?"

"Yeah." Releasing Annie's hand, Rafe straightened in his seat and gave a nod toward the man. "Hope Cindy turns up soon."

Taking his foot off the brake, Rafe barely waited for the man to step back before he was turning the truck around and heading back into town.

"Accident or deliberate?" he growled in low tones.

Annie studied his hard profile in confusion. "What?"

He glanced in the rearview mirror before turning onto a narrow street, and then another. As if he was trying to make sure they weren't being followed.

"This is the first time a car was found."

"What does that mean?"

"He might have been interrupted before he could get rid of it," he said, coming to a four-way stop. "Or Cindy might have escaped and he had to chase her on foot."

She was beginning to know him well enough to suspect he didn't believe either of those explanations. "Or?" she prompted.

His gaze was on the rearview mirror, scanning the empty street behind them.

"Or he's telling us he knows we've made the connection to the gas station," he explained, at last pushing on the accelerator to send them rolling forward. "If that's it, he won't use this place again."

Oh God. Had the stalker been watching them when they were at the station?

Was he watching them now?

Or worse, was he busy cutting the throat of poor Cindy Franklin?

She shivered, her hands clenched in her lap.

The quiet town that'd just minutes ago seemed peaceful was now dark and cramped and oddly menacing. "Will he move from where he's been hiding?"

His expression tightened. "Impossible to say."

He took one last turn and Annie suddenly realized they were pulling to a halt in front of his grandfather's home. "Why are we here?" she demanded in confusion. "I thought we were going to try and search for the missing woman."

He shut off the engine and turned to meet her confused gaze. "For whatever reason, the sheriff is looking for an excuse to get you out of town. If he catches us around a crime scene he might start pointing fingers." He waited for her to grimace before shoving open his door. "Besides, half the town of Newton will be out roaming the fields. The kidnapper is smart enough to disappear for a few days."

They exchanged glances, both knowing it wouldn't be just "a few" days. It would be precisely two days.

The amount of time the Newton Slayer preferred to put between his killings.

Chapter Fifteen

Despite the late night, Rafe woke early, running to the local diner to pick up coffee, doughnuts, and the latest gossip. Then, returning to the house, he gave up on his futile effort to send a weary Hauk back to the motel and instead slipped into the bedroom.

He'd closed the venetian blinds the night before, leaving the room in darkness, but he didn't have any trouble finding his way across the floor and gently settling on the edge of the narrow bed.

Reaching out, he ran his fingers through the honey strands of Annie's hair, spreading them across the pillow. In the shadows she looked young and vulnerable and incredibly fragile.

Christ. All he wanted was to lie down beside her and pull her into his arms. It was the only time he felt he could keep her truly safe.

Resisting the urge, he watched as her lashes fluttered upward and she regarded him with a sleepy confusion.

"Rafe?"

His fingers continued to stroke through her hair. "Morning, sweetheart."

"What time is it?"

"A little after nine."

Her eyes widened as she scooted up on the pillows, the sheet tumbling down to reveal the tiny, white eyelet nightgown that barely covered the sweet bounty of her breasts.

Instantly he was hard, the urge to protect transforming into a sharp-edged hunger.

He still wanted her in his arms, but his desire now included sweaty naked bodies and soft groans of pleasure.

Pushing her hair behind her ears, Annie gave a small shake of her head, as if trying to clear her mind. "I can't believe I slept so long," she said, her voice husky.

Rafe shifted, the press of his erection against the zipper of his jeans downright painful.

"You had a restless night," he pointed out.

She frowned, studying his grim expression. "Something happened."

He nodded. He'd already fought his inner demons that urged him to try and keep the unpleasant news hidden from this woman.

She would eventually learn the truth, unless he handcuffed her to the bed. An option that was far more tempting than it should be.

Besides, she was the one who'd endured the vision.

She deserved the truth.

"Nothing that we didn't already suspect," he admitted with a grimace. "Cindy never turned up."

Annie bit her bottom lip, her eyes darkening with horror. "He has her."

"That's the assumption."

Leaning forward, she reached out to grasp his forearm. "We need to try and find her."

He covered the fingers she'd laid on his arm with his hand, bending his head so they were nose to nose. "After breakfast," he said in firm tones.

She frowned, but he was close enough to see the sudden dilation of her eyes.

He wasn't the only one thinking about sweaty naked bodies and groans of pleasure.

She licked her lips. "Are you always so bossy?"

"Yeah." His fingers trailed up her bare arm and over her shoulder. "I'm also stubborn and I can be bad-tempered before my coffee," he continued, his fingers toying with the narrow ribbon that held up her nightgown. "On the plus side, I'm half-civilized. I can throw a steak on the grill. And I have a ranch that's just begging for a woman's touch. Is there anything else you need to know?"

She sucked in a startled breath, instantly pulling back. She might be willing to indulge their mutual attraction, but she wasn't prepared to discuss their future.

"Do you have doughnuts?"

Rafe forced a smile to his lips, squashing his flare of frustration.

Eventually she would accept that she belonged to him.

Until then he would have to be patient.

Okay, maybe not entirely patient, he conceded, unable to resist the temptation of skimming his fingers down the plunging neckline of her gown.

"I'm beginning to suspect the way to your heart is through the pastry aisle," he teased, satisfaction blasting through him at the sight of her nipples hardening in anticipation.

Her cheeks heated as his finger slid beneath the thin fabric, brushing over the tightly furled nipple.

"Rafe," she choked out.

Bending his head, he pressed a kiss of stark hunger to her lips.

"When this is over I'm taking you to my ranch and locking the door," he growled against her mouth. Unlike Annie, he had no problem talking about their inevitable future. "I want you to myself for the next year."

She shivered, her arms lifting to wrap around his neck. "I haven't said I'm going."

He gave her lower lip a punishing nip. "You will."

"You're right," she breathed, her fingers tangling in his hair as he circled the tip of her nipple with his finger. "You are stubborn."

He dipped his tongue into the warm welcome of her mouth. "You have no idea."

Intent on the arousal that had exploded between them, he ignored the sound of the front door opening. Hauk was still on guard duty. He wouldn't let anyone slip past who didn't belong.

Unfortunately, there was no denying the sharp knock on the bedroom door, or Teagan's impatient voice.

"Rafe."

His hand cupped her breast, a groan wrenched from his throat. "Christ," he growled, forcing himself to pull back as he met her darkened gaze. "A year, sweetheart," he at last said, rising to his feet. "I get you alone for a year."

"We'll see," she hedged, tugging the sheets up to her chin.

"I'm not the only stubborn one." With a half dozen steps he was at the door, opening it just far enough to glare at his friend. "This had better be good."

Teagan was wearing the clothes he'd had on the night before, his expression wiped of emotion. "You're going to want to see this," he said.

Damn.

Rafe already knew he wasn't going to like what Teagan had to say.

Turning his head, he sent Annie a warning frown. "Stay here," he commanded.

A waste of breath.

The words had barely left his lips before she was leaping out of bed and grabbing a robe that matched her nightgown.

"No way." She moved forward. "I'm coming with you."

He blocked her path, his gaze narrowed as he took in the robe that hit her mid-thigh and was thin enough to see through.

"Not like that, you're not," he growled. He might not be able to halt her from hearing Teagan's news, but he'd be damned if she was going to waltz around half-naked.

He loved his friends enough to avoid having any reason to punch them in the face.

She looked puzzled. "What?"

Walking to the small closet, he pulled out a robe that had belonged to his grandfather. Returning to Annie, he efficiently wrapped her in its thick folds.

With an expression of disbelief, she glanced down at the hem that fell to her ankles and the arms that entirely covered her hands. "Are you kidding me?" she demanded.

"I only claimed to be half-civilized," Rafe reminded her, firmly tying the belt around her waist. "The other half is pure male."

She waited for him to step back, her lips pressed into a tight line. "Happy now?"

He swooped down, capturing her mouth in a short, sizzling kiss that promised all sorts of delayed pleasure.

"Sweetheart, the only time I'm going to be happy is when this shit is over and I can get you back in that bed," he informed her.

He could see the pulse race at the base of her neck, but she fiercely refused to be distracted.

"We should go."

"Fine." He claimed one more lingering kiss before he pulled open the door. "Until later," he whispered in her ear as she walked past him.

Following her out of the bedroom, they headed into the kitchen where they found Teagan standing beside the stack of papers arranged on the table.

The man's gaze shifted from Rafe to Annie before returning to Rafe with a rueful grimace.

Teagan was intimately familiar with recognizing a woman who was still flushed with a lingering arousal.

"Sorry to interrupt."

"What've you got?" Rafe asked.

Teagan tapped the stack of papers. "A name."

"For Don White?"

"Yep."

Annie stiffened at his side, her brows drawing together. "What are you talking about?"

Rafe reached to pull out one of the wooden chairs. "I think we should have a seat."

"And some coffee," Teagan muttered, grabbing one of the two Styrofoam cups that Rafe had left on the counter before sliding into the chair across the table. "I'm in dire need of caffeine."

"Did you pull an all-nighter?" Rafe asked, scooting his seat close to Annie.

If she freaked at the news Teagan had to share, he wanted to be able to pull her into his arms.

"It took a while," Teagan admitted.

Annie sat rigid in her chair, her fingers peeking from the arms of the oversized robe to clench the edge of the table.

"This has something to do with my father?"

"There was something sketchy about his background check," Rafe admitted, grimacing as the color drained from her face.

He didn't like having to rip open old wounds, but he didn't know any other way to get to the truth.

"Background check?" She gave a shake of her head. "Why would you run a background check?"

Rafe shrugged. "It's what I do."

There was a long pause as Annie studied him with a narrowed gaze, no doubt realizing he'd run a similar background check on her.

Then she gave a small shake of her head, no doubt filing away her annoyance to toss in his face later.

"What do you mean sketchy?" she instead demanded.

It was Teagan who answered. "There was no history of Don White until he arrived in Newton."

Annie blinked, clearly confused. "Rafe?"

"As I've mentioned before, Teagan is a computer god," Rafe said, ignoring his friend's snort of humor. "He quickly realized that your father's past was bogus."

Her confusion remained. "I don't understand what that means."

"The previous jobs and addresses he listed when he

opened a bank account don't exist," Teagan said. "Even his birth certificate is forged."

"Forged? But . . . why?"

"My first thought was that he was hiding from the law," Rafe reluctantly confessed.

Her eyes widened. She wasn't stupid. She knew why he was concerned that Don White would be using a fake name.

"You suspected he'd killed other women?" she breathed.

He nodded. "It was a possibility."

Annie's lips parted, but no sound came out. Rafe reached to pry one of her hands off the table, wrapping it in his fingers.

Damn. He hated this.

"Your father wasn't on the run. At least not from the law." Teagan swiftly jumped in to end Annie's growing panic, his voice forceful enough to command her attention. "I think he was trying to protect you."

Annie took a second. Actually she took several seconds.

Drawing in a deep breath, she squashed the urge to slap her hands over her ears.

She'd been the one to insist on being a part of this meeting, hadn't she? She couldn't act like a child just because she didn't like the direction of the conversation.

Of course, that didn't ease the nervous tension that twisted her stomach into knots.

"Protect me from what?"

"Your father was a naval officer," Teagan said. "Captain James Emerson."

Annie stared at Teagan in confusion. "That's . . ." She was forced to halt and clear the lump from her throat. "You've made a mistake."

"I'm sorry, babe, it's no mistake," Teagan said, his voice remarkably gentle as he grabbed a stapled stack of papers and slid them across the table. "This is a record of his service.

He was a highly decorated veteran who was well respected and in line to become an admiral, until his sudden retirement."

Feeling oddly numb, Annie glanced over the documents. She didn't have Teagan or Rafe's skills, but they looked official.

"Why would he try to hide this?" she asked. "Most men would be bragging about this sort of career every chance they got."

Teagan held up his hand. "I'm not done." He slid another stack of papers across the table. "Thirty-seven years ago he married Virginia Cole, better known as Ginny, the daughter of a diplomat. They had a son one year later."

"Marty," she muttered, her mind struggling to keep up. She'd known her mother's name was Ginny, but she hadn't known that she was the daughter of a diplomat.

Her father had told her that her grandparents had died when her mother was just a child.

"Actually, your brother was officially named Martin Jacob Emerson," Teagan corrected, saying each name with a deliberate emphasis.

Rafe frowned. "Why is that name familiar?"

Teagan grabbed the top sheet of paper and tossed it toward Rafe. "Because of this."

Rafe's hand tightened on her fingers, his gaze locked on the copy of an old newspaper clipping. "Shit," he breathed.

Dread clenched her heart as his face paled. It had to be bad. Really bad.

"Tell me," she commanded.

Rafe grimaced. "Annie—"

"Tell me."

He shared a worried glance with Teagan before turning back to meet her impatient glare.

"He killed your mother."

She didn't know what she'd been expecting.

But it sure the hell wasn't that.

Barely aware she was moving, she reached to grab the top

of the paper, snatching it from Rafe's hand before he could prevent her.

Nausea clutched her stomach as she read the lurid headline.

FOURTEEN-YEAR-OLD SLICES THE THROAT OF HIS SOCIALITE MOTHER

"Oh my God." The paper dropped from her hand, drifting onto the table. "My father . . ." She shook her head. "He told me they'd died in a car wreck."

"Your father was a good man who wanted to protect you from—"

"Murder," she finished for him.

A shudder raced through her. God almighty, was there anyone in her family who hadn't been accused of some hideous act of violence?

"Not murder," Rafe denied, grabbing the paper to quickly read the article. "Self-defense."

She studied his bleak face. "He killed my mother in self-defense?"

He nodded. "That's what the judge ruled."

"Long-term emotional and physical abuse," Teagan added, sipping his coffee. The morning sunlight slanted through the kitchen window, emphasizing his dark beauty at the same time it revealed the shadows of weariness in his gorgeous honey eyes. "There were a number of witnesses who came forward during the trial to claim they'd seen Martin with bruises and broken bones throughout his childhood. And there'd been more than one friend of the family who said that your mother often locked your brother in a closet for hours, even days, at a time."

Annie surged to her feet, instinctively slamming the door on the image of a young, helpless boy with swollen, black eyes and broken arms.

She told herself it was because she couldn't bear to think of any child being harmed.

Especially not by his own mother.

But the icy chill inching down her spine made her fear that it was something else.

Something terrible that her mind wasn't prepared to accept.

Feeling the male gazes locked on her, Annie paced the narrow floor, her fingers anxiously plucking at the belt of her robe.

Eventually she could give in to the nervous breakdown that hovered like a black cloud on the horizon.

It wouldn't, however, be today.

"But my father," she breathed, refusing to accept he could be involved. It was ridiculous. For years she'd forced herself to believe he was a serial killer. But she couldn't wrap her brain around the idea of him hurting one of his children. "How could he allow someone to hurt his own son?"

"He was a sailor," Rafe reminded her. "He no doubt spent most of his life aboard a ship. It's likely he didn't know what was going on."

He had a point, but Annie wasn't satisfied.

"Then why didn't someone else stop her?" She waved a hand toward the papers spread across the table, her voice thick with the emotions she was determined to keep leashed. "Obviously people knew something terrible was happening."

"She had money. She came from a powerful family," Teagan said, his voice soft as if sensing she was on the edge. "A lot of sins can be swept under the carpet."

"It was also a number of years ago," Rafe added, his expression impossible to read. "People didn't want to admit a mother could hurt her own child."

Annie continued to pace. It was true. Even today, people didn't want to think a woman could give birth to children and then become a monster.

Mother's a monster . . .

A sudden, smothering darkness threatened to drown her as the words whispered through her mind.

No. She gave a sharp shake of her head.

It was a figment of her imagination.

She'd been three years old when her mother had . . . died. There was no way she could have any actual memory of her. Or her brother.

Could she?

Coming to a halt in the center of the linoleum floor, she suddenly realized she hadn't asked the most obvious question.

God. She really was losing it.

"Is he still alive?"

Rafe frowned. "Who?"

"My brother."

Chapter Sixteen

Rafe clenched his hands. He sensed that Annie's brittle composure was about to crack, but there wasn't a damned thing he could do to make this any easier for her.

And that frankly pissed him off.

He was a man of action.

A problem needed to be solved, he solved it.

But this . . .

It was a fucking mess.

And in part, it was his fault.

He was the one who'd insisted Max run the background check on Don White. And allowed Annie to be here when Teagan shared the intel.

But how the hell could he have known that instead of answering questions, it would only open an entirely new set of problems?

Teagan exchanged glances with him, clearly waiting for the sign to continue. Rafe gave a small nod. What else could he do?

Annie already knew that her mother had been brutally killed and that her brother was responsible after he supposedly snapped due to years of abuse.

She was also aware that no one had seemingly done a damn thing to help the poor boy.

She deserved to know if he was still alive.

Teagan turned his gaze to Annie. "Yep. After the trial he was sent to a private institute. The Greenwood Estates. Just outside Madison, Wisconsin."

"He's still there?" she prodded.

There was a momentary hesitation before Teagan nodded. "As far as I know."

Rafe understood his hedging.

Annie was too blinded by the stunning realization that her brother was alive to consider the unpleasant possibilities.

Teagan, however, was well aware it had to be more than just a coincidence that Martin Emerson had sliced his mother's throat with a knife.

"What's his diagnosis?" Rafe asked.

Teagan drained the last of the coffee and reached for a doughnut.

"Hacking into medical files is going to take some time," he told Rafe, taking another bite. "It would be faster to drive there and ask in person."

Rafe frowned, considering the various obstacles.

The drive would only take four hours or so, but he knew enough about hospitals to realize they couldn't just waltz in and start asking questions.

He stilled, his glance shifting to Annie, who'd returned to her nervous pacing.

"I suppose Annie is his next of kin," he reluctantly muttered. "She would have access to Martin and his doctors."

He hated the mere thought of taking her along, but her presence would allow them to cut through the red tape.

"Yep." Teagan reached into the pocket of his jeans, pulling out a small leather wallet. With a flick of his wrist he tossed it toward Rafe. "And just in case."

Snatching the wallet out of the air, Rafe flipped it open,

not surprised to find his picture had been laminated onto a professional I.D.

He cocked a brow. "FBI?"

Teagan shrugged. "Do you want answers or not?"

Rafe felt a sudden warmth press against his back as Annie leaned over his shoulder to glance at the I.D.

"Isn't that illegal?"

He turned his head to study her delicate profile, relishing the sensation of her hair brushing the back of his neck.

He'd never thought of himself as a tactile person.

Not until Annie White . . . or hell, Annie Emerson.

Now he couldn't seem to get enough of her touch.

"Only if we get caught," he assured her.

She bit her lip, and Rafe hid an unexpected smile. It didn't take someone with a lot of insight to suspect that Annie was a woman who'd grown up religiously following every rule.

Not only had she been an orphan who was dependent on the goodwill of her foster parents, but she would have done everything in her power to prove to the world that she hadn't inherited "evil" genes from her father.

He was going to take an indecent amount of pleasure in corrupting that Goody Two-shoes attitude.

Until then, he enjoyed her silent battle to convince herself that his impersonation of an FBI agent was a price she was willing to pay to find her brother.

At last she squared her shoulders and headed toward the living room. "I'll take a shower and we can go," she said.

"Annie—"

Her steps never slowed. "Don't even start," she warned as she disappeared into the tiny bathroom.

Teagan barely waited for the door to close before he leaned his elbows on the table, his expression grim.

"Martin sliced his mother's throat."

Rafe waited until he heard the shower running before he answered.

"Yeah, I got that."

"It can't be a coincidence."

Rafe met his friend's gaze. "What're your thoughts?"

"My first thought is that he escaped his leash and came to Newton to finish his father's work," Teagan said. "It would explain why he was obsessed with Annie, and his childish gifts."

It did.

In fact, it would explain a lot of things, perhaps even her strange visions.

But Rafe wasn't entirely convinced.

"Maybe," he muttered.

Teagan studied him with a too-perceptive gaze. "What's bothering you?"

He didn't try to deny he was worried. Teagan knew him too well.

"Right now all Annie is thinking about is the fact that the brother she thought died in a car crash is alive," he said. "What happens if he's somehow connected to the Newton Slayer?"

Teagan shrugged. "She's had to live with the thought her father was responsible. Could this be any worse?"

Rafe rubbed the back of his neck, his muscles tight with dread.

"It could be a hell of a lot worse," he growled. "She was a child when her father was arrested, which meant that she had at least some protection from the media circus. If it turns out that her brother is involved this time . . . Jesus." He gave a shake of his head, unable to even imagine the shit storm that would follow. "Nothing's going to protect her this time."

Teagan grimaced. "Damn, I didn't consider that angle."

Rafe glanced down at the stacks of papers that were about to change Annie's life forever.

"Even if he's not involved, this will be a nightmare for Annie if word leaks out that the son of the Newton Slayer is in a mental institute after slicing the throat of his mother."

Teagan heaved a deep sigh, leaning to the side so he could pull a folded piece of paper out of his back pocket. "There's something else you should see," he said, shoving it across the table.

Rafe slowly unfolded the paper. He knew it was something his friend had wanted to keep from Annie. That was the only reason to keep it separated from the other intel.

Still, he felt a flare of surprise as his gaze skimmed the copy of the official document.

"A birth certificate?" he murmured in confusion.

"Look at the name," Teagan commanded.

"Annabelle Emerson." His jaw clenched. It was Annie's birth certificate. It had to be. But it wasn't the fact that Teagan had managed to get his hands on the document that was making his blood run cold. It was the spelling of her first name. Annabelle. The same as on the note that had been shoved under her motel door and written in the book left on the porch swing. A name no one in this area could possibly know. Not unless they knew the past her father had been so careful to conceal. "Shit."

Teagan glanced toward the bathroom door that remained firmly shut. "That isn't the only thing."

Rafe swallowed a sigh. Of course it wasn't.

"Tell me."

"Ginny Emerson's parents were responsible for the layers of government protection that hid James Emerson's past," he revealed. "They also set up a very large trust fund to pay for Martin Emerson's extended stay at Greenwood."

Rafe felt a stab of shock. "They're alive?"

"Yep. They're currently stationed in Denmark."

He took a long minute to process the information. "Did they know Annie was in a foster home?"

"It would be hard not to know," Teagan pointed out in dry tones.

Fury exploded through him.

Annie had lost her mother, her brother, and then her father, who had been accused of being a serial killer. She'd been a mere child, alone and traumatized, and her grandparents had done nothing to reach out to her?

What kind of bastards were they?

"They abandoned her," he rasped in angry disbelief.

"They cut their losses," Teagan corrected. "People in their political position can't afford to be tainted by scandal."

"So they hid the grandson who'd been driven to murder—by their own daughter—in an expensive institute and allowed their granddaughter to be taken in by strangers."

"Yep."

Rafe shoved himself to his feet, moving to grab the rapidly cooling coffee off the counter.

"I don't want Annie to know about her grandparents," he growled. "It's bad enough to discover her mother was seemingly an abusive bitch and her brother a murderer. She doesn't need to realize she has family out there who were willing to toss her aside like garbage."

Teagan sprawled back in his seat, his legs stretched out as he studied Rafe with a brooding gaze. "You won't be able to keep it from her forever. Unless . . ."

"Unless?"

"Unless you pack your bags and take your girl to your ranch," Teagan suggested, waving his hand toward the papers spread across the table. "Keep her satisfied and she can forget about this shit."

Rafe snorted. There was nothing in this world he wanted more than to toss Annie over his shoulder and haul her to his ranch. Hell, he was even willing to consider the idea of hog-tying her to the bed until she'd forgotten everything but the pleasure they shared.

Unfortunately, he knew she would never forgive him.

"I wish it was that simple," he muttered.

"Why isn't it?"

"Annie won't leave." He sipped the coffee, briefly wondering if it was too early to pour in a shot of whiskey. A very large shot. He had a feeling he was going to need it before the day was over. "Not until the women are found."

"That's a job for the police."

No shit.

He took another sip of coffee, absently listening as the shower shut off.

"She feels responsible."

Teagan made a sound of disbelief. "Why, for God's sake?"

"Because of the connection to her father—"

"Alleged connection," Teagan interrupted.

Rafe shrugged. Right now the guilt or innocence of the faux Don White was the least of his concerns.

"And because she's convinced her visions can lead us to whoever is responsible for the abductions."

Teagan tilted his head to the side. The younger man never doubted Rafe's intuition.

"Do you believe they can?" he asked.

Rafe didn't hesitate. "Yes, but there's no way in hell I'm going to let her put herself in danger."

"Fine." Placing his hands flat on the table, Teagan pushed himself out of the chair, his muscles bulging beneath his T-shirt. The man looked like he could bench-press a small car. "Then we'll hog-tie her and take her to Texas by force," he said, the darkness in his eyes suggesting he wasn't entirely kidding. "Eventually the crazy bastard will be caught and you two can live happily ever after."

Rafe set aside his coffee, scrubbing his hands over his face.

The rasp of his beard reminded him that he hadn't shaved for the past two days. Christ. He probably looked like a pirate.

Or a drug dealer.

"She'll insist on meeting her brother," he said with a harsh sigh. He was under no illusion he could convince the stubborn female to leave the past in the past. "He's the only family she has left."

Teagan glanced toward the door as Annie scurried from the bathroom to the bedroom.

"Then let's hope he's there."

Rafe nodded, instantly knowing exactly what his friend

was implying. "And not stalking the women of Newton," he muttered.

"Exactly."

Rafe resisted the urge to discuss the possibility of Martin Emerson being the most recent incarnation of the Newton Slayer. The house was too small, and without the shower running Annie was bound to overhear them.

"Where's Hauk?" he instead asked.

"I sent him back to the motel to get some rest." Teagan held up a hand as Rafe's brows snapped together. "I'll keep a watch on the house."

"You're exhausted."

Teagan gave a lift of his shoulder. "Hauk will relieve me in a couple of hours."

Rafe didn't bother to argue. He had a better chance of achieving world peace than changing Teagan's mind. "What about Lucas?" he asked.

"He's having lunch with . . ." With a frown, Teagan pulled out his phone and scrolled through his messages. "With a Dr. Lawrence."

"Who the hell is that?"

"The coroner who performed the autopsy on the alias Don White," Teagan explained. "Lucas hopes to find out if the doctor was coerced by the sheriff into officially listing the death as a suicide."

"Damn." Rafe shoved his fingers through his hair. Was there anything connected to the Newton Slayer that wasn't a lie? He felt like he was stumbling through a minefield completely blind. And worse, he was dragging Annie along with him. "This is a fucking mess."

As if to prove his point, Annie appeared in the doorway of the kitchen, her damp hair pulled into a braid, and wearing a pair of jeans and a Denver Broncos sweatshirt.

"Are you ready?" she demanded, her chin tilted to a stubborn angle.

Clearly she was preparing for a fight.

Rafe ignored Teagan's twitching lips and reached to snatch the keys to the pickup off the counter.

"Yeah, but we're going to have a long discussion about that sweatshirt," he muttered, crossing the floor to take her elbow in a firm grip. "No self-respecting Texan is a Bronco fan."

Turning onto the private road, Rafe drove them past the acres of pristinely mowed grass and large flower beds filled with late-blooming flowers and marble fountains.

Annie frowned. Had they taken a wrong turn?

This didn't look like any mental institute that she'd ever seen before.

Her suspicion only intensified as they pulled to a halt in the parking lot and she was able to see the actual building.

Silently she studied the two-story white brick structure with a red-tile roof. It was constructed in a sleek, modern style with lots of steel and glass. There were two long wings nearly hidden behind a line of pine trees, where Annie assumed the private rooms were tucked out of sight.

The front had tall, arched windows that overlooked the massive terrace elegantly furnished with cushioned wicker chaise longues and glass tables.

"Are you sure this is the right place?" she muttered.

Rafe turned off the truck and unbuckled his seat belt. "I'm sure."

She was slower to unhook the buckle, her gaze moving toward the marble fountain in the center of the circle drive.

"It looks like a high-class motel."

"I think that's the point," he said, reaching to brush back a curl that had escaped from her braid. "Are you ready for this?"

Ready?

She swallowed the hysterical laugh.

Was anyone ever ready to meet the brother they'd thought dead for the past twenty-two years? A brother who'd been brutalized by their mother until he was driven to slit her throat?

Hell, she hadn't even wrapped her brain around the fact that her father was James Emerson, Navy Captain.

"I don't know," she admitted with blunt honesty.

His fingers skimmed down the line of her jaw, his light caress sending a tiny shiver through her body.

"Annie, if you're having second thoughts we can go back to Newton." He leaned forward, his bronzed face savagely beautiful with the hint of beard that shadowed his cheeks. His hand slid beneath her chin. "Hell, we can go anywhere you want."

She grimaced, refusing to allow herself to even consider the temptation of telling Rafe to turn on the engine and just start driving.

Anywhere . . .

"It's just so strange," she instead forced herself to share. "A week ago I believed that my mother and brother died in a car accident and that my father was a farmer named Don White who murdered seven women before committing suicide." She gave a shake of her head, wise enough not to risk fate by claiming her life couldn't get any stranger. Every time she thought that . . . it got stranger. "Now I find out my entire past is a lie. I don't know what's real anymore."

His hand shifted to cup the back of her head, his head lowering until they were nose to nose.

"I'm real."

The hysteria eased as she became lost in the melting darkness of his eyes.

Her entire life was spiraling out of control, but when she was this close to Rafe, none of it seemed to matter.

How was that possible?

She reached up to grasp his wrist, but she made no effort to pull away.

"Out of everything, you're the most unreal of all," she admitted in soft tones.

His warm breath brushed her cheek before she felt his lips press against her mouth.

It was brief. More like a promise than a true kiss. But it was enough to warm her chilled body and soothe her frayed nerves.

Okay. His touch wasn't exactly *soothing*. But the tingles currently making her heart race were a hell of a lot more fun than the mind-numbing panic that threatened to consume her.

"Do you need me to prove how real I am?" he asked, using his tongue to trace her bottom lip.

She sucked in a deep breath, another shiver exploding through her body. He smelled so good.

Raw, delicious male.

"I think you've done enough proving," she choked out as he branded a trail of kisses over her cheek and along the curve of her ear.

He chuckled, tilting her head to the perfect angle to claim another kiss.

This one was deeper. Longer. More of a prelude to paradise than a promise.

"I'm just getting started, sweetheart."

Her breath tangled in her throat as his tongue dipped between her lips. Just that fast her body was going up in flames.

Good . . . Lord.

She pressed her palms flat against his chest. "Rafe, we're in a parking lot."

"I can solve that." Nuzzling a spot just below her ear, his fingers traced down the curve of her neck. "There's a motel just down the street."

"You are . . ." Her words broke off as he deliberately molded her breast through the thick sweatshirt.

"I am what?"

"You really are a hero."

He lifted his head, his gaze lingering on her lips that still trembled from his kiss. "Because I can't keep my hands off you?"

She wasn't fooled for a minute.

She didn't doubt that he desired her. He'd been more than clear on the subject.

But he'd kissed her to distract her from the mess that was her life.

Her hands smoothed over his chest, enjoying the power of his hard body.

Was it any wonder she felt safe when he was near?

"Because you know exactly how to keep me from freaking out."

He heaved a small sigh. "I wish I could make all of this go away."

"Me too, but I have to face this myself," she said.

She wasn't just trying to act brave.

Martin Emerson was her brother.

The only family she had left in the world.

She had to meet him.

"But not alone. Never again," he growled, peering down at her with a fierce intensity. "No matter what happens."

She grabbed his sweatshirt, a nasty premonition inching down her spine. "You suspect something."

"I'm trained to be suspicious." With a smooth motion, he released his grip on her to turn and push open his door.

"Rafe."

"We should go in."

Before she could demand to know what his instincts were telling him, he was out of the truck and headed toward the building.

With a sigh, Annie quickly followed him.

Clearly he wasn't in the mood to share, and she wasn't certain she wanted to know.

Right now it was enough to prepare herself to meet the brother who she'd thought dead and buried twenty-two years ago.

Chapter Seventeen

Rafe waited for Annie to reach his side before pulling open the glass door and crossing the polished white tile floor toward the reception area cloaked in an expensive hush.

The octagon-shaped room was filled with light and decorated with sleek furnishings in soothing shades of gray and silver.

Annie was right, he ruefully acknowledged.

It did look like a fancy-ass hotel.

The sort of place where they left chocolates on your pillow and you could order lobster with a push of a button.

This kind of luxury didn't come cheap.

In fact, Rafe was willing to bet his left nut that Annie's grandparents dished out more every month to keep Martin here than he made per year when he was in the military.

Seated behind a low desk, the receptionist was attired in a gray dress that perfectly matched the decor. She lifted her head at their entry, a professional smile attached to her lips that transformed to one that was far more flirtatious as she caught sight of Rafe.

"May I help you?"

Rafe moved forward. The woman looked like a mannequin,

with her pale face perfectly covered by a layer of makeup and her blond hair so rigidly smooth, it barely moved.

It might be the fashion, but Rafe far preferred the natural beauty of the woman walking next to him.

Still, he was willing to play the game. Conjuring his most charming smile, he leaned his hip against the desk. The receptionist no doubt assumed he was checking out her too-thin body. In truth, the angle gave him an unblocked view of the computer and phone system.

"We're here to see Martin Emerson."

The mannequin perfection was briefly marred as the woman stiffened in shock, her pale eyes darting toward a door across the reception area.

"Martin Emerson?"

Annie moved closer to his side. An unconscious staking of ownership?

He hoped so.

"Yes," she said.

The receptionist discreetly pushed a button on the phone before she tapped on her keyboard, pretending to check her computer.

"I'm sorry," she murmured with faux regret. "I don't have any visits scheduled for Mr. Emerson."

"Surely I don't need to schedule a visit. I'm his sister," Annie insisted, her tone stubborn.

The woman's eyes widened. "Sister?"

"Yes. Annie . . ." She stopped, her throat convulsing before she managed to finish. "Emerson."

Rafe instinctively placed his hand on her lower back, offering a silent comfort.

During the long drive he'd tried to convince himself that they were going to discover Martin Emerson safely stashed at Greenwood Estates, living out his life in peaceful surroundings with the necessary drugs to keep his demons at bay.

The last thing he wanted was for Annie to endure even more pain.

But the knot in his gut hadn't eased. Deep inside, he knew Martin was somehow connected to the most recent disappearances.

And the receptionist's growing discomfort only increased his concern.

"I see," the blonde was saying, once again pressing the button on the phone.

"Is there a problem?" Annie asked.

The woman's smile remained pinned in place. "Not precisely a problem, but I do think it would be better to reschedule your visit for another day."

Annie folded her arms over her chest. Uh-oh. He recognized that look.

Beneath Annie's sweet, rather shy exterior was a spine of steel.

"Why?" she demanded.

"Our therapists prefer not to upset the patients' schedules," the receptionist smoothly explained.

Annie shrugged. "I assume family is allowed to visit?"

"Yes, but it would be better to call ahead so Martin's daily activities can be rearranged," the woman insisted.

Annie narrowed her eyes. Unaware of Rafe's suspicion that Martin was missing, she clearly assumed she was just being jerked around.

"Are you saying I can't see Martin?"

The woman held up a manicured hand. "Please, if you would just—"

"I'll take care of this, Jasmine," a male voice interrupted.

Swiftly turning, Rafe stepped to the side, half blocking Annie from the slender, middle-aged man standing in the center of the reception area.

Rafe made a silent inventory of the dark hair that was threaded with silver and brushed from the lean face that had recently seen the inside of a tanning bed. His gaze lowered, his brow cocked as he took in the designer suit that was a light shade of smoke.

Christ. Did everyone dress in gray?

"You are?" he asked.

The older man's gaze flicked from Rafe to Annie, then warily back to Rafe.

"Dr. Roger Palmer," he said, his tone polite although he made no move to shake Rafe's hand. Unconsciously Rafe lifted his fingers to rub his whiskers. He really needed to shave. "I'm the director of the Greenwood Estates. And you are?"

"This is Annie Emerson," Rafe said, careful to avoid giving his own name. "Martin's sister."

"Sister?" The director visibly jerked before he lifted his hand to smooth his burgundy tie. His attention shifted to Annie. "This is . . . unexpected. You've never been here before, have you?"

"No." Annie tried to step around Rafe, only to make a sound of impatience when he moved to block her. It wasn't that he feared the man would hurt Annie. Not in the middle of the reception room. But he sensed Dr. Palmer would do whatever was necessary to protect his ass. "I lost track of my brother years ago. Now I'm anxious to be reunited."

"Of course." The man flashed a blindingly white smile. "Perfectly understandable."

"Then can we be taken to his room?" Annie snapped.

Rafe could sense Annie's temper rising. She might be nervous about meeting her brother, but she was clearly tired of being blocked from her self-imposed task.

So was Rafe.

Dr. Palmer cleared his throat. "Actually, we prefer visitors to call ahead and make an appointment."

"I've driven a very long way." Annie stubbornly refused to concede defeat. A knowledge that Rafe tucked in the back of his mind. It was no doubt something he was going to encounter over the next fifty years. "I really must insist on seeing my brother."

Dr. Palmer smoothed his tie again. "Unfortunate, but there is really nothing I can do."

Annie sucked in an angry breath. "Are you refusing to allow me to visit with my own brother?"

The man's gaze darted toward the receptionist, as if seeking inspiration.

None was forthcoming, so he repeated his lame excuse.

"As I said, we prefer not to disrupt our patients without prior notice."

Rafe stepped forward. Enough.

He'd let Annie take charge because he truly hoped Martin Emerson was safely tucked in one of the expensive rooms and she could enjoy a long-overdue reunion without it being marred by Rafe's ugly suspicion.

Now it was obvious Dr. Palmer was going to continue to stonewall them unless he took command of the situation.

"I'm afraid we're going to have to insist," he said, his low tone edged with an unmistakable command.

The man licked his lips, his gaze taking in Rafe's casual attire.

"Are you related?"

"Not exactly." Reaching into his back pocket, Rafe pulled out the leather wallet and flashed the badge Teagan had made.

The director leaned forward. "Agent Torres," he read out loud, his face paling beneath his tan. "FBI?"

Rafe flipped the wallet shut and shoved it back into his pocket.

"That's right."

"Is this an official visit?"

Rafe shrugged. "I can make it official."

"No, please." Turning to the side, the director pointed toward the door nearly hidden in a shallow alcove. "Can we speak in my office?"

"If you want," Rafe agreed.

The director nodded toward the wide-eyed receptionist. "Jasmine, hold my calls unless it's an emergency."

Without waiting for her agreement, Dr. Palmer headed

toward his office, his Italian leather shoes clicking against the tile floor.

Rafe returned his hand to Annie's lower back as they followed in the man's path. Even through the thick fabric of her sweatshirt he could feel the tension that hummed off her body.

She wasn't stupid.

She knew this was about more than disrupting a patient's schedule.

They entered the office that was surrounded by tinted glass walls. The furnishings were the same as in the reception area . . . modern, sleek, pretentious, but instead of tiled floors there was an expensive gray and silver carpet.

The director instantly took the position of power behind his desk, waving his hand toward the two black leather chairs across from him.

"Have a seat." Waiting until they were settled, he glanced toward a silver machine set on a low table. "Coffee? Espresso?"

Rafe grimaced. The office was making him nervous as hell.

Who had glass walls? It was a sniper's paradise. And the seats were so low and deeply curved there would be no way he could get his gun out quickly enough.

If the stalker had managed to follow them to Greenwood Estates, then Annie was a sitting duck.

A knowledge that wasn't doing anything to improve his temper.

"No, thank you," he said in clipped tones.

The director cleared his throat. "I assume this has something to do with Martin's disappearance?"

Annie sucked in a shocked breath. "He's—"

Shit. Rafe reached out to grab her hand, giving her fingers a warning squeeze.

"As you might have guessed, I'm a friend of the family." Rafe firmly took command of the meeting. He needed Dr. Palmer to believe he was an FBI agent investigating Martin's disappearance. Otherwise the man was going to clam up and not give them a damned thing. "They asked me to come with Annie and discover exactly what happened."

The director carefully placed his palms on his desk, his expression revealing the perfect combination of regret and sympathy.

Rafe briefly wondered how often the man practiced the look in front of the mirror.

"Martin was last seen at breakfast three weeks ago."

"Three weeks?" Annie breathed.

Dr. Palmer gave a nod. "Yes."

Rafe leaned forward, his elbows on his knees, hands casually dangling between his legs. The position meant his fingers were just inches from the gun holstered at his ankle.

"He just left?" he demanded.

The thin face hardened with a defensive expression. "This is a residential center, not a prison."

Rafe glanced toward the windows that overlooked the gardens. The building was isolated enough to make it difficult to approach or leave without being noticed, but it wouldn't be that hard to slip away.

Obviously it had been decided that Martin Emerson would be treated as a victim instead of a criminal.

Still, he would have assumed there would be some sort of limitations to his movements.

"Your patients are free to come and go as they please?" he demanded.

"We strongly discourage them from leaving the clinic unless they have a suitable chaperone, but on occasion they do decide to spend a few hours or even a few days on their own," the director confessed.

Great. Just fucking perfect.

"Do you have surveillance cameras?"

"Yes."

"Can I see them?"

The man squared his shoulders, his lips thinning. "Not without a warrant."

Rafe didn't press. This man would know the laws regarding patients' rights far better than he did.

"Did the surveillance tape show Martin leaving?" he instead asked.

Dr. Palmer nodded. "It did."

"Was anyone with him?"

The man looked surprised by the question. Which meant Martin rarely had visitors.

"No, he was alone."

"No one picked him up?" Rafe pressed. "Not even a taxi?"

The director shook his head. "Not as far as we could tell. He walked out the door and through the gardens. He must have used a side entrance to leave the grounds."

Rafe grimaced. There was no way to know if Martin had called for a taxi to meet him. Or if he had someone waiting down the street to pick him up.

Or hell . . . he might have hitchhiked.

He turned his attention to what might have prompted Martin's sudden departure.

"How was Martin before his disappearance?"

The director shrugged. "He seemed fine."

"There was nothing strange in his behavior?"

Dr. Palmer tapped a slender finger on the desk, clearly annoyed at being put in a position of having to answer questions from nosy officials.

On the other hand, he wouldn't be stupid enough to do anything that might provoke unwanted attention on his clinic. People didn't pay an enormous fee for pretty gardens and smiling receptionists.

They paid for discretion.

"Not that we could detect," Dr. Palmer assured him.

"No unexpected guests?"

The man's gaze briefly flickered toward Annie before he answered. "Martin didn't have guests."

"Never?"

"Never."

Damn. Another dead end.

Time for a new line of questioning.

"Did you contact the authorities?"

The lean face hardened, his eyes guarded. "No. As I said, we're not a prison."

"You weren't concerned that something had happened to him?"

"Naturally we were concerned."

Rafe narrowed his gaze. "But?"

The director gave a lift of his hands. "But after we reviewed the tapes, it became obvious he intended to stay away for a few days."

"Why?"

"He was carrying a suitcase."

He sensed Annie tense at the reluctant revelation. Clearly she'd assumed that her brother had wandered off in a fog of confusion and would eventually return. Now she was forced to consider the fact that it had been a deliberate act.

And that Rafe had suspected Martin was missing before they ever arrived.

Ignoring her searching gaze, Rafe willed himself to concentrate on the man behind the desk. "Did you make any effort to trace his whereabouts?"

"No."

Annie made a sound of distress. "Why not? He could have been hurt."

"We didn't want to cause any . . ." The director paused, licking his lips as he sought the best way to explain he didn't want to piss off the people with the massive checkbook. "Waves."

Annie scowled. "I don't understand."

Rafe reached to grab her hand, his gaze never leaving Dr. Palmer. "They didn't want to risk the very lucrative fee they charge to keep him here."

The director stiffened, but before he could protest the blunt description of his motives, Annie was speaking.

"Oh, wait." Her brows tugged together in confusion. "How could my brother possibly afford to stay at a place like this for so many years?"

Dr. Palmer sent her a puzzled glance, unaware she didn't have any contact with her grandparents.

"There was a trust fund set up for his care."

"Set up by—"

"I assume the money would be cut off if Martin was no longer a resident?" Rafe interrupted.

Annie had enough shocks. The MIA grandparents would have to be saved for another day.

Dr. Palmer pursed his lips, the air vibrating with his indignation. "Agent Torres, we are a highly respected residential center that is renowned for our cutting-edge treatment and our caring staff."

Rafe smiled. He wasn't going to be intimidated by a bureaucrat in a thousand-dollar suit. "You didn't answer my question."

The man clenched his teeth, clearly wishing he had the balls to have Rafe tossed out on his ass.

"Certainly if Martin was no longer our patient, the funds would be transferred to his new caregivers," he managed to respond, his tone clipped. "But that isn't the reason we haven't contacted his family."

Rafe cocked a brow. "No?"

"Not entirely," he conceded.

"What's the other reason?"

Anxious to prove he wasn't a heartless mercenary, the director babbled a lame excuse. "This isn't the first time Martin has decided to disappear for a few days."

Rafe's gut twisted. He wasn't entirely certain why.

He just knew something bad was coming.

"He does this often?" he demanded.

"No, not often, but I know that he did leave once before."

Dr. Palmer shrugged. "He was gone several weeks, then he returned. It's quite possible that he will show up and everyone will be pleased we didn't make an unnecessary fuss."

Sickness swirled through the pit of Rafe's stomach. "How many years ago?"

Another shrug. "Several."

Rafe leaned forward. "Precisely."

The man frowned, clearly sensing the sudden tension in the air. "I would have to look up his files to be sure."

"Do it," Rafe snapped, his hand keeping hold of Annie's fingers as the director swiveled his chair to tap on the keyboard of the sleek computer.

It took several minutes as the man scanned through Martin's records.

"Ah, here it is," he murmured, lifting his head to meet Rafe's fierce gaze. "It was fifteen years ago."

Annie sucked in a sharp breath. "Oh my God."

Chapter Eighteen

Annie didn't even realize she was clinging to Rafe's hand. She was way too busy trying to sort through the implications of Dr. Palmer's words.

Implications that were making her palms sweat and her mouth dry.

The director easily picked up the prickles of unease in the air, his gaze shifting toward Annie before returning to Rafe.

"Is there a problem?"

Rafe rose to his feet, tugging Annie out of her seat to stand close at his side.

"Can we be shown to his room?" Rafe asked.

Dr. Palmer slowly pushed himself upright, his expression wary.

"Has something happened to Martin?"

"That's what we're trying to determine," Rafe informed him, his natural air of authority making it easy for him to play the role of FBI agent.

Which was why she bit back the thousand questions that thundered through her mind.

If she accidentally revealed that Rafe didn't have the right to demand answers, she might ruin everything.

"He isn't hurt, is he?" Dr. Palmer demanded.

"Not so far as we know, but clearly the quicker we can

find him, the better." Rafe jerked his head toward the door. "His room?"

"Yes." There was the slightest hesitation before the director was rounding the desk and headed out of the office. "Follow me."

Rafe placed an arm around her shoulders as they crossed the reception room and went through the double doors that led to the private quarters.

There was a blur of hushed corridors intersected with small lobbies where the patients gathered to watch TV or play games. Distantly she was aware of the expensive artwork hung on the walls and the staff who occasionally appeared with trays of food, but her thoughts were consumed with the fact that the brother she'd just discovered was alive, was now missing.

A task made easier by the sensation of Rafe's strong grip on her hand.

For today, he was her anchor.

They reached the end of the hallway when the director shoved a hand into his pocket to pull out an I.D. badge, swiping it against the electronic reader beside the door.

She heard a faint click and then the door swung open to reveal a long, narrow room that doubled as a bedroom and small sitting area.

Hesitantly she stepped inside, feeling like an intruder.

The furnishings were elegant and the decor was dominated by shades of gray and silver. Across the room, a large window allowed the fading afternoon sunlight to brighten the space, at the same time emphasizing the air of sterile emptiness. As if whoever lived here hadn't bothered to stamp the place with his own personality.

Annie frowned as she felt the air heat as Rafe moved to stand directly behind her, his hand resting on her lower back.

She wasn't sure what she'd been expecting, but it wasn't this fiercely tidy room that looked like a model home.

There just for show.

"This is it?" she muttered.

"Yes." The director stepped toward the middle of the room, the practiced smile returning to his thin face. "As you see, we offer each of our guests a private apartment with all the comforts of home."

Annie grimaced. "It's so . . . bare."

Dr. Palmer shrugged. "I believe the therapist did try to encourage Martin to surround himself with pictures or books that gave comfort, but there are some patients who prefer to keep their private space uncluttered."

Annie gave a reluctant nod. It seemed reasonable that Martin might be bothered by too many distractions in his living space. But this . . .

There was nothing on the walls, nothing on the empty shelves, nothing on the low coffee table.

Nothing that could connect her to the brother she'd thought she'd lost.

Or answer the questions that were making her stomach twist with dread.

Standing close at her side, Rafe was studying the room with an unreadable expression. "Did he leave anything?"

Dr. Palmer waved a hand toward the door next to the bed.

"There are clothes in the closet as well as his private diaries," he said, then he pointed toward a curio cabinet in the corner of the room. "As well as his pictures."

Annie's breath was trapped in her lungs. Even at a distance she could see that the matching silver frames held pictures of her.

And not just when she was a baby.

They were school pictures, as well as a few candid shots of her on a tractor and one of her picking apples.

Where the hell did he get them?

"Good Lord," she breathed.

"Those pictures were his most treasured possession," the director said. "That's why we assumed he would be back."

Rafe nodded. "Do you mind if we have a minute alone?"

The older man hesitated before catching sight of Annie's

pale face. Then, with a grudging nod, he headed across the room, pausing at the door to send him a questioning glance.

"You haven't said what interest the FBI has in Martin."

"As I said, I'm a friend of the family," Rafe smoothly lied. "We want exactly what you want. Martin found and safely returned."

"Yes." There was no missing the fervent sincerity in the director's voice. Whether it was genuine concern for Martin's welfare or the fear the clinic was about to lose the mystery money that was paying the no-doubt outrageous fees was debatable. "Quite right."

"We'll return to the reception area after Annie has a chance to leave a note for her brother," Rafe said.

It was an unmistakable dismissal, and with a last nod of his head the director left the room, closing the door behind him.

They waited in silence until they heard the sound of his footsteps echoing down the hallway, then Annie turned to meet Rafe's dark gaze.

"Did you suspect he would be gone?" She blurted out the question that had been burning the tip of her tongue since Dr. Palmer had been forced to confess that Martin had been missing for the past three weeks.

Without warning Rafe yanked her against his body, burying his face in her hair. "Annie, we don't know if this room is secure," he muttered in low tones.

Her heart stuttered with excitement until she belatedly realized he was using their embrace to pass along a warning.

Good Lord.

She had it bad.

"What do you mean?"

His lips brushed her ear, sending tiny tingles down her spine. "As much as this might look like a hotel, it's a very expensive clinic. I'm sure the patients are monitored twenty-four seven."

She stilled. Damn, she should have thought of that herself.

"There are cameras?" she muttered, trying to covertly glance toward the ceiling.

"We have to assume there are," he said, speaking directly into her ear. "We'll discuss Martin later. First I want you to cover your face as if you're crying."

Crying?

"Why?"

"It will give us an excuse to go into the bathroom."

Without hesitation, she pressed her hands to her face, her head bowed. For now she was willing to let him take the lead.

It wasn't like she had any experience in covert ops.

But once the danger was over, she was going to have a word about his habit of snapping out orders and expecting them to be obeyed.

"Like this?"

"Perfect." He turned, keeping one arm wrapped around her waist. "Lean against me."

With slow steps they crossed the floor and entered the small bathroom. Reaching behind them, Rafe pushed the door shut and released his hold on her.

Annie took a brief inventory of the white tiled shower that was surrounded by glass walls and the toilet tucked in one corner before returning her attention to Rafe, who had squatted down to pull out the bottles of shampoo and soap and shaving cream from the cupboards beneath the long marble vanity.

She crouched down beside him. "What are you doing?"

He pulled out the last of the toiletries before he stuck his head into the empty space. "I'm assuming they don't have this room under surveillance, which means if Martin had anything to hide he would put it in here," he muttered. "Do you have your phone with you?"

"Yes." Digging into her purse, Annie pulled out her phone. "Do you want me to call someone?"

"No, I want you to shine the light in here."

"Oh."

Grimacing at her lack of cool spy skills, she hit the app for her flashlight and held it toward the cupboard. Rafe ran his hands over the bottom of the vanity before he rolled onto his back and continued the search behind the pipes leading to the sink.

At last, he gave a small grunt of satisfaction.

"Found it."

She scooted back as he wiggled his way out of the cupboard.

"Found what?"

Rafe shoved himself to his feet, holding what looked like a wad of terry cloth in his hands. Laying it on the counter, he pulled away the towels to reveal a stack of leather-bound journals.

"His real diaries," Rafe said.

"The doctor said his diaries were in the closet."

Rafe's lips twisted. "I'm beginning to suspect your brother is a very, very clever man," he said. "Clever enough to keep diaries full of crap that he would know could be easily found in the closet. My guess would be they're meant to placate his therapists." He tapped a finger on the thick leather journals. "All the while he hid the truth in these books."

Annie bit her lower lip, able to see there were pictures and newspaper clipping stuffed between the pages.

"I'm afraid to look."

Rafe studied her pale face, the hint of sympathy in his gaze sending a horrifying chill through her.

Oh God.

She bit her bottom lip, but before she could speak, he stepped forward to press the journals into her hands.

"We need to take these with us," he said, the sudden urgency in his tone forcing her to squash the questions that were hammering through her mind. "Can you put these under your shirt?"

She awkwardly shoved the journals beneath her heavy sweatshirt, wrinkling her nose at the large bulge that couldn't be disguised.

"Not without them showing," she said.

"I'll take care of that," he assured her, leaning down to grab the purse she'd left on the floor. "Are you ready?"

No, she wasn't ready.

Her knees felt weak and she had to struggle to breathe.

It wasn't just the fact they were about to commit a crime. Stealing, no matter how worthless the item, was against the law, wasn't it? Not to mention the fact that Rafe was posing as an FBI agent.

But the feel of the journals pressed against her stomach made her skin crawl.

She didn't know what they were going to find inside them, but she was fairly confident it wasn't going to be old family photos and love notes.

Still, staying in her brother's private rooms wasn't an option.

"Let's go," she finally muttered.

Tugging her toward the door, Rafe wrapped his arm around her shoulder and turned her until the journals were pressed tight against his side. Then, without warning, he reached up to tug her hair out of its braid, spreading the strands until they partially covered her face.

"Stay close," he warned, leading her out of the bathroom and through the living room to the outer hallway. She shivered, weirdly aware they were being monitored by some unseen security system. His arm tightened around her, his cheek brushing against her forehead. "Keep your head lowered."

"Do you think they'll try to stop us?" she demanded.

"Not if they believe you're crying."

"Why would that matter?"

"Trust me, men give sobbing women as wide a berth as possible," he assured her dryly.

She barely resisted the urge to tilt back her head so she could send him a punishing glare.

She had to settle for deliberately kicking his ankle. "Nice."

He gave a stifled sound that might have been a laugh. "It's the truth." They both fell silent as they passed by various residents who eyed them with open suspicion, at last reaching the open reception area. Feeling her tense, he gave her a small squeeze. "Hang on, sweetheart, just a few more feet and we're out of here."

Rafe didn't allow Annie to hesitate as he ruthlessly swept her forward, ignoring the receptionist, who rose to her feet as they headed out the front door.

Even then he continued toward the truck at a brisk pace, knowing that Dr. Palmer might very well be contacting the local FBI office to discover if they had an Agent Torres.

It wasn't until they'd left Greenwood Estates far behind that he at last released the breath he'd been holding and glanced toward the woman sitting rigidly at his side.

"You did good, Annie," he assured her softly.

Pulling the journals from beneath her sweatshirt, Annie carefully laid them on the floorboard before she turned to stab him with a frustrated glare. "You suspected Martin wouldn't be there, didn't you?"

He didn't bother to lie. As much as he wanted to protect Annie, there was no way he could hide the truth.

She was too clever not to put two and two together.

"Yeah, I suspected."

"How?"

"Gut instinct."

He glanced in the rearview mirror as he circled a block and then another before heading out of town. He didn't really think they were being followed, but it was natural instinct to take precautions.

"No." She shook her head, her fingers twisting together in her lap, a sure sign she wasn't as composed as she wanted him to believe. "It was more than that."

Bypassing the merge that led to the highway, Rafe instead took the narrow county road. They would return to Newton later. For now he was looking for a remote location where they could have some privacy.

"The book he left for you and the nursery rhyme . . ." He

shrugged. "They all pointed toward someone who knew you as a child."

"And?" she pressed.

Rafe glanced around as the suburbs were replaced by dairy farms and rolling hills.

"He called you Annabelle." Rafe slowed the truck, turning onto a small side road that wound through a thick cluster of trees. "That's the name listed on your birth certificate."

"Annabelle. God." She sucked in a sharp breath, her knuckles turning white as she struggled to contain her seething emotions. "There's more, isn't there?"

Well, shit.

How did she know?

He didn't have Lucas's ability to hide his emotions behind a charming smile, but he could usually hold his own in a poker game.

Annie, however, seemed capable of seeing right through him.

"And he killed your mother by slicing her throat," he gently reminded her.

Silence filled the truck. A pulsing, thick silence that scraped against his nerves as Annie was forced to accept that her newfound brother wasn't going to fill the void of the family she so desperately wanted.

In fact, he was more than likely a demented killer.

With a tiny cry, Annie pressed her hands to her face. "He's the Newton Slayer, isn't he?"

"It's a possibility," he hedged. It wasn't just to protect her feelings.

He was willing to follow his hunches, but he preferred cold, hard facts before he came to a conclusion.

She lowered her hands, her face set in grim lines. "It's more than that and we both know it."

Pulling to the side of the road, he unhooked his seat belt so he could lean to the side and grab her chilled hands, rubbing them between his.

He wanted to assure her that everything was going to be

okay. That they could drive to his ranch and forget all about Martin and his connection to the Newton Slayer.

But he wasn't a fool.

Neither of them was walking away from this.

Not when there were still women missing.

Smothering his instinctive urge to protect, he gave Annie's fingers a small squeeze.

"We need to look at the journals," he reluctantly confessed. "Are you ready for this?"

Her jaw clenched, but she gave a firm nod. "I have to be ready."

Holding her darkened gaze, Rafe bent forward to grab the stack of journals. Then straightening, he made a sound of impatience when a stack of Polaroid pictures slid out of the back.

Snatching them off the floorboard, he felt his heart miss a beat.

Jesus. The pictures were grainy, but there was no mistaking the images. Each photo was of a different woman, but they were all bound to the same wooden chair in the middle of the same empty room.

Women he recognized as the first victims of the Newton Slayer.

He grimaced, trying to ignore his fury at the unmistakable terror on the women's faces. It was obvious they were heartbreakingly aware that they were about to die.

The bastard.

Instead, he concentrated on looking for any clue that might help him get into the twisted mind of Martin Emerson.

There wasn't much.

The photos were dark, with little to see in the background. Beside each chair was a shallow bowl of water and a cloth, as if Martin had washed the women after stripping them naked. But there was no distinguishing feature that would indicate a precise location.

It could be the bomb shelter, or it could be a thousand other places.

Still, something nagged at the edge of his mind.

He shuffled through the pictures again and again, trying to pinpoint what was bothering him.

"Damn," he at last muttered.

Beside him, Annie pressed a hand to her mouth, her face completely white with horror. "Are these the women who died?" she choked out.

"Yeah."

Belatedly sensing his distraction, she lifted her head with a frown. "Rafe?"

He gave a short shake of his head. "There's only six."

She blinked in confusion. "Six?"

He held up the pictures. "He only photographed six of his seven victims."

"Oh." She licked her dry lips. "He was interrupted after the seventh," she pointed out. "Maybe he didn't have the time."

"True," Rafe murmured, far from satisfied.

The pictures were all taken before the women were killed.

Had he known the sheriff had found his hideout and was in a hurry? Or was there something special about the last victim?

Oh hell.

He stiffened, abruptly recalling who exactly the last woman was.

She was the sheriff's wife.

Clearly it'd been Martin's final act of defiance before disappearing.

Disturbed by the depth of the man's depravity, he tossed aside the photos and began reading through the cramped writing that filled the pages of the journal.

He heard Annie drag in a shaky breath, her hand lifting to push back the thick strands of her hair. "What else?"

Rafe shrugged, skimming from page to page. "Mostly it's ramblings about the evils of mothers who don't love their children."

Annie stiffened, her fingers reaching to dig into his arm. "Were all the women who were killed mothers?"

He gave a slow dip of his head. "Yeah."

"God." She shivered, leaning forward to glance at the pages he was rapidly flipping past. Obviously not fast enough as she caught sight of her name repeated over and over. "What's that?" she demanded.

"Just gibberish," he muttered.

"It's about me," she argued. "What does it say?"

Rafe swallowed a curse. She was already freaked out enough. He didn't want to let her know that her brother had devoted the last twenty-two years to his obsession with her.

"He clearly felt the need to protect you," he at last conceded.

She scowled. "Protect me from what?"

"At a guess, I would say your mother," he said.

Her pale face took on an ashen shade as she pressed a hand to her stomach.

She looked . . . broken.

"My God," she breathed.

Rafe tossed the journals back on the floorboard.

He'd seen enough to accept that Martin was the most likely candidate to be the Newton Slayer. Later he'd go through the journals in greater detail. Or better yet, have Max travel to Newton and let him take a look.

The forensic expert had a much greater eye for small details.

For now, he needed to take care of the woman who was once again dealing with the realization a member of her family was a killer.

Taking the time to send out two quick texts, he tossed aside his phone and shoved the truck into gear.

"Hang on, sweetheart," he murmured, heading toward the winery he'd spotted just down the road.

Chapter Nineteen

Hauk strolled into the tiny house to discover Teagan seated at the kitchen table with two computers running a dozen different searches.

At his entrance, Teagan rose to his feet, stretching his big body as if he was working out the kinks. No surprise. The man had probably been sitting in front of the computers the entire day.

Once Teagan was on the hunt, he was like a bloodhound.

Crossing toward the counter, Hauk set down the groceries he'd traveled to LaClede to buy.

"Any word from Rafe?" he asked as he turned back to watch Teagan scrub a weary hand over his face.

"They left the clinic," Teagan said.

Hauk's lips twisted.

He loved Teagan like a brother, but the man had the social skills of a rabid badger.

"What did they find?" he pressed.

Teagan shrugged. "Rafe sent a text that said he's fairly certain Martin Emerson is not only the current Newton Slayer, but that he was responsible for killing the women fifteen years ago. Oh, and that he'd be back with Annie in a few hours."

Holy. Shit.

Hauk gave a shake of his head.

Unlike his companion, he couldn't treat the thought of chasing a serial killer like another day at the office.

This was serious shit that put them all in danger.

"Do we have a photo of Martin Emerson?" he asked.

Teagan reached over the computers to shuffle through a tall stack of papers he'd obviously spent the day printing off, pulling out a photo that he shoved into Hauk's hand.

Hauk silently studied the enlarged picture of a man with a narrow face, brown, curly hair that tumbled onto his forehead, and guileless blue eyes.

"This is the most recent I could find," Teagan told him.

Hauk felt a flicker of surprise.

He wasn't stupid. He knew that killers rarely looked like the bad guys in the movies.

One of the bastards who'd tortured them while they were imprisoned in the Afghan hellhole had the face of an angel.

But this man was . . . average.

So average he would melt into the background, no matter where he was.

"He's not the sort of guy a person would remember seeing," Hauk muttered.

"Exactly." Teagan folded his arms over his chest, stretching his black T-shirt to the limits of its endurance. "He could be walking the streets of Newton without anyone giving him a second glance."

Hauk narrowed his gaze, studying his friend's face in the gathering gloom. Teagan always vibrated with a seemingly endless supply of energy, but there was no mistaking the shadows beneath his eyes.

When the hell was the last time the man had slept?

"You need to rest, amigo," Hauk abruptly announced, reaching into his pocket to pull out the old-fashioned key. "Go back to the motel."

Teagan gave a shake of his head. "I'll crash on the couch later."

Hauk tossed him the key. "Have you seen that couch? It looks like it was built for a fucking leprechaun."

"Then I'll stretch out on the floor." Teagan shrugged. "I've slept on worse."

Hauk hesitated, sensing a tension in his companion that had nothing to do with Rafe or the Newton Slayer.

"Is there a particular reason you're hanging around?" he demanded.

"No point in driving to the motel when Rafe will be back in a few hours," Teagan said, the smooth excuse tripping off his tongue. "I want to hear what he discovered."

"Right." Hauk leaned against the edge of the counter. "Was Rafe the only one who called?"

Teagan abruptly smiled, flashing his perfect white teeth. "Hell no. The women of Houston are in collective mourning without their Teagan loving. I've spent the past two hours trying to pacify a dozen different women who were hoping to climb into my bed."

"Jesus." Hauk held up his hand. "No need to share."

Teagan's smile widened. "You asked."

Hauk wasn't about to be deflected. "Did Max call?"

There was a pause, as if Teagan was considering lying, then he gave a lift of one shoulder. "He phoned to check in."

It didn't take a genius to read between the lines. "Was there another note left for me?"

Teagan grimaced. "A picture."

Hauk lifted his brows. His unknown stalker was clearly upping his game. "A picture of what?"

"A satellite shot of the Afghan village where we were rescued."

Hauk hissed in shock.

He hadn't even considered the possibility that the nutcase might be a haunting reminder of his time in the Middle East.

"This is connected to Afghanistan?"

He tried to conjure up the various enemies he'd made during the war. It was a depressingly long list.

"That, or . . ." Teagan let his words trail away with a shrug.

"Or what?"

"Someone's trying to make us believe it is."

"Shit." Hauk gave a shake of his head. He didn't care what grudge the bastard was holding against him, he just wanted him caught so they could concentrate on building ARES into a world-class security business. "Where was the picture left?"

"It was sent to the office by courier," Teagan revealed.

A courier? Hauk frowned. The stalker was becoming more ballsy by the day.

"Max doing a trace?"

"Yep."

Hauk heaved a resigned sigh. His stalker was a worry for another day.

For now, they had a serial killer to catch.

"Then we need to let him do his thing and we need to concentrate on keeping Rafe alive," he said.

Teagan's expression hardened. "Maybe you should think about a vacation."

Hauk didn't hesitate. "No."

Teagan made a sound of frustration. "Don't be such a stubborn bastard."

Hauk met his friend glare for glare. He wasn't trying to be a hero. He was too smart to let macho pride put him in danger.

But he understood that running from shadows was going to drive him crazy.

"Look, I don't know who is harassing me, but I do know if I let him screw with my head, then he's won," he said in low, fierce tones. "Got it?"

Teagan didn't look happy, but he did give a reluctant nod. "Got it."

Hauk's lips twisted. His friend might accept that Hauk was done discussing the stalker, but he knew there was no way in hell he was going to be able to talk Teagan into returning to the motel to get some much-needed rest.

Instead he shifted his attention to Rafe's current troubles. "Did Max have any other intel?" he asked.

"He got the book and pictures I sent," Teagan said. "He said that something was wonky."

"Wonky?" Hauk frowned. Max was brilliant, but he could be . . . eccentric, to say the least. "What the hell does that mean?"

Teagan held up his hands. "He didn't know. Just a feeling he was overlooking something."

Now Hauk truly was curious. Max was a scientist. Pure and simple. "I thought Rafe was the only one with gut instincts?"

Teagan's lips twitched. "Max would tell you that gut instinct is nothing more than our unconscious mind rationally solving a problem and attempting to bridge the gap with the conscious mind."

"Yeah, that sounds like him." Hauk shoved his fingers through his hair, which was still damp from his recent shower. Christ, he couldn't wait to get back to his luxurious apartment in Houston. The bathroom in the motel was not only cramped, but the water pressure was epically shitty. "So until he's figured out what's wonky, he doesn't have anything to help us?"

Teagan glanced at the watch strapped around his wrist. "He'll let us know when he gets here."

Hauk blinked. Well, hell. What else had he missed during his short nap?

"He's coming to Newton?"

"Yep. Rafe texted him to ask if he would meet him here," Teagan explained. "He has some sort of journals from Martin Emerson he wants Max to take a look at."

"Makes sense," Hauk said. Max had a freaky ability to see what others missed. "What about Lucas?"

"He said he had lunch with the coroner and that the guy didn't deny he was under a great deal of pressure to close the case on Don White."

"And to make sure it was officially classified as a suicide?"

Teagan nodded. "The doctor was cagey, but that was the implication."

Hmm. It didn't take a giant leap to guess who was putting the pressure on the coroner.

"The sheriff?"

"That was my first thought," Teagan surprisingly hedged.

Hauk studied his friend with a flare of puzzlement. "And now?"

Teagan waved a hand toward the stacks of paper. "Now I know that he wasn't just plain Don White, but a high-ranking naval officer. And that there are powerful people in very important places who desperately wanted to keep the shit storm that was swirling around him from landing on them."

Hauk took a minute to consider his friend's words.

It was true.

He didn't have Lucas's experience with the rich and influential, but he understood they played by a different set of rules than most mortal men.

It really was true that the more you had to lose, the more you were willing to risk.

Even having a man killed while he was sitting in a jail cell to prevent a scandal from ruining their career.

"Fair enough," he murmured.

A silence fell as they both considered the fact that a decent, potentially innocent man had been so easily sacrificed fifteen years ago.

It was something they'd both had to endure during their years in the military.

Wars were a messy, brutal business.

Sometimes peace was even worse.

At last Teagan shook off his air of brooding and nodded

toward the brown paper sacks that Hauk had placed on the counter. "What's in the bags?"

"Ah." Hauk flashed him a smile of anticipation. "I'm about to treat you to the best damned Swedish meatballs you've ever eaten."

Teagan widened his eyes. "God almighty. I don't know whether to be excited or terrified."

"I also brought beer."

Teagan laughed. "Okay, now I'm excited."

Annie was lost in a fog.

A part of her had already accepted that her brother was responsible for killing at least seven women . . . and likely at least three more, unless they managed to find those poor missing females.

It wasn't like she could ignore the evidence that was piled against him.

His tortured past. His obsession with her. His disappearances from the clinic. The journals filled with pictures of the dead women . . .

And more importantly, the visions that had plagued her.

It made sense that she would have some sort of psychic connection to her brother.

But another part of her couldn't help but mourn the loss of him.

Again.

How could fate possibly be so cruel as to dangle the hope she had at least one family member still alive, only to snatch it away?

Lost in dark thoughts, it took a minute for Annie to realize that the truck was parked in a nearly empty parking lot.

With a frown she peered through the growing dusk at the two-story brick building with green shutters and a pretty, fenced-in verandah on the side.

Above the heavy wooden door was a sign that read:

HALL'S MILL WINERY & EATERY

"Why did you stop?" she demanded.

Shutting off the engine, he unhooked his seat belt and stepped out of the truck.

"I told you, I need a drink," he said, rounding the hood to open her door. "And you need to eat."

She grimaced at the mere thought of trying to swallow food. "I'm not hungry."

Without warning he reached to grab her hands, his bronzed features grim in the streetlights.

"Please, Annie," he said in husky tones. "I need to feel like I'm doing something to help."

Meeting his dark gaze, she felt her heart clench with regret. She'd been so caught in her own drama, she hadn't considered what it was doing to Rafe to have to reveal the truth of her past.

For whatever reason, he felt an overwhelming need to protect her. It couldn't have been easy to allow her to travel to Wisconsin, suspecting what she would find. And now he was no doubt consumed with guilt that she'd been hurt. The last thing she wanted to do was make him feel worse.

Unbuckling her belt, she slid out of the truck. "Okay."

Wrapping an arm around her shoulders, he led her across the lot and through the front door.

They entered a small lobby with wood plank floors and open beams overhead. The walls were hidden behind shelves filled with local wines and barrels overflowing with various cheeses.

Immediately they were wrapped in the warm scent of freshly baked chicken pot pie.

On cue, Annie's stomach growled.

She went at warp speed from not being hungry to starving.

She heard Rafe give a low chuckle before a young waitress appeared with blond hair pulled into a high ponytail and a pretty face.

Her bored expression was instantly replaced by shocked fascination as she caught sight of the tall, dark, and delectable man standing in the center of the lobby.

Annie didn't blame her.

Most women were starstruck when first confronted by Rafe Vargas.

"A seat on the terrace," he said, his arm still wrapped around Annie's shoulders.

"I'm sorry," she breathed, sticking out her chest to make sure Rafe could have a full view of her bountiful breasts, which were shown to advantage in the stretchy black dress. "It's only open on the weekends."

Rafe flashed a charming smile. "No exceptions?"

Predictably dazzled, the young woman gave a small giggle, glancing over her shoulder as if looking for her boss. "I suppose I could make one exception," she murmured.

Rafe gave another smile. "Thank you."

Sashaying her way across the lobby and out a side door, the waitress led them down the steps to the sunken terrace. The air was cool, but the potted trees provided a barrier to the breeze and gave a sense of complete isolation.

Annie suddenly understood why Rafe had insisted on sitting out here.

It was secluded enough that there was no way any conversation could be overheard.

Smoothly moving past her, Rafe pulled out a wrought-iron chair at the nearest table, waiting for Annie to take a seat before settling next to her.

The waitress procrastinated for a long minute before she turned to hurry back inside, probably headed toward the bathroom to put on another layer of lipstick and plump her boobs.

Annie gave a rueful shake of her head, turning to meet Rafe's curious gaze. "It should be illegal."

A dark brow flicked upward. "What should be illegal?"

"Your smile," she explained. "It's lethal."

A wicked heat smoldered in the depths of his eyes as his

hand slid beneath the table to skim over her knee and up her inner thigh.

"I like the sound of that."

Her heart forgot how to beat as the heat of his hand seeped through the denim of her jeans. Their gazes tangled and she suddenly wished they were someplace far more private than a winery.

She didn't want to think about her brother. Or the brutal abuse he'd endured that had made him into a killer.

She wanted to lose herself in the passion that sizzled between them.

She was actually swaying forward when there was the sound of approaching footsteps and the waitress returned, carrying a tray.

Setting down two glasses of water and a basket of rolls, she kept her gaze laser-locked on Rafe. "Would you like to look at a menu?"

His fingers continued to stroke up and down Annie's inner thigh as he glanced toward the giddy waitress. "What smells so delicious?"

"Our special chicken pot pies." A flush stained the girl's cheeks, as if Rafe had just called her delicious. "We're famous for them."

"Bring us two of them along with a bottle of your favorite local wine," Rafe ordered.

At any other time, Annie would have protested a man ordering her dinner. She was shy, not a doormat. She didn't need anyone telling her what she wanted to eat.

But tonight she just wanted to get rid of the waitress with all possible speed.

Besides, the pot pie really did smell delicious.

"Anything else?" the waitress asked, a hopeful edge in her voice.

"No." Rafe gave a firm shake of his head. "Thanks."

"Just let me know if you need anything." Once again she spoke directly to Rafe, completely ignoring Annie. "My name is Suzi."

When Rafe remained silent, she heaved a faint sigh. Turning on her heel, she returned to the main restaurant.

Annie rolled her eyes. "Lethal."

Leaning forward, Rafe pressed his lips to the curve of her neck, his fingers squeezing her knee. "It's all yours, sweetheart," he murmured.

Annie shivered, tiny quakes of pleasure racing through her body.

His lips barely brushed her skin, but she felt as if she'd been branded.

"Hmm," she vaguely muttered.

He gave her knee another squeeze. "Someday you'll trust me."

Returning with a speed that made Annie wonder if the girl had raced all the way to the cellar or simply snatched one of the bottles off the display shelves, Suzi uncorked the bottle and poured a small amount in Rafe's glass, clearly waiting for him to take a taste.

Rafe ignored the way she pressed against his shoulder, instead reaching to tug the bottle from her hand.

"I'm sure it's fine. That will be all," he said, his smile taking the sting from his unmistakable dismissal.

Suzi didn't attempt to stall. Rafe had made his disinterest clear.

Pausing long enough to flick on the muted lighting that was concealed in the vine-covered rafters overhead, the waitress left them alone on the terrace.

Rafe leaned to the side to fill Annie's glass with the white wine.

"Here," he said. "You look like you could use a drink."

She grimaced, reaching for her glass as he poured his own drink.

If any night called for a drink, this was it.

"I don't understand," she said, taking a sip of the wine.

"Don't understand what?"

"Why don't I remember Martin?" She gave a frustrated shake of her head. It didn't matter how hard she tried, she couldn't dredge up any memory of her life before she moved to Newton with her father. "Surely I shouldn't have completely forgotten my mother and brother?"

Lifting his hand from her knee, Rafe gently tucked a stray curl behind her ear. "Don't beat yourself up, sweetheart," he urged softly. "You were only three when your mother died and your brother was taken away."

"Still—"

"Your father obviously tried to protect you from the past." Rafe overrode her protest, his hand cupping her cheek. "He would have made sure to replace your bad memories with happy ones."

Annie bit her lip. She couldn't argue with his logic.

Her father had done his very best to make her childhood as close to *Leave It to Beaver* as possible. She'd always assumed he was trying to make up for the fact her mother and brother had died when she was so young.

Now she had to wonder if it was to erase any potential nightmares.

"He did. He . . ." She forgot what she was going to say as she was struck by a startling realization. Christ. Her mind was clearly mush for it to have taken so long. "Oh."

Rafe was instantly concerned. "Annie?"

She met his worried gaze. "If Martin was responsible, that means my father was innocent."

His expression softened. "Yeah."

A strange rush of relief surged through her, healing a wound that she'd carried for the past fifteen years.

"There was a small part of my heart that always hoped," she breathed, remembering the nights she'd pulled out her father's picture to kiss it good night. "Even when it seemed a ridiculous wish." Her lips twisted. "It shouldn't make me feel better to know that my own brother is responsible, but it does."

His fingers lightly brushed her cheek, an oddly comforting gesture that warmed her deep inside.

"We're going to get through this," he assured her, his thumb tracing the curve of her lower lip. "I promise."

When he said it, she believed him.

There was just something so . . . solid about him.

Still, she knew this was bigger than either of them.

"We have to tell someone," she abruptly announced.

He cocked a dark brow. "Tell someone?"

"The authorities," she clarified. "They need to see the journals so they can search for my brother. He has to be found before he can take another woman."

He nodded, the muted light emphasizing the stark beauty of his face.

"Once we get back to Newton I'll have Max use his contacts with the FBI to pass along the information," he promised, his fingers skimming down the line of her jaw. "Okay?"

She grimaced. No, it wasn't really okay. It was what she'd just demanded, of course. It wasn't like she had a choice. Martin had to be stopped. But while it would be a relief to bring an end to the Newton Slayer, she wasn't ready for what came after the arrest.

The nasty publicity. The finger-pointing when she walked down the street. The loss of yet another family member.

"I wish—" She broke off her futile words with a shake of her head.

Rafe slid his fingers beneath her chin, forcing her to meet his searching gaze. "What?"

"That Martin had been different," she confessed in low tones. "That I had someone."

He leaned forward. "You do."

"Rafe."

"Tell me what you want."

Her mouth went dry at the fierce expression that tightened his features. He was asking for something she wasn't sure she was prepared to give.

Not until she could be sure he wanted her as a flesh-and-blood woman, and not a damsel in distress.

"Chicken pot pie and wine," she lamely tried to tease.

The dark eyes narrowed. "For your future."

She pulled away from his lingering touch, taking a sip of the crisp white wine. "I don't know."

"You have to have some idea," he pressed, a small breeze sneaking through to ruffle his hair. "What did you want to be when you were a little girl?"

"First I thought I wanted to be one of the Olsen twins."

He cocked a brow. "Olsen twins?"

"They're famous actresses." She grimaced. "But after my father died, I wanted to be John Wayne," she ruefully admitted.

After her life had been turned upside down, she'd desperately longed to be strong and brave and capable of facing any enemy without flinching.

And of course, he was a kick-ass cowboy.

"Perfect." Rafe's lips twitched. "My ranch happens to have an opening for the Duke."

A soft sigh escaped her lips as she became lost in his dark eyes. He always knew exactly what to say, exactly how to tempt and tease until she lost all sense of reality.

"That's when I was little," she said, speaking more to herself than the man who was plucking the wineglass from her hand so he could lace their fingers together. "Now I'm an accountant."

He shook his head. "Your heart isn't in it."

She wrinkled her nose. She wasn't a good enough actress to pretend that sitting in a cubicle crunching numbers was as exciting as being John Wayne.

"Not all of us can afford to be choosy," she instead said. "I have a condo and rent to pay."

He shrugged. "Move in with me and I promise not to charge you rent." He lifted her fingers to press them to his lips. "Plus there will be some perks to your new position." He turned her hand over, planting a kiss to the center of her palm. "Or should I say . . . positions?"

Heat darted straight between her legs, a thousand butterflies fluttering in the pit of her stomach.

"Rafe," she chided, her voice not entirely steady. Damn. He shouldn't start things in public they couldn't finish. It was downright frustrating. "Behave yourself."

He nipped the tip of her fingers. "Come to Texas with me."

She shook her head. "I can't just walk away from my life."

"Why not?"

For a crazed moment she didn't know why not.

She had a job she hated. A condo that felt empty. And an endless number of years stretching before her with a terrifying lack of direction.

So why not give in to madness and head off into the sunset with Rafe Vargas?

"My foster parents went to a lot of effort and spent a great deal of money to make sure I had a viable career." She finally latched onto one of the few excuses she had left.

"And you feel indebted?"

She flinched. "Indebted" was an ugly word.

But she couldn't entirely deny that there was a part of her that felt as if she would be a traitor not to accept her foster parents' plan for her life.

"They deserve my loyalty," she muttered.

"Fine, you can help me straighten out my accounts. God knows, they're a mess. Plus we'll invite your foster parents to visit once you're settled at the ranch." He held her gaze, his expression sending a chill of . . . something . . . down her spine. He looked smugly satisfied. As if their future had just been decided. "Any other roadblocks you want to put between us?"

"We barely know each other, Rafe," she whispered. "You can't expect me to walk away from everything that's familiar to me."

Obviously he did.

His smug expression remained firmly in place.

"You'd be a fool to stay in a boring job and some impersonal condo that your foster parents chose for you instead of taking a risk to be happy," he informed her.

She couldn't halt the faint smile that tugged at her lips.

He was a master at hiding his arrogant bossiness behind an irresistible charm. "How can you be so sure you'd make me happy?"

He leaned forward, brushing her lips with a kiss filled with endless promise.

"Because I intend to devote my life to that particular goal."

Chapter Twenty

She was missing.
Again.
It was unacceptable.
Clearly Rafe Vargas didn't understand the role he was supposed to play.
His only duty was to keep Annabelle safe, not to interfere in things that were none of his business.
Dammit. The man was as worthless as Annabelle's father had proven to be.
Which meant that once again his work had to be interrupted. This time, however, he wasn't taking any chances.
He was going to get rid of Vargas, then he was taking sweet Annabelle far away from here.

The trip back to Newton was made in near silence.

The adrenaline rush that had allowed her to endure the shocking revelation that her brother was the Newton Slayer, followed by sneaking his journals out of the clinic, had abruptly disappeared just minutes after they'd finished their pot pies, leaving her barely capable of keeping her eyes open.

Or maybe it was the bottle of wine she'd polished off.

Either way, she found herself dozing as they drove through the darkness, soothed by the sway of the truck and the comfort of knowing Rafe was just inches away.

She was dreaming of an isolated ranch and Rafe lying naked in a pile of straw when she sensed they were slowing and turning off the highway.

Giving a shake of her head to clear it of the cobwebs, she forced herself to peer out the window at the sleeping town of Newton. "Wait," she muttered.

Instantly slowing, Rafe sent her a startled glance. "What's wrong?"

"We haven't searched for the missing woman."

Rafe deliberately glanced toward the dashboard where the clock displayed the time.

2:12 a.m.

"It's too late tonight."

She grimaced, her weariness abruptly replaced by a sudden need to be doing something.

Anything.

It was almost as if she could *feel* her brother's growing sense of urgency.

"We could at least see if I can recognize something from my vision," she said.

He blinked, clearly wondering if she was still dreaming. "It's dark," he slowly pointed out. "Even if there is something you could recognize, you wouldn't be able to see it."

She frowned. Did he have to make sense? "I know, but—"

"Sweetheart, I realize it's hard, but there's nothing that can be done until the morning," he firmly interrupted.

Annie bit her bottom lip, shoving her fingers through her tangled curls. "What if he takes another woman?"

"He won't."

She glared at his profile as he rolled to a halt at the four-way stop.

"How do you know?"

"It hasn't been two days."

She flinched, wrapping her arms around herself as Rafe pressed on the gas.

"God," she breathed, shivering at the thought of what the women endured. Whether they were alive or dead, they must have suffered an unimaginable terror when they realized they'd been kidnapped by a crazed serial killer. "Why two days?"

"I don't know why, but most serial killers have a pattern they're compelled to follow," he said with a lift of one shoulder. "I suppose it makes sense to them even if it doesn't to us."

Another shiver racked her body as they turned onto a narrow road and she caught sight of the flashing lights.

For a horrified second she was terrified that something had happened to Rafe's home, or worse, one of his friends. Who knew what Martin would do if he felt threatened?

Then she realized they were still a couple of blocks from the house and that the lights were yellow instead of the typical blue or red of an emergency vehicle.

She leaned forward, trying to read the words painted on the side of the truck blocking the road.

"What's going on?"

"Must be some trouble with the gas lines." Coming to a halt, Rafe glanced around the dark streets, his body tense. "I don't like this."

"Why?"

"It feels like a trap."

Releasing his seat belt, Rafe leaned down to pull out his gun, keeping it in one hand as he put the truck into reverse.

Annie followed his lead, undoing her belt and shoving it aside. She didn't want to get tangled up if she had to run.

Continuing to scan their surroundings, Rafe slowly backed down the empty street. They'd reached the corner when there was the shrill peel of tires and a blinding flash of headlights being turned on.

Rafe cursed, shoving the truck into drive, but it was too late.

Before they could move out of the path of destruction, the car slammed into the side of the truck, sending them skidding across the narrow road and into a fire hydrant.

An explosion of pain shot through Annie's head as she was thrown into the windshield. Distantly she could hear the sounds of twisting metal and the burst of water from the destroyed hydrant, but shoving herself back into her seat, her sole focus was on the man who was crumpled over the steering wheel.

Her heart halted as she tried to reach over the console to touch him. Even in the dark she could see he was unconscious and that there was a trail of blood running down the side of his face.

Or at least she was praying that he'd just been knocked out.

She wouldn't allow herself to even contemplate the possibility that he could be dead.

That was unacceptable.

"Rafe." Ignoring her own injuries, she managed to brush his hair off his forehead to reveal a cut that was still seeping blood at an alarming rate. "Oh God, Rafe."

She had to do something.

He was alive, but it was obvious he was badly injured.

Phone. She latched onto the thought like a drowning woman. She needed a phone to call for an ambulance.

Leaning down, she desperately patted the floorboard in search of her purse. It'd been in her lap when the car had slammed into them. Which meant it could be anywhere.

She was still searching when the passenger door was abruptly yanked open to reveal a slender man with brown curls and clear blue eyes.

Her lips parted to demand he go for help when he leaned forward to offer her a gentle smile.

"Hello, Annabelle."

Annabelle.

Annie's blood ran cold.

Dear God. She'd been so fixated on Rafe, she'd shoved aside the suspicion that the wreck hadn't been a random accident.

Now she knew beyond a shadow of a doubt that the car had deliberately rammed them.

In silence, she studied the man who had to be her brother, her hand covertly sliding behind her back. Rafe had been holding a gun when they were hit. If she could just reach it . . .

"We need help," she said, pretending she didn't know who he was as she tried to keep him distracted.

Even if she couldn't locate the gun, the crash had to have attracted attention among the neighbors. Someone surely had called the police?

Almost as if capable of reading her mind, Martin offered a heartrendingly sweet smile and leaned forward. "Forgive me," he said, just before he grabbed her by the arm and hauled her toward him.

She felt a pinprick at the back of her neck as she struggled against his astonishingly strong grasp. Her lips parted, but before she could release her scream of sheer horror, she felt her muscles freeze, immobilizing her as surely as if she'd been dipped in cement.

Oh . . . hell. He'd drugged her.

Still smiling, Martin wrapped an arm around her waist, ruthlessly tugging her out of the truck.

Annie grunted, unable to do anything but to tumble bonelessly into his waiting arms. Even worse, darkness was creeping at the edge of her mind, warning that whatever drug he'd given her was about to knock her unconscious.

Her last thought was oddly one of relief. Whatever happened, she could cling to the belief that Rafe would soon be found and taken to the hospital.

She could endure almost anything as long as she knew he was safe.

* * *

Rafe hovered on the edge of consciousness, knowing that a shitload of pain was waiting for him once he fully committed to waking.

For a minute he continued to hover, contemplating the pleasure of sinking back into the beckoning darkness. Then the sound of sharp, steady beeps penetrated his fog of sleep.

Shit. He recognized that sound.

A heart monitor.

He was in a hospital.

Jerking himself awake, he managed to lift his heavy lids.

As expected, the pain slammed into him as he glanced around the excruciatingly white room filled with bright lights and strange machines.

Yeah, definitely a hospital room.

So what the hell had happened?

On cue a lean face with brilliant blue eyes and a worried expression came into view.

"Welcome back to the world of the living, amigo," Hauk said.

Rafe grimaced, not convinced that being in the world of the living was worth the agony that thundered through his poor body.

"What hospital is this?" he managed to rasp.

"The emergency room in LaClede."

He glanced down to see his clothing had been replaced by an ugly hospital johnny and his arm was being used like some sort of science experiment. He could see a blood pressure cuff, a heartbeat monitor and, stuck into his flesh, a needle that was attached to a clear bag above his head.

"How bad?" he demanded.

"A couple bruised ribs. A cut on your forehead that's been stitched, and a possible concussion. No internal injuries beyond the ribs, although you're going to be as sore as hell for the next few days," Hauk answered with concise detail.

They'd all spent time in emergency rooms. They knew the drill.

Rafe frowned. The fog was clearing, but he struggled to remember how he'd been injured. "How'd I get here?"

Hauk's face was unreadable. "Ambulance."

"Smart-ass," Rafe growled. They both knew he was asking how he'd been hurt. But as his lips parted to insist his friend share the details of his accident, he had a sudden memory of being in his truck as headlights blinded him from the side. "Oh . . . hell. There was a car," he said slowly. "It came out of nowhere to ram into us." He gave a low groan, his ribs protesting as he inched up higher on the narrow gurney. "Is Annie okay?"

Hauk's face looked pale in the bright light. "I don't know."

Rafe hissed in shock at the blunt words. "What the fuck do you mean?"

"Teagan and I were waiting for you at the house," Hauk explained. "We didn't realize anything was wrong until we heard the sirens. By the time we got to you, the sheriff and EMT were there and you were being pulled out of the truck. There was no sign of Annie."

Terror exploded through Rafe as he struggled to sit up, ignoring the searing agony that ricocheted through his body.

"Shit." He reached to remove the various torture equipment strapped to his arm, ignoring the annoying beeps and alarms as he ripped out the IV needle stuck in his vein. "It was a setup."

Hauk blinked in confusion. "What was?" he demanded.

Rafe groaned, forced to lean his head back against the gurney as a wave of dizziness threatened to overwhelm him.

"There was a utility truck blocking the road," he muttered, frantically trying to recall each detail.

It was that or lose his mind at the thought of Annie in the hands of a psychotic killer.

If he went into that rabbit hole he'd never come out.

And Annie needed him.

Now more than ever.

"You're right," Hauk said, his brows tugging together. "I remember seeing it."

Rafe muttered a curse.

He'd been suspicious of the truck, but he'd assumed it was there to keep him from reaching the house. It hadn't occurred to him that it was a deliberate means to force him to back down the street.

"Whoever attacked us couldn't know exactly when I would be returning, but they were smart enough to block the road assuming I'd have to come to a halt. It gave him the opportunity to get ready for me before I started backing up." His teeth clenched in frustration. He'd failed Annie. "Christ, I couldn't have made it easier for the bastard."

Hauk shook his head. "You didn't suspect it was a trap, Rafe."

"I should have."

Rafe once again shoved himself upward. The dizziness threatened, but he grimly concentrated on the clock hung on the far wall until his brain settled into place.

It was only when he was upright that his eyes focused enough to actually see the hands on the old-fashioned clock weren't pointing to 2:30 as he first thought.

"Christ, it's six thirty," he snarled in disbelief, shoving aside the sheet that was tangled around his legs.

Annie had been missing for over four hours.

Four fucking hours.

"Hold on." Hauk placed a hand on his shoulder, careful not to press too hard. "What are you doing?"

"Getting the hell out of here." He swung his legs over the edge of the gurney, his ribs screaming in protest at the twisting movement. "I have to find Annie."

"Teagan and Lucas are already out searching."

"Good." The knowledge his friends were on the hunt for Annie helped to ease a portion of his thundering terror, but that didn't stop him from pushing to his feet. More pain, more dizziness, but he didn't collapse. It was a start. "The more the better."

Hauk stood close at his side, his hands twitching as if he was considering the possibility of physically throwing him back on the gurney.

"And Max is at the house, sifting through the journals."

"You found them?" Rafe felt a stab of relief. He'd forgotten about the diaries they'd found in Martin's bathroom.

Now he had to hope there was some clue in them that would help track the bastard down.

With a curse, Hauk followed Rafe's pained shuffle across the short space to the chair where his clothing had been neatly folded.

Thankfully he was smart enough not to try and stop Rafe from pulling off the gown and reaching for his jeans. Instead he grabbed Rafe's upper arm, holding him steady as Rafe stepped into the wrinkled denims.

"I caught sight of them when they were putting you in the ambulance," the older man revealed. "Since I doubted you wanted the local authorities to get their hands on them, I snuck them out of the truck and shoved them in a nearby bush along with your guns." He shrugged. "Max dug them out when he arrived in town."

Releasing a string of foul words as he wrangled his sweatshirt over his head, Rafe shoved his feet into his tennis shoes. He was breathing hard and his entire body was drenched in sweat, but he was dressed.

"Max needs to let his FBI contact know he has them," he ground out, willing to include anyone who might be able to help. Hell, he'd call in the National Guard if he thought they'd come. Anything to get Annie back safely. "Maybe together they can find something."

Hauk tightened his grip on Rafe's arm. "I think he already gave them a call, but it's going to be hours before they can get an agent here. Newton is too far from a major city to have any regional offices nearby."

Rafe grimaced. Dammit. Annie couldn't wait.

He had to get to her.

"Let me go," he said as Hauk tried to steer him back to the gurney.

"At least let the doctor finish taking X-rays," the older man pleaded.

"No, dammit. I—"

"In a hurry, Vargas?" a male voice drawled as the door to the ER room was shoved open and the sheriff strolled across the tiled floor.

Rafe stiffened, instantly feeling the urge to punch the man in the face.

It wasn't just the fact the man had tried to bully Annie, although that was enough to deserve a broken nose. But there was something about the cocky attitude that set Rafe's nerves on edge.

Sheriff Graham Brock was a small-town petty tyrant who routinely used his authority to intimidate anyone who stood in his way.

Unfortunately, Rafe couldn't afford to indulge his dislike.

He might not trust the man any further than he could throw him, but he was the local law. Which meant he had the resources to mount a search for Annie. "Annie is missing," he said in sharp tones.

The lawman's lips twisted into a sneer. "That's convenient."

Rafe narrowed his gaze, caught off guard by the man's response. "What the fuck do you mean?"

Perhaps sensing the sudden danger that crackled in the air, the sheriff held up his hand.

Like all tyrants, he was no doubt a coward at heart.

"Settle down," he muttered. "It's not uncommon for someone to flee the scene of an accident. People who are driving drunk or—"

Rafe wasn't appeased. In fact, his hands curled into fists as the need to wipe the smirk off the man's face became irresistible. "Are you trying to imply she took off because she was drinking?"

"No." The man shifted uneasily, but his expression remained defiant. "It was obvious you were behind the wheel, but there could be other reasons she might not want to be taken to a hospital. Doing drugs might be legal in Colorado, but we don't allow it here in Iowa."

"Look, you piece of—"

Hauk moved to stand directly in front of him, his face hard with warning. "Easy, Rafe."

Rafe glared at the sheriff over his friend's shoulder. It was lucky he was too weak to do something stupid.

Otherwise there would be a new patient for the ER to stitch back together.

"The only thing Annie had in her system was the wine that I insisted she drink with her dinner," he snarled. "Now, if you aren't going to help me find her, then step aside."

The man scowled, clearly not used to having his authority challenged. "You need to make a statement about the accident."

Rafe pushed aside his friend. He wasn't going to kill the sheriff.

Not with so many witnesses.

When this was all over, however . . .

All bets were off.

"Later," he snapped, taking a step toward the door.

Instantly the sheriff was blocking his path. "Now."

Hauk reached out to give his shoulder a sharp squeeze.

It was a timely warning.

Sheriff Brock might be a conceited jackass, but he had a badge.

Which meant Rafe was going to have to make a token effort to play by the rules. For the moment.

"I'll call Teagan and see what's happening," Hauk said, heading for the door.

Rafe watched his friend stride from the room before returning his attention back to the sheriff, who was pulling a small notebook from his pocket.

"Maybe you should sit down," the sheriff suggested as Rafe lifted a hand to touch the bandage on his forehead.

Rafe folded his arms over his chest, ignoring the acute flare of pain. He'd be damned if he would show weakness.

"This won't take long," he said, his impatience a tangible force in the air. "I was returning to my grandfather's house with Annie."

"Coming from where?" Graham Brock demanded.

"That's irrelevant." Rafe scowled at the interruption. "When we got two blocks from the house, I discovered the road was blocked by a utility truck."

The sheriff's lips thinned as he futilely attempted to gain an upper hand. "Do you know how it got there?"

"How would I know?" Rafe demanded.

"The gas company claims it was stolen from their lot."

"Then you should be talking with them." Rafe took a step forward. It wasn't a threat, but with at least six inches on the sheriff, it was a silent form of intimidation. "Or better yet, you should be searching for Annie."

Brock tilted his chin, looking like a belligerent bulldog. "What happened next?"

Rafe trembled with the effort not to knock the idiot out of his way. God dammit. He didn't have time for this shit. Annie was missing. And every passing second felt like an eternity. "I was backing up to go around the block when a car came from a side street and rammed into my truck," he said between clenched teeth.

The sheriff jotted down something in his little notebook. "Did you see the driver?"

"No."

"Did you recognize the car?"

"It was dark. All I saw was headlights," Rafe snapped. "Then the world went black. That's all I know."

The man lifted his head to study Rafe with a searching gaze. "Do you think Annie was kidnapped?"

Fear clutched his heart at the blunt question. "Yeah, I think she was kidnapped."

"Why?"

Was the jerk kidding?

Or just trying to piss Rafe off?

"The same reason you instantly assumed that Cindy Franklin was missing when she was late for work," he snapped. "There's a crazed madman out there snatching women."

Sheriff Brock stilled, abruptly shoving the ridiculous notebook back into his pocket. "You know something," he accused in flat tones.

Rafe's lips twisted. So, the man wasn't as stupid as he'd assumed. "I have my suspicions," he grudgingly admitted.

"Are you going to share them?"

Was he?

Rafe wavered. He'd resigned himself to the fact he would never trust the lawman. Just as he'd resigned himself to the fact that he was the legal authority in this town, with the ability to organize the locals into a full-blown search for Annie.

"I recently discovered that Annie's brother wasn't killed in a car accident as she always believed," he revealed.

The man looked confused. "He's still alive?"

"Yeah."

"Why the hell did Don White lie about his son being killed in an auto accident?"

"Because until recently Martin Emerson was a patient at the Greenwood Estates."

"What's that?"

"A private mental facility."

"Christ." The sheriff's face twisted with disgust. "He's a whack job?"

Rafe's aversion for the man amped up another notch.

Sheriff Graham Brock truly was a nasty waste of space.

"He was severely abused by his mother and killed her in self-defense." He ridiculously found himself defending Martin even as he knew he would kill the tortured man without hesitation to rescue Annie.

The sheriff shrugged. "What does this have to do with the fact your girlfriend is missing?"

Girlfriend.

It wasn't a term Rafe had used since he'd left junior high. But suddenly it sounded right.

Of course, once this madness was over he intended to make sure his bond with Annie was wrapped up legally, spiritually, and any other way he could think of to tie her to him on a permanent basis.

But for now, girlfriend would do.

Giving a shake of his head, Rafe shoved aside his odd musing. Shit. This was no time to lose focus. "I think it's possible that he's the Newton Slayer."

The man sucked in a shocked breath. "What?"

"Martin Emerson sliced his mother's throat when he was fourteen."

"Holy fuck." The sheriff grimaced, his hand unconsciously lifting to touch his throat. "He's obviously a sicko, but it doesn't mean he killed those women."

"I just got back from the clinic where he was living," Rafe said.

The sheriff frowned. "And?"

"And he's been missing for the past three weeks," Rafe said.

"Shit." The sheriff scowled. "That doesn't necessarily mean he came to Newton."

"I might agree if Annie hadn't been receiving notes," Rafe admitted.

"Notes?" Brock's scowl only deepened. "Why didn't she tell me?"

Rafe shrugged. "At first she thought they were pranks."

"But you don't?"

"The notes were addressed to Annabelle, not Annie," Rafe said. "No one knows that name in Newton. No one except for Martin Emerson."

The sheriff snatched off his hat to run a hand over his nearly bald head. "Goddamn," he at last muttered, accepting that Rafe might be right. A fact that clearly rubbed at his pride. "I suppose blood will tell. First the father and now the son."

Rafe shook his head, then winced when a sharp pain sliced through his brain.

Damn, he felt like he'd been through a blender.

"No, not the father," he told his companion.

The sheriff looked predictably baffled. "Don White wasn't her father?"

"He wasn't the Slayer," Rafe corrected. "Don White was actually Captain James Emerson, a well-respected naval officer. It was Martin who was killing the women of Newton fifteen years ago."

Rafe watched as the man absorbed his words, the chunky face paling to a strange shade of ash. "Impossible," Brock breathed.

"Trust me, I had the very best investigator searching through his records," Rafe insisted, annoyed by the idiot's refusal to accept the truth.

He didn't have time for this shit.

Brock shook his head. "I found him myself in the bomb shelter. He wouldn't have been there if he wasn't guilty."

"At a guess I'd say he was trying to protect his son," Rafe rasped with an impatience that could no longer be restrained. Who cared how or why Annie's father had been in the shelter? "Or Martin forced him down there to use as the fall guy."

"No." With quick, jerky steps the sheriff paced the cramped

space of the hospital room. Sweat poured down his round face, staining the collar of his uniform. "It was him."

"Think what you want," Rafe muttered. "But all the evidence points toward Martin being the Slayer."

Without warning, Brock swung his arm and smashed his fist into a metal cabinet, sending a tray of equipment crashing to the floor.

"Fuck," he burst out, his face flushed an ugly red.

Rafe frowned before he belatedly realized why the sheriff looked like he was on the edge of a complete meltdown.

It was very possible that the lawman had killed Don White thinking that he was the man responsible for murdering his young wife and unborn child.

Now he was forced to accept that he'd made a hideous mistake.

"It seems an innocent man died in your jail cell, sheriff." Rafe stepped around Brock, who was staring absently at the far wall. "Now I intend to find Annie. I suggest you do your job and get a search organized."

"Wait."

Rafe didn't hesitate as he headed out the door. "You have any more questions for me, contact my lawyer."

Chapter Twenty-One

Annie was running down a long tunnel. It was cramped and cold and no matter how fast she ran, she couldn't reach the entrance, which remained frustratingly out of reach.

She didn't understand the terror that was making her heart thunder, but she was convinced that there was someone running behind her. And that if she didn't get out of the darkness soon she was going to die.

That simple.

With an effort, she forced her heart to slow, assuring herself that this was no different from any other vision she'd endured.

Okay, this time she wasn't watching from a distance. Instead, it was directly happening to her.

But soon she would open her eyes to discover she was lying in her bed, drenched in sweat.

She was still telling herself that when she finally managed to force her eyes open.

Only this time she wasn't in her own bed.

Forcing herself not to twitch a muscle, she took in her surroundings.

Above her head were open beams. Not a decor statement, but instead the bottom of the floor above her. Combined with the plain cement wall that was just inches from her face, it was easy to guess she was in an unfinished basement.

There was a small slit of a window at the top of the wall that allowed in the first rays of morning sunlight. Not enough light to banish all the shadows from the basement, but she could tell she was lying on a narrow cot and that her arm was handcuffed to a steel pipe bolted to the cement floor.

Oh shit.

This was real.

As in . . . real, real.

But how had it happened?

She'd been with Rafe. She remembered that much. They were returning from the clinic and there was something blocking the road. A gas truck. Yes. And then . . .

Her breath tangled in her throat, her heart missing a beat.

Oh God.

A car had appeared out of nowhere to smash into the side of the truck, injuring Rafe and leaving her vulnerable to her crazy-ass brother.

"Rafe?" she breathed, turning her head to the side as she heard the sound of approaching footsteps.

Instantly she stiffened, sheer terror exploding through her at the sight of the man who appeared from the shadows to crouch beside the cot.

Martin.

Even through her panic she inanely found herself searching the narrow face surrounded by a halo of brown curls for some sign of recognition.

Some flicker of memory.

There was nothing, but as she studied the shape of his blue eyes and the curve of his lips, Annie had to admit they resembled one another. Not exact duplicates, but close enough that it was obvious they were related.

It was creepy. And oddly reassuring that she wasn't completely alone in the world.

God almighty, she was truly screwed in the head.

"At last. You're awake," he murmured softly, his expression tender as he reached his hand toward her. "How do you feel?"

"No." She instinctively shrank away from his touch, eyeing him as if he were a cobra about to strike. "Don't touch me."

"Shh." He lightly stroked her hair. "I won't hurt you."

She shivered, her head aching and her mouth dry. "You already did."

His gaze shifted to the lump on her forehead, genuine regret twisting his delicate features. "I'm sorry," he said softly. "It was necessary."

Annie forcibly swallowed her urge to scream. She didn't know where she was, or how long she'd been out.

The only thing she knew beyond a shadow of a doubt was that she was going to find some way to escape.

Either she would convince Martin to release her, or she would keep him distracted long enough for Rafe to find her.

Because there was no doubt in her mind that Rafe was searching for her.

Even if he had to crawl out of his hospital bed to do it.

Until then . . . well, she just had to stay alive.

"Why?" she demanded.

His lips thinned as his fingers continued to stroke over her hair. "I'd hoped that Rafe Vargas could be a suitable companion when I couldn't be near to protect you," he said, the faintest edge in his voice hinting at his disappointment in Rafe. "But he's become far too possessive."

She licked her dry lips. "He was only trying to help."

Martin frowned. "He took you away."

Her stomach cramped at the knowledge he'd been keeping such close track of her movements.

"Took me away from what?"

"From me." Martin's fingers tightened in her hair. Not hard enough to hurt, but enough to make Annie's heart stutter with fear. "I can't allow that. Not again."

"I . . ." She was forced to halt and swallow the lump in her throat. "I didn't realize we were supposed to be together."

His burst of frustration eased and the tender expression returned to his face.

Annie hid a grimace. It was unnerving just how normal he looked.

As if he was just an ordinary young man and not an unbalanced killer who sliced open women's throats.

"You don't remember me, do you?" he asked.

She briefly considered her answer.

She could lie and say she had memories of their childhood together.

Or she could go the other extreme and pretend she didn't have any idea who he was.

In the end, she went for the truth. She wasn't a good liar under the best of circumstances. And these were far from the best of circumstances.

"No, I don't remember you, but I suspect you're my brother," she said.

"How did—?" He bit off his words, his brief confusion replaced by a rueful smile. "Ah. Vargas must have discovered our little secret."

Annie frowned. She didn't think hiding the fact that her brother had murdered her mother and was currently living in a private clinic was a "little secret."

"All these years I thought you were dead," she accused, her voice revealing the grief she'd endured for the past twenty-two years.

Genuine regret darkened his blue eyes. "I know, sweetie, and I'm sorry," he murmured. "When I went to the clinic, I insisted that you be told I had died in a car accident."

"I should have been told the truth."

He gave a sharp shake of his head. "No, I would have rather you believed I was dead than to have you growing up knowing that I killed Mother. You would have thought I was some sort of crazed maniac."

Once again his fingers tightened in her hair, revealing the turbulent emotions that seethed just below the surface.

Annie hastily pinned a soothing smile to her lips. God. She had to be more careful.

"I would never have thought that," she assured him. "I know that she . . . wasn't a good mother."

"Yes, you would have," he argued, his voice petulant. As if he was six, not thirty-six years old. "Father would have poisoned your mind against me."

"Why would he do that?"

"He was always jealous of me," he growled. "He resented the fact that you loved me more."

Annie gave a startled blink. She understood his seething hatred for their mother. She'd clearly been a psycho bitch.

But their dad had been a kind, gentle man who would never hurt anyone.

"No, Martin—"

"Marty," he firmly interrupted her protest. "You always called me Marty."

"Okay . . . Marty," she conceded. She'd call him whatever he wanted if it kept him calm. "Dad loved you. When he talked about you I could see how much he missed you."

His jaw clenched, the cresting sunlight revealing the unmistakable pain that flared through his eyes. "If that was true he wouldn't have abandoned us."

"Do you mean after . . ." Her words faltered, not sure how to discuss the murder of their mother. "After you went to the . . . clinic?"

"No." He scowled, clearly disturbed by the thought of their father. "I mean when we were young."

She gave a jerk of surprise, the handcuff rattling against the steel pipe. "He abandoned us?"

"He might as well have," Martin amended, thankfully removing his fingers from her hair as he shoved himself upright. "He was always gone," he said, his eyes growing distant as if he was suddenly lost in the past. "Being a sailor was more important than taking care of his own children."

Annie grimaced. It was difficult to remember her father

had once been an ambitious naval captain who'd married the daughter of a diplomat.

As far as she could remember, he'd been a farmer who was content to work his land during the day and spend his nights taking care of his daughter.

Now she found herself instinctively defending the fact he'd clearly failed his son, even if it had been unintentional.

"It was his career," she said softly.

Martin snorted in disgust. "A convenient excuse."

"But someone had to work to pay the bills, didn't they?"

Her brother glared down at her, a faint flush touching his pale cheeks. "Now you sound like him," he snapped. "He came to the clinic pleading for me to understand that he had no choice." He shook his head. "As if I would ever forgive him."

Annie tried to find a more comfortable position on the cot. Not easy when her arm was cuffed to the pipe at an awkward angle and her head continued to throb.

"How often did he visit you?" she asked, not only to keep Martin distracted, but because she was truly curious.

How had her father managed to keep so much of his life a secret from her?

Granted, she'd only been ten when he died. But still . . .

"During the first couple of years he came every week," Martin said with a shrug. "After I refused to see him, he started coming once a year on my birthday."

Annie's breath caught in her throat as she abruptly recalled her father's annual fishing trip with an old college buddy.

It was the one time he'd allow Annie to sleep over at a friend's house.

"March twenty-fourth," she whispered.

"Yes." Martin abruptly smiled. "He would bring pictures of you and leave them with the doctors."

Ah. Well, that explained the framed pictures of her that they'd seen in Martin's private rooms.

"He didn't see you?"

"I refused." The words were stark. Unforgiving. "I will never forget that he left us in the hands of a monster."

Mother's a monster . . .

The words echoed through the back of her mind.

Had Martin whispered them to her?

"Do you mean Mother?" she demanded.

Without warning Martin turned to pace the cement floor, his hands clenched and his back rigid. "Don't call her that," he snarled, stepping toward her as if he would strike her. Then, seeing her wince in fear, he sucked in a deep breath and made an obvious effort to calm down. "She was never a mother. Not to either of us."

The early morning sunlight was making a valiant attempt to combat the frost that'd coated the leaves and grass in front of the small house.

Moving like an old man, Rafe limped across his grand-father's porch, wryly aware of Hauk walking a few inches behind him, clearly prepared to catch him if he fell.

His friend was hovering around him like a mother hen, but Rafe didn't have the energy to complain.

Besides, if he was being entirely honest, he wasn't sure he wouldn't take an unexpected tumble.

The murkiness in his brain might have cleared during the drive from the hospital, but the cut on his forehead throbbed, his knees were weak, and taking a breath hurt like a bitch.

It was only his fierce need to find Annie that kept him upright.

Managing to pull open the door, he crossed through the living room, acutely aware of the lingering scent of cherry blossoms that clung to the air.

The smell of Annie.

Jesus. He was swayed as a wave of fear threatened to over-whelm him.

He was trying hard not to think of her terrified, perhaps even injured, in the hands of the Newton Slayer.

He wouldn't be able to function if he gave in to his fear.

Right now Annie didn't need a panicked lover.

She needed a covert ops specialist.

And that's what he intended to be.

Entering the kitchen he wasn't surprised to see that it'd been turned into a command center by Max and Teagan.

The countertops had been cleared of dishes, towels, and small appliances. Hell, even his coffeemaker was gone. And in their place were four separate laptops running various search programs.

On the nearest wall they'd taped up an enlarged map of the county, along with the latest satellite shots. And the kitchen table was nearly buried beneath stacks of paper.

"Max," Rafe murmured, intensely pleased at the sight of the large man, dressed in jeans and a long-sleeved tee stretched over his massive chest, who turned from one of the computers.

He considered all his friends as brothers, but Max had a calm, steady presence that Rafe desperately needed today. He clapped the forensics expert on the shoulder. "Thank you for coming, my man."

Max held his gaze, his expression somber. "All you have to do is call."

Rafe gave a careful nod, stepping back. He hadn't doubted for a second that his friends would drop everything if they thought he was in trouble. "I know."

The astute gray eyes lingered on the stitches that ran the length of his forehead.

"How do you feel?"

"Like I got hit by a car," he ruefully admitted. "But I'll heal. Any word from Teagan and Lucas?"

Max leaned against the edge of the countertop, his arms folded over his chest. "Teagan has been doing door-by-door interviews."

Rafe cocked a brow. "Interviews?"

"A crash in the middle of the night had to attract a lot of

attention," Max pointed out. "Someone might have seen Annie being taken from the scene."

Of course it would attract attention. Especially in a town where people considered spying on their neighbors an art form. Dammit. He should have thought of that angle himself.

Clearly his brain was still sketchy.

"And Lucas?" he asked.

"He went to LaClede." It was Hauk who answered, moving to open the fridge and grab a bottle of water. "He arranged with a friend to have a helicopter flown in." He reached into his pocket of his jacket to pull out the medicine given them before they left the hospital. Shaking out a little white pill, he handed it to Rafe along with the water. "The search will be easier with eyes in the sky. And once she's found, it will be a quick way to get her out of danger."

Rafe swallowed the antibiotic as he glanced toward Max.

"Can you make sure that we're in constant contact?"

Max nodded. "Of course."

Forcing himself to drink the entire container of water, Rafe moved to stand next to the table. His hand reached to touch the leather-bound diaries that were spread open.

"Did you discover anything in the journals that might help us?"

"Martin Emerson is a sick fuck," Max said without hesitation.

Rafe's gut twisted. "Yeah, I got that from the pile of women with their throats slit."

Max studied his pale face. "Are you sure he's the one who's taken Annie?"

Was he?

Rafe grimaced. He was smart enough to know the danger of leaping to conclusions. They always came back to bite you in the ass.

But they didn't have the luxury of debating whether there

was any chance Annie had been taken by anyone but her brother.

Even if the person guilty of kidnapping Annie didn't intend to hurt her, he was most certainly on the run. They had to hunt them down before the trail went cold.

"We have to assume he's responsible for now," he said in decisive tones, holding Max's gaze. "Can you tell me where he would have taken Annie?"

Max frowned in confusion. "I'm not a profiler."

"Guess."

"Dammit, Rafe," his friend growled, running his hand over the short strands of his blond hair.

It wasn't fair to press his friend. Max's expertise was hard science, not the psychology of criminals. But Rafe couldn't afford to feel guilt. "Guess."

Max glanced toward the silent Hauk before heaving a sigh of resignation. "His mind is cluttered, but he's meticulous. Maybe because his mind is cluttered," he at last muttered, shoving away from the counter to stand next to Rafe. He pointed toward the nearest journal, which was open to a series of newspaper clippings that were fifteen years old. Each of them had a headline that included the words "Newton Slayer." Rafe's blood ran cold. "See how carefully he's cut the edges of the paper?" Max demanded, his finger tracing the clipping before pointing toward the yellowing bits of tape at each corner. "Even his pieces of tape are cut exactly one inch. And I mean *exactly* one inch."

"So what does that mean?"

"Shit, I hate guessing," Max muttered. "But I would assume he would choose a setting that he can control. No squatting in some random field or sleeping in his car. He'll be in a permanent structure with electricity and running water."

It made sense to Rafe. It also gave him a flicker of hope.

In such a rural area it would be impossible to check each patch of woods or abandoned barn.

"That should make him easier to find."

Max shook his head, flipping shut the journal. "I'm not sure about that," he warned. "He's extremely clever. I doubt he came to Newton without careful planning."

Rafe shrugged, refusing to contemplate failure. "He might be clever, but he's not as good as us."

Max nodded. It was true. But his expression remained hard with concern. "Have you considered the fact that he might already have left the area?"

Rafe grabbed the back of a kitchen chair, partially to keep himself upright and partially to keep himself from running through the streets, searching for Annie like a maniac.

"Of course I have," he admitted. "But I don't think he'll leave Newton until he's finished."

Hauk moved to stand at his side. "Finished what?"

Rafe carefully reached for one of the diaries, flipping it open to search for the pages he'd noticed when he'd glanced through them earlier. "This."

Hauk and Max leaned forward to read the nursery rhyme that'd been copied over and over.

> *One for sorrow,*
> *Two for luck.*
> *Three for a wedding,*
> *Four for death.*
> *Five for silver,*
> *Six for gold.*
> *Seven for a secret,*
> *Not to be told.*
> *Eight for heaven,*
> *Nine for hell*
> *And ten for the devil's own sell.*

Hauk made a small sound of shock. "That's the poem that he's been sending to Annie, right?"

Rafe nodded. "Yeah."

Max glanced from Hauk to Rafe, his brows pulled into a confused frown. "What does this have to do with the bastard staying in town?"

Rafe took a minute, organizing his vague suspicions.

He'd sensed from the first note that the rhyme was somehow important to the stalker. And that it had some connection to Annie, as well as the missing women.

But it wasn't until he'd seen it written on page after page that he'd realized the depth of Martin's obsession with the words.

"I think the poem has some special meaning to Martin Emerson," he said slowly. "And I think he intends to murder a woman for each verse."

There was a tense silence as his friends considered his theory.

"There's ten verses." Hauk was the first to speak, pointing out a flaw in his logic. "There were only seven women killed the first time."

"Because he was interrupted," Rafe reminded him, shivering at the mere thought of seven innocent women being slaughtered. Jesus. He'd seen his share of horrors during the war, but Martin Emerson took it to a new level. "This time I don't think he'll quit until he's finished his job." He deliberately paused. "Or he's dead."

Max furrowed his brow, the logical scientist in him not impressed with Rafe's gut instincts.

"That's a pretty big leap," he said.

It was.

In fact, it was fairly close to grasping at straws. But at this point, Rafe didn't have much choice.

"It's all I have," he admitted with a shrug.

They all froze as a shadow fell across the back porch. Then, with a blinding speed, both Max and Hauk had their guns pulled and pointed toward the back door, which was being shoved open.

Completely ignoring the tension, not to mention the guns pointed at his head, Teagan strolled into the kitchen. Halting at the center of the floor, he took a slow survey of Rafe's pale face and tousled hair.

Despite the cold morning air, the computer genius was dressed in jeans and a short-sleeved black tee with a leather holster strapped across his chest. "Amigo, you look like shit," he said, planting his hands on his hips.

"Thanks." Rafe sent his friend a wry smile. "Tell me you found something that can help us."

The younger man didn't hesitate. "No one claims to have seen the accident or who disappeared with your woman, but I traced the car that smashed into your truck to a farmer just north of town."

Rafe's lips twisted.

Why hadn't he questioned the sheriff about the car that had crashed into him?

Either he was suffering from a concussion or his fear for Annie was screwing up his brain.

Thank God he had his friends around as backup.

"You're sure it was stolen?" he asked.

Teagan gave a nod. "Yep."

"When?"

"The man didn't know it was missing until I called him," Teagan said, his expression revealing his disbelief that anyone could not know his car had been stolen. Of course, Teagan lavished as much love on his automobiles as most people gave their children. Maybe more. "He said it was usually parked in a shed behind the house."

Which meant they didn't have any time line for when it was stolen.

"Damn," Rafe muttered.

"Wait." Teagan held up a hand, his eyes glinting with gold in the morning sunlight. "He did say he'd noticed a battered black pickup parked at the end of his drive before he went to bed."

"He didn't investigate?" Hauk demanded in surprise.

They'd all discovered that while the locals could be friendly, even with strangers, they took a very dim view of trespassers.

Especially since the explosion of meth labs in the area.

Few of them would hesitate to shoot anyone who strayed onto their land at night.

Teagan gave a lift of his shoulder. "By the time he got his shotgun, the truck had taken off."

"Tell me he at least got the plate number?" Rafe pleaded.

"No, but he was certain it was a 2000 Ford F150 Super-Cab with a mounted toolbox."

"Shit," Hauk muttered. "Half this county drives Ford trucks."

Teagan moved forward, a smug smile on his lips as he began to shuffle through a pile of papers stacked on the kitchen table.

"True, but I already pulled the pics from the security cameras at the gas company," Teagan said, collecting several 8x10 photos. "Whoever installed them should be shot," he groused.

Rafe gave a short laugh. "Not everyone can be a techno wizard," he reminded his friend.

"They could at least be competent," Teagan muttered, standing at Rafe's side to reveal the black-and-white images of a parking lot. Rafe studied the three utility trucks lined side by side, as well as a small shed, shaking his head as he understood Teagan's frustration. The majority of the picture was centered on a brick wall.

Why?

"Shit," he muttered.

"The cameras cover less than half the lot and none of the street, but I did manage to narrow down a few images of cars that didn't look like they belonged," Teagan continued, sorting through the pictures until he found the one he wanted.

He pointed toward the front cab of a black Ford pickup that was parked next to one of the gas trucks. "This is our guy."

Fury as corrosive as acid scoured through Rafe's blood as he tilted the picture toward the window where the morning sunlight streamed into the kitchen. The image was fuzzy and too far away to make an exact I.D., but there was no mistaking the driver of the truck had a mop of curls and a thin face that were remarkably similar to Martin Emerson's.

Max moved to peer over Rafe's shoulder, grabbing his upper arm as if sensing he was about to explode.

"Good work, my friend," Max told Teagan. "Unfortunately, it doesn't tell us how to track him down."

Teagan grabbed the pictures and tossed them back on the table before nodding toward the computers humming away on the counter.

"There's two businesses on the edge of town that have ATMs," he said. "Thankfully they both use the same security company. Once I hack into their system, I should be able to review their cameras and see if the truck passed them."

Rafe nodded, not at all surprised that Teagan had the ability to break into the company's private computers. He could hack his way into Homeland Security if he wanted.

"What are you looking for?" he asked.

"Hopefully we'll be able to see if the truck headed for the highway and if he went north or south after leaving town." Teagan hesitated, his gaze locked on Rafe. "And if he had a passenger."

Pain lanced through Rafe, nearly sending him to his knees.

"God dammit," he growled.

Max tightened his hand on Rafe's arm while Hauk moved to stand at his other side. Without words they were giving him the support he needed.

And that was why he loved them.

"So how the hell did he pull it off?" Hauk rasped, no

doubt as much to distract Rafe from his blinding fear as to discuss how Annie had been snatched from beneath his nose.

It was Teagan who answered. "If it was me I'd steal the farmer's car and park it on the side street before going back for the gas truck to block the street," he said, pausing as if he was considering the various logistics of pulling off the kidnapping. "After that it was only a matter of placing his own truck close by and waiting for Rafe to fall into his trap."

Teagan's explanation made sense, but it left a hell of a lot to fickle fate.

"Still, he couldn't have known when I would return," he muttered, futilely wishing he'd kept heading south.

Annie might have been pissed if he'd hauled her to his ranch and locked her in his house, but she'd be safe in his arms.

Right now he'd take pissed.

"True," Teagan agreed. "There was a calculated risk that the farmer would miss his car or that someone would call the gas company demanding to know if there was a leak. But the return on a successful execution of his plan more than made up for the chance of having it interrupted." The golden eyes narrowed. "I have to admit the bastard can think quick on his feet. A damned shame."

Rafe made a sound of frustration.

He'd tried to be so careful. He'd assumed that as long as he was close to Annie she would be protected.

Shit.

One well-placed gas truck, one stolen car, and one untimely accident later and he'd been easily incapacitated.

Hauk muttered a foul word, giving a shake of his head. "Why now?"

They all turned to study the older man's troubled expression.

"What do you mean?" Max demanded.

"Why not take Annie as soon as she got to town?" Hauk clarified. "Or hell, while she was in Denver. She would have been easy to snatch before we got involved."

Rafe absently pressed his fingers to the aching cut on his forehead.

It was a legitimate question.

There'd been a hell of a lot easier ways for Martin to get his hands on Annie.

So why take such a risk last night?

The answer came like a strike of lightning.

"It's *because* we got involved," he growled. "Or at least because I got involved."

Teagan tilted his head to the side. "He's jealous?"

"Exactly." Rafe met his friend's disgusted gaze and gave a small shake of his head. "Not in an incestuous way. The diaries are clear that his obsession with Annie is brotherly, not sexual," he said. "But she's his to protect, as far as he's concerned. He can't let me usurp his position."

Max gave his arm a squeeze. "Which means he won't hurt her," he assured Rafe. "He's obsessed with keeping her safe."

Rafe wasn't nearly so certain. He didn't have experience with a serial killer, but he did know that their thought processes were whacked.

Who the hell knew what was going through Martin's twisted brain? "He's unstable," he said, his voice harsh with fear. "He might decide the only way to protect her is to kill her."

Max held his gaze. "We'll find her."

"Damn straight," Teagan muttered.

Rafe sucked in a deep breath.

They would find her.

Any other outcome was unthinkable.

Period.

A fierce, ruthless need to be out on the search exploded through Rafe, propelling him toward the large map that was pinned to the wall.

Annie was out there somewhere. Waiting for him to save her.

He wasn't going to fail her again.

Waiting for his friends to join him, Rafe used the tip of his finger to draw a small circle around Newton.

"When Lucas calls in, tell him to concentrate on this area."

Max pulled out his phone, tapping in the GPS coordinates. "Are you sure you want it so limited?" he demanded when he was done.

Rafe didn't hesitate. "Yeah."

Max glanced up from his phone, studying Rafe with a small frown. "You have a reason to think he's going to be there?"

He nodded. "Annie's visions."

"Rafe—" Teagan started, only to snap his lips shut when Rafe held up a hand.

"Plus, I suspect all three missing women were taken from this convenience store," Rafe continued, pointing toward the gas station along the edge of the highway. "He has to be near enough to have kept a close watch on the parking lot without attracting notice."

Teagan considered his words before giving a slow nod. "Fine."

Rafe stepped back, glancing toward Hauk. "I'll need you to drive until the last of the painkillers get out of my system," he informed his friend.

"Where are we going?"

"Annie's out there. I'm going to find her."

Hauk hesitated, as if he was going to try and convince Rafe he was in no condition to be out riding over rough country roads. Then, catching sight of Rafe's grim expression, he gave a slow nod of resignation. "Fine." He conceded defeat. "But first we need to stop by the motel so I can get my equipment."

They all knew that Hauk's "equipment" included his high-powered sniper rifle.

The retired soldier could kill at a thousand yards.

Not a bad wingman to have around.

Rafe turned back to Teagan. "Once you get into the surveillance cameras, let me know," he commanded. He was used to taking charge. "It will help us narrow down the search if we know which direction the truck went."

Teagan nodded. "Will do."

Rafe glanced toward Max, who was looking less than pleased with Rafe's sudden burst of restless energy. "Will you run point?"

Max grudgingly nodded. "Of course."

It was Teagan who stepped forward to express what was on all their minds. "Be careful, Rafe," he warned in somber tones. "Martin Emerson will be desperate to keep Annie. If you cross his path, he won't hesitate to kill you."

Chapter Twenty-Two

Annie didn't need to see the ugly flush on her brother's face to sense his rising agitation.

Eyeing him with a growing concern, she tried to think of some way to ease his distress.

"Can I have some water?" she at last demanded.

It was an embarrassingly clichéd diversion tactic, but surprisingly it worked.

"Of course, sweetie."

The fevered glitter in the pale eyes was instantly replaced with concern as he turned to hurry across the cement floor to a small refrigerator that was hooked up in the distant corner.

His distraction gave Annie a limited opportunity to take an inventory of her surroundings.

It was without a doubt a basement. The floor and walls were cement, with two miniscule windows that allowed in a small amount of sunlight.

From her position on the cot, she could see a wooden shelf shoved against a back wall filled with home-canned vegetables, old Tupperware, and broken appliances covered in cobwebs. Closer to the cot was a stack of bikes that looked like they hadn't been used in years.

Beyond that there was nothing to be seen except the

small fridge and a washer and dryer that had obviously been bought in the seventies.

No tools that she could use as a weapon. No telephone or computer she could use to contact Rafe. Nothing she could even use to set a fire to attract attention.

Annie sent a quick glance toward a narrow flight of stairs that led to the main house, catching sight of a closed door that was no doubt locked, before Martin returned with her water.

Taking the bottle with her free hand, Annie cautiously scooted up to lean against the chilled wall behind her.

"Where are we?" she asked, taking a deep drink.

She hadn't entirely been trying to divert Martin.

She truly was thirsty.

Probably a side effect of being drugged.

He stood next to the cot, his lean body covered in a pair of loose jogging pants and a matching jacket.

"My temporary home," he answered, casting a dismissive glance around the musty basement. "Very temporary."

She took another drink. "Where are the owners?"

"They're an elderly couple who are spending the winter in Arizona," he explained. "I rented the house from them for the winter."

Annie choked on the water.

She didn't know what shocked her more.

The sinking knowledge that there was no hope the owners might return and call the police, or the fact that Martin had actually gone to the time and effort to arrange a place to stay.

"You rented it?" she managed to ask in a strangled voice.

"Yes." Martin looked pleased with himself. "It's amazing what can be accomplished on the Internet these days."

"True." Annie struggled to force a smile to her stiff lips. "So you . . . planned to come to Newton?"

"Of course." He hesitated, briefly lost in an unpleasant thought. "I had to."

"Why?"

He blinked, as if coming back from a great distance.

"Because we hadn't finished our game."

Game? An icy premonition inched down her spine.

"I don't understand."

He leaned down to gently remove the empty bottle from her hand.

"You will."

She watched as he turned to toss the bottle into a nearby trash can. There was a strange tension humming around his slender body.

Not the same agitation as when he was forced to think of their mother.

This was . . . excitement.

Which was even more disturbing.

"Did you know that I would come to Newton?" she asked, not entirely sure she wanted to know the answer.

"Of course."

"How?"

He reached out to lightly brush her hair from her cheek, his touch making her shudder. "Because we can share our thoughts."

She gasped, her eyes wide.

Wasn't it bad enough she'd been forced to see into the mind of a killer?

No one wanted to live with that kind of curse.

But to think that the killer could actually see into her mind . . .

God almighty.

She pressed her head against the wall, futilely trying to avoid his lingering touch.

"The visions," she breathed.

"Yes." He smiled his sweet, sweet smile. "They began when you were just a baby. At times it was the only way I could comfort you."

Sickness rolled through her stomach.

If Martin knew that she could share his thoughts, then he had to know she'd seen him stalking the poor women. And that she would feel compelled to try and stop him.

"So you deliberately lured me here," she muttered.

Something that might have been genuine regret darkened the blue eyes as he abruptly turned away and paced back to the corner of the basement. He reached into the fridge before returning to the cot and shoving an apple into her hand. "Here."

She furrowed her brow, wincing as a pain shot through her head.

"I'm not hungry," she muttered, dropping the apple on the cot.

Martin clicked his tongue, a chiding expression on his thin face. "You should eat more fruit. You're too pale." He lowered himself to perch on the edge of the cot, his hand cupping her cheek. "From now on I'll ensure that you take better care of yourself."

She shrank against the wall, turning her head to knock away his hand.

In her mind all she could see was the women screaming in fear as this man chased them through the dark.

"No, please . . ."

Martin stiffened, his eyes troubled as he studied her terrified expression. "Annabelle, don't be afraid of me."

She licked her lips, knowing it would be impossible to lie. Not only was her heart pounding a thousand miles an hour, but her entire body was trembling.

"I'm trying, but it's not easy when you drugged me and now have me handcuffed to the bed."

His lips thinned. As if he didn't like to be reminded that he'd kidnapped his own sister. "It's necessary," he muttered.

"Why?" She ignored the tiny voice in the back of her mind that warned she didn't want to probe into Martin's obsession with her. For now, she had to cling to the belief that she could forge some sort of connection with her brother and hope she could lull him into a sense of complacency. Maybe then he would release her from the handcuffs and she would have a chance to escape. "If you wanted to see me, you could have knocked on my door. Or better yet, you could have contacted me through the Internet," she pointed out. "I would have come to you without hesitation."

His lips drooped in a petulant frown. "I told you, we hadn't finished our game."

Game.

There was that word again.

She searched his delicate features. He looked so innocent. Like the typical boy next door.

It seemed impossible to accept that beneath the All-American good looks was a ruthless killer.

"Does this game have anything to do with the missing women?" The words were out of her mouth before she could halt them.

On cue, Martin's face flushed, a feverish glitter entering his eyes as he abruptly shoved himself to his feet. "They must be punished," he rasped.

Oh God. She hadn't intended to stir up his crazy.

What if she'd triggered some need to kill and he went after another woman?

God, she would never be able to live with herself.

"Martin—"

"Marty," he corrected with a distinct edge in his voice.

She sucked in a slow, deep breath. "Marty, they didn't do anything to deserve to be punished," she said in careful tones.

"You don't understand."

"Then tell me," she urged.

As long as he was in the basement talking to her, he wasn't out hurting other women.

Yet another bonus to keeping him focused on her.

"She's evil." His features twisted into a mask of pure hatred. "So evil."

Annie's chest tightened. "Who is?"

"Mother," he snarled. "Do you remember?"

She gave a hesitant shake of her head. "No."

A tight smile curved his lips. "I'm glad."

So was Annie. She was growing certain that her mother had been just as twisted as her brother.

"Did she hurt you?" she asked in a soft voice.

Absently Martin shoved up the sleeve of his jacket, turning over his arm to reveal the dozens of round scars that marred his skin. "Sometimes."

There was the scrape of metal against metal as Annie leaned forward, the handcuff biting into the flesh of her wrist. Not that she noticed. She'd braced herself for some sign of abuse. Rafe's research had revealed that her brother's childhood had been far from ideal.

But not . . . mutilation.

"Oh my God," she breathed. "Those are cigarette burns."

He jerkily shoved the sleeve back down his arm, his face tight with remembered pain. "She told everyone that they were an accident. Just like my broken arms and black eyes were accidents." He grimaced, pressing a hand to his chest. "Later she became smart enough to hurt me where my scars could be hidden by clothes."

Oh . . . God.

Annie felt pity clench her heart.

It did nothing to lessen the horror of what this man had done. Or blind her to the fact that he might snap at any moment and slice her throat.

But the thought of any young, vulnerable child having to endure such agony from his own mother made her want to cry.

"I'm so sorry," she said, her sincerity unmistakable.

He gave an absent nod, his eyes haunted by a past that had destroyed his future. "The beatings weren't the worst," he admitted, his voice hoarse. "It was the days I spent locked in the closet that I hated the most." He glanced toward the windows, almost as if making sure they were still there. "I can't breathe in the dark."

A tear trailed down her face. How many nights had she lain in her bed, somehow convinced that she'd gotten a raw deal? She couldn't think of anything worse than having a father who was the renowned Newton Slayer.

Now she realized just how immature she'd been.

She'd been raised by people who loved and protected her. First her father. And then her foster parents.

It was a gift she'd taken for granted.

But never, ever again.

"Oh, Marty," she murmured.

"I tried to be good." Martin jerkily walked toward the stack of bikes near the end of her cot before turning to pace back toward the washer and dryer. He appeared lost in the past. Almost as if he'd forgotten she was even there. "I tried to do whatever she wanted, but it was never enough."

Annie wiped away her tears, her heart aching. "She was sick."

"No." He spun back toward her, fury vibrating in the air. "I told you . . . she was evil."

Her heart missed a beat. Dammit. She felt like she was walking through a minefield, never knowing what was going to set her brother off. "Okay," she quickly agreed.

He clenched his hands, visibly regaining command of his composure.

Then, with one of his mercurial changes of mood that she was beginning to suspect was par for the course with Martin, his expression cleared and the sweet smile returned. "The only decent thing she did in her miserable life was give me you." He moved back to the edge of the cot, gazing at her with blatant devotion. "You were a blessing that saved me."

Annie believed him.

She wasn't a psychiatrist, but she could understand how Martin would have latched onto her.

He was an abused young boy who was no doubt kept isolated from the world. He would be desperate to love and be loved.

Tentatively she returned his smile. If she could keep him focused on his happy memories with her as a baby . . . she might just survive.

"I was very lucky," she told him. "Most boys wouldn't consider a younger sister a blessing."

"You were mine to love," he said in fierce tones. He

angled his chin, the gesture oddly familiar. It was what she did when she was feeling defensive. "Mother barely remembered she had a baby, and Father was never around. I was the one who fed you and rocked you to sleep. I kept you clean and warm and safe."

She held his gaze. "You took good care of me."

He leaned down, brushing his fingers over her hair. She had a feeling it was something he'd done a lot when she was little.

"It was what I was meant to do," he said softly. "I'm your guardian angel. Which is why I had to stop her."

"Mother?" she asked, even though she already knew who he meant.

"Yes."

"I understand," she hastily assured him, hoping to keep him from shifting back into his scary mode. "I truly do, Marty. No one should have to endure what she did to you."

Despite her effort his face tightened as he abruptly straightened, his hands clenched into tight fists.

Definitely scary mode.

"I didn't care about me," he informed her, returning to his pacing. "The bitch no longer had the power to hurt me. But I couldn't bear having you tortured."

Annie made a sound of shock. "She tortured me?"

Martin sent her a puzzled glance, as if he was caught off guard by her reaction. "Of course she did," he said, his tone matter-of-fact. "First it would be a slap or a shove when you were in her way. Then she started to lock you in the closet for hours and hours." He rubbed his arms, as if suddenly feeling the chill in the air. "I couldn't bear to hear you cry."

Annie bit her bottom lip, a long-forgotten memory trying to surface against her will.

She was in the dark. Alone and terrified.

But there was a voice that she could hear over her sobbing. A low, soothing voice that helped to ease her fears.

"You talked to me," she muttered. "Through the door."

"Yes." His expression lightened. Was he pleased she could

remember? Annie wasn't. She wanted to forget the horrible memory. Along with the mother who'd do that to a little kid.

"I used to read to you," he continued. "*The Velveteen Rabbit* was your favorite."

Annie hid a grimace. That explained the book that'd been left on Rafe's porch swing.

"And the nursery rhyme you sent to me?" she asked, oddly confused that she would remember the book and not the poem. "Was it a favorite too?"

His expression tightened, his eyes wary. "No, that was my promise you wouldn't be hurt."

She gave a shake of her head. "I don't understand."

"I know."

"Martin—"

"That last day she took you into the bathroom," he interrupted, clearly unwilling to explain the significance of the poem. Probably because the meaning was only in his twisted brain. "She told me she was going to stop your crying once and for all."

It took a minute for the meaning of his words to penetrate.

Hell, she hadn't yet managed to wrap her brain around the fact her mother had locked a three-year-old child in a closet. Now Martin was telling her . . . what? That the coldhearted bitch intended to kill her?

"Oh my God."

Martin nodded at her horror, his somber expression revealing that he truly believed what he was telling her. "She was going to drown you," he said in insistent tones. "I had to stop her." A spasm of pain seemed to clench his entire body. "I had to."

Annie felt a stab of guilt.

It might be ridiculous, but she felt as if it was somehow her fault that Martin had been driven to the point of murder.

He had, after all, confessed that he'd become so inured to his mother's abuse that she no longer had the power to hurt him.

Not until she'd been born.

Then she'd become the tool to punish him even more.

Instinctively she reached out to grasp his hand. "You saved me, Martin," she assured him. "I'm alive."

He gazed down at her, his eyes oddly glazed. "But you're still in danger."

She frowned. Something was happening. Something that was making the air prickle with a dangerous tension.

"No, Marty," she murmured in soothing tones. "You saved me."

He shook his head, the flush returning to his face as he squeezed her fingers. "She's after you."

She flinched, covertly trying to pull her out of his painful grip. "Who?"

"Mother."

Mother? Oh hell. Annie's blood ran cold. She was losing him. She could almost *feel* him slipping into his madness.

But how was she supposed to stop it?

She tried the obvious.

"Martin, Mother's dead."

"No." He gave a violent shake of his head. "She's here."

Annie glanced around the basement. "In this room?"

He leaned down until they were nose to nose. "Everywhere."

The outdated kitchen was a world away from the high-tech offices Max had designed in Houston. It was cramped, the electricity was dodgy and the Internet service slower than molasses.

But while Teagan stood in front of the computers lined up on the counter, muttering his opinion of wireless service that was from the Dark Ages, and Max was struggling to hear Lucas as the phone faded in and out, they'd both been in far worse conditions.

Tough to beat a trench dug in the desert, with bullets flying just inches from your head.

Ending his connection with Lucas, Max instantly called Rafe.

"What's up?" Rafe demanded.

"Lucas is in the air," he said, his gaze locked on the large map pinned to the wall. "He should arrive in the search zone in less than fifteen minutes."

"Got it," Rafe said. "We just reached the convenience store."

From across the room, Teagan gave a sudden grunt. "I'm in."

"Hold on, Rafe," Max commanded. "Teagan's pulling up the pics from the ATM."

Max moved to stand beside his friend as Teagan clicked the mouse, fast-forwarding through the grainy video.

It took several tense minutes before Teagan stopped the search, pointing toward the black truck that was clearly visible as it drove past the ATM.

"Gotcha, bastard," Teagan growled. "He went north."

Max spoke directly into his phone. "Did you hear?"

"Yep," Rafe answered. "I'm going to concentrate my search from two miles north of the store and three miles east. That will include the Roberts farm that Annie saw in her vision."

Max grimaced, but he didn't bother to argue. Whether there was any truth in visions or not, they had to start the search somewhere.

The Roberts farm was as good a place as any until they had better data.

"I'll let Lucas know," he assured his friend before ending the connection and heading toward the map.

Once he was certain of the GPS coordinates, he sent them along to Lucas.

"That's still a lot of ground to cover," Teagan muttered as he moved to stand next to Max, lifting his finger to trace the area Rafe intended to search.

Max nodded, keeping the phone clutched in his hand.

It was that or throw it across the room.

He didn't easily show his emotion. When he'd been young

he'd been bigger and stronger than most boys his age, which meant that when he lost his temper, someone ended up hurt.

He'd learned to use his clever brain, not his fists, to settle conflicts.

Today, however, his discipline was being severely tested.

Not only because Rafe was out chasing a serial killer when he should be in a hospital bed. But because there was a clue gnawing at the edge of his mind.

He'd seen or heard or picked up something by fucking osmosis that he sensed was important.

But as hard as he tried, he couldn't put his finger on it.

And it was driving him nuts.

Trying to shake away the aggravating distraction, Max studied the map. Right now he needed his full concentration on finding Annie.

Later he would go back through the evidence they'd collected and discover what was troubling him.

"A large chunk of it is farmland," he pointed out. "That should help narrow down the search."

Teagan nodded, his large body humming with tension. Unlike Max, the younger man rarely tried to contain his emotions.

"I'll pull up the property owners in that area," Teagan said, abruptly returning to his computers. It was obvious he felt the need to keep busy. Max shared his frustration. "See if any homes are for sale or in foreclosure."

"Good idea," Max said, leaning against the table as he watched his friend tap on one of the computers, working his magic.

"Naturally," Teagan agreed without glancing away from the screens popping up on his computer.

Max gave a short laugh. Teagan never lacked for confidence.

Then slowly his smile faded, his thoughts on Rafe and his grim search for the woman he loved.

Christ, he couldn't bear the thought of what it would do to Rafe if they didn't track down Annie.

It might just destroy him.

"I hope we find her." He spoke his thoughts out loud, absently noting Teagan's shoulders tightening as he continued to work.

"No shit. No one wants another woman to be added to the Newton Slayer's tally," Teagan muttered.

"I mean for Rafe," Max said, shifting so he could watch Teagan's profile tighten. "I'm not sure he can survive if he feels he failed her."

"He's not the only one." Teagan's expression was grim. "We all let Annie down."

"I didn't think you cared," Max retorted, surprised by Teagan's response.

They all knew that Rafe had it bad. Hell, he'd obviously been a goner from the minute he'd met Annie. But Teagan had been suspicious, to say the least.

Teagan snorted. "Rafe is going to keep her, so she belongs to us."

Max crossed the small distance to stand directly beside Teagan. "I have to admit, I'm surprised."

"Why?"

"You were concerned that she was going to be bad for Rafe."

Teagan sent him a wry glance. "She's being hunted by a serial killer. What else was I supposed to think?"

Max frowned.

His friend had a point.

There was no doubt that until the Newton Slayer was captured, everyone around Annie was going to be put at risk.

"True," he murmured.

"But Rafe has made his choice," Teagan said. "And that means we support him. That's what friends do."

There was an edge in his friend's voice that made Max suspect there was more to Teagan's fierce urge to help Rafe than just friendship. "This has the feel of something very personal."

Teagan rolled his eyes. "You're a nosy bastard, you know that, Max?"

"And you're not?" Max countered.

"Not really."

Max tilted back his head to laugh. "Teagan, you've run enough computer searches on me to know that my parents are serving thirty years in jail for fraud, the number of my bank account, and the fact I just bought tickets to spend Christmas in Switzerland. Christ, you probably know the size of my damned underwear."

Teagan's lips twitched. "Okay, I'm nosy."

Max narrowed his gaze. "So tell me what's going on."

Teagan punched a key on the computer before he pushed away from the counter and moved to yank open the door of the fridge. Reaching inside, he grabbed a small bottle of orange juice. Tearing off the plastic top, he downed most of the juice in one long swallow. "Rafe doesn't half-ass his emotions," he at last said. "He has no filter for his heart."

"No shit," Max instantly agreed. Rafe was impulsive and hopelessly addicted to his gut instincts. And he had the sort of generous nature that anyone could take advantage of. "He was broke two days after he got paid because every scrounger in camp knew he was an easy touch."

"And when he decided he wanted us to stay in contact after we returned to the States, he didn't just set up a reunion in Vegas," Teagan continued. "He started a damned business."

"What's your point?"

"When he's in, he's all in." Teagan tossed the bottle toward the box that Rafe had placed next to the back door. Old Man Vargas hadn't been big on recycling. Hell, it didn't look like the old man had bothered to throw anything away, Max acknowledged with a shudder. Which meant that Rafe was still trying to separate the mess. "Especially when it comes to choosing the woman he loves."

Max held his friend's gaze. "Isn't that how love is supposed to be?"

The golden eyes darkened with a pain Max suspected had been a part of Teagan for a long time.

"Yep. And why we have to make sure that nothing, not even a damned serial killer, can tear them apart."

Well, well. Max studied his companion. The five of them might be as close as brothers, but they'd met in Afghanistan.

Which meant that despite the fact they'd faced hell together, and of course, done the sort of intrusive background checks that only men with scary security skills could run, there were still large chunks of their pasts that remained a mystery.

He couldn't remember Teagan ever mentioning a woman.

"Does she have a name?"

Teagan's face closed down, for once his expression impossible to read. "I don't know what the hell you're talking about."

Naturally it only made Max more determined to dig out the story.

"The woman who ripped out your heart?" Max clarified. "She have a name?"

"Fuck off," Teagan muttered, then headed back to his computers.

Max had a feeling his friend did that a lot. Surrounding himself in the cyberworld to avoid reality.

"At least tell me she was pretty," Max teased.

There was a long silence before Teagan sent him a dark glare. "She wasn't pretty. She was gorgeous."

Max widened his eyes. So there had been a woman.

"What happened?"

Teagan's gaze snapped back to the computer. "It's not open for discussion."

"Fair enough." Max instantly backed down.

Each of them might have done what was necessary to make sure they weren't about to go into business with someone with open warrants or a shitload of debt, but they didn't pry where they didn't belong.

Well, not unless they thought it was necessary.

Then . . . all bets were off.

Max returned to the table, pulling open the nearest journal to study the painfully precise script. It seemed unlikely that a man as smart as Martin Emerson would reveal his plans for returning to Newton, but there was always a chance Max could find some clue to his intentions.

If nothing else, he might locate a name of a friend or acquaintance who might have helped Martin after leaving the clinic.

He was reading through the news clippings when a sound from outside penetrated his concentration. With a frown he lifted his head. "Did you hear a car?"

Teagan was already headed out of the kitchen and into the living room to peer out the front window. "Shit," he muttered.

"What's going on?" Max demanded.

Teagan glanced over his shoulder, his expression grim. "Sheriff."

Shit was right.

"Stall him," Max ordered in sharp tones, rapidly collecting the journals Rafe had taken from Martin Emerson, along with the pictures that'd been snuck out of the courthouse before it'd been burned to the ground.

Sheriff Brock might be a blowhard, but he was the law in this small town.

If he learned they had evidence that should have gone directly to the authorities, there wasn't much that Max could do but hand it over.

Something he had no intention of doing until Annie was safely back in Rafe's arms.

Chapter Twenty-Three

Annie gasped as her fingers were squashed together in a grip that went well past painful to actual damage.

"Martin." She was forced to halt and clear her throat as she caught sight of the frenzied heat that smoldered in his eyes. God almighty, he was lost in his madness, completely unaware that he was crushing her hand. "Marty," she pleaded in soft tones. "You're hurting me."

Another long minute passed before Martin gave a blink, slowly returning from whatever hell had been tormenting him.

With a sound of distress he abruptly released her fingers, stepping back from the cot with a jerky movement.

"I'm sorry." He wiped a hand over his forehead, which was beaded with sweat despite the chill in the air. "Forgive me, Annabelle."

She tucked her hand into her lap, pretending it didn't throb. Martin didn't need any reason to flip out. Not when he was clearly at the very edge of his control. "It's okay."

He grimaced, lowering his hand to press against the center of his chest. Standing in a shaft of sunlight, he looked far younger than his years, and oddly vulnerable.

Annie, however, wasn't stupid enough to let her growing pity for her brother blind her to the fact he was a ruthless killer who'd murdered innocent women.

"I'm frightened," he at last breathed in a tortured voice.

"Frightened?" She shifted on the cot as she tried to ease a cramp in her lower back. How long had she been in the basement? And more importantly, how the hell was she going to get out of it? "Of what?"

"I won't be able to keep you safe."

"But I am safe," she assured him.

"No." He scowled, annoyed by her refusal to accept she was in danger. "I've seen her."

Annie licked her lips, pretending a calm she was far from feeling.

"Marty, listen to me. That's not possible." She tried to soothe him. Maybe it would be better to humor him. He clearly didn't like having her argue with him. But she didn't want him sinking any deeper into his delusions. She was never going to convince him to unlock the handcuffs and let her out of the basement as long as he thought their mother was lurking in the shadows. "She's dead."

He gave a sharp shake of his head, glancing toward the stairs. "She reaches out from her grave," he said, lowering his voice as if afraid he would be overheard. "I didn't understand until I came to see you."

"What?" She gave a shake of her head, baffled by his words. "You came to see me?"

"Yes." His expression lightened. "It was your tenth birthday."

Assuming that any visit had just been a figment of his twisted imagination, Annie froze in sudden horror.

Her tenth birthday.

That was when the killings had started.

In fact, they'd heard the news of the first missing woman just the day after her birthday.

She remembered it clearly.

Which meant . . .

None of those women would have died if it hadn't been for her.

"Oh my God." A wave of guilt crashed through her. "You came to Newton because of me."

Clearly misunderstanding her horror, Martin lifted a hand.

"I didn't intend to bother you," he hurriedly assured her. "I just wanted to see you. Maybe even pretend I was an old friend of the family so I could watch you blow out your candles." His expression was wistful, as if he was just a young man wishing to spend time with his sister. "That didn't seem so much to ask."

She battled through the darkness that threatened to overwhelm her.

Later she could sort through her feelings of responsibility for creating the Newton Slayer. For now, it was all a matter of staying alive long enough to escape.

Or for Rafe to find her.

She'd take either one.

"I don't remember you at the party." She managed to speak past the lump in her throat.

He moved back to the cot, perching on the edge. "Because I realized that you were vulnerable," he said, gently brushing a finger down her cheek. "Mother was all around you. I could sense she was preparing to hurt you."

Her skin crawled, but she forced herself not to jerk from his touch. "If Mother was there I would have known."

"No, you wouldn't." His fingers clamped on her chin, his grip just shy of painful. "She was hidden in those women."

She held herself perfectly still. She sensed any sudden movement might set him off.

"The women you . . ." Her words faltered.

What could she say?

The women you kidnapped, tied up, and murdered?

Martin didn't seem to notice. Or perhaps his sickness allowed him to twist the heinous acts he'd committed into acceptable behavior.

"They were evil. I knew as soon as I saw them," he insisted, a trickle of sweat inching down the side of his face. It was clearly an effort to maintain his composure. "So I watched and I waited, always protected by the shadows while they revealed their taint."

She shivered, wondering if he'd been hidden in the bomb shelter while she'd been playing in the yard, completely unaware she was being watched.

The mere thought was going to give her nightmares for years to come.

"Not all mothers are evil," she muttered.

His brows snapped together. "I know that."

"Then—"

"You didn't see it in their eyes, but I did." He overrode her protest, his fingers tightening on her chin.

Annie winced. "See what?"

He leaned forward, their noses almost touching. "Mother had returned and I had to stop her before she could find you."

"Oh God." She closed her eyes, unable to bear the madness twisting his features. "It wasn't Mother, Marty."

As if sensing she was on the edge of panic, Martin released her chin and surged back to his feet.

"It was. She was back," he insisted, pacing the floor as he tried to contain his seething emotions. "But I was smarter than she was. I knew exactly how to get rid of her."

Annie forced her eyes open.

It was unexpectedly difficult.

A part of her wanted to keep them closed and pretend that she wasn't handcuffed in a basement with her crazy-ass brother.

Cowardly?

Hell, yeah.

Worse, it was dangerous.

She wasn't going to escape by pretending she was lying on a warm beach with a margarita, as tempting as it might be.

"You thought you could get rid of Mother by kidnapping the women?" she instead asked.

He nodded, as if relieved she was finally listening. "It was our secret game, you see."

"Game?"

A muscle in his jaw twitched. "Mother was very angry when I flunked my English test in school," he explained. "She said I wasn't trying hard enough, even though I studied and studied."

Annie lifted her brows. From what she was discovering about her mother, she wouldn't have thought the woman gave a shit about Martin's grades.

It was a surprise he even made it to school.

"I'm sure you did the best you could," she assured him.

"No. I'm an Emerson." He abruptly stiffened his spine and squared his shoulders. Like a soldier snapping to attention. "And that means nothing less than excellence is acceptable. I failed to memorize the poem and I had to be punished."

Annie nearly missed the significance in his explanation.

It was only because she'd been so freaked out by the notes Martin had left for her that the mention of a poem triggered the connection.

"'One for Sorrow,'" she slowly said. "That was the poem."

His eyes darkened. "Yes."

"What did she do?"

"She tied me to a chair and made me recite the poem. Over and over." He halted his pacing, absently rubbing his inner arm. "Every time I got a verse wrong, she would remind me of the price of failure."

She silently warned herself that she didn't want to know what price her demented mother had forced Martin to pay. It wasn't like she could change the past, was it?

But even as the rational thought formed, her lips were already moving.

"Remind you? You mean . . ." She gave a small gasp as her gaze lowered to where he continued to rub his arm. She had a vivid memory of the small scars that dotted his inner forearm. "She burned you," she rasped. "With a cigarette."

Martin instantly dropped his hands to his side, as if he'd

given away more than he intended. "It was part of the game," he muttered.

She clenched her hands until her nails dug into her palm. God. Even if she was sick, how did a mother tie up her son and burn him with cigarettes?

It was . . . unimaginable.

"That's not a game," she breathed.

He hunched a shoulder. "It was to Mother."

A soul-deep regret ripped through Annie.

Who knew who her brother might have been if Virginia Cole Emerson hadn't been a psycho bitch? If his childhood hadn't been one of brutal torture, and he hadn't been forced to kill his own mother.

For the first time, Annie felt a flare of anger toward their father.

He might have been devoted to her, but there was no denying he'd failed his son.

Failed him completely and utterly.

Captain James Emerson had been a well-educated, extremely clever man. He should have known that his wife was unstable. And that his son was being injured.

And he should have been the one who was there to stop Annie from being drowned in the bathtub by her mother.

Instead he'd put his career ahead of his family and turned a blind eye.

"I'm so sorry," she said with genuine regret. "For everything."

He stiffened, blatantly offended by her sympathy. "I'm not," he insisted, another trickle of sweat zigzagging down the side of his face. "It made me realize I had to be smarter than her. I couldn't beat her unless I became better at her own game."

How was he sweating? The basement was freezing.

"You did, Marty," she reminded him. "You beat her."

"No, I tried, but the game was interrupted." He slammed his fist into the palm of his hand, returning to his pacing.

"This time I'll finish it and she'll be gone." He nodded as if hearing a voice in his head. "Yes. Truly gone."

Suddenly any thought of escape was lost beneath a sharp-edged fear that seared through her.

Oh God. She shuddered. He was going to continue killing women.

She had to do something to try and stop him.

"Please, Marty." She held out her hand, which still throbbed from his earlier grip. "Those women are innocent."

"They're not." Martin's breath sawed in and out of his lungs as he glared at her. "She's inside them. I can sense her."

"They—"

"No more," he interrupted with a snarl. The very air seemed to heat with the force of his annoyance. "Once she's gone we can leave here and be together. Just the two of us." With an obvious effort he fought to leash his growing agitation, leaning forward to take her hand. "You'd like that, wouldn't you, Annabelle?"

She swallowed her groan of pain as her fingers were once again squeezed together, and tried her best to force a smile to her lips.

"Yes, that's exactly what I want," she assured him, holding his wary gaze. "But let's go now. Right now."

"I . . ." He frowned, clearly tempted. "I can't."

"Of course we can," she urged. How did she convince him that he could keep her safe without sacrificing innocent women? "We'll leave Newton and go far away."

He shook his head. "She'll find us."

"No." She leaned forward, ignoring the handcuff that bit into her wrist. "We can go to my condo in Denver. She can't follow us there."

He faltered, a tragic expression of hope softening his features. "We'll be together?"

Her heart squeezed, the pain of what might have been bringing tears to her eyes.

"Just you and me."

* * *

Max had just finished shoving the journals in the oven when he heard the front door open.

"Yeah?" Teagan demanded with his usual lack of tact.

"Where's Vargas?" the sheriff demanded.

"Searching for Annie." There was a deliberate pause before Teagan delivered his jab. "Isn't that what you're supposed to be doing?"

Max didn't need to see the sheriff to know his face was getting flushed and his hands were clenched.

Teagan could piss off a saint.

"That's why I'm here," the man said between gritted teeth. "The dogs are going to need something of Annie's to get her scent."

There was an insulting pause before Teagan blew out a resigned sigh. "Fine. I'll get something."

Max grimaced, moving to pull up the screen savers on the laptops. The approaching footsteps warned him that the sheriff was going to come in and try to snoop.

From all reports, the lawman was running scared.

Maybe because he was afraid his murder of an innocent man was going to be discovered.

Or more likely, he had a healthy fear that he wouldn't keep his job once it was discovered he'd allowed the real Slayer to escape so he could return to kill again.

Either way, Max didn't intend to allow him to screw up their search for Annie.

The sheriff entered the kitchen dressed in a starched uniform and a matching hat on his round head. All very official if you didn't notice the bloodshot eyes and the smell of whiskey that clung to his breath.

It seemed a little early in the day to be hitting the bottle, but Max was far more concerned with the sheriff's suspicious glance, which took in every inch of the room.

Was he just nosy? Or was he searching for something in particular?

At last turning his attention toward the silent Max, he gave a small grunt. "This is quite an operation you've got going on."

Max shrugged, his own face devoid of expression. "We're just trying to help."

The suspicion remained as the man folded his arms over his chest, as if trying to emphasize the shiny badge pinned to his shirt. "Vargas said he went to see the boy . . . Annie's brother." He managed a fake frown of confusion. "What's his name?"

"Martin Emerson," Max said, even though they both knew that Brock had rushed back to his office to run a check on Annie's brother the minute he'd left the hospital. "I'm sure Rafe told you that he wasn't there."

"Yeah, but he must have learned something?"

"Enough to suspect that he's the Newton Slayer." Max shrugged. "And that he's kidnapped Annie."

The sheriff twitched. Just enough to reveal that beneath his good-old-boy bluster, he was edging toward a meltdown.

Clearly he wasn't one of those lawmen who rose to the occasion.

"If he didn't get to talk with the guy, then how did he leap to the conclusion that he was the killer?"

Max leaned against the wall, choosing his words with care. Sheriff Brock might be an asshat, but he had a badge. Max preferred to avoid outright lies that might lead to a messy tangle with the law. "I believe there were journals and even pictures hidden in his rooms," he hedged.

"Journals?" Brock's gaze darted toward the table, his face flushed. "Where are they?"

"Rafe said he wanted them sent to the FBI." Which was perfectly true. Max just left out the part where they were currently hidden in the oven.

Brock muttered a foul curse. "They should have been

given to me." He thumped his fist against his chest. "I'm in charge of this case."

Max cocked a brow, careful to hide his amusement. The sheriff was a common bully. He didn't cope well with people who weren't easily intimidated.

"You have no jurisdiction in Wisconsin," he smoothly pointed out. "I assume the authorities will contact you if they decide to share any info."

The man glared at Max. "What did they say?"

"I think most of it was gibberish."

"Bullshit." The sheriff growled, his face so red it was almost purple. "He found out something."

"You'll have to ask Rafe."

Brock narrowed his eyes. "If I find out that you're deliberately withholding evidence, I'll have you thrown in jail."

His threat was still hanging in the air when Teagan stepped into the kitchen. The younger man was instantly bristling with aggression as he shoved a sweatshirt into the sheriff's hand.

"Here," he growled, his golden eyes smoldering with blatant dislike. "I thought you were anxious to start your search."

Brock clutched the sweatshirt in one hand, continuing to glare at Max.

"It would be considerably easier if I hadn't been kept out of the loop," he snapped. "It makes me wonder if you're trying to hide something."

"What would we want to hide?" Max demanded, his expression giving nothing away.

He might not have Lucas's talent as a smooth talker, but he was no rookie when it came to lying.

His mother had taught him how to grift when he was barely out of diapers.

"Maybe the fact that Annie is working with her brother," the lawman blustered.

Wrong answer.

Instantly Teagan was in his face, vibrating with the urge

to smash in the sheriff's smug expression. "Not even you are stupid enough to believe that," he snarled.

"Watch it, nacho," Brock warned even as he hastily backed away.

He was a blowhard, not a complete idiot.

He had to know that Teagan could rip him into a dozen bloody pieces.

"If you intend to be a racist, then at least get it right, bubba," Teagan drawled. "I'm Polynesian, not Hispanic."

Knowing how easily things could go south, Max grabbed his friend's arm and gently tugged him away from the lawman.

"Teagan," he warned in soft tones, ensuring his friend didn't intend to go apeshit, before he returned his attention to the sheriff. "How did you find the Newton Slayer the first time?"

Brock warily turned his head to meet Max's gaze, his brow furrowed with confusion. "What?"

"You were the one to discover the women were hidden in the bomb shelter fifteen years ago," Max said. It was a question that had nagged at him since he'd read through the police report, but more importantly it provided a much-needed distraction. Teagan could be a pain in the ass, but Max didn't want to see him shot by the aggravating prick. "How?"

The man hesitated. Did he intend to ignore the question?

"Someone called in, the dispatcher didn't catch the name," he at last admitted.

"You never identified the caller?"

"No."

Max had the feeling no one tried very hard to trace the snitch.

But why not?

"Did they actually go into the bomb shelter?"

"What the fuck does it matter?"

Max wasn't sure. He only knew that there was something about the murders that continued to nag at him.

"If Martin has a pattern that was spotted by a local citizen, it might help us track him down," he said.

The sheriff thinned his lips. "Someone called nine-one-one and said there was a foul smell coming from the Whites' garage. I went to investigate. Satisfied?"

Not hardly. Max eyed the lawman.

Was he reluctant to discuss the discovery of the bodies because he'd screwed up by arresting the wrong man or because he'd done something illegal to track down the kill site?

Hard to say.

"You didn't notice anyone lurking around?"

"I don't have time for this shit," Brock snapped. "I want to know what the hell Vargas found in those journals—"

His angry words were cut short as Max's phone vibrated in his hand.

A glance revealed that it was Rafe calling.

"I have to take this," he muttered, pressing the phone to his ear. No way in hell he was putting his friend on speaker. "Yeah?"

"Is that Vargas?" Brock demanded, moving until he was nearly pressed against Max.

"The sheriff is here," he warned Vargas, even as he lifted his hand to press the intrusive bastard away from him. Christ, he didn't even like his women standing that close. Unless they happened to be naked. "Personal space, my man," he growled.

Brock refused to budge. "Where is he?"

Max scowled at the sheriff as he concentrated on Rafe's voice.

"Got it." He grudgingly passed along the information to the sheriff. For this, the idiot might actually come in handy. "He says that they found the cars belonging to the missing women."

The lawman stiffened. "Where?"

"Here."

Turning toward the wall, Max pointed toward a spot on the map that looked like an empty field. The sheriff leaned forward, studying the area surrounding the area.

There was a tense silence before the lawman at last breathed out a low hiss. "Fuck."

Max studied the chubby face that had abruptly paled. "Do you know where he is?" he demanded.

The sheriff hesitated, clearing his throat before he finally pointed toward a small dot on the other side of the field. "That's the Gilbert place."

"Do they have any buildings that could be used by Emerson to hide the women?"

Brock nodded. "They have a dairy barn they don't use any more and several empty silos. Tell Vargas I'm on my way."

Max passed along the information to Rafe while Teagan texted them to Lucas before he returned his attention to the sheriff, who was already headed out of the kitchen.

Happy to be rid of the aggravating jerk, Max grimaced when Brock halted in the doorway to flash a humorless smile.

"One more thing," he said, back in full bully mode. "Warn Vargas to keep his eyes open, but to stay in his vehicle. If I catch him anywhere near the crime scene I'll shoot his ass."

Max rolled his eyes, turning the phone on speaker as Sheriff Doofus left the house.

"Did you get that, Rafe?" he asked.

There was a string of curses before the connection was abruptly cut.

Max grimaced as he met Teagan's wry smile.

"He isn't going to wait, is he?" the younger man demanded.

"Nope." Max raised a hand to massage the tense muscles of his nape. "This has all the potential to become a cluster-fuck."

Chapter Twenty-Four

Annie's fingers ached from her brother's punishing grip and her entire body was shivering from the chill in the air, but she held his gaze.

If she couldn't escape, then she at least had to do something to get him out of Newton.

If she didn't, then he was certain to kill again.

"Please, Marty, we should go," she urged.

His expression briefly softened. Annie held her breath. Was it possible he was going to give in?

Then the glimpse of vulnerability was blanked out and the fanatical glitter returned to his eyes.

"Not yet." He dropped her hand and rose to his feet, his gaze shifting toward the stairs. "I still have things that have to be done."

A stab of panic pierced her heart.

She couldn't let him leave.

Not only because she feared he was going to kidnap another woman. But what would happen to her if he was captured or in an accident or simply decided to take off?

She could be trapped in the basement for days, maybe weeks.

The mere thought was enough to make her stomach twist with dread.

"There's no time," she said in an urgent tone.

He frowned, studying her with a mounting suspicion. "Why are you in such a hurry?"

She arranged the pillow behind her, stalling in the hope that inspiration would strike.

It didn't.

Instead she was forced to latch onto the only excuse that came to mind.

"They'll be searching for us."

Martin glanced around the basement, as if expecting a hidden intruder. "No one will find us here."

"You don't know Rafe very well," she muttered. "He has an entire team of ex-military friends who could probably locate Bigfoot if they wanted to."

A petulant scowl settled on Martin's face. "I'm not afraid of them."

"You should be," Annie insisted.

His expression hardened. He clearly disliked her faith in Rafe's skill. "You like him," he accused in dark tones.

"He's been a good friend," she hedged.

He flattened his lips, a dangerous glint of anger shimmering in the depths of his blue eyes. "Do you want to be with him?"

Annie knew better than to admit the truth.

Her brother clearly had an obsessive need to be her one and only protector.

"No, I've told you, I want us to be together," she hastily assured him, "but that won't happen if we get caught."

Martin's anger faded, but his frown remained as he considered the danger that Rafe posed to his twisted plans.

"You can send him a note," he at last decided, speaking with the confidence of a man who'd been isolated in a private clinic for years. He wasn't used to dealing with trained soldiers who didn't understand the word "quit." "You'll tell him you're with your family and that you want him to leave you alone."

She gave a disbelieving shake of her head. "That's not going to stop him."

He stilled, a scary-ass expression twisting his features. "Then I'll make him stop."

A chill inched down her spine.

Well, hell.

Her only thought had been to try and urge Martin to leave Newton. But dealing with her brother was like walking through a minefield.

Each time she thought she had found a way to coax him into doing what she wanted, he went off the rails into crazy.

And this time, it was even worse.

She'd deliberately encouraged her brother to think of Rafe and his friends as enemies who needed to be eliminated.

"No," she rasped. "You're right. I can send him a note. Once he's convinced I'm okay he'll forget about me."

Instantly his expression softened. "Don't worry, Annabelle," he murmured. "It'll only be a few more days."

Annie nodded, accepting that she had to try a new strategy.

She wouldn't dangle Rafe as a target, not even to save a helpless woman.

She just wouldn't.

But there were others she was willing to throw under the bus, she wryly acknowledged. Starting with the prick of a sheriff.

"What about the cops?" she asked.

Impatience rippled over her brother's face. "What about them?"

"They're looking for you."

He made a sound of disgust. "They're idiots."

Annie grimaced.

Hard to argue with that.

If the other police even remotely resembled Graham Brock, then they'd be lucky to find their way out of the parking lot, let alone track down a serial killer.

"Maybe," she conceded, holding his gaze. "But they're persistent. They won't stop until they've tracked you down."

"Let them look," he easily countered, far less concerned with being caught by the law than he had been by Rafe. "I'm too clever to be found."

She gave it one last try.

"You nearly got caught the last time."

His brow furrowed at the unwelcome reminder.

"I was sloppy," he groused. "And it wasn't the cops who stopped me."

Annie froze, her urgent need to leave overshadowed by an unexpected flare of curiosity.

For fifteen years she'd been tormented by the mystery of what had happened the day she'd ended up tied and gagged in the bomb shelter.

She suddenly realized that she had to know the truth.

No matter how painful it might be.

"Then who was it?"

"Father."

Annie grimaced. Since discovering that Martin was actually the Newton Slayer she'd futilely hoped their dad had never realized his only son was the one responsible for killing all those women.

It was bad enough to think that her father had been senselessly murdered. She didn't want to think that he'd gone to his grave blaming himself for Martin's killing spree.

"How did he find you?" she asked.

"I was searching for Mother." Martin moved to the fridge to pull out a bottle of water, thankfully missing Annie's shudder. His casual attitude toward stalking his victims was . . . unnerving. "And when I returned to the farm I realized I hadn't sealed the door properly."

Annie hurriedly smoothed her expression as he turned back. It was a waste of breath to try and convince her brother that their mother wasn't returning from the grave.

She suspected only professional help, along with a large dose of pharmaceuticals, was going to ease his demons.

"The door that led to the bomb shelter?" she asked.

"Yeah." He took a deep drink of water before rubbing the chilled bottle over his face, as if it was ninety degrees in the basement instead of barely above freezing. "When I came into the garage I could hear Father calling the cops on his cell phone."

"He'd seen the women?"

Martin shook his head. "Not yet, but he was telling them there was a bad smell that he wanted investigated." His brow furrowed. "I think he already suspected what was down there. And that I might be involved."

Annie gave a slow nod. At least her father had been spared the sight of the murdered females. "What did you do?"

"At first I tried to convince him of the truth." Martin's eyes were unfocused as he became lost in the past. "I thought that once he accepted that I was protecting you, then we could work together."

"He didn't agree?"

"He pretended he believed me." Martin gave a sharp, humorless laugh. "He even said he would help me, but I knew he was lying."

Annie wondered how her brother had been so perceptive.

Their father had lied to her for years and she'd never suspected that he might be anything but truthful.

Of course, she'd just been a child, she reminded herself.

All children believed their parents.

"I'm sure he only wanted what was best for you," she murmured.

"That wasn't it," Martin argued. "He just didn't want to share you with me."

Annie met his angry gaze. "I'm sure he was worried," she conceded.

Martin wasn't appeased. "He intended to hand me over to the cops." He abruptly threw the half-empty bottle of water across the basement. "His own son. It was just like the first time I protected you from Mother."

She instinctively pressed against the cement floor. Martin might claim that he wanted to protect her, but his emotions were too volatile to predict.

He could kill her before he realized what he was doing.

"He didn't let them put you in jail," Annie reminded him in gentle tones.

"That wasn't Father's decision. It was Grandmother," he argued, unaware that he'd just shaken the very foundation of Annie's world. Again. "I heard her telling the cops that she'd called the governor and if they tried to arrest me they'd lose their jobs. She said I was going to the Greenwood Estates, and Father did nothing to stop her."

"Grandmother?" Annie struggled to wrap her brain around the word. "We have a grandmother who's still alive?"

Martin lifted a brow in surprise, seemingly baffled by her question. "You haven't met her?"

"I . . ." Annie paused to gather her scattered thoughts. Her father had told her that her grandparents had all passed away before she was born. Of course she'd believed him. Why wouldn't she? And even after learning that he'd lied about virtually everything in her past, she still hadn't considered the possibility that she had other family out there. "No."

"What about Grandfather?" Martin asked.

There was a grandfather, too?

God almighty.

"No."

Martin grimaced, not bothering to hide his blatant disdain for their elderly relatives. "Lucky you."

"Grandparents," she breathed, the word unfamiliar on her tongue.

For a golden moment, all she could think about was the fact that she had a family beyond her deeply disturbed brother. And not just distant cousins or weird uncles.

No, this was far, far better.

In her mind, grandparents meant sleepovers with hot

chocolate and Sunday dinners and birthday cards with money tucked inside.

It actually took a while to recall that none of those things had happened.

In fact, they'd been complete no-shows when she'd needed them the most.

Where had they been when she was burying her father? Or when she'd been locked in a mental institution?

Even if they were too old, or in too poor health to take in a traumatized child, they should at least have rushed to Newton to stand at her side.

Unaware of how deeply she'd become lost in her thoughts, Annie nearly jumped out of her skin when Martin brushed his fingers down her cheek.

"Annie?" he murmured in worried tones.

"Sorry," she said in hoarse tones, grimly acknowledging she would have to deal with this latest betrayal when she wasn't handcuffed in a basement with her crazy brother. "Hard to believe my family could get any worse."

He straightened, something that might have been pity darkening his eyes. "They don't love you, but I do," he assured her in gentle tones.

"I know that, Marty," she said, returning to the original point of the conversation. Later she could deal with missing grandparents. Or better yet, she could forget they even existed. Clearly they weren't interested in her. Why waste a minute thinking about them? "What happened with Father?"

Martin stepped back, his expression defensive. Almost as if he was afraid she was going to be angry with him.

"I didn't want to hurt him. I swear I didn't," he said. "He may have been a shitty father, but he didn't deserve to die."

Annie believed him. "You were the one who knocked him out," she said.

"Yes." He kept his gaze lowered. "I just needed to keep him out of the way until you got home from school and we could find a new place to hide."

A shiver shook her body.

He'd been there when she'd gotten home that day?

"You waited for me?"

"Of course." His head snapped up as he studied her in puzzlement. "You don't think I would leave you there, do you?"

"You tied me up?"

"No," he denied in horrified tones. Which was a little ridiculous considering he currently had her handcuffed. "I was waiting in the house, but then the car pulled into the driveway and I had to hide."

Good Lord, how many people had been at the house that day?

And why couldn't she remember?

She gave a confused shake of her head.

"Was I there?"

"Not yet," Martin said. "The bus hadn't arrived."

She watched as her brother paced to the center of the floor, his fingers drumming against the side of his leg.

"What happened?"

"A man got out of the car and went into the garage."

"What man?"

Martin shrugged. "He was wearing a uniform."

She frowned. Her father didn't have any friends who wore uniforms. Although she supposed one of his old military buddies might have stopped by.

Then she abruptly remembered Martin's earlier words.

Her father had called 9-1-1.

"Was it a cop?"

"He was an interfering bastard," Martin muttered. "He went down to my private hideout."

"Then what?" she prompted.

"Then he went back to his car."

Yeah. Annie had seen the pictures of the bodies piled in the shelter.

If she'd been the cop, she would have been fleeing in horror.

"Did he leave?" she asked.

"No." Martin paused, and she sensed that this was the

first time in fifteen years he was allowing himself to recall the events of the day. "He pulled a woman out of the car and took her into the garage."

Annie frowned in confusion. "A woman? You mean a female cop?"

Martin shook his head. "No. I think she was his wife." His hand touched his stomach. "She was fat, like she was pregnant."

Annie shook her head. Could her brother have imagined the cop and his pregnant wife?

He was delusional, after all.

She studied his tense profile as he turned to pace back toward her cot, his movements jerky.

"Why would he take his wife into the garage?"

"I don't know." He wrinkled his nose. "She didn't seem very happy. She was screaming nasty words and trying to hit him."

"Did you follow them?"

"No, I left the house and hid myself across the road," he admitted. "I couldn't let the man see me."

The throbbing behind Annie's right eye picked up speed. Her brother had to be mistaken. No man would drag his pregnant wife into the lair of a serial killer.

"Did they go into the shelter?"

"Yes."

"And then?"

"Then she stopped screaming," Martin said with a stark simplicity.

Annie started to give a disbelieving shake of her head only to feel her muscles clench in shock as she was struck by a disturbing, utterly gruesome suspicion.

The last Slayer victim was a pregnant woman, wasn't she?

"Oh my God." She squeezed her eyes shut before forcing them back open to meet her brother's steady gaze. "Martin, do you remember how many women . . ." She faltered, not entirely sure how to say the words. "That you had to get rid of to protect me the first time you came to Newton?"

He didn't hesitate. "Six."

Her heart stopped beating. There were seven victims.

"Not seven?" she pressed. "You're certain."

His brows snapped together. "It was six."

She instantly changed tactics. She wouldn't get any answers if she pushed her brother too hard.

It was the one thing she'd learned about him. He was like an adolescent boy who shut down the second he felt threatened.

"What happened next?" she instead demanded.

Again he hesitated, trying to dredge up the memories he'd kept buried for over a decade.

"The bus came," he finally burst out, his hands clenching at his sides. "But before I could get to you, the man sneaked into the garage. He kept watching the house, and when you came out the back of the house he grabbed you before you could see him." His face twisted with a soul-deep regret. "I'm sorry. I couldn't stop him."

Annie lifted her free hand to press against her pounding head.

She'd gone out the rear of the house?

Yes. She had a fuzzy memory of walking down the back stairs. She'd been hoping to find her father in the barn.

And then darkness . . .

"He knocked me out?" she muttered.

"He must have," Martin reluctantly conceded, not wanting to admit he'd done nothing to help her. In his mind he was her most loyal guardian. "Then he carried you into the bomb shelter. I was trying to decide how to get you out when another car arrived and I had to leave."

She leaned her head back, her stomach churning with the suspicion that there was a man out there capable of murdering his pregnant wife and then blaming her father.

"He killed her, didn't he?" she whispered her dark thoughts aloud.

"Who?" Martin demanded in confusion.

"The cop who brought his wife into the shelter."

"Yes," a male voice drawled from the steps leading to the upper floor. "I'm afraid he did."

Chapter Twenty-Five

Rafe was certain he'd never been more miserable.

Not even when he'd been a prisoner in Afghanistan.

His ribs ached, his head ached, and every step felt like someone was shoving a hot poker up his spine. But it was the gnawing fear twisting his gut and squeezing his lungs that transformed discomfort to sheer hell.

After speaking with Max, Rafe and Hauk had driven straight to the Gilbert farm, parking behind an abandoned shed before heading toward the house.

There was no way in hell he was waiting for the cops to show up.

If the sheriff wanted to shoot him, fine. As long as Annie was safe.

But after spending the past quarter of an hour doing a thorough sweep of the area, he'd grudgingly returned to Hauk's SUV. From what he'd been able to discover there was nothing to indicate Emerson was using the place as his temporary home. Or even his dump spot.

Everything was recently painted, the hinges oiled, and the various farm implements carefully stored in the barns.

Tough to believe the owner would overlook a stranger creeping around his property.

"Well?" Hauk demanded as he stepped around the SUV, his gaze skimming their surroundings for any hint of danger.

Rafe covertly leaned against the bumper of the vehicle. He had no intention of revealing how close he was to complete collapse. "Nothing in the shed," he growled, his words vibrating with impatience.

Hauk grimaced. "There's nothing in the silo."

"Dammit." Rafe scrubbed a weary hand over his face. "What are we missing?"

Hauk pulled his phone out of his pocket, studying the screen with a frown. "Teagan sent me the specs on the property," he said, scrolling through the files. "There's no basement and no bomb shelter listed in the tax records."

"What about a cellar?"

"Hard to say." Hauk lifted his head with a twist of his lips. "Outside the city limits you don't need a permit to build or dig on your own property. But I don't see any electrical wires that lead away from the house."

"Shit."

Frustration exploded through him and Rafe closed his eyes, forcing himself to take a deep breath.

The only way to rescue Annie was to keep his emotions tightly leashed.

His meltdown would come later.

"Do you want me to speak with the owners?" Hauk at last broke the silence.

Releasing his breath, Rafe opened his eyes, glancing toward the ranch-style house with painted green shutters and a ceramic goose on the porch dressed in a flower print dress.

Why would a goose wear a dress?

"It's unlikely," he pointed out the obvious. "But I suppose they could be involved."

"Wait," Hauk muttered as there was a low buzz and he pressed the phone to his ear.

"What is it?" Rafe demanded.

"Lucas," Hauk said, heading around the hood of the SUV to yank open the driver side door. "He spotted a black truck."

"Where?"

"Two miles east of here."

Moving with much less grace, Rafe crawled into his seat and held on as Hauk did a U-turn and headed down the narrow road at a speed that sprayed gravel like confetti.

He didn't slow until they caught sight of the helicopter hovering over a large oak tree. Rafe's heart kicked against his ribs as he caught sight of the truck parked in the shadows.

Pulling next to the ditch, Hauk glanced toward Rafe.

Together they cautiously stepped out of the SUV, both holding their handguns as they edged toward the truck.

The helicopter pulled away, no doubt looking for somewhere to land, while Hauk circled the vehicle from the north and Rafe took the south. There was no need to speak. They'd both been trained to deal with situations with a silent efficiency.

Waiting for Hauk to give the all-clear sign that indicated there was no one hiding in the tree line, Rafe approached the vehicle, quickly determining that no one was inside.

"Damn," he growled, turning to glance toward the Gilbert house, which was easily visible across the open field. "This doesn't make sense."

Hauk took a position at the edge of the road where he could keep a lookout.

"What do you mean?" he demanded.

Rafe pointed toward the truck. "Why would he park so far from his hidden lair?"

Hauk sent him a startled glance. "Hidden lair?"

Rafe gave an impatient shrug. "Batcave?"

Hauk allowed a tight smile to touch his lips before his grimly focused expression returned. "He couldn't leave it in the driveway," he pointed out.

Rafe tried to put himself in Emerson's mind. The bastard

might be crazy, but he'd managed to remain undetected for weeks.

Which meant he was cunning enough to fly beneath the radar.

"Maybe not, but there's no way he carried the women he kidnapped two miles down an exposed road."

Hauk gave a lift of his brows. "I wouldn't call it exposed. Hell, there's nothing here but cows and corn."

Rafe wasn't deceived. Such a rural area might not have the traffic of a big city, but it wasn't completely isolated.

There were always farmers, hunters, mail carriers, and conservation officers cruising along the roads. And there would be absolutely no way to predict when someone might drive past.

"You would have to use the main road to reach the Gilberts' from here," he said. "Why wouldn't he have parked on the other side of the property where he could have remained hidden behind the barn?"

Hauk shrugged. "He might have pulled up close to his batcave and unloaded the women before moving the truck to a place that would give him a quick getaway if necessary."

It made sense. But . . .

"It doesn't feel right," he admitted with a burst of fury.

Dammit. He was wasting time, but he didn't know how the hell to speed up the process.

Hauk nodded. "I agree. Emerson isn't stupid. If he parked here, it was for a reason."

Rafe turned his attention to the tracks that led directly into the thicket of trees.

"We need to see what's on the other side of those trees."

Rafe moved forward, only to be halted when Hauk grabbed his arm. "Where are you going?"

"Up there." Rafe nodded toward the deer stand that was built in the upper branches of the nearby tree. "I should have a clear view of the area."

"Don't be an ass," Hauk growled, shoving his gun in the holster at his side. "There's no way you can climb up there."

Any other day Rafe would have argued.

He had too much testosterone to let a few bruised ribs put him on the sidelines. But today he didn't give a shit about his manly pride.

There was no way he was going to risk doing anything that might incapacitate him before they could find Annie.

Instead he kept a careful watch on their surroundings as Hauk easily climbed the tree and stepped onto the stand.

"Anything?" Rafe demanded.

"Yeah, I can see the convenience store from here."

Rafe nodded. The stand would be a perfect place to keep watch. "Anything else?"

"There's a house less than half a mile away—" Hauk's words were abruptly cut off. "Shit."

Rafe's fingers tightened on his gun. "What?"

"I just caught sight of the sheriff's car."

Rafe swore beneath his breath. He'd hoped he could find Annie before he got shoved out of the search by the prick of a lawman.

"Is it headed this way?"

"No." Hauk moved to the edge of the stand and stepped off the side, easily landing at the bottom of the tree. "It's parked at the neighbor's house. The sheriff must have gotten a tip."

What the hell?

Rafe pulled his phone from his pocket and hit speed dial.

"Teagan," he said as soon as the connection went through. "Get me a name and info on the house just south of the Gilbert farm."

Hauk moved to his side as they listened to the tapping of Teagan's computer.

"It belongs to the Hesters," Teagan at last said. "An elderly couple. Looks like they live in the house, but rent out their land to a nephew."

Which meant that they wouldn't spend much time out in the fields.

"Did you notice any buildings that Emerson could be using?" he asked Hauk.

The older man gave a shake of his head. "A few sheds and a barn. Nothing that couldn't be easily seen from the house," he said. "Impossible to know if there's anything underground."

"We don't have time for this shit," Rafe snarled, a sickening sense of urgency thundering through him. Annie needed him. He could *feel* her growing terror. He spoke directly into the phone. "Do you have anything else?"

There was no tapping. "Not that . . . Christ."

Rafe stiffened. There was no mistaking that tone.

Teagan had found something.

"What is it?" he demanded.

"The owners of the house have their mail being forwarded to a condo in Arizona."

Teagan had barely finished speaking when Rafe was limping back to the truck and pulling open the door. "Let's go," he commanded.

Hauk didn't hesitate as he started the engine and headed the SUV directly through the trees.

"Hold on," he warned.

Screwing any hope of stealth mode, Hauk gunned the engine, nearly sending them airborne when they hit a shallow ditch.

"Damn, Hauk," Rafe ground out between clenched teeth, his hands on the dashboard to keep him from being catapulted through the front windshield. "I hope you bought insurance when you rented this thing."

Aiming for the detached garage, Hauk screeched to a halt behind it. The position gave them a full view of the house as well as the nearby barn.

Rafe shook his head, once again struck by the bucolic peace of their surroundings.

This was a place you planted a garden and went fishing with a stick pole.

It was just wrong to think there was a serial killer lurking in the shadows.

"Stay here," Rafe ordered, shoving open his door.

Hauk sent him a frown of disbelief. "No fucking way."

He slid out of the truck and sent his friend an impatient glare. "Look, I don't think the sheriff was kidding about shooting us if we try to interfere."

Hauk matched him glare for glare. "Then we wait here for the bastard to do his job."

Rafe shook his head, holding up his gun to make certain the safety was off. "You know I can't do that." Rafe's voice warned he wasn't going to argue. "Besides, we don't know if Emerson is in the house. We need eyes out here to make sure he can't escape while my back is turned." He slammed the door shut, only to lean through the open window. "And call Max and let him know what's going on. And tell him to get my bail money ready. I have a feeling I'm going to need it."

Teagan paced the cracked linoleum floor, his gaze locked on Max as he finished his call with Hauk.

Christ, he hated this waiting.

Especially when he wasn't in the position to provide electronic backup.

"Well?" he demanded as soon as Max shoved his phone back into his pocket.

"They're headed to the Hester house," Max said, clearly no happier than Teagan at being left to twiddle their damn thumbs while their friends were in danger. "Hauk asked me to get Rafe's bail money ready."

Teagan's lips twisted into a humorless smile. "I don't mind hauling his ass out of jail, as long as he doesn't have a bullet in it."

"True." Max nodded, but it was obvious he was distracted.

Teagan planted his hands on his hips and studied his friend. "What's on your mind?"

Max turned to study the map. Looking for answers? Or inspiration?

"If the sheriff believed that Emerson was holding Annie at the Gilbert farm, why did he stop at the neighbors'?"

Teagan walked the short distance to join his friend, instinctively sorting through the various possibilities. He'd learned to look for angles when he'd been young and trying to survive on the street.

It was a talent that'd kept him alive.

"Maybe someone called in a tip," he suggested. "Or he spotted something suspicious."

Max shrugged. "I have a feeling."

"A feeling?" Teagan gave a bark of laughter. It was a running joke that Max used scientific equations in place of emotions. "You?"

"I think the sheriff knew the Hesters were out of town," Max said slowly, speaking his thoughts out loud. "People who leave for months at a time ask the local police to keep an eye on their house."

Teagan nodded. His friend was right. "And?" he prompted.

"And I think he deliberately led Rafe and Hauk on a wild-goose chase."

A chill of foreboding raced through Teagan. "It could be nothing more than a way to keep them away from the action," he muttered, trying not to jump to conclusions. "If the sheriff manages to capture the Newton Slayer, it might make up for having arrested the wrong man fifteen years ago."

"It could be," Max muttered, turning his head.

Their gazes locked, both thinking the same thing.

"Or it could be something we're missing." Teagan spoke their concern out loud.

"Exactly."

Max walked to pull the journals out of the oven where he'd hidden them during the sheriff's unexpected visit, and dumped them on the table. The impact was enough to jiggle a stack of files, and Teagan instinctively reached out to steady them.

He managed to keep the files off the floor, but a dozen black-and-white pictures slid out of the top folder to land on the table.

Teagan frowned, reaching to grab the grisly photos of the bomb shelter. "These are the pictures that were taken out of the courthouse before it burned, aren't they?" he muttered, his stomach twisting as he studied the pile of women in the corner of the room.

It was obscene.

Wrong on a deep, fundamental level.

Max flicked a brief glance toward the photos in Teagan's hands before returning his attention to the journals. "Yeah."

Shuffling through the pictures, Teagan was about to shove them back into the file when his attention was captured by the woman who was separated from the others.

He hesitated, his brows snapping together at the blatant clue he'd overlooked.

What the hell was wrong with him?

"Christ," he muttered.

Max snapped his attention back to Teagan, no doubt sensing his sudden tension. "What do you see?" he asked.

"Where are the pictures of his victims before they were killed?" Teagan demanded, pointing toward the journals.

Max obediently flipped through the pages of the bottom journal to pull out the pictures of the women who were tied and gagged in a wooden chair.

He handed them over with a frown. "What are you looking for?"

Teagan spread the pictures over the table, grimly ignoring the expressions on the women's faces that varied from terror to heart-wrenching resignation. "The women are all naked."

Max grimaced. "And?"

Teagan reached for the crime scene photo that had been destined to be burned.

He pointed toward the woman who was lying a few feet from the rest of the victims.

The photo was aged, but it was easy to see the female was

wearing a loose denim dress that was popular with pregnant women. "And this one isn't."

"She was the final victim," Max said with a shrug. "He was in a hurry."

"No." Teagan pointed toward the pictures that Emerson had taken of the women, the tip of his finger lingering on a shallow bowl of water and towel that'd been left by each of the chairs. "He stripped and washed them before he killed them," he said. "It was a ritual he wouldn't have skipped. Not for any reason."

"Fuck." Max stepped away from the table, his face white. "She was the sheriff's wife."

Teagan's thoughts had veered in the same direction. "She was still warm when the deputy arrived, right?" he growled.

"Call Rafe," Max snapped, already pulling out his own phone to speed-dial Hauk.

Teagan returned to his pacing, a bad feeling lodged in the pit of his stomach. "He isn't picking up," he growled as the call went straight to voice mail.

"Hauk," Max spoke into his phone, clearly having more luck. "The sheriff's not there to arrest Emerson. He's intending to execute him," he said, not giving the other man a chance to interrupt. "Get Rafe the hell out of there."

Chapter Twenty-Six

Annie watched the sheriff with a numbed sense of disbelief.

A part of her understood she was in shock. Otherwise she would be screaming at the top of her lungs.

Instead she watched in silence as the lawman warily moved down another few steps, his eyes darting around the basement as if afraid there might be someone hidden behind the jars of pickles.

He was wearing his uniform, and in his hands he had a pistol that was pointed directly at Martin.

"That's the man," her brother muttered, heading to stand next to the cot.

"Don't move," the sheriff growled, halting halfway down the steps.

She gave a slow shake of her head.

Distantly she was aware of a bone-deep fear racing through her, and a primal urge to survive. But within her bubble there was nothing but horror at the growing acceptance this man had committed cold-blooded murder.

"You're supposed to protect people," she rasped. "Instead, you killed an innocent woman."

The round face twisted with a sneer that was blatantly absent of any guilt. "It was my wife," he drawled. "And she was far from innocent."

Annie shuddered, feeling as if the entire world had gone mad. "Oh my God."

Brock leaned to the side, keeping the gun trained on Martin as he glanced over the railing, trying to see behind the stairs.

"It wasn't intentional," Brock said. Then, returning his gaze to Annie, he gave a small shrug. "Or more precisely, it wasn't premeditated."

She tried to swallow the lump in her throat. "Then why?"

He moved down two more steps. "I discovered she'd been banging the local football coach and that she'd told one of her girlfriends that the baby wasn't even mine. Bitch." His eyes narrowed as Martin shuffled his feet. "I told you not to move."

Martin hunched his shoulders, his face twisted with anger. "You're a bad man."

"Not bad," Annie muttered. "Obscene."

The sheriff shrugged. "I did what anyone would do."

Did he really believe that?

It seemed excessive, but there were men who were so shallow that nothing was more important than their inflated ego.

Graham Brock seemed like that kind of man.

"Cheating doesn't deserve a death sentence," she stated in grim tones.

"Like I said, it wasn't planned."

She studied his pudgy face. There truly wasn't the smallest hint of remorse. "Are you trying to say it was an accident?"

"In a manner of speaking." He took another step, swaying slightly, as if he was having trouble with his balance. Had he been drinking? "I told her that morning to pack a bag and get into the car. I intended to drop her off at her loser boyfriend's house," he continued. "Then I got a call to swing by the White farm and check out a suspicious smell in the garage. It was on my way and I didn't want to have to drive back, so I stopped." He gave a short laugh that echoed eerily through the basement, his gaze shifting to Martin. "I had no idea what I would find in that shelter. You truly are a demented freak."

Martin scowled. "I was protecting my sister."

The sheriff's lips twisted. "I wish I'd known that you were responsible at the time," he said. "I saw Don White passed out on the bed and I assumed he was the Slayer. It was too good an opportunity to miss."

"Opportunity?" A horrified breath was wrenched from her throat.

You had to be an amoral SOB to be able to stumble across six dead women and consider it your lucky day.

"I'm not stupid," he insisted, taking another step as he glanced toward the stack of bikes. He was dangerously twitchy. One sudden movement and he was going to start shooting. Annie didn't like her chance of survival, or her brother's. "My wife was not only a slut, but she was the daughter of a shyster lawyer," Brock continued, the words falling off his tongue with ease. Obviously he'd spent a lot of time convincing himself that his wife deserved to die. "There was no doubt she was going to try and take me for every penny she could get her grubby little hands on."

Annie gave a slow shake of her head, feeling the urge to puke. "You're crazy."

"No, your brother is the whack job. I'm just a man who sees the potential to get rid of a problem."

Martin took a step forward, his hands clenched into tight fists. "Don't call me that."

"Martin, don't," she hissed, trying to keep him from provoking the sheriff. Her brother clearly needed to be locked away from society, but she was terrified he might be shot. "Your wife was a human being, not a problem," she said in loud tones, drawing Brock's attention back to her.

The man curled his lips with disgust. "She was trash."

Annie sucked in a sharp breath, abruptly realizing that this man must have been the one who'd dragged her down to the shelter and tied her up. "Did you intend to kill me?"

His brows snapped together, as if he was offended by her question. "Of course not. I don't kill children," he growled, his face flushing. "I only meant to keep you out of the way so I could finish arranging the crime scene and kill your father." His gaze swept toward the washer and dryer before he took another step down. "But I'd barely gotten started when my deputy came down the stairs. I had to pretend I was in the act of releasing you."

Annie tried to sort through her memories, but she couldn't pull up anything beyond a sensation of darkness. And fear.

The same fear that pulsed through her now.

Clearly, her young brain had blanked it out in an effort to maintain her sanity.

That was fine with her.

She didn't want the memory now that she knew what'd happened.

"Then you waited until you had my father in your jail and you murdered him," she accused with unconcealed revulsion.

His expression settled into defensive lines. Almost as if he had a smidgeon of remorse for killing an innocent man who was locked in his cell. "I still assumed he was the Slayer," he muttered. "I couldn't let him talk to a lawyer. Or worse, the FBI. If he confessed to six of the murders, they'd start to question the death of my wife—"

"Your pregnant wife." She couldn't stop herself from reminding him.

Just seconds ago the sheriff had claimed he didn't hurt children.

Bastard.

He shrugged aside her words, reaching the bottom of the steps. "It was a risk I wasn't willing to take."

Annie wrinkled her nose as the sheriff stepped into a pool of sunlight that revealed his pasty skin and bloodshot eyes. Lord, he reeked of whiskey.

The realization only added to the potential for disaster.

"So what do you intend to do now?"

A creepy facsimile of a smile twisted his lips. "Obviously I'm here to save you." Keeping the pistol pointed toward Martin, he reached behind his back to pull out a large butcher knife. "A shame your brother already slit your throat."

Martin made a sound of indignation. "I would never hurt Annabelle," he snapped, incapable of realizing that the sheriff was explaining how he intended to get away with murder.

Brock ignored the interruption. "Then, of course, I would have to shoot the crazed killer who was trying to attack me," he concluded.

The protective bubble that'd allowed Annie to maintain a false sense of composure abruptly burst.

Agonizing fear brought her to her knees, her handcuff rattling against the pipe.

The man wasn't stupid. He had to realize that the chances of getting by with a double homicide were slim to none.

But at the moment his brain was clouded with panic and alcohol. It was a toxic combination that was quite likely going to get her dead.

Perfect.

"You can't," she pleaded.

"Of course I can. I'll be a hero." The sickly smile was still pasted to his face as he headed toward the cot, the knife clutched in his hand. "If you don't fight, it will be over before you know it."

Concentrating on Annie, the sheriff seemed unaware that Martin was watching him with an increasingly desperate expression.

"No," her brother breathed, his hands lifting as he launched himself at the sheriff.

"Martin, stop," Annie cried out, desperately trying to grab his jacket as he leaped past her.

It was useless.

Even as the tips of her fingers brushed the jersey material, there was a deafening explosion as Brock squeezed the trigger of the pistol.

Annie felt a blast of hot air as the bullet skimmed past her and hit her brother in the center of his chest.

She was held immobilized with shock, her brain shutting down as she watched her brother stagger back a step. Then, as Martin looked down in confusion, a round stain of blood began to spread over the front of his jacket.

"Marty," she gasped, a wrenching sense of loss stabbing through her as she watched Martin tumble to the floor. "You shot him." She stretched her arm over the edge of the cot, unwilling to accept what she'd just witnessed. No matter what her brother had done, she couldn't bear to watch him die. "You . . . bastard."

"He didn't leave me any choice," the sheriff muttered.

Her brother made a gurgling sound, his eyes sliding shut as his head rolled to the side.

Oh . . . God.

He was gone.

She didn't need to feel for a pulse to know.

She could sense it in the hollow depths of her heart.

"You're worse than my brother," she rasped, turning back to glare at the man who had shot him down like an animal. "Martin was sick. He couldn't see what he was doing was wrong. But you." Her voice was thick with loathing. "You're evil."

Brock swung toward her, the bloodshot eyes narrowing in accusation. "This is your fault," he muttered.

Her breath sawed in and out of her lungs as her mouth dropped open in disbelief.

Was the bastard serious?

"Mine?"

"You should never have come back to Newton."

He stepped toward the cot, the knife still clutched in his hand.

Annie instinctively scuttled to the end of the cot, a pain shooting up her arm as the attached handcuff brought her to a sharp halt.

Dammit. She was trapped.

Ironic really, considering that her brother had locked her in this basement with the sole intent of keeping her safe.

The sheriff took another step forward, then they both froze at the unmistakable sound of approaching footsteps.

"Annie?" a mercifully familiar voice echoed down the stairs.

Deep, profound relief raced through her.

Rafe.

He'd found her.

She didn't know how, and right now she didn't care.

All that mattered was that he was only a few feet away.

"I'm down here," she screamed. "The sheriff is trying to kill me."

"Fuck," Brock growled, moving with surprising speed to the end of the cot. Then, tossing aside the knife, he slapped his hand over her mouth. "You just signed his death warrant, bitch."

Annie frantically reached up to try to pull his hand from her mouth, her eyes wide as she watched Brock aim his gun toward the stairs.

Stupid. She'd been so stupid.

How could she not have realized that calling out like that would lead Rafe straight into a trap?

Pressed painfully against the wall, she found it impossible to shove aside his hand. Worse, he'd turned his body enough that there was no way to reach his gun.

Rafe was going to be a sitting duck.

It was raw desperation that had her lifting her foot, preparing to try and kick the man before he could squeeze the trigger. At the last second, however, she altered the path of her foot, hitting the stack of bikes leaning against the wall.

She'd hoped to make enough noise to startle Brock and disrupt his shot. But what she hadn't expected was that the bikes would go over like dominoes, quickly picking up steam until they crashed into the nearby shelves.

Jars of pickles, beets, and green beans shattered, while a half dozen paint cans rolled off the top shelf to bounce against the cement floor.

It was loud.

Shockingly loud.

But even as she caught sight of Rafe diving off the edge of the stairs, Brock tightened his finger on the trigger and emptied the remaining bullets in the clip in Rafe's direction.

If Rafe had been thinking clearly he would never have charged into the basement like a maniac.

But he wasn't thinking clearly.

In fact, his brain had shut down the very second he'd heard the gunshot echo through the house. And then he'd heard Annie's frantic cry . . .

Suddenly nothing mattered but getting to her.

Which was why he'd nearly gotten his damned head blown off.

If it hadn't been for the sound of shattering glass he would never have taken the dive over the handrail just as a shot was fired in his direction.

As it was, he'd been grazed on the shoulder by the first bullet. Nothing more than a flesh wound, but it still pissed him off as he crouched behind the washer and sucked in a steadying breath.

At the same time, he felt a continuous buzz in his pocket that indicated someone was desperately trying to contact him.

Holy . . . fuck.

He pulled out his phone, but didn't bother to answer the persistent calls. He couldn't afford to be distracted.

Instead he hit a button on the screen and dropped the phone to the ground as he peered around the edge of the washer. He frowned at the sight of a man lying on the floor who he assumed was Emerson.

A frown that deepened as he watched the sheriff lean over Annie, who was handcuffed to the wall.

First the lawman had shot at him, and now this.

What the hell was going on?

"Step out where I can see you, Vargas," the sheriff ordered.

"Rafe, don't listen to him," Annie abruptly called out. "He killed his wife and blamed it on the Newton Slayer."

The sheriff made a sound of frustration. "Shut up, bitch."

Rafe grimaced. Brock murdered his own wife?

Shit.

So that was why the bastard had sent him on a wild-goose chase to the Gilbert farm earlier. He must have suspected this was where Martin had taken Annie and hoped to sneak here and kill them both before his sins could come back to haunt him.

"Don't do anything stupid, Brock," he called out, stalling for time.

He didn't doubt for a second that Teagan had contacted Hauk.

The sniper would already be getting in position to take a shot.

The sheriff gave a humorless laugh, his gun thankfully pointed in Rafe's direction, although he'd forced Annie to her knees on the cot and was using her as a shield.

Cowardly ass.

"I think we both know it's too late for that," the man muttered.

"It's never too late," Rafe countered. If the man thought Rafe intended to let him walk away, he might lower his guard. "I don't give a shit what you did to your wife. It was fifteen years ago."

"Yeah." The sheriff's gaze darted toward the dead man on the floor, his pudgy face drenched in sweat. "Do you really think I'm that stupid? There's no way you're going to keep your mouth shut."

"I'm willing to trade my silence for Annie," Rafe promised.

"Just drop your gun and we can discuss this situation like grown men."

"I don't think so."

"Look, if we tell the authorities you killed Martin in self-defense, there won't be any reason to bring up the past," he said in soothing tones. "No harm, no foul. Do we have a deal?"

"Fuck that," Brock growled. "What's going to happen is that you're going to throw me your gun and step out so I can see you."

The man was on the edge of panic.

Any second he was going to do something desperate.

Rafe's gaze made a sweep of the basement, trying to think like a sniper.

Where would he set up for a shot?

He glanced toward the stairs before giving a quick shake of his head. There was no way for Hauk to get into position without revealing his presence. He shifted his attention to the small window just behind him. It gave a view of the basement, but the air conditioner unit blocked half the window.

Which left the window just above the cot.

It faced the side of the house that was shaded from the sun, so no shadows to alert that someone was approaching. A clear view of the basement. Level ground.

Perfect.

The only problem was getting Brock far enough away from Annie for Hauk to get a clear shot.

"I have a better idea," Rafe said, his mind racing with possibilities of how to lure Brock toward the center of the room. "We both lower our guns and—"

"Do you think I won't kill her?" Brock interrupted with a snarl, abruptly turning the gun toward Annie.

Rafe's heart slammed against his ribs, his gaze locked on Annie's pale, grimly resolute face.

She was terrified. Even from across the basement he could see her entire body trembling. But it was obvious she wasn't going to go down without a fight.

Christ. He had to keep her from doing something crazy.

"Shit, Brock," he rasped, his gaze still locked on Annie as he willed her to trust him. "Settle down. If you'll just listen, we're going to get out of this without anyone getting hurt."

A beat passed before she gave the smallest nod, understanding the words had been meant for her.

The sheriff, on the other hand, was becoming increasingly agitated. "I'm going to count to three," Brock snapped, the edge in his voice warning he wasn't screwing around. "One. Two."

Without hesitation, Rafe leaned to the side and slid his gun across the cement floor. "Here."

"Now put your hands above your head and come out," the sheriff ordered.

Holding Annie's worried gaze, Rafe slowly rose to his feet, his hands shoved above his head as he stepped from behind the washer. "Fine."

Instinctively Brock aimed his gun back in Rafe's direction, clearly prepared for any sudden movement. The lawman was unaware that he was doing exactly what Rafe needed him to do.

"Turn around so I can see you don't have another weapon," Brock commanded.

Rafe willingly complied, turning in a slow circle with his hands over his head.

He had a small pistol strapped around his ankle that the sheriff couldn't see, but he was hoping he wasn't going to need it.

"Satisfied?" he demanded as he completed his circle and faced the sheriff, who looked like shit.

Brock's face was flushed and streaked with sweat, his eyes bloodshot. But his hand holding the gun was steady, and his jaw clenched with stubborn resolve.

He was like a cornered badger, ready to kill anything that threatened him.

"Not hardly," the sheriff growled. "Who's outside?"

Rafe didn't even consider lying. Brock would never believe he'd traveled here by himself. Besides, he wanted to keep the bastard distracted until he could make his move.

Whatever the hell that was going to be.

"Hauk. Lucas is keeping an eye from the air," he said with a shrug. "There's no way you're getting out of here."

A muscle twitched beside the sheriff's eye, as if he knew escape was a long shot. But still he wasn't ready to concede defeat. "I will if you call to tell them to back the hell off," he snarled.

"Why would I do that?"

Brock's face twisted with an unexpected flare of fury. "Because I'm going to shoot your bitch in the head if you don't tell them to go," he warned, waving the gun around like a madman.

Rafe sucked in a sharp breath. Shit. The man wasn't only desperate, he was dangerously unstable.

He had to get him away from Annie.

Now.

"Let Annie go and I'll make the call," he swore.

The bloodshot eyes squinted. "Do I have 'stupid' tattooed on my forehead? The bitch goes with me."

Rafe shook his head. "How far do you think you'll get?"

"Far enough." On the point of yanking Annie off the cot, Brock seemed to belatedly recall the fact that she was chained to the wall. "Shit. I need the key to the handcuffs." He pointed his gun at Rafe. "Check the stiff."

"You bastard," Annie abruptly hissed, her gaze resting on her brother, who was stretched on the ground.

Brock gave her a vicious shake. "You should tell her to shut up, Vargas," he rasped, spittle forming at the edge of his mouth. He was a man on the edge. "Maybe she'll listen to you."

Rafe held Annie's gaze as he moved to kneel beside Emerson's dead body, silently urging her to hang on for just a few more minutes. "It's okay, sweetheart."

"I'd be doing you a favor to get rid of her. Women aren't worth the trouble," Brock muttered, turning his head to glare at Annie.

Rafe swiftly took advantage of the man's distraction to glance through the window. It took less than a second to catch the sight of the rifle barrel peeking through a nearby bush.

Hauk.

Knowing his friend would be watching him through the scope, he used one hand to reach into the front pocket of Emerson's jacket, easily finding the key. He remained kneeling, however, long enough to shut and open his other hand four times.

Twenty seconds.

Hauk would know what he meant.

"I've got it," he said, straightening with one fluid movement.

He held the key up in his fingers while he did a silent countdown.

Seventeen, sixteen, fifteen . . .

"Toss it here."

"Release Annie," he insisted.

Ten, nine, eight . . .

"No way in hell," Brock snapped. "I'm not playing. Throw me the key."

Five, four, three . . .

"Fine."

Tossing the key in a high arch, Rafe waited until Brock leaned forward to catch it before he lunged forward.

Instinctively assuming that Rafe was coming for him, the sheriff dodged to the side. Rafe, however, angled to the side, tackling Annie backward.

He landed on top of her, the force of his weight collapsing the cot even as there was the sound of shattering glass, followed by a sickening thud.

Rafe didn't need to look to know that Hauk's bullet had

gone through the window and caught Brock in the back of his head.

Hauk didn't miss his target.

Not ever.

"Shh," he instead softly murmured, wrapping Annie tightly in his arms. "It's over, sweetheart. It's all over."

Epilogue

The next three weeks passed in a blur for Annie.

After carrying her out of the basement, Rafe had driven her straight to the police station, where the FBI had been waiting to take her statement. They'd already located the bodies of the three women her brother had stored in a large freezer in the garage. And Rafe had been clever enough to hit record on his phone, so the sheriff's threats had been captured.

It'd taken hours, but at last Rafe had bundled her back to his grandfather's house and she'd collapsed in his bed, wrapped tightly in his arms.

The next few days had been consumed with police interviews and dealing with her brother's affairs, which included a cremation and a very private funeral. They'd also finished cleaning out the small house so Rafe could hand over the keys to the Realtor.

Thankfully, Rafe had stood staunchly at her side.

Perhaps it'd been stupid, but she hadn't been able to shake the fear that once the danger had passed, he would lose interest in her.

But his steadfast devotion had never wavered. And certainly his desire had remained . . . avid, to say the least.

And more surprisingly, his friends had adopted her into

their small group, offering her the same fierce loyalty that they gave to Rafe.

The first morning when they'd awoken to discover the yard filled with yammering reporters and TV cameras, it'd taken Teagan and Hauk less than a quarter of an hour to get them cleared away. And when Annie had to make her appearances in front of the various officials who were investigating the Newton murders, they'd surrounded her with a wall of silent protection.

No one was allowed to approach her without their say-so, including her grandparents, who'd reached out after seeing a picture of her in the company of Lucas St. Clair. Rafe's friend seemingly had powerful connections that had impressed her grandparents.

Annie would decide later if she wanted to meet the elderly couple who'd willingly turned their backs on her.

Instead she'd focused on completing her unpleasant duties with a brisk efficiency, allowing Rafe to help her when she needed him, but making her own decisions.

She felt a growing confidence that came not only from knowing that the nightmare was over, but also from opening her heart to the man she loved.

The past was done, and for the first time in her life she looked forward to the future.

Once the most pressing obligations had been accomplished, Rafe had accompanied her to her condo in Denver to pack her belongings, and then they'd made a quick trip to her foster parents' home.

She'd expected their need to fuss and fume over her. She'd even managed to bite her tongue as they'd smothered her with kisses even as they'd called her all kinds of fool.

It was how they showed their deep relief that she was okay.

But she hadn't expected their open welcome of Rafe. They'd treated him like a long-lost son. And amazingly, their delight in him hadn't diminished even after he'd informed them he intended to whisk her away to Texas.

Hell, they'd already started planning the wedding.

Giving a shake of her head, Annie pulled her thoughts back to the present as Rafe slowed the truck and turned onto the drive that led to his ranch just an hour west of Houston.

Her heart gave a small leap at the long, wooden house with a covered porch, and nearby stables where she could see a dozen horses in the attached paddock.

Behind the homestead were wide, open plains with a few rolling hills that filled her heart with joy.

"Rafe," she breathed, completely enchanted.

"What do you think?" He pulled the truck to a halt in front of the house and turned off the engine before sending her a wary glance. "I warned you that it was still rough."

She smiled, indifferent to the lack of paint on the house, and the barn that was clearly one stiff breeze away from complete collapse. "It's perfect."

He reached to cup her cheek with his hand. "Are you sure?"

"Positive," she assured him softly.

His eyes darkened with a familiar heat, but even as his head lowered, his gaze shifted toward the porch, where over a dozen people had suddenly appeared.

Obviously the visitors had parked their vehicles behind the house to surprise them.

"Shit," he muttered, a wry smile curving his lips. "It looks like the welcoming committee has beat us here."

Giving her a swift kiss, Rafe exited the truck and was instantly surrounded by his friends. Annie hesitated.

Not because she feared she was unwanted, but simply to savor the sensation of being a part of something so special.

It was Teagan who came to help her out of the truck, shoving an ice-cold beer in her hand as he leaned down to press a light kiss to her cheek. "Welcome to the family," he said softly, dodging Rafe's fake punch as he strolled back to the group.

"Family," she murmured in wonderment, leaning against Rafe as he wrapped an arm around her shoulders.

"Yeah, family," he said. "Is that okay?"

Her heart swelled with a happiness she never dreamed was possible.

Not for her.

"It's more than okay." She wrapped her arm around his waist, smiling as she watched Max and Lucas arguing over who should be in charge of the grill they were in the process of firing up. "It's home."

"Yeah, it's home."

She knew that beneath jokes and lighthearted teasing, they were all worried that Hauk was being stalked by evil.

And they had a business that was just getting off the ground.

But for tonight, they were all together. And that was enough.

Arm in arm, Rafe and Annie walked onto the porch.

Blessed and cursed by their hidden abilities,
the Sentinels have no choice but to live, and love,
on the edge of humanity . . .

The Sentinel assassin, Bas, is facing the greatest challenge of his outcast existence. His young daughter, Molly, has been kidnapped. But her disappearance has brought the return of her mother, Myst, whom Bas has never forgotten—or forgiven.

Haunted by a vision that she's destined to create a weapon that will destroy thousands, Myst was never impulsive—until she met the irresistibly handsome Bas. But with the Brotherhood, the enemy of the high-bloods, hunting for her, Myst had to stay on the run, to keep her child, and the world, safe. Now, with the most important thing in both their lives at stake, she and Bas must embark on a treacherous journey to save Molly, to confront the truth of Myst's fate—and to face their fierce desire for one another.

Please turn the page for an exciting sneak peek of

BLOOD LUST,

the next exciting installment of Alexandra Ivy's
SENTINELS series!

**Coming in June 2016
wherever print and eBooks are sold!**

Prologue

It had been over a century since the high-bloods revealed themselves to the norms.

In that time they'd established Valhalla, the main compound for the high-bloods, and built it smack-dab in the middle of the United States, as well as several satellite compounds around the world.

It was a way to try and convince the mortals that the witches, healers, psychics, necromancers, telepaths, and clairvoyants were just like them . . . only with special powers.

And that the monk-trained warriors called the Sentinels could be trusted to maintain order among the high-bloods.

What they didn't bother to share was that there were several high-bloods with rare, sometimes dangerous powers who were kept hidden from sight. And that while the guardian Sentinels—who were covered in intricate tattoos to protect them against magic—and the hunter Sentinels—who remained unmarked to be able to travel among the people unnoticed—had been revealed along with the other high-bloods, there was another sect of warriors . . . the assassins.

The faction of ruthless killers had been disbanded years ago, but a few had managed to survive.

And a rare few had managed to prosper.

Chapter One

Bas had retreated to his penthouse suite in the luxury Kansas City hotel after fleeing from the clusterfuck that recently destroyed his highly profitable business.

Not that he gave a shit about the money.

He had enough wealth stashed in various properties around the world to last him several lifetimes.

And he gave even less a shit about ending his role as the leader of a renegade band of mercenary high-bloods who defied the laws of Valhalla to sell their various talents for an indecent price.

It'd been fun, not to mention highly profitable, to create his merry band of misfits, but he'd made more than his fair share of enemies over the years. A fact that had come back to bite him in the ass when a former employee had kidnapped his precious daughter and used her as leverage to try and gain control over a volatile high-blood who could have started Armageddon.

Now all he wanted to do was find someplace safe to raise Molly.

He could, of course, have gone underground. Keeping a low profile was easy for a man who had his talent for altering his appearance. But he wasn't going to drag Molly from one seedy location to another.

She needed love and peace and stability in her young life.

Things he fully intended to give her. Once he figured out how to avoid being arrested and thrown into the dungeons of Valhalla.

He was in the process of plotting his future when he heard the pitter-patter of tiny feet.

He turned to watch Molly enter the salon, her stuffed hippo, Daisy, clutched in her arms.

Joy pierced his heart as he studied his daughter's sleep-flushed face surrounded by her silvery curls. Christ, he still got up a dozen times a night to make sure she was safely tucked in her bed. Molly, on the other hand, barely seemed to remember her time as the witch's captive. Thank God.

"What are you doing out of bed? Did you have a bad dream?"

She flashed a smile that could light up the world. "Mama called me."

Bas swallowed a curse. Molly often spoke about Myst, almost as if she was a constant companion instead of the woman who'd given birth to her and then promptly disappeared.

"Called you?" He gave a teasing tug on a silvery curl. "On the phone?"

She giggled, the dimple he loved appearing beside her mouth. "No, silly. In my head."

"It was a dream," he gently assured her.

Her bronze eyes that perfectly matched his own widened. "No. It was real."

"Molly."

"She talks to me all the time."

Bas bit his tongue. He couldn't tell his daughter that five years ago he'd had a one-night stand . . . no, it hadn't even been that.

Myst had come into his office, desperate for a job. She'd

claimed to be a clairvoyant, but she hadn't been capable of providing even one reading of the future.

He hadn't had much choice but to tell her that he didn't have a place for her on his payroll.

Not only because she didn't bring the skills that could make his business money, but because he'd been rattled by his intense reaction to her fragile beauty.

He was nearly three centuries old. He'd had countless lovers. Some had been passing acquaintances, some he'd enjoyed for several years.

But none of them had ever come close to making him a conquest.

Which was why he hadn't been prepared when Myst had stepped into his office, nearly bringing him to his knees with the force of his instinctive, gut-wrenching desire.

Even now the memory of her beauty haunted him.

Her pale, exquisite face that was dominated by a large pair of velvet-brown eyes. And the long, silvery-blond hair that looked as if it was spun silk.

She was danger. Pure female danger wrapped in the warm scent of honeysuckle.

Unfortunately, before he could get rid of her, Myst had caught him off guard when she'd burst into tears.

He might be a bastard, but he'd been unable to toss a sobbing woman out on her ass. So instead he'd given her a good, stiff drink to calm her nerves. And then another.

And the next thing he knew they'd been naked on his couch and he was lost in the spectacular pleasure of her body.

Bas gave a sharp shake of his head, his hand reaching into the pocket of his slacks to touch the locket he'd carried for the past five years.

He'd wasted too many nights recalling just how good it'd felt to have Myst pressed beneath him, her legs wrapped around his waist.

The only thing that mattered was that she'd disappeared from his office the second his back was turned. And then, nine months later, slipped through his security to abandon Molly in his private rooms.

What kind of woman did that?

"Okay," he murmured, fiercely attempting to disguise his opinion of Myst. "What does she say?"

"That she has something she has to do, but she misses me," Molly said. "And that soon we'll be together again."

"I don't want you to be disappointed if she can't come," he said gently. He tenderly smoothed her silken curls. "You have me. And I'm never going away."

"But she is coming." Molly bounced up and down at the sound of the door to the suite being opened. "See? I told you."

Bas surged upright, his hand reaching for the gun holstered at the small of his back.

What the hell? How had an intruder gotten past his security system?

"Molly, go to your room."

"But it's Mommy."

There was the unmistakable scent of honeysuckle drenching the air before a silver-haired female stepped into the salon, her yellow sundress swirling around her slender legs. Bas hissed, feeling as if he'd been punched in the gut.

Christ.

She was just as beautiful as ever.

Perhaps even more beautiful.

"Myst." The name was wrenched from his lips.

Her delicate features were impossible to read. "Hello, Bas."

He gave a shake of his head, trying desperately to dismiss his potent, intoxicating response to the sight of her.

"What the hell are you doing here?"

Her gaze shifted to the tiny girl standing beside him, a luminous smile lighting her fragile features.

"I've come for my daughter."

* * *

Myst had learned to endure living in a constant state of terror.

It wasn't like she had a choice.

For years she'd attempted to avoid her inevitable fate, always on the run, always looking over her shoulder.

Stupidly, she assumed that she'd become so accustomed to her sense of dread that nothing could rattle her.

Until five years ago.

The day she'd first met the man who was standing in front of her like an angel of retribution.

Not that she'd felt dread when she'd walked into his office. She only wished she had.

No. If she wanted to be brutally honest, she'd tumbled into instant lust. Who could blame her? Bas Cavrilo was a stunningly beautiful male.

His features were carved by the hand of an artist. A wide brow. A narrow, arrogant blade of a nose. Full, sensuous lips that hinted at a passionate nature beneath his stern façade.

His skin was a pale ivory and satin smooth unless you counted the small eye-shaped emerald birthmark on the side of his neck and the thin horizontal lines tattooed beneath it.

In contrast his hair was as black as midnight and cut short to emphasize his male beauty.

And his eyes . . . Lord, those eyes.

A tiny shudder had raced through her at her first glimpse of the metallic-bronze eyes that held a cunning intelligence.

She'd felt as if something vital had been switched off in her brain. That would explain why she'd so recklessly chugged the Scotch he'd offered after refusing to give her the job she so desperately needed.

And then another Scotch had been chugged . . .

The next thing she knew she was giving in to the passion that had exploded between them with electric force. Once sanity had returned, she'd slipped away, hoping to put the crazed incident behind her.

Of course, she couldn't be so lucky.

Instead she'd discovered that she was pregnant, and she'd learned the true meaning of terror.

Now she licked her lips, her heart thundering like a freight train in her chest as she forced herself to meet the scorching bronze glare.

"How did you get past my security?" Bas snapped.

Before she could speak, Molly was darting forward, ignoring her father's biting fury with the confidence of a child who knew that she was well loved.

"Mommy, Mommy!" she cried.

Myst fell to her knees, enfolding the wiggling bundle of sunshine in her arms.

For a perilous second she closed her eyes, savoring the pure joy that briefly drove away the nightmares that were Myst's constant companion.

"Hey, baby," she murmured softly.

A shadow fell over her as the tall, lethally dangerous assassin moved to tower over her. "I asked you a question."

She pressed her cheek to the top of Molly's soft curls, staring at the original Renoir painting that was hung on a far wall.

"I heard you."

"Then you have no excuse for not answering."

"You didn't hire me, remember?" she muttered.

There was a startled silence. "I remember everything," he at last said, the words oddly husky.

Myst shivered. Heavens. His voice was magic. Low, and whiskey-smooth. Sometimes she woke in the middle of the night, imagining she could still hear him whispering words of pleasure in her ear.

"You're not the boss of me."

He snorted, unimpressed. "And?"

"And I don't have to answer to you."

Tiny arms wrapped around her neck as Molly smacked a moist kiss on her cheek. "I missed you, Mommy."

Her arms tightened around her daughter, tears filling her

eyes. "I missed you too, baby. More than you could ever imagine."

She heard Bas swear beneath his breath.

"Molly, go back to your bed so Mommy and I can have a little chat."

"No, I don't want to go to bed," Molly pouted, burying her face in Myst's neck. "I want to stay with Mommy."

"Molly." The edge in Bas's voice warned that he was at the end of his patience.

Keeping her arms around the fragile little girl, Myst rose to her feet and carried Molly toward the door that led to the back of the suite.

"It's okay." She brushed her lips over Molly's forehead. "I'll tuck you in."

Molly gazed up at her with shimmering bronze eyes. "I don't want you to leave."

Pain sliced through Myst. She'd known this was going to be difficult. But she hadn't realized it was going to feel as if her heart was being ripped out.

She forced a smile to her lips. This was for Molly.

After everything her daughter had been forced to endure over the past week, a visit from her mother was the least she could do for her.

"I'm not leaving," she said, pretending to ignore the large male form prowling behind her like a panther shadowing its prey.

The hair on her nape stirred, her mind urging her to flee as she walked down the short hall that led to two bedrooms. She chose the nearest, heaving a silent sigh of relief at the sight of the toys piled in the corner of the elegant black and gold room.

The last thing she wanted was to accidentally intrude into Bas's privacy.

Not that she feared he would toss her on his bed and strip off her clothes. Her lips twisted. His expression when she'd entered the suite had revealed what he thought of her.

And it was nothing good.

But it would have been . . . unnerving.

"You swear you won't leave?" Molly pleaded as Myst crossed the lush black carpet to settle her daughter on the bed. "A pinkie swear?"

She gently tugged the gold comforter over Molly's tiny body. "I swear."

"You shouldn't make promises you can't keep," Bas growled from behind her.

"We can discuss it later," Myst muttered, concentrating on her daughter, who was snuggling into the mattress with her stuffed hippo pressed to her chest.

Although they'd been in constant mental contact, she'd never had the opportunity to savor Molly's delicate beauty or the pure innocence of her soul, which glowed around her with a golden aura.

She was . . . perfect.

And worth every sacrifice that Myst had to make.

"Will you tell me a story?" Molly pleaded.

Myst gently pushed a silver curl off her daughter's cheek. "Of course."

Molly flashed her a dimpled grin. "I want to hear the one about the princess who saves the troll and he turns into a prince. That's my favorite."

"Her favorite?" Bas growled, abruptly grabbing Myst by the arm to tug her away from the bed. "What's she talking about?"

Myst made a sound of impatience as they halted near the doorway. Okay, Bas had every reason not to trust her. She got that. She truly did.

But she only had a limited time with Molly.

She couldn't afford to waste a minute.

"It's a fairy tale that I made up," she confessed, forcing herself to meet the bronze male gaze even as tiny shudders raced through her body.

Who wouldn't shudder when an assassin was scowling at

her as if he was considering where he intended to dump the
body?

It had nothing at all to do with the fingers that had loosened
their grip and were absently stroking up and down the bare
length of her arm.

"Fairy tale?" he snapped.

She shrugged, wishing she wasn't such a shy, timid mouse.

If she was one of those beautiful, sophisticated women
that seemed born with the knowledge of how to manipulate
men, she could use her wiles to convince this man to let her
stay.

As it was . . . she had no flipping idea how she was going
to perform that particular miracle.

"It's a harmless story."

The stunning metallic eyes narrowed, the air heating. Bas
was not only a witch, he was a born Sentinel, which meant
his body temperature ran hotter than other people's. Especially when they were pissed off.

Or in the throes of passion . . .

She slammed shut the door on that agonizingly vivid
memory, watching as his bronze eyes narrowed, his heat
spiking.

Almost as if he'd managed to catch her wicked thoughts.

"Myst—"

"Mommy," Molly called from the bed.

Myst released a breath she didn't know she was holding.
Thank God for a timely interruption.

"Coming." She moved to step around the male only to
come to a halt as his fingers tightened on her arm. She tilted
back her head to glare at his painfully beautiful face. "Let me
go, Bas."

He refused to release his grip, but his fingers instantly
eased. She blinked in confusion. Was he afraid he was hurting her?

That seemed very . . . un-assassin like.

"Have you been sneaking in to see Molly?" he growled.

She shook her head. "No."

"Then how did you tell her a fairy tale?"

Myst hesitated. She wanted to lie, but she feared he would sense she wasn't telling the truth.

Probably not the best way to convince him that she could be trusted with their daughter.

"We're psychically connected."

His dark brows lifted in surprise. "You told me that you're a clairvoyant."

"That's one of my gifts," she agreed, her voice carefully devoid of emotion.

"One?"

Her lips twisted in a wry smile at the disbelief in his tone. She was used to being dismissed as a mere scribe with meaningless powers.

"Yes."

He looked . . . offended.

"You didn't tell me you were a telepath."

She shrugged. "You didn't ask."

"You applied for a job. I assumed you would have shared your complete résumé." He leaned down, wrapping her in the scent of clean male skin and Scotch. "Or were you keeping secrets even back then?"

His lips brushed the top of her ear, sending streaks of lightning through her body.

Danger, excitement, and pure lust twisted her stomach into a knot.

Dammit. She'd spent the past four years isolated in the bowels of a Russian monastery. She wasn't prepared to deal with the cascade of sensations.

She struggled to suck air into her lungs. "I wasn't a telepath when I applied for the job," she said in hoarse tones.

He frowned, his fingers resuming their absent path up and down her arm. Was he even aware what he was doing?

Her skin shivered with delight.

"Is that supposed to be a joke?" he demanded.

She grimaced, understanding his annoyance. High-bloods were born with their mutations, even if some didn't reveal themselves until after puberty. Most people only had one, but a rare few could claim a combination.

Like Bas, who'd been born with both the magic of a witch and the superior strength of a Sentinel. And even more rare were those powers that appeared later in life, seemingly out of nowhere.

None of the healers had an explanation.

It simply happened.

"The talent didn't reveal itself until I was pregnant," she grudgingly confessed.

He lifted his head, genuine amazement in his eyes. "A spontaneous manifestation?"

"Yes."

He studied her with a searing intensity. "Fine. You should have told me you were in contact with Molly."

She forced herself to hold that raptor gaze. Bas was a natural leader with a male confidence that easily intimidated others.

In other words . . . an arrogant ass.

He would run her over completely if she didn't try to stand her ground.

"As I said, you're not my boss."

"No, but I am Molly's father."

"I know that . . ." she started to snap, only to bite her tongue. Well, hell.

He was right.

"And?" he prompted.

She grimaced. It was true he was an arrogant ass, but he'd taken in a baby that he hadn't known existed, without question and without hesitation, and surrounded her with the sort of love every little girl deserved.

As much as it might pain her to stroke his bloated ego, she owed him her eternal gratitude.

"I'm truly grateful that you've done such a wonderful job

with Molly." She managed to force the words past her stiff lips. "She's a very special little girl, and I know that you had a very large part in that."

He blinked, a flare of color staining the sharp line of his cheekbones.

Had she managed to knock him off guard?

Amazing.

Then his lips abruptly thinned. "You're very good at deflecting my questions," he accused.

She dropped her gaze to his thousand-dollar Italian shoes. "Then stop asking them."

"Myst." His finger curled beneath her chin, tilting her head up. "Why didn't you let me know you were in contact with my daughter?"

A fresh pain sliced through her heart. "*Our* daughter," she corrected in fierce tones.

His lips parted, but before he could deny her right to be a mother, Molly's plaintive voice interrupted their tense confrontation.

"Daddy, I want Mommy to tell the story."

Myst glanced toward the tiny girl who was perched on the edge of the bed before returning her wary gaze to the predator who was nearly vibrating with the urge to toss her through the nearest window.

"Let me go to her, Bas," she said in low tones. "Please."

Frustration tightened his stark features, but dropping his hands, he forced himself to take a step back.

"Tell her the story. Then we talk," he warned, turning his head to send his daughter a smile that held uncomplicated affection. "Good night, pet."

Bas stalked from the room, his phone pressed to his ear as he reached the main room of the suite.

"Kaede," he snapped as soon as his enforcer picked up. "I need you in Kansas City. I'll explain when you get here."

He shoved the phone back into his pocket and paced to the bank of windows that overlooked the Kansas City skyline.

Un-fucking-believable.

After five years of paying a fortune to trackers, witches, and even a human private investigator to hunt down Myst, she'd waltzed into his penthouse as if she had every right to be there.

Worse, he discovered that she'd been in constant contact with Molly.

A short, humorless laugh was wrenched from his throat.

No, that wasn't the worst.

The worst was the undeniable fact that he found her just as damned exquisite as the first time she'd sashayed that tiny body into his office.

His fingers had twitched with the urge to run through the moonlit silk of her hair. To yank off her pretty sundress and explore the pale ivory skin that had haunted his dreams. To crush the soft curve of her lips until they parted in helpless surrender.

Emotions are the enemy.

He'd been taught that by the monks who'd honed him into the perfect killer.

But Myst managed to shatter a lifetime of training, stirring his passions with an ease that was frankly terrifying.

He needed her gone.

Now.

Pacing toward the long bar that was set near the leather sectional couch, Bas grimly poured himself a Scotch. Tomorrow he would have the suite cleaned from top to bottom. Maybe that would get rid of the lingering scent of honeysuckle.

He was on his second drink when he heard the sound of approaching footsteps and he whirled to study the woman who came to a hesitant halt in the center of the room.

His brows snapped together. He told himself it was because

she was an unwelcome interloper and not because she looked as delicate and ethereal as a moonbeam.

A very sexy moonbeam.

She wrapped her arms around her slender waist, making a visible effort to meet his gaze.

"There's no need to glare at me," she chided.

He set aside his empty glass, smoothing his face to an unreadable mask.

It was something that should have come easily. He was a cold, ruthless assassin, wasn't he? Unfortunately, this woman had a unique talent of getting under his skin.

In more ways than one.

"You've been screwing with my daughter's mind," he said between clenched teeth, still unnerved by the revelation that this woman had been speaking with Molly without his knowledge.

Her chin jutted to a defensive angle. "I'll admit that I've often communicated with Molly, but I was hardly screwing with her mind. We talked like any other mother and daughter."

He narrowed his gaze. "You knew very well that I was unaware of your telepathic powers. You deliberately used that lack of awareness to take advantage."

"Molly was the one to reach out to me."

His scowl deepened. "How? You're not trying to claim she's a telepath?"

"No, but I could sense her," Myst muttered. "She needed to know that her mother loved her."

"A mother who loves her child doesn't abandon her."

She flinched at his deliberate attack. "I didn't . . ."

"Didn't what?"

"Nothing."

He studied her pale face.

She was hiding something. But what?

"Why are you here?"

"You know why." She hunched a shoulder. "I'm here to see my daughter."

"Why?" he pressed again. "Four years ago you left her on my bed and walked away without looking back. Surely you can understand my confusion as to why you'd be struck with a burning need to see her now."

Her lovely face that looked far too young to be a mother's flushed at his accusation.

"Molly was traumatized when she was kidnapped."

His breath hissed between his teeth.

The memory of Molly's kidnapping was still a raw wound that made him think about killing things.

"You don't have to remind me," he snapped. "We were all traumatized when she was taken."

The velvet-brown eyes widened with something that might have been confusion.

"I'm not blaming you."

"Then what are you doing?"

"Trying to explain that after Molly was taken she reached out to me in terror," she said, her voice trembling as if she'd been as tormented as he'd been by her abduction. "She couldn't tell me where she was, or who'd taken her, so all I could do was try to give her comfort and swear to her that I would come and visit if she would be a good girl and do everything they told her to do until you could come for her."

Her soft words should have infuriated him. What right did she have to make promises to his daughter?

Instead, he went hunter-still. "You were so certain I would find her?"

"Yes," she said without hesitation.

Shit.

He struggled to keep his face devoid of emotion at the insane flare of pleasure that raced through him at her absolute confidence in his skills.

What the hell was wrong with him?

It wasn't as if this woman's opinion mattered, did it?

"Is that why it took you a week to get here?" he snapped,

angered by his ridiculous reaction to this female. "Or were you just too busy to care that your daughter was in danger?"

Her head snapped back, an unexpected fury tightening in her delicate features.

"Don't ever say I don't care about Molly," she spit out, her hands clenched into tiny balls. "I left the second I knew she'd been taken. If I hadn't had to make sure I wasn't being followed I would have—"

She bit off her impulsive words, stiffly turning to walk toward the bank of windows.

"Followed?" he instantly pounced. Was this a trick? A lame excuse for not rushing to help in the search for Molly? "By who?"

"It doesn't matter."

Bas kept his gaze locked on the fragile profile reflected in the window.

"It does if you're in danger."

She hunched her shoulders, a visible shiver shaking her body.

"All I'm asking is a few days to spend with my daughter," she said in low tones.

Bas was moving before he could halt his forward progress, grabbing her shoulders so he could turn her to meet his searching gaze.

"I want to know why you think you're being followed," he insisted.

Her ridiculously thick lashes lowered to hide her expressive eyes. A sure sign she was about to lie.

"You're always in hiding," she muttered. "I didn't want to accidentally give away your location."

"Bullshit."

Her jaw tightened, but her gaze stayed lowered. "Can I stay?"

His grip eased on her shoulders, his fingers compulsively stroking the satin-soft skin of her back.

"For how long?" he demanded.

"A few days."

"And then you intend to disappear into the ether once again?"

"Yes."

Some indefinable emotion clenched his stomach at her blunt admission that she couldn't be bothered to spend more than a handful of hours with her child.

His hand moved from her shoulder to grasp her chin, tilting back her head so he could study her delicate features.

So innocent.

The face of an angel.

How the hell could she be so cruel toward her only child? Unless . . .

"Do you have another family?" he abruptly demanded.

She blinked, as if confused by his question. "Do you mean parents or siblings?"

His lips thinned. "I'm asking if you have a husband and pack of kids. Is that why you treat Molly like a dirty secret?"

"Of course not," she breathed, a genuine outrage darkening her eyes. "And I don't treat Molly like a dirty secret."

Dropping his hands as if he'd been scalded, Bas took a step back.

He didn't want to feel a sharp-edged relief that he'd been wrong in his suspicion that Myst was already claimed by another male.

He didn't want to feel anything for this woman.

"No," he said abruptly.

"No what?" she asked in bewilderment.

"No, you can't stay," he informed, retreating behind his icy composure. "It isn't fair to Molly."

She sucked in a sharp breath, her expression stricken. "A visit from her mother isn't fair?"

"You can't just appear and disappear from her life whenever you want." He shrugged. "It's too confusing."

"All I'm asking is a few days."

"No."

"Bas . . ." She held out a slender hand. "Please."

Her soft, pleading expression didn't touch him, he fiercely assured himself.

He was turning away and heading out of the room because he needed to check on Molly, not because he was trying to avoid the blatant yearning on her beautiful face.

And the strange emotion that was currently twisting his gut into tight knots wasn't guilt.

Or regret.

No way.

"Lock the door on your way out," he commanded, refusing to glance at her.

"I'll return in the morning," she said, the words soft but stubborn.

His steps never faltered. "You're wasting your time."

"It's my time to waste," she muttered. "I'll be back."

Bas had reached the end of the short hallway when he heard the sound of Myst's retreating footsteps, followed by the closing of the door.

Coming to a sharp halt, he pulled out his phone and made a swift call to his security team.

"There's a silver-haired woman leaving the building," he said in clipped tones. "I want her followed."

Keeping the phone in his hand, he quietly entered his daughter's room, standing beside her bed to savor the sight of her tiny body curled beneath the blankets.

Usually he loved these moments. When the world was quiet and he could enjoy the knowledge his daughter was safe in his care.

But tonight his peace was disrupted by the lingering scent of honeysuckle that stirred sensations he hadn't felt in far too long.

Damn Myst.

Damn her to hell.

His phone vibrated, and with long strides he headed out

of the door and into his bedroom across the hallway that was decorated in shades of black and gold.

"You got her?" he demanded as he pressed the phone to his ear. He stiffened as the hunter Sentinel shared the bad news that Myst had somehow managed to slip past them unnoticed. "Shit."

Throwing the phone across the room, Bas watched with satisfaction as it shattered in a spray of worthless technology.

Books by Bestselling Author
Fern Michaels

___	**The Jury**	0-8217-7878-1	$6.99US/$9.99CAN
___	**Sweet Revenge**	0-8217-7879-X	$6.99US/$9.99CAN
___	**Lethal Justice**	0-8217-7880-3	$6.99US/$9.99CAN
___	**Free Fall**	0-8217-7881-1	$6.99US/$9.99CAN
___	**Fool Me Once**	0-8217-8071-9	$7.99US/$10.99CAN
___	**Vegas Rich**	0-8217-8112-X	$7.99US/$10.99CAN
___	**Hide and Seek**	1-4201-0184-6	$6.99US/$9.99CAN
___	**Hokus Pokus**	1-4201-0185-4	$6.99US/$9.99CAN
___	**Fast Track**	1-4201-0186-2	$6.99US/$9.99CAN
___	**Collateral Damage**	1-4201-0187-0	$6.99US/$9.99CAN
___	**Final Justice**	1-4201-0188-9	$6.99US/$9.99CAN
___	**Up Close and Personal**	0-8217-7956-7	$7.99US/$9.99CAN
___	**Under the Radar**	1-4201-0683-X	$6.99US/$9.99CAN
___	**Razor Sharp**	1-4201-0684-8	$7.99US/$10.99CAN
___	**Yesterday**	1-4201-1494-8	$5.99US/$6.99CAN
___	**Vanishing Act**	1-4201-0685-6	$7.99US/$10.99CAN
___	**Sara's Song**	1-4201-1493-X	$5.99US/$6.99CAN
___	**Deadly Deals**	1-4201-0686-4	$7.99US/$10.99CAN
___	**Game Over**	1-4201-0687-2	$7.99US/$10.99CAN
___	**Sins of Omission**	1-4201-1153-1	$7.99US/$10.99CAN
___	**Sins of the Flesh**	1-4201-1154-X	$7.99US/$10.99CAN
___	**Cross Roads**	1-4201-1192-2	$7.99US/$10.99CAN

Available Wherever Books Are Sold!
Check out our website at www.kensingtonbooks.com